PAUL SEAN HILL

The Last Butterfly

For information about this title or to order other books and/or electronic media, contact the publisher:

Atlast Press

https://AtlasExec.com
pshill@AtlasExec.com

Library of Congress Control Number: 2023910791

ISBN:
978-0-9986343-7-1 (hardcover)
978-0-9986343-8-8 (softcover)
978-0-9986343-9-5 eBook

Printed in the United States of America

Cover and Interior design: 1106 Design

For Pam, my fierce butterfly

CONTENTS

PROLOGUE

She simply followed her nature.

Only a few people in their cars or on the sidewalk looked up to see her as she flew across the street and over the schoolyard, but those who did smiled and counted themselves lucky. Every now and then, someone said out loud what most who saw her thought, "Oh cool, look at that, a butterfly!" Whether it was the flash of brilliant color as she flew by, or the improbability of her flight or even her existence, just the sight of such a fantastical and rare creature was usually enough to brighten someone's day, if just for a few moments.

To those who watched her go by, the butterfly simply zigzagged away, apparently aimless if not helpless in the breeze. But she was neither aimless nor helpless. She knew the direction she must travel—towards the warmth and away from the cold winds that were coming—while also searching for the scent of a place she had never smelled or seen but was compelled to find. It was October, and she had already flown several hundred miles. She would endure more than a thousand miles more before she could rest and wait for the winter to retreat again next spring.

For now, though, she needed to pause for a few moments to concentrate and regain two important scents she had just lost. One would lead the butterfly to the blooming plants whose nectar enabled her to continue the journey. The other would lead her to many more of her own kind and the place where they will spend the nighttime huddled together before flying on in the morning.

She just happened to alight on a high windowsill in a brick wall overlooking a darkened high school gymnasium from where she could search the wind for scents. Although the butterfly was of course oblivious to the goings-on inside, had she looked, she would have seen the school's student body filling bleachers along the walls and in rows of folding chairs across the large floor. A man stood at a podium lecturing passionately while pictures flashed across a large white screen above his head. He was saying,

> Life is tenuous.
>
> In his book, *A Short History of Nearly Everything*, Bill Bryson wrote, "It is a curious feature of our existence that we come from a planet that is very good at promoting life but even better at extinguishing it."
>
> He was right.
>
> With the 4.5 billion years of our world's history as a guide, not only are the odds against flourishing, but just surviving is a long shot. More than 99 percent of all species that ever

> lived on Earth have become extinct. This isn't a new phenomenon. It is seen in the oldest fossil records.
>
> In the beginning, so to speak, the right conditions come together, and a species emerges, is able to thrive, and spreads—in some cases like wildfire. Then, something changes. Once-favorable conditions become less so or downright hostile. Whether this stems from changing climate as ice ages and tropical periods ebb and flow, competition from other species for resources, or predators, to survive a species must adapt to the change. That adaption can be behavioral, physiological, or both. In any case, some less-dominant trait becomes a strength in the new environment, while some previous strength becomes less important.
>
> In this way, every species adapts to change . . . until it can't. Then the population shrinks, sometimes rapidly, until a once-prolific species disappears. And most do.

As he listened while leaning on his dust mop by an exit, Ed Schmutz thought, *Great, another professor from the junior college, blathering on about science, like these brats care.* To their credit though, unlike Ed, the kids crammed into the gym appeared to be mostly paying attention.

Ed cocked his head and glanced sideways at the nearest rows of students. *Not that it's going to do them any good. This bunch just ain't right, and everyone knows it. Dr. Smarty Pants up there surely doesn't think he can teach them anything, does he? Because no one else does, that's for durn sure. They're just the next in a long line of dumb and coddled kids, who ain't going anywhere.*

Ed wasn't all wrong. In fact, the Orange Independent School District had been grasping at straws for several years, because they knew they were losing the fight. Grayton High School was failing, but they couldn't figure out why or what to do about it. Every grade level's test scores, both in the standardized tests required by the state for graduation and in the college board exams, had not just lagged the state average for a decade, they were steadily dropping. Everyone, from Grayton's city hall to the school district and the Texas Education Agency, was now in the school's business, either giving advice or controlling some part of the day-to-day administration. And the results kept getting worse.

Today's school assembly was just another opportunity for the students to hear something—anything—that might interest them, might make them curious enough to retain something, to ask anything, and maybe learn, even if just one fact. God knows the faculty was open to trying just about anything.

The professor was still talking:

> Take the monarch butterfly, *Danaus plexippus*, as an example. These complex creatures who start as caterpillars, turn into these marvelous flying artworks. As they visit flowering plants for nectar, they're also pollinating them—helping the plants they touch stay healthy and productive. In this way, they contribute to the health of countless others who benefit from the plants they've touched.
>
> For over 1 million years, these little guys have thrived in a repeatable pattern. Two generations migrate up through North America and into Canada from April through August. The third and fourth generations then return to the same

very small area in Central Mexico to wait out the winter months before starting the annual cycle again.

While there is much that we know about the monarch, there's much also that we don't fully understand about how they do what they do. How does each generation know its changing role? How do they navigate so unerringly to far distant destinations they've never seen, and haven't seen for three generations?

One sad fact we do know about them, as this map shows, is that in the last ten years the monarch population in those Mexican wintering grounds has shrunk dramatically. With this steady and rapid decline, there is wide speculation that their extinction is imminent.

With such low, historical odds for any species' long-term survival, it isn't likely we can do much to protect any particular species forever. But we can definitely hasten their demise. Man-made pressures contribute to the environment changes that affect species around the world, including our friend the monarch. Whether it's our contribution to climate change, habitat destruction, or simply making the environment more hostile through our use of pesticides and herbicides, people have increased pressure on this wondrous and fragile species.

How terrible—and terribly easy—it would be, with just the "right" carelessness, to hasten their extinction.

> And when the last butterfly is gone, with it go all of their contributions in the world, the wondrous and enriching uniqueness they are in creation, and the simple joy of their existence.

Ed scowled as he only half-listened. *Oh, boo-frickin'-hoo, we're killing butterflies! Who really cares? They're just caterpillars! Sprouting wings doesn't change where they came from or what they really are. Darwin's big ol' boot is coming down on them, and then splat, one less bunch of useless bugs. If it's going to happen anyway, who cares a whit if we helped them right on out of our way and out of our world?*

Say now, there's an idea!

With that thought, Ed's day just took a turn for the better. Listening to that professor had turned out to be quite inspiring! He'd have to really think this one through, but he was onto something, however sketchy.

Ed turned and strolled out of the building while the lecture was wrapping up. As he pushed open the heavy door and stepped through, a rush of air blew past him from inside the large hall, turning up the outside wall and adding a faint stir to the air around the butterfly, high above the ground. In that new mix of air, the butterfly picked up the scents that she had lost, and they told her it was time to go. She lifted into the breeze almost effortlessly, following those scents into the last leg of today's journey, all the while still feeling and following her internal guide to that other, distant, and compelling place.

As the butterfly flew away, a little girl waiting with her mother in front of the school saw the flash of yellow wings and squealed with delight, "Oooh, Mommy, look! A butterfly!"

Not many noticed Ed as he went on his way. Those who did were surprised to see a rare smile spread across his face and a spring in his step as that idea and a sense of purpose came to life in his head. And for some reason, something in that observation darkened their day just a little.

Chapter 1

FINDING LIGHT

Some winds ushered her to where she needed to go and into clear skies.

Ed and Margo Schmutz spent most of their lives as thoroughly mean, bitter, and angry people, in some of the same ways, but each in their own way and both through and through. This was no ordinary meanness. It was a slow-burning desire to lash out, avenge so many wrongs, right all of the injustices, strike down the undeserving and prideful, punish the unenlightened, yoke the undeserving blessed, and share the hurts, agonies, and injustices of life.

They nurtured their meanness, and it was an active, glowing source of energy that sustained each of them as they fed it. They both were secure in the knowledge that no one suspected them of any bad feelings. Hell, they both were sure they had no *bad* feelings. They felt exactly as they should. They were simply playing the lousy hands they had been dealt at every turn, as they watched the rest of the world gather all the lucky breaks.

Further stoking Ed and Margo's resentment were the endless irritating reminders, year after year, that other people didn't have their own dreams of happiness, hope, and love ripped from them. After twenty angry and hopeless years, Ed and Margo began to see a dark light at the end of the dreary tunnel that was their lives; they weren't powerless after all, and there might be ways they could share their misery and sense of injustice. So they each put schemes into work to do just that—remind the world around them that nothing in life matters, and there is no enduring happiness or beauty that couldn't be taken away.

They hadn't come into the world this way, of course, but the lessons that life taught them eventually sank in indelibly, corrupting them to the core.

• • •

Times were lean when Ed was growing up in the 1950s and '60s. Like so many other small East Texas towns, Grayton didn't have much to offer besides shiftwork in the lumber mill or a chemical plant. That suited Ed's father, Carl, just fine, since he wasn't looking to get rich. Having grown up through the Depression and then coming back from World War II already an "old man" of thirty-four, his only real ambition was to make his own way and not be beholden to anyone—no one telling him where to go or what to do with the rest of his life. Carl bought thirty cheap acres out where the town gave way to the woods and started building his own junkyard just off the two-lane state road.

He was content with his routine and what little he had until he met a pretty, blue-eyed teller named Hildie at the First National Bank. It didn't take many dates for coffee or the occasional blue plate special (when he could scrape a little cash together) before Carl and Hildie were both smitten. Hildie saw so much strength and simple honor in this quiet, good man. Carl loved everything about Hildie, including the reflection of himself as she saw him. He found himself happily wanting to be the man Hildie already saw him to be. They were married three months after their first date.

After they were married, Carl ran the junkyard, and Hildie managed the books, the household, and Carl's spirits. When business was slow and money even slower, Hildie reminded him as he went out the door, "Keep your chin up, husband. Remember, you're no *junker*. You're Carl Schmutz, my *salvage-man*." That, and the kiss that went with it, always made him laugh as he lifted her off her feet in a bear hug.

The salvage-man idea had really grown on Carl. Thanks to Hildie, he now had bigger dreams for the yard, the business, and a family. He knew that each dream led to the next. They just had to put in the hard work, and in time it would pay off. That's just how the world worked. Fortunately, Hildie saw it the same as Carl and wasn't interested in spending money they didn't have for things they didn't need.

That levelheaded way of thinking is also how they ended up waiting nine years to have Ed, making sure they could "pay as we go" and not get in over their heads. That meant Carl was a forty-three-year-old with a newborn, and Hildie was a still-young thirty-six.

Hildie tended to young Ed's spirits just as she did Carl's, telling him at night before bed with a hug and a kiss, "Dream big things, and remember your mama loves her little man." When he was old enough, she sent him off to school every morning with another hug and reminder, "Go learn big things, and remember your mama loves her little man."

In between, Ed lived what he considered an idyllic life. Although they lived in the same old, wood frame house that also served as the yard's office, there were touches of Hildie everywhere, from the bright curtains on the windows, to the smell of homemade bread and coffee that filled the place. Walking through the door always felt like walking into a hug from Hildie. When he wasn't in school, Ed could often be found "driving" some of his favorite wrecks in the yard while imagining he was flying down roads all over the world. Even better were the weekends when Carl would take him along in the truck, especially when they made long drives to deliver a load to a buyer. It was just Ed and his dad, bouncing along in the old flatbed with the windows down, enjoying the ride the way best buddies do. They even shared the driving job, sort of, with Carl working the clutch and Ed shifting the gears. It was a team effort, alright, and Ed knew they were a team—a salvage-man team—taking care of business for Mom.

As they drove through the thick, piney woods from one small town to the next, Carl would share his dreams with his son, "Oh, we're going places, bud. There's money in all this old stuff. We just need to build a system to separate the best parts, the best rebuilds, the best metals for recycling, and the customers to go with it. We'll figure it out, Ed. You and me. With a lot of help from your mama, course." After the delivery, they'd stop beside the road and feast on whatever lunch she'd put together for them, and then it was back home to Hildie.

She was definitely the rock. Carl may have done the heavy lifting in the yard, but it was Hildie that kept Carl and Ed grounded, happy, and dreaming.

When Ed was in the third grade, life changed.

What Hildie thought had been a summer cold and cough, turned into weeks of what she referred to as, "Just feeling a little puny." After a few weeks more, Carl noticed his already-slim wife losing weight and looking as puny as she so often felt. Instead of making the rounds in his truck one morning, he took her to Orange to see a doctor. Rather than going home with a prescription, they found themselves driving over to Beaumont to consult with a big-city doctor.

Two days and many tests later, the big-city doc confirmed what theirs already suspected. "That dark patch on the back of your leg is a kind of cancer called melanoma. This is an especially bad one, it tends to spread, and it moves fast when it does."

The doctor took Hildie's hands in his, "I don't really have any good news about this, young lady. It isn't exactly everywhere, but it may as well be. It has already metastasized to so many other organs. I'm so sorry. I know this isn't what you want to hear."

Two weeks later, as if overnight, Hildie was gone. She had been stunned and disbelieving as she faded. Now Carl and Ed were left stunned and bewildered by the hole in their lives she once filled. Feeling very small and helpless, a bewildered Ed watched from the truck as a dazed Carl laid down beside Hildie's freshly sodded grave, asking out loud, "How do I do this without you?"

As the evening sky darkened, a teary and broken Carl climbed back into the truck and vacantly drove home, neither he nor Ed uttering a word. The last of the dinners Hildie had made and frozen for them before she turned too sick ran out that night. It was just as well, since it made them miss her that much more to taste her food and not have her here to wrap them in her joy.

Now, more than ever, Ed needed his dad to be his best buddy and the other half of their salvage-man team. But instead of holding on desperately to his memories of Hildie for the warmth and sense of life she exuded so effortlessly, Carl simply disappeared into the loss. *His* loss, where nothing made sense, and nothing mattered beyond getting through each day.

As months turned into years, Carl progressed only barely through the stages of grief, finding himself stuck in anger and depression. Being a junkman hadn't become any easier—he had given up on the crazy salvage-man dream—and now he was having to pick up all of the things Hildie had made look easy. After a long day hauling parts and wrecks around, Carl was barely able to take care of the books and manage all of the paperwork the state and the feds demanded from the business, while also trying to drum up new business. It always felt like there was something he was dropping the ball on, just one too many things to keep things together.

And there was Ed.

As Carl became silent and detached from the world, so did Ed.

He did what he had to at school, but his broken and lonely heart wasn't in it, any more than Carl's. Ed felt a new and nagging envy when he listened to kids at school as they talked about their lives. Hearing about someone's family outing over a weekend, or a movie they'd seen with their moms, or pretty much anything about other kids' moms, were little, ongoing reminders of who and what he didn't have—the voice, face, and hugs no longer waiting for him at home.

Not really understanding the need he felt to fill the void from Hildie's absence, Ed was pulled towards groups like Little League, soccer, and Cub Scouts. Carl was indifferent to any of Ed's ideas, muttering things like, "Why waste time with that stuff? What's the point of it?" which Ed answered by dropping each new activity in turn, until he gave up and stopped trying altogether.

Ed turned to more solitary things. His favorite was trying to read the stack of books his mom had collected for him. "One day I know you'll get lost in these, just as I did," she'd tell him as they flipped through them together. "They'll take you to places and help you build your dreams." Maybe now they could also help him dream about her, or even just remember the sound of her voice.

After months of coming in from the yard to find Ed reading, Carl went from shaking his head and scowling to saying, "Son, if you have time to just sit around, why not do something useful? Come on and help me pay the bills."

So it was that just before his eleventh birthday, Ed began spending all of his free time bouncing along once more with Carl moving junk. This time, though, it wasn't like the old days with two buddies taking care of business. No, this was two silent partners doing what they had to do to survive another day. And they *were* mostly silent, except when Carl would tell Ed what to do at each stop, after which they'd climb back into the truck and move on to the next stop.

They'd finish every day in the same silence with some meal poured out of a can or a frozen TV-dinner tray. After cleaning up the mess, they'd sit in front of the TV to watch shows neither of them cared much about and go to bed. The years went by with very little change, both to the routine and the quiet detachment. Carl was never overtly abusive; in fact, he still loved Ed. He just never recovered from being broken without Hildie and couldn't find it in himself to move past it, to heal. It was as though allowing himself any tenderness again in life would come at the expense of his love for his wife, and his still-broken heart couldn't face that thought. However unintentionally, this is also how Carl led his son into a very similar silent detachment.

By the time Ed could drive, he knew the business as well as Carl, at least the business in the yard and on the truck. Once Carl figured that out, Ed inherited most of the hauling responsibility after school and on weekends, and Carl handled the books and paperwork. That was okay by Ed, since he had long before stopped enjoying the time with his brooding father. He had also started to enjoy the work, surprisingly enough. He found ways to better organize the yard and identify higher-profit equipment for salvage, and each step gave him more energy in the job. Although not really sure where it was all going, Ed was confident it was the right direction.

Although he was finishing high school with no friends other than a few regular junkyard customers and no real life outside of school and the business, nine years after Hildie's death, Ed could see a flicker of light at the end of the tunnel. With it came the faintest memory of his mother telling him to learn and dream big, and that they were a salvage-man team.

That's when Ed met Margo.

• • •

Margo's parents, Cy and Lois Cormier, were high school sweethearts. There was never any doubt that they'd be married once Lois graduated a year after Cy, even when their life together was put on hold when Cy was drafted and sent to Korea. Three years later, Cy didn't waste any time and married Lois a week after he came home to Grayton. Although twenty years younger than Carl and Hildie, like them, Cy and Lois weren't looking for much more than life with each other.

Cy had always been pretty handy, from fixing cars to patching walls to plumbing. If there was a tool for it, he could probably do the job. With Lois to come home to every night, he didn't care much about what he did or where he did it, as long as she was there and happy. Which is how he ended up as a maintenance man and custodian at Grayton High School. It kept him close to home for Lois, gave him a never-ending list of repairs to put his mind to, and it paid the bills. It sure beat working long shifts on nights, weekends, and holidays down at one of the chemical plants where most of Cy's friends worked.

In 1954, a year after Cy and Lois were married, Margaret Anne was born, coincidentally in the same year as Ed. Once life with a newborn settled down, Lois started taking in laundry and ironing from some of the well-to-do families living in the big houses around the Liberty Pines Country Club. It allowed her to work at home while also juggling her mom-time with Margo, and still help put a little money in the bank.

Between the two of them, Cy and Lois made enough to cover all of their bills, set a little aside for rainy days, do a little camping, and go on a summer vacation every year, usually to some white-sand beach from Gulfport to Panama City. If they lived an unglamorous life, they also lived one free of a lot of other people's stress, thank you very much, and spent all of their free time together.

Growing up, Margo delighted in riding along with Lois for laundry pickups and deliveries. Besides enjoying the ride with her mom, as she got older Margo would point out her favorite big houses: "Ooh, look at the 'castle.' I like their fancy new front door. That's the door I want it to have when I buy it for you," both of them grinning as Margo described life in their new palace. They both enjoyed their rides so much that when Margo started school, Lois waited until she was home before making deliveries, to ensure they didn't lose that time together.

Margo had her first "there-is-no-Santa-Claus" moment on her way to the school cafeteria one day in fourth grade. As she walked up to the group of girls who she ate lunch with, the conversation stopped with several muffled giggles. An especially snooty Jeannine Rezak stepped between Margo and the other girls, waving her hands as she said, "Ewww, watch out. Don't let her touch you. Her mom washes other people's underwear!" Jeannine stuck out both hands stiffly and turned her face away with a wrinkled nose.

Margo stopped in her tracks, dumbstruck as she wondered why anyone would be talking about her great mom like this. And why these girls . . . her *friends?*

"I see her with her mom in our neighborhood all the time. Carrying everyone's clothes. My mom said she can't imagine ever being that desperate." Margo was even more confused as all the girls giggled and ran down the hall and into the cafeteria.

When she walked up to her usual seat at the long table, girls slid away to avoid contact, laughing as they did it. Hearing various cries of, "Ew, don't touch," and "Don't get any in your food," Margo's confusion gave way to tears. She bowed her head and ate in silence.

When Margo got home, as usual, Lois was waiting for her to ride along on the day's laundry delivery. Instead of racing out the door to the car, Margo asked quietly, "Mom, are we poor?"

Lois turned to her, puzzled, and said with a chuckle, "No, honey, we're not poor. I mean, we're not rich, but we're not poor. We have everything we need and then some. Really. Look around at our great place. I love our house, and we have *us!* We're good. Now what in the world brought this on?"

Staring at Lois's feet, Margo could barely get it out, "Jeannine was mean to me today. She said you have to wash rich people's underwear. Because we're desperate. Are we?"

Try as hard as she could, Margo couldn't keep the tears from coming.

Lois pulled her in for a hug, "Hey, hey, kiddo. It's okay. We're fine. Don't you let that Jeannine get under your skin. Who cares what she thinks anyway?"

"It wasn't just her. The rest of them laughed at me too, and no one would sit next to me. They didn't even want me to touch them," Margo cried a little harder.

Lois hugged her tighter, "Oh, my sweet girl. I do this work because I can, not because we're poor or desperate. This has always let me stay close to you while still helping to pay a little of the bills. Don't you listen to anything that Jeannine or any other of those girls say. We don't need to care what they think about anything. Our little family is what matters most to us, and we're great. Okay?" She kissed Margo on the head and turned for the door. Two steps later, she looked back and asked, "You coming?"

Margo, her tears still flowing, said, "No, I have homework to do." She hated to lie to her mom, but the idea of riding through that neighborhood now made her feel just as alone as she had at lunch when none of the girls would come close to her. She also couldn't tell her mom that she didn't want to get other people's dirty underwear on her.

Lois gave her another kiss on the head, "Hey, that's okay. You do what you need to do, kiddo, and I'll be back in a jiffy. By then your dad will be home too, and I bet he'll put a smile back on that face." And as Lois had predicted, by bedtime, Margo was feeling almost back to herself. Several hours of life-as-usual with Mom and Dad always had that effect on her, helping her find her happy place after any hurt.

But Margo never rode with her mom again on the laundry runs. They also never spoke of it again.

After a few days, the giggling girls in Margo's class forgot their fun at her expense. The hurt didn't fully go away, however. For the first time, Margo saw the difference in some of the girls' clothes and noticed the expensive cars their parents drove. The big houses she had ridden past on laundry runs with Lois were no longer part of a dream Margo had for her mom. They, like the rest of the contrasts she now saw, were sober reminders. *We're not friends. You think we're different. You think that you're better than me.*

With those thoughts, Margo pulled away. It started simply with her eating lunch at another table, but over time she spoke less and less with most of her classmates. She didn't become mute in protest; she simply didn't join in the little conversations in the hallway or in class before the teacher began talking. She minded her business and had nothing to do with theirs. Over the next several years, if she spoke to the "rich kids" at all, it was usually to point out some stupid remark or mistake they made in class. With practice making perfect, she had become quite skilled at both catching gaffes and pointing them out for everyone else's amusement, and doing it during class was always the best payoff with the largest and most attentive audience.

In the seventh grade, she found out she had been antagonizing more than just the rich kids—her math teacher was not a fan either.

To be fair, Mr. Thomas wasn't a fan of most kids, any more than he was of teaching. But here he was, year after year, trying to teach the same basic and mind-numbing arithmetic to another group of kids who either didn't care or were just dumb as rocks. As bad as that was, most days before class was over, a group of the rich kids sitting in the back became bored and started throwing paper at each other or making goofy noises, infuriating Mr. Thomas. Rather than taking them to task, he'd simply grumble, "Alright, calm down. We're almost done," almost always eliciting barely suppressed chuckles from the clowns in the back. As if on cue, Mr. Thomas then became even more visibly angry as his entire pale head flushed, and he squinted at them through his thick round glasses.

More than once, he caught a glimpse of Margo rolling her eyes. Once, Jimmy Faison threw a paper airplane that bounced off of Mr. Thomas's head while he was droning on. As Jimmy and his buddies cracked up in the back of the room, Mr. Thomas looked up to see Margo's eyes roll and her headshake. *Alright, smart ass, go ahead and smirk,* he thought. *Your parents aren't high rollers who rub elbows with the school district execs like those hooligans in the back.* You *are not untouchable.*

At the end of the year, Mr. Thomas got his chance. Although there were several seventh grade math classes, only a single class full of them could move up to algebra in the eighth grade. Grades alone weren't all that mattered, since there were more than enough A-students. Each math teacher was allowed to rank order their top students however they saw fit. At the end of the year, only the top few from each class were allowed to move up.

To announce his recommendations, Mr. Thomas sat at his desk in front of the class and called up each student one at a time. After a somewhat hushed conversation, each student returned to their seat, most of them shrugging their shoulders with a, "Whatever. Regular math it is."

Jimmy Faison was one of the few who bounced back to his desk with a crazy grin, "Yeah, dudes!. Al-ge-braaaa with the *rest* of the smart kids."

Margo made her usual eye roll and headshake. *Great, another year with that clown.* When Margo finally sat next to Mr. Thomas's desk, he smiled slightly, "Well, what do *you* think I should do with you?"

"Uh, I uh, I have straight A's. Always have in math. Guess I'm good at it," shifting self-consciously in the seat and cocking her head to the side. "So, algebra, right?" she said matter-of-factly with a shrug of her shoulders.

"Yeah. Well, hmmm. No, it's *regular* math for you again next year, young lady," Mr. Thomas said casually, but he was now positively beaming.

While his answer alone had her immediately confused, Margo was stunned by his apparent pleasure in giving her such hurtful news. The class was now clearly listening to the not-so-private conversation, which became much easier as a shocked Margo spoke more loudly, shaking her head, "Wait, wait. Why? I think I have like the second or

third best grades in the class. And I *have* to move up to algebra next year. If I don't, I'll be a year behind and won't be able to take calculus in high school."

Still smiling, Mr. Thomas sneered through his teeth, "Yeah, but I don't like your *attitude*. Never have. You're not mature enough for algebra," he hissed, glancing down his nose at her.

She fell back in the chair and blurted out incredulously, "Really?" She turned and nodded towards Jimmy and his pals, "*Those* clowns? You're letting *them* move up and not me? Because of *maturity!?* Are you kidding!?"

After a deep breath, she said in a more even tone, "Those guys, who throw things at you, make jokes all through class, and copy each other's work? *They* move up. *I* don't?"

She shook her head slightly, looked down at his desk, and said slowly in a hushed voice, "But I can't participate in the college prep program in high school without this. And if I don't do that, I won't qualify for the scholarship that I need just to start college. It messes up *everything*. All because of this . . . this . . . algebra class that you *know* I can do!"

"Life doesn't always work that way. Maybe this will teach you something about the price of your behavior, a little *life* lesson. What goes around comes around, Missy." Mr. Thomas leaned slowly towards her, the smile now gone, narrowed eyes peering over his glasses, "You don't want to roll your eyes about that? No? Huh. Guess not. Go sit down."

He turned back to his list, crossing out "Margaret Cormier" with a flourish and a renewed smile and called the next kid up.

Margo sleepwalked back to her desk as Jimmy and the back row yucked it up at her expense. She heard them only vaguely as her own thoughts drowned them out. *HOW CAN HE DO THIS? IT ISN'T FAIR! Oh my God. College . . . Now what?* Margo dropped into her seat.

She stared down at her desk until class was over, barely stopping the tears from flowing, and was out the door before the bell stopped ringing.

Margo accepted that Mr. Thomas's decision was final and uncontestable. He was the adult in charge, and she was just a kid, not that she would have thought to tell her parents anyway. She couldn't tell them she had snuffed out her college plan thanks to her own behavior, whether it made sense to her or not.

However, Mr. Thomas had opened her eyes to two things: Life doesn't always turn out right or fairly, even when it could or should; and worse, some people are okay with that.

The next year was uneventful as Margo became even more guarded and just plodded through. Leaving middle school felt like a parole. She was genuinely excited to finally be at Grayton High School, where, besides making a fresh start, she could now ride with her dad as he went to work and she went to school. As she and Cy rolled into the school parking lot on the first day, it felt a lot like the good old days riding with her mom on laundry runs.

Walking up to the front doors, Margo kissed her dad happily on the cheek, "Thanks, Dad. See you at home tonight."

"See you, high school girl. Go get 'em and have fun," and he squeezed her shoulder as she walked past him.

As she walked through the hallway towards her first class, Margo gritted her teeth as she heard a familiar voice from behind, "Soooo, your dad is the *janitor?* Oh, that's too cooool." Jimmy Faison added, in his dramatic and incredulous best, barely camouflaging the sneer, "How awesome. Must be a real Einstein."

Jimmy brushed past her and into the room as she turned and glared without a word. *Great. Let the sucking of the next four years begin.* An already-quiet Margo went from guarded to detached and almost stoic around classmates throughout that year, which, although relatively uneventful, included regular barbs from Jimmy and his admirers about the janitor and wash maid's daughter.

Fortunately for Margo, her serious demeanor and good grades got the attention of her homeroom teacher, who recruited Margo as a paper-grader in the tenth grade. That led to working in the school's office as an administrative assistant in the eleventh grade. In January of Margo's senior year, the school secretary announced she was retiring at the end of the year and wanted to work only half-time until then. By then, it was an easy transition for Margo to fill in as the secretary in the afternoons.

Life was definitely looking up for Margo. While she still didn't have a plan for college—especially for paying for it—as she spent more time out of class and working, she put more distance between herself and the Jimmy Faisons of the world and began to come back out of her shell.

That's when Margo met Ed, in January 1973.

• • •

One afternoon, Cy had tried everything he could to unjam the large trash compactor behind the high school. No luck. Realizing it may finally be down for the count, he shook his head as he thought the school may finally have to buy an expensive new motor for the old contraption. About that time, a lanky kid walked up, peeking over Cy's shoulder, "Hey. Motor problem? We have some of those same motors, mostly bigger ones. Probably just bearings, you know."

Cy raised his eyebrows and gave a quizzical, almost amused look at the kid, "Well, I've kept this thing running for a long time, and it don't sound like bearings to me. If it is, I'll have to see what I can do to find replacements for this old thing."

The kid shrugged, "Seriously, I can pull one of ours and bring it in tomorrow. That will give me time to rebuild this one over the weekend, and we can trade them back next week."

Cy was smiling now, "You don't say? I'd hate for you to go to all that trouble." *Where'd you come from, boy? And how do you have a bunch of electric motors lying around?* For all Cy knew, the kid didn't know the business end of a screwdriver from a hammer.

"No, it's not a big deal. I do stuff like this all the time anyway. I sort of run my dad's junkyard," said the kid, grinning.

"Well, okay. Bring one in tomorrow, and we'll see what we can do. And thanks. By the way, I'm Cy. Cy Cormier. You've probably seen me around, I'm the repair guy around here," Cy said, sticking his hand out for Ed to shake.

"Oh. Uh—yeah, cool, I'm Ed Schmutz," was the awkward response, but he gave Cy a firm handshake. "I'll see you in the morning then."

The next morning, Cy was surprised to see a flatbed truck already parked by the dumpster when he got there. Walking around it, he found Ed connecting the ground wire to finish attaching the replacement motor. Ed looked up and smiled, "Oh, hey! Let's give her a test."

Cy flipped the switch, and the compactor whirred into life. "Alright then! Wow, that was my easiest repair job yet! Thanks, young fella! What do we owe you?" he asked, happily surprised.

"Nah, no charge. I'll rebuild the old one from parts we already have. It will be good as new, and I'll just swap it back in. Wish they were all this easy," Ed huffed a little as he put the old motor on the truck.

Cy, still grinning, slapped Ed on the back and cocked an eye at him, "Boy, oh boy! I could use some help from someone as handy as you. How'd you like to spend a couple hours helping me around here as sort of an assistant in the afternoons? Who knows, maybe you'll learn something. And just maybe *you'll* teach *me* something."

"Huh. Well . . . we *are* kinda slow right now at the yard," Ed said, rubbing his chin and thinking about it. "I could probably give you the last two periods every day, since I'm already on early release as a senior."

"You're on. Let's start tomorrow!"

A week later, Margo walked up to find them working on some pipes outside the building, "So? This is *him?*"

Ed looked wide-eyed from Margo to Cy, who chuckled without looking up from the patch he was finishing, "Yeah, this is Ed. He's my kind of guy. He can do stuff." Ed couldn't help but smile hearing that.

"Oh, well okay then. So hey, Ed Who Can Do Stuff. I'm Margo."

"Hey Ed," said Ed. Instantly turning red, he blurted out, "Margo. I mean: Hey *Margo*."

She raised her eyebrows and nodded. Rolling her eyes at her dad, she then headed down the hallway to the office. Cy looked sideways from Margo to Ed and smiled to himself.

After that, Cy looked for more excuses to do work around the office with Ed in tow. That strategy finally paid off months later when Ed hung back at Margo's desk as he and Cy were leaving. After shifting his weight back and forth several times and staring at the ceiling, Ed noticed Margo watching him, again eyebrows up and curious. He finally said quietly, "So, ah, you know, I don't really do stuff like this or go to things. You know. Like dances and things and stuff. And Cy told me you don't either. I know he and your mom want you to go to prom. So. I mean, if you want, you could go with me. It doesn't have to be any big thing or anything. If you want. Or not . . ." his voice trailed off. As painful as it was to hear his own voice sounding like an idiot, Ed was consciously thankful that Cy had already walked out the door and didn't hear it too.

Thanks Dad, as Margo fought rolling her eyes and instead just stared back at Ed, her lips pursed like she was deep in thought. After a quick look around the office to make sure no one was listening, she let out a breath and said, "Oh, sure. I don't know why we'd *want* to be around these people any more than we already are, but sure. I know *Dad* likes you, but it would probably be weird if you take *him*. So, yeah, why not? I mean . . . thanks?"

To both of their surprise, Ed and Margo enjoyed prom, or at least they enjoyed each other's company. Unlike so many of their peers, they found each other grounded and thoughtful. What started as a one-time thing quickly became a regular Friday-night outing, then Saturday night too, and finally Ed found himself eating dinner at home with the Cormiers once or twice a week. Cy and Lois had both taken to Ed, in great part because they saw the light shining again in Margo's eyes.

1973 was a banner year for Ed and Margo. They graduated from high school in May, and they were married that summer. They knew they were young and that this would complicate their plans, but so be it. As Ed said to Margo, "We can do this. I'm taking the yard and the business to another level like my dad used to talk about. We'll figure out how to get you into business classes so you can take over the money stuff. Until things are really going, you can still work in the high school office for some extra money. It'll work."

Cy and Lois turned their garage into an apartment for them. Cy assured Ed it was all good, "It's not permanent or anything. Might as well save as much as you can for now while you get this business thing going. It's the least we can do for you two since we really can't pay for Margo to go to college."

It was all a blur of simple happiness for Ed and Margo. Even though they had essentially set up their homestead under Cy and Lois' roof, Cy and Ed had done a fine job in converting the garage into a separate apartment, giving them as much privacy as they wanted. But part of the newlyweds' happiness was also in sharing dinners and other time together as a bigger family, which included Cy and Lois. Having missed so much of this with Hildie's absence, Ed couldn't get too much of it. Cy added to it by hiring Ed part-time to keep him on for help now and then at the school. The two of them would come home some evenings mulling over some next project and continue the conversation right through dinner—two peas in a pod, happily working through another set of details. Some days, Margo and Lois wondered out loud who exactly Ed had married, Margo or Cy!

None of them could imagine a better or happier arrangement: The young'uns were in love and together; Cy and Lois had them both close to watch them grow together; Cy had his dream helper in his own son-in-law, who was just as fascinated with fix-'em-up projects as he was; and Ed was rebuilding a best-buddy relationship again with a father figure who he admired and looked up to.

Ed kept spending a couple of afternoons each week at the school, but true to his word, he also went to work laying out plans to evolve Carl's junk business into a real and more profitable salvage business. He began tracking monthly cash flow and categorizing buys into reliable, smaller revenue and the high-value single items, and taking notes on the trends that influenced higher profits over the longest amount of time. All of this he kept in a notebook that went with him everywhere, and every idea that came along went into that book to help focus the business.

A year later, early in the fall of 1974, Ed was eating lunch in a roadside diner on a pickup run near Winnie. As usual, he had his notebook wide open on the table and was scribbling away, oblivious to the people coming and going around him. Across the aisle a stranger watched him, glancing curiously towards Ed's truck full of worn-out farm equipment. The stranger finally spoke, causing Ed to look up in surprise as the stranger pointed at his notebook, "I admire people who are serious and take care of business. Do you mind if I ask what you're working so hard at?"

Ed shrugged, "Sure. It probably isn't much interest to someone else, but I'm right on the verge of expanding our junk business into something more, something really great." Ed then got lost in one idea after another that he'd gleaned from poring over the books. Along the way, the curious stranger had moved over to sit across from Ed and look through the notebook as Ed told his story.

After a while, Ed realized he'd been giving a sermon and hadn't let his visitor say a word, "Sorry about that. One man's junk and all. I just know I'm onto something, and this can be big for my family."

The stranger leaned back in the booth, smiled, and chuckled slightly, "Yeah. Life is funny. You just never know which way the wind is going to blow some days. Take me. I'm really just passing through on my way to Houston, where my company is interested in starting a few heavy-metal salvage and recycle yards. Not really mom-and-pop stuff, but large farm implements and heavy machinery. We identify the equipment we can either quickly refurb, part out, or easily scrap straight to meltdown, or we pass on it altogether. No long-term storage of junk for future pennies."

Ed slapped his hands on the table incredulously, "Wow. I have to tell you, that's exactly where I want us to go!"

The man chuckled again and tapped the notebook, "I gathered that from your business plan."

After sizing Ed up for a minute, the stranger said, "Listen, my name's Sam Iverson. Here's my card. I'm from an outfit called Ransom Steel. We have a few candidate yards we may partner with or buy to give us a foothold in the region. But to tell you the truth, I've always advocated buying into the right man more than the place."

"I get that, alright," Ed said, nodding with a grin. "I've run into some outfits I'd do business with over a handshake any day. There's others I wouldn't trust under any conditions."

"Ed, I'd like to come around to this yard of yours and talk a little business. If we can work things out, Ransom is in a position to step you up to the next level of heavy equipment you'd need to run the kind of yard you're talking about, which just happens to be the kind of yard we need."

A stunned Ed looked down at his notebook and back to Iverson, and then stuck his hand out with a smile, "Well alright, then. Come on down. You can follow me there now if you like!"

An hour later Ed was showing Iverson around the yard, talking nonstop about his plans. After a while they went into the house to talk it over with Carl. After hearing them out, Carl nodded to himself, grabbed a beer out of the fridge, then sat at his desk again looking out towards the yard, "Tell you what, let me think about it."

Ed leaned towards Carl, "Dad, *this is it*. It's *exactly* what I've been working on, but it puts us years down the road from where we could get to on our own! You see that, don't you? Come on, let's do this!"

After watching Carl's reaction, Iverson said, "Tell you what. We'll pull up some papers and send them to you. After you've read them, I'll come back down to talk over the details, not just about the contract and the deal, but how we'll do business. It'll be great for you and a good way for us to make a start here. You don't have to take my word for it; I'll have it all spelled out on paper. What do you say?"

Seeing Ed staring holes through him, Carl shrugged, "Okay, okay. We'll have a look and then see what we see."

Ed wasn't really listening as he shook Iverson's hand again. His mind was reeling over all of the next steps and possibilities. *Man, this is it!* It was all he could do to not jump up and yell it.

Iverson, not being one to spoil progress by continuing to sell after the sale, decided to head on to Houston and let this idea settle in with the Schmutz boys. The old man may be standoffish, but this kid Ed sure seemed like the real deal, was ready to go, and there was just something Iverson liked about him. Iverson was also eager to take advantage of the quick win for the company in this part of the world. "I'll be in touch soon, fellas, and we can go over the details line by line to make sure you're comfortable with how this will go. It was damn good to run into you like this, Ed. And Carl, this boy of yours is going to do big things for us both."

The screen door slammed closed behind him, and he didn't waste any time driving out on his way to US-90 and places west. As soon as he was gone, Ed jumped up with a grin, slapped Carl on the shoulder and almost yelled, unable to contain his excitement, "Man, I gotta go tell Margo about this! This is going to be great, Dad. I mean, I really think this is it! Yeehaw! Alright, alright, I'm gone," and he was heading out the same door.

"Hey now, hang on there," Carl said as he waved Ed back into the room. "Let's wait and see this contract he's going to send us before we get all stirred up and stir up anyone else. No use getting everyone all excited about something that might not happen. There'll be plenty of time for that if we decide to do this crazy thing. I mean it, now."

Ed gave his dad a frustrated glance and sighed. He knew by Carl's tone that this wasn't up for negotiation. "Okay. I'll wait, I guess, but I don't see why this has to be a secret. That darn contract better get here pretty quick!" He walked out the door with a little less bounce in his step.

The next month crawled by. At home with Margo and her folks, Ed had become outwardly quiet and detached, while inside he was tied up in knots waiting for the contract from Sam Iverson and the opening of the door to their new future. As time went on, Margo seemed to grow distracted too. One afternoon, after installing some new hallway lights with Cy at the high school, Ed saw Margo walk through the front entrance and turn into the office, and he decided he should clear things up with her.

As Cy went on to other chores, Ed went into the office to find Margo at her desk, her face in her hands, staring at the wall, while two student office aides rifled through file cabinets chatting away. "Hey, you look serious. I hope it isn't me. I know I've had some things on my mind, and maybe we should talk," Ed said with a nervous smile.

Margo turned to look at him, wiped a tear from her eye and said quietly, "Well, I guess we're going to have company soon." Seeing his puzzled look she said, "I just got back from a doctor's appointment. I've been feeling weird and some other things. So, anyway, he tells me I'm eight weeks along."

"Along? Along what?" Ed stared, still looking just as puzzled. Margo cocked her head at him with raised eyebrows and patted her belly, then Ed's eyes went wide, "What?! You're pregnant?! Holy cow!" Ed lifted Margo out of her chair and whirled her around the office in a bear hug.

"I hoped you'd be happy. I have some things to figure out, but . . ." Margo didn't finish the sentence before Ed cut her off.

"Hey, hey, listen, we'll figure it out when we figure it out, whatever it is. For now we celebrate." After kissing her, Ed said, "Look, I have to go tell my dad. Why don't you ride home with your dad, but don't tell him yet. When I get there, we'll tell both your folks together."

She nodded and said, "Sure, I have about an hour to go, but we'll be home by 4:30. Hug your dad for me and tell him I'll come by this weekend."

Ed hugged her again and bolted out the door. The two office aides, who had stopped chattering to watch, giggled and congratulated Margo. Past them through his open office door Principal Edgar Clanton stood smiling, "I guess you have some news, and we may have some planning to do." He waved his hand and said, "Ed's right, it can wait though. Go on home."

Margo walked past him into the office and said, "You know me. I'm a planner. I have an idea in mind because of this." Mr. Clanton chuckled to himself as he sat at his desk and knew from experience that he should just let Margo have her say.

"This may sound crazy, but I think we could start a day-care program right here at the school." Seeing Mr. Clanton peering over his glasses she hurried on, "Look, like it or not, we lose girls every year who drop out to have babies and don't come back. What if we start a day care here, run by student aides with some staff oversight? Maybe we could help those poor girls with a chance of staying in school, and the aides will get some new job experience."

"And you have a place to bring your kiddo right here at school while you work? Yeah, I get it . . ." Mr. Clanton trailed off, looking out the window. After a minute that seemed like an hour, "Tell you what, let me make a call to the junior college. I've known the president over there for years. I know they have a program like that, maybe not for the same reason, and he'll get us in the door to learn some start-up tips—if the Superintendent will let us do this in the first place, that is."

Margo was stunned, "That would be great, Mr. Clanton, and—"

He interrupted her before she could go on, "You need to hear me out. Assuming it all comes together, I'd need someone to spend part-time at the junior college for a while and then to set our program up based on what she learns."

"Well yeah," Margo nodded.

"I'd like *you* to do it. Before you tell me no, think about it. We'll bring in another student aid for the hours you'd be gone. And who's better motivated to make it work?"

"Gosh," Margo stammered, "I can try. Sure. But I was going to start taking night classes in business management for Ed's yard."

He agreed, "Yes, yes, I know. I remember 'the plan.' First things first though. If you want to get this day care thing up and going, we'll have to start now. Once it's rolling along, we'll make the time for you to take those business classes."

He paused to let her digest the idea, then he went on, "So if you're really up for it and agree to my terms, I'll make some calls to make sure I can coax the system along. This ain't New York, you know, I'll have to ease the district into it. And we'll have to bring in a guidance counselor or faculty member for some official supervisory stuff, at least for a while. But I think it may be time," Mr. Clanton said with a deep breath.

Margo nodded, "Okay, let's do it. I'll talk to Ed about everything. I'm sure he'll like the idea too."

"For now, go home, young lady, and celebrate your good news. We'll work out the details," and Mr. Clanton walked around the desk, patted Margo on the shoulder and sent her on her way.

Ed was in for another shock when he reached the junkyard and found Carl at his desk with a beer in one hand and a large, open envelope in front of him. "Guess you can see for yourself what came in the mail," Carl said indifferently and tilted his head at the papers.

Ed didn't know what to do first and simply started laughing, "Does it get any better than today? Holy cow!"

Ed kept talking nonstop, first the news about Margo's condition, and then about the business prospects with Iverson, hardly hearing an oddly calm Carl say, "Hey, that's great, boy. That really is. You guys have a regular family going and everything."

Carl sipped silently on his beer, keeping his gaze on his boy as Ed read excitedly through the stack commenting here and there about some detail or other. When Ed finished, he slapped it back on the desk with a flourish. Beaming at Carl, Ed tapped on the papers and said, "Dad, I was *right.* Mr. Iverson was *right.* This is *it.* This is how we start the new plan. What do you think? You read it, right?"

Carl took a slow breath, "Well, yeah, I read it. Look, Son, it's a big deal. I see it. But it's a lot of new work, things we haven't done. A kind of business we haven't done. And I'm not getting any younger, you know. Besides, I may not be a banker, but it looks like any profit comes after his company's end. So if this don't go the way your plan says it will go, Iverson's deal says we don't make anything. We just get a pile of new equipment taking up space that don't help pay the bills. You see what I'm saying?"

Ed was stunned when he answered, "You know that's just as true for the yard as it is today. If we don't keep finding business, we don't have business. This new deal with Iverson and Ransom Steel sets us up to handle a better-paying business and helps bring in that business too. If we're ever going to make the leap from a junkyard to a real, heavy salvage outfit, this is it. I don't know how else to say it, and surely you see it, right? This is it, *right?!*"

Ed's question was really rhetorical. He just knew his dad saw this too. All the confirmation he needed was Carl's shrug, "Yeah. Sure."

Ed snatched up the phone and dialed home. When Margo answered, she whispered into the phone, "Me first, before Mom and Dad come in," and she told Ed about the plan she and Mr. Clanton talked about.

"Whoa, you're way ahead of me, but that all sounds good. Here's mine," and Ed started explaining the Ransom Steel deal.

As he started going into the long-term business strategy, Margo cut him off again, "Hey, hey. Let's talk about that tonight. You still need to get home so we can tell everyone else *all* the news, remember?"

Ed stopped, "Alright, alright. Tell you what, tell your folks we have big news and want to celebrate by taking everyone to dinner. We'll spring it all on them over dinner somewhere nice, like the fancy steakhouse out by the country club."

"Okay, big spender, but come on home quick. I can't sit on this news forever," Margo laughed.

Ed thought about it, "Better yet, you guys hop in your dad's truck and meet us there. The steakhouse it is. I'll bring Dad. We can meet you there in thirty minutes, okay?"

"Sure. But come on. It feels like it won't be real until everyone knows," Margo said with mock impatience.

"Alright. We're getting on the road right away. See you in a few, little mama," and Ed hung up to see Carl still sitting passively and staring at him.

"Come on, Dad, let's lock up and hit the road," Ed said, turning for the door.

"No son, that's okay. You go." Seeing Ed turn around shaking his head, Carl waved his hand, "Naw. The big, public group stuff isn't my thing. You know that. Look, it's great. It is. Go have your nice dinner with the family. Really. It's all good. But I'm good *here*. Really now, just go. Bring Margo over this weekend, and we'll grill something."

Sighing, Ed relented, "Sure, Dad. It wouldn't kill you to come along, but whatever. I've gotta go, so I'm not late. But we're gonna talk about this this weekend, alright? *And* we'll talk about business! Later." A still very happy Ed bounded out the door and across the drive to his truck; all the while his thoughts ricocheted from baby to Margo to business and back.

Chapter 2

NIGHT COMES

Other winds took her astray and into darkness.

Lost in his thoughts about life's new possibilities, Ed took no notice when Carl narrowed his eyes and shook his head as the door closed on Ed's way out. It wouldn't have mattered to him anyway. As he pulled the truck onto the road, happiness rushed over Ed in such a flood of thoughts that he couldn't focus on any one of them.

Margo, pregnant. Oh man. And Iverson, holy cow! Look at this sunset, it's going to be a beaut. Bet she'll like that. It's all coming together! What a life! Man, I know Cy is going to love this Iverson plan. Oh hey . . . and Margo is pregnant! He'll love that too, and wait until Lois finds out!

Turning west onto the brand-new interstate highway, he said out loud to himself, "Even this darn road is awesome. You could land a jumbo jet on this thing!" He laughed at his sudden mental image of himself delirious and babbling. "It's alright, Ed, just breathe."

Less than ten minutes later, Ed was almost to Beaumont and parked. With no sign of Cy's truck, he went in and got a booth towards the back, where he sat almost in a dream state, still letting the happiness pour over him.

On the other side of town, Margo hurried her mom and dad out the door and into Cy's pickup. The three of them sat across the bench seat, with Margo in the middle in her traditional seat. Trying to sound grumpy through a smile, Cy said, "I don't know what all the fuss or the secrecy is about. And we have food here at home, you know. We don't need to put other people's kids through college just so we can have dinner."

"Dad, it isn't a secret. We have news that's a big enough deal that Ed wants to celebrate. It's all good." As she said it, she glanced at her mom and saw Lois was looking at her through squinted eyes.

Lois turned away, smiled to herself, and in a low voice Margo could barely hear said, "Hmm. Well, I wonder. I guess we'll see what this day has in store, won't we?" Margo snapped her gaze to the front and sat quietly and wide-eyed, wondering just how much her mom had already guessed. It was going to seem like an even longer ride now. They'd be traveling twice as far as Ed, and all of it on Main Street as it wound its way into State Road 105, not the fancy new interstate.

At the same time, another celebration was getting started not far away. Five pals who had gone separate ways after high school were home for a party weekend together. After an hour of drinking beer at Branson Pond out on Duncan Road, they realized it wasn't as much fun as it had been as teenagers. The ringleader, Margo's old "friend" Jimmy Faison, said, "Dudes, let's go back to my house. My dad has a full bar and a pool table, plus it's going to be dark soon, and we can go out on the golf course and blaze up a few."

That perked up Mark Hammock. "Cool!" As he started into a trot, Mark said over his shoulder, "Let's see who can get there first. C'mon, dudes." Tommy Jenks and Greg Logan threw beer cans down and broke into a run towards Marks pickup.

"Oh, no way man! Not fair!" now Jimmy was running towards his Trans Am. "Let's go, Speed Racers!"

Mark already had the truck's engine roaring to life as Jenks and Logan piled in. The tires were spitting gravel before Logan had his door closed. Behind them, Jimmy's Smokey and the Bandit Trans Am was cranking as Steve Mallet leapt into the shotgun position, but the old Chevy pickup was quickly pulling away down the gravel road.

Mallet pointed at Mark's truck, "Dude, no way he can beat this race car, can he?" In answer, Jimmy just grinned and punched it. The Trans Am fishtailed briefly then found its traction and was off like a bullet. A half-mile down the road, the black race car pulled next to the pickup, as Mallet taunted Mark through an open window, "Hah, you suck, Dude!"

With that as his cue, Jimmy pressed the gas pedal and shot past the pickup. Mark yelled, "Oh, I'm mad now! Faison's not the only badass in the world!" and he jammed the truck's gas pedal to the floor.

Next to him, Jenks and Logan were bouncing off the seat and howling, with Logan leaning out through the open passenger window and pounding the outside of the door with his fist, "Come on man, get 'em!"

At just that moment, Cy was rounding a sweeping leftward bend in the two-laned state road, with not much more on his mind than a good steak dinner with Ed and his two gals. All he could do was smile as he only half-heard Margo's "Geez Dad, could you drive any slower? Ed's going to eat without us at this rate."

As they drove along, Lois was taking in the scenery and also smiling to herself about their happy family and simple life. She noticed a cloud of white dust blowing behind a black car that was racing along a dirt road off to the right of them, with a pickup not far behind it. *Boys and their cars. They all seem to go through a second childhood until they fully grow up, and even then . . .* Lois shook her head slightly, sighed, and turned a smile to Margo and Cy. Cy's attention was naturally drawn towards the oncoming traffic to his left and the nifty Mustang convertible full of teenagers that was approaching. Unseen by Cy off to his right and creating the cloud of dust Lois saw, Jimmy Faison was still rocketing up Duncan Road which merged straight onto the state road at the end of the curve.

Seeing Cy's truck off to his left, and then seeing Mark's Chevy closing in his rearview mirror, Jimmy thought, *Damn. If I just get in front of that dude, I'm golden, and Mark's blocked!* He stood on the gas and the Trans Am accelerated to over 60 miles per hour, barely holding the road as it danced across the rough gravel surface with Mark's pickup only a few car lengths behind him.

Cy saw a dark blur to his right at the same time he heard Lois gasp loudly and Margo yell, "You assholes!" He was startled by the Trans Am, as it launched off of the dirt road in front of them and kept flying down the road after just missing Lois's side of the truck. He instinctively took his foot off the gas, tapped the brake, and grabbed the wheel with both hands.

"Ho, that was close," Cy said wide-eyed while watching the Trans Am zoom away.

Mark had been so fixated on catching Jimmy, that he hadn't noticed they were merging onto the state road. That, and the cloud of white dust the Trans Am was kicking up meant he never even saw the pickup that Jimmy had only narrowly missed. Mark wasn't as lucky as Jimmy—he plowed directly into the passenger door of the old white pickup, and he could see the woman inside looking directly at him with surprise in her eyes. They hit at an angle, reducing the impact somewhat, and Mark slammed on the brakes at the same instant.

Seeing motion in the corner of her eye, Lois had turned quickly to look out the passenger window and flinched back away from it with an "Oh!" punctuated by a loud, muffled sound like kicking a cardboard box. The passenger door instantly buckled inward and the window exploded glass like shrapnel across the cab. Cy felt his truck lurch sideways and start to spin slightly to the left. At the same time, wind and noise roared through the cab from the now-shattered passenger window drowning out almost everything, including his own thoughts. The sound of a racing engine and screeching tires sounded like they were inside the truck with them. Mark's Chevy went into a long, straight skid, following the white pickup as it careened towards the far shoulder.

Cy was doing everything he could to keep the truck on the road and going straight. The truck had now spun almost sideways on the road, as it still slid along. As the skid slowed, the tires began to bite again, and the truck jerked back to the right, straddling the center line. Feeling he was regaining control of the truck, Cy glanced up the road where he saw the wide-open eyes of the young Mustang driver, who had seen and heard the collision and was now frozen behind the wheel. Too late. The convertible smashed into Cy's side of the truck, barely missing a full head on collision. With that impact, the pickup lurched to a sudden stop, and Mark's Chevy, which was still skidding, slammed again into the back. Both pickups screeched to rest almost side-by-side across the road, each facing a different direction. The convertible had rebounded off of Cy's truck and into the deep ditch beside the road, rolling upside down and slamming to a stop at a culvert, engine still running and wheels spinning.

Jimmy stopped when he saw the commotion in his rearview and backed up the road almost to where Cy's mangled pickup sat. He parked on the shoulder and faced a surreal scene as he walked towards the wreckage. Both pickups were in the middle of the road, with Cy's looking like it had been driven off a cliff—crumpled in front and on both sides, and the windshield and a window had blown out. Mark's truck was accordioned in the front, and the left front wheel had broken at the axle. Shattered glass covered the pavement behind the trucks, and both trucks were hissing as their destroyed engines spewed steam, antifreeze, and oil, and the air smelled like burning rubber.

In the midst of the chaos, Jimmy heard something familiar, and it didn't make sense to him. *Is that Lynyrd Skynyrd? Yeah, play it, son. I love that song! Sweet Home Alabama, where the skies are so blue . . .* Jimmy's thoughts about the music stopped, and he shook his head realizing it was coming from the crashed, upside-down car in the ditch. *Whoa.*

Margo started awake in the pickup, confused as she found herself slumped forward over something heavy in her lap. Her first groggy thoughts were, *What is on me? Wait, why am I sleeping? What are we doing?* She opened her eyes and realized her mom was lying across her lap, and Margo had been leaning against Lois's back.

Her head pounded as Margo turned towards Cy, "Dad, help me . . ." Then she saw her dad laying awkwardly against the steering wheel, his face turned away from her. She tried to roll Lois into a sitting position, but Margo's belly erupted in pain like it was on fire, forcing her to stop. Margo looked up and noticed a couple of men walking up to the front of the truck. Although her vision was not quite clear, she thought she could make one of them out. *Am I seeing this? Why is Jimmy Faison here? What . . . ?*

Before she could utter a word, she faded to black again, overcome by pain and shock, and she bent forward, still holding her mom.

Squinting at the shattered windshield, Jimmy could barely see a couple people in the old white pickup, but it was hard to make them out in the shadows. As Jimmy craned his neck to look, his attention was interrupted by the passenger door on Mark's Chevy creaking open, then out stumbled Logan and Jenks. A few seconds later Mark slid out the passenger door. The three of them huddled on the side of the road, looking lost.

More cars were now stopping, and a couple of drivers ran to the guys standing with Mark. One of them asked, "You boys okay?"

Logan answered incredulously, "Y-yeah. Dude, holy shit!"

Jimmy walked up wide-eyed and shaking his head, "I can't believe that just happened. I can't believe he missed me, but I thought you were going to stop, man! What the hell?"

Mark was looking from side to side like a bobblehead, staring at the ground and rambling, "I didn't see him, man. We were just flying, and then *BAM*, I hit him. I just hit him. I mean *BAM!* Didn't even see him, 'cause I was just watching your ass, man. Oh shit. What did I do? I saw her look right at me like she knew I was going to hit 'em. And then I did. Oh shit. Oh shit. How am I gonna get out of this one? Oh shit."

Seeing one of the guys who had run up staring at Mark and taking all of this in, Jimmy grabbed Mark by the shoulder and started leading him up the road and away from the wreck, hissing urgently, "Dude, you gotta get it together!" Looking back over his shoulder as he picked up the pace, Jimmy said loudly, "Hey man, you know that's not what happened. You couldn't have done anything when that guy hit you. I saw it all."

A few seconds later the stranger turned back and jogged toward the wreck and started talking with another man who was looking into Cy's truck. Jimmy hustled his friends to his car, "Get in. We gotta call my old man. He'll know what to do." No one seemed to notice the sound of the Firebird cranking up and hurrying away.

Jimmy raced home and ran inside to call his father at work while the others were piling out of his car. After hearing Jimmy's story, Jimmy Faison, Sr., attorney-at-law, did what he did best. He took charge and started controlling the damage, "Damn it! They shouldn't have left the scene. Alright, look, take those idiots to Baptist Hospital in Orange. Check Mark in at the ER for pain and shock from the accident. Be sure to say those words—'pain and shock.' Get there as soon as you can, and make it clear you went straight there from the scene. I'll make sure they're expecting you, and I'll meet you there. Now go."

"Great. Like I need this," Jimmy Sr. sighed to himself. "Darla, get Al Tailor on the phone for me. His hospital number. It's urgent." A few minutes later Jimmy Sr. jumped right to the chase, "Al, Jimmy. I need some help."

"Hey, Jimmy boy! Whatever you need, my friend. What's up?" Dr. Al Tailor just happened to be a managing physician at the hospital, not to mention a member of Jimmy Faison Sr.'s golf foursome. After Jimmy Sr. relayed the story, Al assured him, "No problem. I'll have a look at them myself. Want me to call you back after I see them?"

"No, no. I'll be up there as soon as I can. But listen, the kid who was driving was Mark Hammock."

Al nodded on his end, "Ah, I see. As in County Commissioner Ken Hammock?"

"Yeah. And Jimmy tells me the kid is very confused . . . disoriented, babbling nonsense that could be misinterpreted as incriminating. Look for that, will you? I wouldn't want him to do something stupid before I'm there to counsel him."

"You got it. I'm on it. See you when you get here, Jimmy. Come straight to the ER," Al hung up and headed to the ER himself.

As Jimmy Sr. walked out of his office, he didn't break stride and told his secretary, "Call Ken Hammock. Let him know his boy has been in an accident and Jimmy has taken him to the ER in Orange. I'm on my way there now from my office in Beaumont."

Jimmy parked at the ER door and hustled Mark, Jenks, and Logan to the desk, leaving Steve Mallet with the car. He told the nurse, "These guys were in a bad wreck, and I brought 'em here so you could see how bad any of 'em are hurt. Uh, they're in pain and shock of some kind."

Al Tailor was already waiting for them, "I'm Dr. Tailor. Your dad let me know you were on your way. Are any of you hurt, and which of you is Mark?" They all shook their heads, and Mark meekly raised his hand halfway. "Alright, fill out those forms from the nurse and come on back to Number 3."

A few minutes later, the four boys shuffled into examination room 3, and Al pulled the curtain closed around them. "Alright, let's have a look at you, Mark." As the boy started to protest, Al held up a hand, "Standard procedure. You just never know. Sometimes shock hides the injury for a while."

As the doctor poked and prodded him for signs of pain and swelling, Mark went back into auto-babble, shaking his head, "No, no. Nothing hurts. I'm good, but holy cow, I didn't even see the guy in that white pickup. I was watching Jimmy and didn't see any other cars or even the road, until it was too late. Shit. It was all my fault. I'm so screwed." Mark hung his head.

"Hmm, well. Nothing too severe so far," Al said, looking pensive. Mark figured the doc was thinking about all of the things that could be wrong with him. Al was actually considering Jimmy Sr.'s call and worrying about the direction of Mark's babbling. "Tell you what, let's get you a sedative to calm you down some and help us have a good look at you. I'll be back shortly." Al looked in the waiting room for Jimmy Sr. and then hustled back to his office to ensure he hadn't called.

A nurse came in a few minutes after the doctor left and gave Mark a shot. Minutes later he was lying back on the examination table and looking glassy-eyed at the ceiling. As Mark drifted in and out of light sleep, Jimmy, Jenks, and Logan wandered back out to the car to wait with Steve "away from all the sickos" in the ER.

Mark paid no attention to the commotion as some EMTs rolled in with stretchers. The ER staff kicked into high gear, surrounding the stretcher and taking it right into an elevator, leaving the EMTs to walk back outside with their heads down. As they went out, an Orange County Deputy Sheriff walked in and patted one on the shoulder, "Hey guys, it happens. You did good to get her here. The rest of them in that wreck weren't so lucky."

Hearing that, the nurse looked up and said, "Was this the same wreck the boys in Number 3 were in?"

Curious, the cop walked over and stuck his head in Number 3. He looked back and asked the nurse, "Anything wrong with this guy? Can I talk to him?"

"Oh, Dr. Tailor said he seems fine, but we gave him a sedative because he was so wound up. He can talk, if you can keep his attention," and the nurse kept flipping through a clipboard full of paper.

Jimmy Sr. walked into the ER like he walked into a courtroom: He owned the place, and it's best if these folks understood it from the get-go. His son followed quietly behind him after having filled him in on their visit with Dr. Tailor, "He's down there, Dad."

The deputy sheriff could be heard through the curtain as they walked up, "Okay, okay. I got it, and it's the same as I heard at the scene. That's good, at least. I need to make a call, but I'll be right back."

Stepping into the tight space and between the officer and Mark, Jimmy Sr. was all business, "Officer, I'm not sure what is going on here, but I am Mr. Hammock's attorney, James Faison. Anything you have to ask him will, of course, need to be in my presence, and for now, young Mr. Hammock is in no condition to speak with anyone except his medical team."

Mark's eyes opened wide and he started gibbering, "What? Oh. Hey Mr. Faison. I was just telling him—"

Jimmy Sr. waved his hand dismissively, cutting Mark off, "There will be time for that."

Turning back to the deputy sheriff, he said, "I want to be clear. My client has been in a severe and traumatic car accident. Between his injuries and the medication, he is not sufficiently lucid to give any reliable witness statements."

"Sir, everything he tells me corroborates what I was told on the scene. This isn't really so much about witness statements as it is a confession for being the cause of this accident. He told people at the scene—and has told me—that it was all his fault, and his recollection matches the scene perfectly. Based on the severity and the number of fatalities, I'm sure charges will be filed," said the deputy sheriff calmly while putting his notepad in his pocket.

Mark was blinking back tears when Jimmy Sr. shook his head and sighed, "Charges? So far, we have several witnesses, one of whom is being treated in the emergency room, and no police report on what actually occurred on that highway. I suggest you take this one step at a time, and I'll talk with my client and his doctor. Here's my card. Please contact my office if you have further questions for him after he has been treated."

• • •

After sitting alone in the booth for forty-five minutes, Ed was tired of waiting and couldn't drink another glass of water. He called Cy and Lois's house from a pay phone but didn't get an answer. *Surely they'd be here by now. What the heck?* He finally gave up and told the hostess, "If a man and two gals come in looking for someone named Ed, will you tell them I went to the house to check on them and to call me there?"

He pulled onto State Road 105, driving south towards the house, wondering where along the way he'd pass the family driving to meet him. Ten minutes later he was stuck behind a line of cars, and down the road he could see flashing lights. *Great, no wonder they're late.*

After inching his way along, he was finally passing the wreck that caused it all. Off to his right was an upside-down car in a ditch, with emergency responders all around it. Just past it, two very smashed pickups had been dragged off the road across a culvert into a clearing. Neither pickup looked great, but one of them looked like it got the worst of the deal, with missing windows and doors. As he drove by, he couldn't help but take one more look at the wrecked vehicles, and his heart felt like it stopped, "Holy shit, that's Cy's truck!"

Ed jammed on his emergency break, jumped onto the road, and ran to the pickup. There was no one in it, but it was covered in shattered glass. *Is that blood on the seat and the floor?* "Oh God, no!"

A cop walked up, "Hey, buddy, get back in your vehicle and get the hell out of here. This is a crime scene and none of your damned business!"

Walking towards the cop and barely keeping it together, Ed asked, "Where are they? The people in this truck? I know them. They're mine . . . my family, my wife, her parents!"

"Uh huh, well . . . Ah, all I know for sure is there have been some fatalities from some of the vehicles involved, but I know at least two women have already been taken to the Orange hospital. One of them was pregnant, and the EMTs were worried about the baby."

"What? Oh no, Margo! How could . . . Oh man, I got to go! What the hell?" Ed yelled as he sprinted back to his truck.

Twenty minutes later, Ed hurried into the emergency room at Baptist Hospital. "Ma'am, my wife was brought in here. She was hurt in a car wreck. Cop said the EMTs were worried about her baby."

The nurse looked genuinely concerned, "Oh, sir, she's up in surgery now. They're doing everything they can for them. You can take that elevator to the fourth floor and follow the signs to the surgical waiting room, and they'll be able to tell you more. I'll let them know you're on your way." Ed was already running to the elevator.

As Ed stepped out of the elevator, a concerned-looking volunteer in the surgical waiting room was standing at her desk, "Please make yourself comfortable. All I can tell you now is that she's in critical condition. I'm so sorry."

"Is there a doctor or nurse who can tell me how she is? And how about her parents?" Ed was desperate for anything.

"Well, someone on the team will come out before long, I'm sure, but I can't say when. I'm not sure her parents are here, but I'll let you know if I hear something." After Ed had taken a seat in front of the doors into the surgical suite, the volunteer sat at her desk and whispered into her phone.

After what seemed like hours to Ed, the door opened and a tired-looking man in scrubs came out. "He the dad?" the surgeon asked the volunteer, who nodded slowly.

"Well, young fella, I'm very sorry, but we couldn't do enough for Mom. Her injuries were just too severe. I know it's a shock for someone so young, but she's gone. Again, I'm very sorry," the surgeon said matter-of-factly. Ed felt his heart stopping again, like he did when he saw Cy's truck. He sat down heavily, putting his head in his hands. *What? No! Oh my God, Margo . . .*

"But the baby is fine. We got there just in time, and she's going to be fine."

The volunteer hung up the phone, "Doctor, the girl's parents are on the way up."

Thank God, Cy and Lois are alright, Ed thought and could feel his hope rising. *But how could Margo possibly have delivered a baby? What was she, six weeks pregnant? Eight?*

The elevator chimed, and Ed sprang out of his chair and ran to the doors. As they slid open he asked in a rush, "Cy? Lois? What happened?"

Two people edged out as Ed walked in looking for his in-laws, only to find an empty elevator. Ed stepped back out and saw the volunteer watching him in puzzlement. She asked him, "Aren't these her parents?"

"No, I don't know these people. I'm looking for Cy and Lois Cormier."

The volunteer looked down at her clipboard, "Cormier? No, no. The patient's name is Lucky. Sarah Lucky."

The worried-looking woman who had just come up the elevator perked up, "That's our daughter! Has there been a mix-up? Is she alright?" Ed could see she had been crying. She was now gripping her husband's arm and looking desperately at the doctor who was still standing in the waiting room looking from Ed to the couple from the elevator.

The doctor spoke quietly to the volunteer, then pulled the couple aside to repeat what he had told Ed. As the woman sat down sobbing, the doctor told her husband, "Again, your daughter's baby is going to be fine. She's on her way to the NICU now as a precaution. Sarah's injuries were just too bad for us to help her. I'm very sorry."

Now standing at the desk, Ed's head was spinning, "Look, I'm Ed *Schmutz*. My wife is here somewhere. *Margaret Schmutz*. And her parents should be here too, Cy and Lois Cormier. They were all in the same car and were in some bad wreck out on 105."

The volunteer made several hushed phone calls. Minutes later a white-coated doctor stepped off the elevator and went into the surgical suite. When he came back out, the volunteer nodded toward Ed. The doctor approached Ed and asked, "Sir, are you Mr. Schmutz?"

Ed jumped up, "Yes. What can you tell me?"

"Well, first . . . your wife . . . Margaret, right? She's been very badly injured and is in critical condition. She's still in surgery, and we're doing everything we can. She should be out soon, but she'll be going to the ICU and probably has a long road ahead of her. Her surgeon will be able to tell you more, when he comes out."

"And what about her parents? Where are they?" Ed asked while looking through the windows in the doors.

"Ah. The Cormiers, right?' The doctor paused, looked down briefly, took a breath, and said, "I'm sorry to have to tell you they did not survive the accident. They were deceased when they were brought in. I'm very sorry, Mr. Schmutz."

Ed sat down hard. *Cy and Lois. Gone? How could this be? I just had coffee with them at home this morning. We were going to dinner! We hadn't told them about . . .* He looked up at the doctor, "What about the baby?"

"Baby? Your wife was pregnant? Oh, Mr. Schmutz, I didn't realize." He looked gravely at the volunteer, then back to Ed and said, "I'll make sure the surgeon gives you a full picture." The doctor walked back into the surgical suite, leaving Ed bewildered and feeling like a drowning man.

Hours later, another tired man in scrubs walked out and approached Ed, who was now alone in the waiting room, "Mr. Schmutz, I'm Dr.

Willis. I operated on your wife." Although he felt like he had lived in that room for days, Ed was now wide awake and almost afraid to hear what the doctor had to say.

"She tolerated today's surgery as well as can be hoped. She'll be in ICU for some time and will need more surgery. But so far so good."

"She was very badly injured in this accident from multiple physical traumas, the most serious one probably from the seatbelt, which saved her life but also caused considerable abdominal damage. It either lacerated or ruptured the abdominal wall at impact, as well as tears in the colon and a few other organs. We've repaired and stabilized the colon and temporarily closed her belly. We're going to have to watch the healing on this step for a few weeks before we can go back for final repairs to her abdominal muscles for long-term stability."

"In the interim, as soon as we think her system can tolerate it, we're going to schedule her for surgery to repair some broken bones around her eye socket, as early as next week if we can. Any questions so far?"

Ed clasped his hands together, leaned towards the doctor, and pleaded, "Yeah, how bad is this for her overall? Is she going to come out of this? Will she be okay?"

"Again, her injuries were severe, and she has some tough recovery ahead of her. But she's young and fit. That's in her favor and will help her recover as much as possible."

"And the baby?" Ed asked quietly, blinking back tears.

After a pause, the doctor took a breath and said, "Son, I'm sorry. The tears in her uterus and the blood vessel damage surrounding it were severe. The only way we could stop the bleeding and save your wife's life was to remove it. Believe me, we had no choice. The baby could not have survived in any case, and we had to take care of your wife."

Ed sat down and hung his head, taking it all in, and feeling shock give way to grief. Margo was physically shattered. Their baby was gone. Cy and Lois were gone. "They didn't even know," he sobbed softly.

The doctor put a hand on Ed's shoulder, "Get some rest if you can. She's going to need you when she starts coming around," and the doctor disappeared through the double doors, leaving Ed alone and feeling very small.

The weeks that followed were a blur of sameness and sadness for Ed. He haunted Margo's ICU bedside, waiting for a sign that she was coming back, but also dreading what he had to tell her. Late at night, he'd drive home to eat, shower, and sleep fitfully for a few hours, and then return to her bedside in the morning. As terrible as it was to watch her like this and wonder, it was worse for him at home where every sight, sound, and smell compounded the pain in his heart, reminding him that Cy and Lois were gone.

Ed called his dad from the hospital the morning after the accident, and Carl had spent an hour or two with him in ICU each day after that. They didn't speak much. Falling into their old habit, they simply soldiered through each day and did what needed to be done. For Carl, that meant watching his son grieve for a family and a life that Carl wasn't really part of, having lost interest in the world when he lost Hildie.

Margo woke up in the ICU three days after her first surgery. Most of the day she was in and out of consciousness and then gradually became more lucid after the nurses cut back the sedative. With Ed holding her hands, Margo's eyes went to Carl and then back to Ed before croaking, "Mom and Dad?"

The tears running down her husband's face told her what she needed to know. Ed slowly filled in some of the details of the accident, stopping as Margo's eyes swelled with tears. She shook her head, "No, tell me the rest. What happened, and when can we go home?"

Ed explained the accident as he understood it from what he saw at the scene and from a deputy sheriff who had come to see him in the waiting room in hopes of talking with Margo. "I don't know how soon we'll get you home. The doc said something about needing a little more fixer-upper work. We'll get you home though," Ed tried saying confidently.

Margo's hands went to her belly, and she asked, "What do they say about the baby?"

Ed held her hands in both of his, closed his eyes, and explained what Dr. Willis had had to do. When he finished, he found Margo looking up at the ceiling, tears running down her face. She closed her eyes with a heavy sigh, and something changed in her countenance. She looked again at the ceiling, and when she spoke, her voice was quiet and sounded almost defeated, "I want to talk to the cop who you talked to. I need to tell him about the car that cut us off before the other guy hit us."

Even in the ICU, Margo was all business. Ed nodded and bowed his head, thankful that she was still with him.

Carl sat quietly and watched his son and daughter-in-law. He knew he didn't have words to make any of this go away or make the pain more bearable. *I wish things like this didn't happen. But this is just how it goes. I hate to see it, I do, but it is a heartless, cruel life we live.*

A few days later Margo got her wish when the same deputy sheriff accompanied Ed into the ICU to see her. After telling him everything she could remember, the officer nodded and said, "Ma'am, everything you're telling me lines up with what the driver who hit you has already said, both to witnesses at the scene and to me in the ER. I'll be sure your statement is in the report to back it up. Thanks for letting me talk to you. I know this isn't an easy time for you. Now just heal up, and we'll take care of this."

The next two weeks remained eventful for Margo. She underwent two more surgeries to correct the rest of her injuries, from the bone fragments and fractures in her face to rebuilding her abdominal wall. All of this left her in ICU and heavily sedated once again.

After visiting her one morning, Ed walked the two blocks from the hospital to the District Attorney's office near the county courthouse. The deputy had let him know there would be a formal review of the case, and the DA would be making a decision that morning regarding charges. Ed wanted to be there to hear something he could bring back to Margo. When he arrived, the DA was still behind closed doors, so Ed sat just outside in the hallway waiting for news.

Inside, seated in front of the DA's desk were the deputy sheriff as the investigating official, Jimmy Faison Sr. representing Mark Hammock, and several of the DA's staff members. Bobby Dorcas, the District Attorney, summarized what he'd heard as he flipped through the case file, "Well, it's all pretty cut and dried: three car pile-up; two fatalities in the pickup driven by one Cyrus Cormier; four teenage fatalities in a car that ended up upside down in a ditch. All the witness statements agree except for one—from someone in one of the vehicles involved—and that young gal was not really in a position to see the first collision. The other witnesses are all in agreement that the driver of the pickup that was on State Road 105—Mr. Cormier—was driving recklessly, creating the conditions that led to this terrible accident, colliding with Mark Hammock's pickup, then crossing the center line and colliding with a car that was traveling in the opposite direction."

The deputy was indignant, "But sir, I personally took the statement from Mr. Hammock not long after the accident in which he was very clear that he caused this accident, not Mr. Cormier."

Jimmy Faison, Sr., didn't miss a beat, "And that statement will not be admissible in court. Mr. Hammock is a witness and was under medical care. In fact, he was under the influence of both traumatic shock and medication when the deputy spoke with him."

Ignoring Jimmy Sr., the deputy leaned towards Dorcas and went on, "And yet his statement to me still agreed, word-for-word, with comments he made to others at the scene."

The DA shook his head and waved dismissively, "Doesn't matter, Deputy. Bystander recollections of what young Mr. Hammock said are hearsay at best. At worst, there was a violation of Mr. Hammock's Fifth Amendment rights, since you were seeking confirmation of criminal guilt without first advising him of his rights and while he was under the influence. No, Mr. Faison's right, unsurprisingly. Mr. Hammock's comments in your report are inadmissible on multiple counts and just as unreliable as the little gal's . . . what's her name, Smut?" Dorcas looked around the room to a chorus of muffled laughs.

The deputy spoke up, "It's *Schmutz*, Margaret Schmutz. And she was in the pickup that Mark Hammock hit. Mr. Cormier was her father, and he and her mother both died in the accident."

Dorcas went on, "Well, however you say her name, my point is that, independent of his Fifth Amendment rights, Mr. Hammock's statement is no more reliable than hers. They were both traumatized in the accident and heavily sedated when you took their statements. There are other statements that are in agreement, however. These are from uninjured young men in Mr. Hammock's vehicle and from Mr. Faison's own son, who just happened to be there and was narrowly missed by Mr. Cormier before the first collision."

"So look, we're not ever going to know what really caused this accident and cost six people their lives. As terrible as that is, there is still nothing credible that points towards Mark Hammock. There not only isn't a case here against young Mr. Hammock, but there are statements and circumstantial evidence that support this was the fault of Mr. Cormier."

Bobby Dorcas looked at Jimmy Sr., who nodded, "Sounds just about right, Mr. District Attorney. I expect Mr. Hammock to seek compensation from Mr. Cormier's insurance company for his totaled vehicle and medical expenses, but we're probably all best served to let it go at that."

Chuckling, Dorcas said, "Oh hell, you do beat all some days, Counselor." He walked around his desk and opened his office door, "Alright, we're done here. My staff will close this out with the court. Deputy, thank you for your diligence. Mr. Faison, see you on another day in court."

The deputy shook his head, looked from Dorcas to Jimmy Sr. and walked into the hallway. As they walked out the door, Jimmy Sr. patted Dorcas on the back and said, "Thanks, Bobby. I'll let Ken know he can rest easy about Mark. All's well that ends."

"Yes it 'tis, Jimmy, yes it 'tis. See you tomorrow night at the club," the DA answered with a chuckle and a wink as he stood in his office doorway and watched Jimmy Sr. walk away.

Sitting in the hallway, Ed took all of this in. Seeing him waiting there, the deputy walked over to him and said in a low voice, "Mr. Schmutz, I don't know how to tell you this, but it's done. No charges. The DA's conclusion is that it was your father-in-law's fault."

Ed stood, narrowing his eyes and said, "You know that's not true. Margo was there. She was an eyewitness to the whole thing. She told you what happened. Mark Hammock told you it was his fault."

"Yeah, I know, I know. But there are other eyewitness accounts that contradict your wife's statement, and the DA found them compelling." The deputy summarized the witness statements from Jenks, Logan, and Jimmy Faison, the DA's opinion about Margo's and Mark Hammock's statements, and the basis for the decision. "For what it's worth, I believe your wife and Mr. Hammock and don't believe justice was served here."

Ed bit his lip and looked down. Then, nodding his head, he turned slowly away from the deputy and walked away, not really hearing the deputy's, "I'm sorry, Mr. Schmutz."

• • •

With Margo still out of it in ICU, Ed went to the yard to see his dad, the only other family he and Margo had left. Maybe Carl could make sense of it all. As Ed pulled up, he was confused by what he saw. A couple of large flatbed trucks were driving off the lot with some of Carl's and Ed's heavy equipment, including parts of their largest crusher. *What the hell?*

He walked into the house and found Carl sitting at his desk in the darkened front room, a stack of papers scattered across the desktop. "Dad, who the hell is that with our equipment and where are they going with it?"

Carl looked up tiredly, "Well, I was going to tell you about this after Margo was doing better, but I guess now the cat's out of the bag and all." Carl watched as Ed strode through the room and looked out the window surveying the yard.

"Listen, it's time, son. I know you've had a lot to deal with, but I've been thinking about this for a while now. I'm not going to live forever. I'm sixty-three years old. I can already start taking social security. That's a damn sight easier than scratching a living out as a junkman. So I sold it all. Cashed out to retire as best I can."

Shaking his head, Ed said, "No, Dad, you can't! This Iverson deal is going to change things. This is how we'll move up to better money, regular money. It's all lined up, we just have to stick to the plan. We already signed the Ransom Steel contract!"

Carl grimaced, "Well, no, *we* didn't. I just hung on to it for a few weeks, and now I've torn it up. I've already talked with ol' Iverson and told him he'll have to find another yard somewhere. And old Henry Peake made me an okay deal for most of the heavy equipment and is going to clear the yard, moving our scrap to his place in Port Arthur."

"That can't be worth much in real money, Dad. What we're really sitting on is the value of the work we're going to do with Iverson!" Ed was incredulous.

"No, Son," Carl said calmly. "I got some real money for the *property*—the real estate. That pompous bastard Harry Rezak wants to put a motel of some kind right on the highway, and he's been wanting our parcel to fill it out. He's even going to let me keep the house on it, since it's out of the way of his construction site. I'll clear enough to keep my bills paid along with the social security checks, and then no more of this heavy lifting."

"Heavy lifting? Dad, I do most of the heavy lifting around here! Come on, we have a plan! What are you thinking?"

Carl glanced down at the desk and back at Ed, "You know you've been pretty scarce around here for a while now. Don't get me wrong. You had to do what you had to do after the accident and all. I get it. But even before that, you had a good thing going with Margo and her folks. I figured for a while now that you had moved on to a better life than I ever gave you. Hell, I'm glad you set yourself up with something better. You saw your chance with them, and you took it. You were in a family again."

He could see Ed was confused. Sighing heavily, Carl said, "Look, this is done, Son. Just like you did, I needed to do something to take care of *me*, and this is it. I ain't getting rich in this deal, but I'll keep making ends meet without worrying where the next load of junk is coming from, day after day and week after week.

"In time, you'll see this is the right thing. This keeps things simple. And, hey, life hasn't exactly gotten easier for you and Margo right now, so this should simplify things a bit for you too. The Iverson thing? *Not* simple, and it's likely to end bad anyway. What does an outfit like that need with us and this yard? Nothing. It was just a matter of time before they pulled something over on us with their damned lawyers and their contracts. Well, screw that and screw them. We're out—*I'm* out. Instead of them screwing me, this will keep me in beer and groceries."

Carl looked towards the window without really seeing it and lowered his voice, "I've tried telling you, boy. This is how the real world is. Life don't bring us happy endings. It takes and it takes. It takes everything, even when you're just minding your own business, taking care of your own, and happy just being left alone." He paused, lost in thought, and then muttered, "Happy? Yeah, right. It ain't real, at least not for long and not for keeps. It's just the calm before the storm that takes it all away.

"You know I'm right about this. Think about it . . . your new family with Cy and Lois? Gone. Margo's baby? Gone. And it damned near took her too. And for what? Huh? Some grand purpose?" Carl's voice trailed off, and he closed his eyes.

Carl looked down at his desk then turned to Ed, shook his head, and waved his hand dismissively. His voice now shifted from sadness to a sharp, bitter edge, "No. It was just the same for your mom, the most precious thing God ever breathed life into, happiness and goodness incarnate. *Gone*. Life just took her. Because that's just how it is. We get what we can get, when we can get it, and then we wait for life to take it all. There is no happy ending. There is no justice, no meaning, no reward for goodness. There is just this life until there isn't. You get what you get, and you shouldn't get your hopes up, because there ain't anything more."

Ed was reeling. The business—their *future*—was gone, but that wasn't all. Looking around the room, it was like he was seeing it for the first time in years. Everything was lifeless. A coat of dust covered the floor and countertops. The couch and chairs showed years of spills on threadbare cushions and had sweaty grime worn into the armrests. The once cheery curtains had faded to white and were starting to give in to dry rot. The area rugs that once decorated the place had shredded over the years, only to be thrown out and replaced with streaks of dirt and mud tracked in from the yard on work boots. The happy tastes of life that once wafted from the kitchen had long since been replaced by stale beer and burnt coffee. It looked, smelled, and felt soulless and lifeless.

Twelve years after Hildie's death, there was no remnant of her anywhere in the house. Carl had long since given in to the loss and his grief with no hope of seeing through them to any happy memories of his wife. The last few weeks of pain and fear now turned to a despair that was crushing Ed, and as it did, the last light of Hildie's memory also winked out. There was nothing left of her, not just in the house, but in their hearts. Her death had now become truly absolute.

In that moment of realization, Ed felt a darkness swelling up inside to fill the void. He could feel hope, happiness, and his dreams fading away into that same soulless and lifeless darkness that permeated what was once his home. One thought came to him like a last lifeline: *Margo!* He rushed from the house without a word, leaving Carl still sitting where he found him.

Ed spent the rest of the day sitting next to Margo, either bewildered as he kept frenetically rehashing mentally what he'd heard from his dad, or desperate as he watched for any sign of consciousness on his wife's face. Margo was now the last person left who could help, who could push back this darkness. Just before nightfall, she stirred, and after fussing over her and consulting with Dr. Willis, the nurses moved her to a regular room where she would spend another several days recovering from her last operations.

As she settled in, Margo rallied a little as she turned towards Ed, "Hey, how long have you been babysitting me?"

Ed gave her a worried smile and took her hands, "Oh, I've been here as much as I could. I go home every day for a while to shower, if nothing else, before the people here complain. How are you feeling? Any pain, want me to get a nurse or anything?"

"Nothing I can't handle. I guess some of this might hurt more as the anesthesia wears off, but I'm okay right now. My memory's kind of foggy though. I know we had a wreck. Someone hit us," her eyes welling up, and she paused. "I know Mom and Dad are gone, and . . ." Margo shook her head, and her chest shuddered as she worked to stifle the sobs behind the tears that were now flowing. "What happened, and where are things now?"

Ed leaned over her, taking her hands and nodding, "Okay, okay. I'll tell you." He took a breath and explained everything, starting with the accident. He told her the deputy's best theory on how the accident happened, and that in addition to losing Cy and Lois, those four poor teenagers in the convertible never had a chance. He told her about her surgeries and everything that Dr. Willis had fixed along the way. Then he paused, desperately wishing there was no more to the story.

"What else? I know you. There's something you're not saying," Margo said quietly. "Just say it. All of it."

He sighed and dropped his eyes from hers as he explained the District Attorney's decision about the accident. As he talked, Margo's hands went to her belly and her eyes became more set and her jaws clenched. Finally, he told her about his last visit with his dad, and Carl pulling everything out from under them with the yard, Iverson, and Ed's grand plan.

When he finished, Margo spoke slowly, seething through clenched teeth like someone trying not to lose control, "So it really is all over. They win, and we lose everything."

Ed started to speak, but Margo shook her head and cut him off, "No, no. Your dad is right. Mom and Dad are gone. Our baby is gone, and not just that baby—any baby. They took *that* away from us too. And the bastards who did it not only will walk away, they're getting credit for setting the record straight. They're the good guys in this! That Jimmy Faison and his punk buddies—those sons-a-*BITCHES*—took everything from us and can now laugh about it all—again!"

Red-faced and breathing hard, Margo paused, took a breath, and went on more quietly, "Yeah, your dad is right. Rat bastard that he is for selling us out, but he's right. There is no real happiness for long in the world. The good guys don't win. Nothing keeps the rest of the world from taking whatever they want from you, whenever it suits them, for no good reason other than they can. All we can do is wake up each day and get through it until we don't. Nothing really matters." She crossed her arms and looked away.

He shook his head slowly, started to speak with tears in his eyes, but Margo cut him off, still not facing him, "Go home, Ed. Get caught up at work so you don't lose your job. I'll be here until they release me."

Ed felt that familiar darkness well back up in his heart and in his soul. That darkness that he had only barely escaped when he left Carl to find Margo. But there would be no lifeline for him or for them. She had given up. She was gone, so *they* were gone, because he could not escape this darkness on his own. Instead, he accepted that it was all gone—their joy, their dreams, and any hope for the future.

He turned away unsteadily and without a word. As he walked out of the room, the light dimmed in Ed's and Margo's eyes, this time for good.

Chapter 3

OTHER SUNS RISE

She had no real destination, just a direction;
she knew not how, only that it was right.

Unnoticed in Ed's despair, a quiet and preoccupied couple walked out of the hospital right in front of him. Had he seen them, he may have recognized the couple that had been mistaken for Cy and Lois by the hospital staff on that terrible day a month before. A generation older than the other new parents who were going home on this day, Ben Lucky held the door for his wife Dina, who was carrying their month-old granddaughter in her arms. Both grandparents were somber in the still-new reality that their daughter Sarah had died with three young friends in that terrible car accident, and the new grandmother held the infant closer, anxious to protect her as she stepped outside.

Still, Ben and Dina couldn't help feeling gladness when they looked into the baby girl's innocent young eyes and saw so much of their daughter there. That gladness, renewed every day by a living reminder of someone so precious to them, made them cherish her all the more. It also meant that instead of walling her off from the world that took their daughter at such a young age, her grandparents filled Jodie Lucky with a joy in the gift that her life was. That joy and overt sense of life personified how Jodie experienced her world, and were central to what she considered an idyllic and happy childhood.

Like their friends and neighbors, the Luckys weren't especially well-off, but they got by just fine. Ben had worked at the Dupont plant in Orange for more than twenty years when Jodie was born. Dina had worked as a bookkeeper at the Sears Roebuck, but quit to stay home with Jodie. Thankfully, as a senior process supervisor, Ben made good enough money on his own to make ends meet, even if he did still work periodic night shifts.

From some people's perspective, Jodie's childhood was unremarkable. She enjoyed school from elementary to high school, participated in group activities like choir and band, but she felt no competitive drive to play sports. Although she was well-liked by her classmates, she tended not to draw attention to herself and simply enjoyed each day as it came. And although she was not in the "in" crowd, which suited her just as well, she also did not have any detractors. It was almost like she had navigated her first eighteen years not really being noticed much by others. More important to Jodie was reflecting back the great warmth she felt every day from her grandparents. They were a happy and close threesome.

The summer of 1994, after she graduated from Grayton High School, Jodie both got and took notice.

The same age as Jodie, Joe Deming grew up in the woods just north of Grayton in a true, East Texas, working-class home. The Demings lived on a few acres in an old but tidy wood frame house with an old barn out back that they used as a woodshop. Joe's mother, Jessie, drove a school bus twice a day and worked in the high school cafeteria in between. That meant her hours were Joe's hours during the school year, and when he was out of school, she was too. Joe's father, Hal, worked at the lumber mill north of town in Buna. Like a lot of country folk, Hal could do just about anything with his hands and some tools. On weekends, he could be found either in his shop tinkering away at some project for Jessie, or one of the many chores that came up on their property, from cutting fallen wood to repairing a section of fence.

As Joe grew up, he could always be found out in the shop with his dad, where he learned how to work with his hands at an early age. By the time he was in middle school, Joe was big and handy enough that he and Hal began building fences on weekends for a little extra money. During his high school summers, Joe worked with Hal at the lumber mill, and then went full-time there after he graduated.

The two of them became quite a team. By then, the apprentice carpenter's skill exceeded his father's, to Hal's delight. That spring, they cut back some on their fence building, and Joe designed and installed a new set of kitchen cabinets as a surprise to Jessie. The surprise was on them as the word went around from their astonished friends about the craftsmanship in Joe and Hal's work. They soon realized they would have to stop their weekend fence building altogether in order to keep up with the cabinet orders that had now piled up. They had one last fence to put up, and they'd then be free and clear to fill their time with cabinet jobs.

For a June morning in southeast Texas, it wasn't too bad out, so Jodie was sitting on the back porch reading the Lamar State College course catalog with a scowl when Hal and Joe walked through the backyard with tool bags. She had forgotten her grandpa had someone coming by to replace their fence. Although not really friends, she recognized Joe from school, "Oh, hey. Is this what you do now?"

Joe smiled and kept walking towards the fence, "Sometimes, weekends anyway. During the week I work at the lumber mill with my dad," nodding back at Hal. That was Joe, a man with a mission who probably didn't even notice the pretty girl as he kept walking.

When they started taking down the old fence, Jodie went inside to escape the noise. Unlike Joe, she had noticed *him*. Watching him work, she liked what she saw. He didn't act like the other boys she'd been in school with. It wasn't that he seemed overly serious, but he acted like he had a sense of purpose, that this is what he was here to do, and he was getting it done. In fact, his dad seemed to just go with the flow, taking his cues from Joe.

With the old fence torn down and new fence posts set, Joe and Hal were wrapping up for the day, when they heard the back door close and saw Jodie walking towards them with two glasses in her hands. "I thought you could use something cold to drink before you go. I hope tea is good enough," she said with a big smile.

After they'd taken the glasses, Jodie turned and walked back toward the house. Hal nudged his son and grinned, "Say something, dummy."

"What? Alright, okay. Um, we have our water jug, but this is good too I guess," stammered a bewildered Joe.

Hal shook his head, "Thanks, young lady. This will be great." After the door had closed, he gave Joe's shoulder a squeeze with a grin, "And that's why you're still hanging out with the old man."

Since the next day was Sunday, they waited until noon before showing up to finish the new fence. There sat Jodie again. She jumped up and with a big smile said, "I was wondering when you were going to show up. Mind if I watch and learn how you do this?"

Hal raised his eyebrows and smiled back, turning to Joe with a curious look on his face. Joe shrugged, "Sure. It's not all that hard to catch on once you see it done." Hal smiled even more and picked up his step as he carted fence boards from the trailer into the backyard.

Jodie stood back and watched as Hal and Joe marked the posts and nailed up the fence rails. After watching them mark, cut, and nail up the first six feet of fence boards, she gave it a try for herself. It took her a few boards to start getting the hang of nailing without bending the nails or missing them altogether, but she kept at it. An hour later she heard her grandfather's voice behind her, "You fellas seem to be doing alright now that my granddaughter has it all under control. Maybe I should get a discount."

"Oh Grandpa," Jodie laughed at him. "I think I slowed them down some, but they're good teachers. And I'd rather help than watch." She kissed his cheek as she walked past him to grab another fence board.

Hal smiled at Ben and said, "She's a quick learner and doesn't mind pitching in. She can come work with us anytime."

"Yeah, she's some punkin,'" Ben chuckled and went in the house.

They finished and had cleaned up by 5:30 P.M. While Hal and Joe were stowing their tools, Jodie went in the house to get them all more of yesterday's tea. Hearing the rumble of the truck as Hal was pulling it out of the driveway, Jodie ran out the back door to catch them, running right into Joe, who had been sheepishly staring at the door wondering if she was coming back. "Oh! Sorry, I just wanted to see if you wanted something to drink, even if it was to-go," Jodie said with a gasp.

"Yeah okay, but we weren't leaving just yet. Dad was just pulling the trailer off the driveway and out of your way. He'll be back around in a minute," and Joe just stood there smiling at Jodie, lost in his thoughts.

"So, do you work all the time, or do you sometimes take a break and live a little?" Jodie asked innocently.

"Well, we do work at the mill all week, and then we're usually putting in a fence or building cabinets for somebody on weekends. More cabinets nowadays. It's better work and pays better too. But we live alright," Joe said with a satisfied nod.

"Then how about you come over Friday night for dinner?" Jodie asked. "This time I'll show *you* how to do a thing or two."

Joe took a step back and scratched his neck, "That'd be nice, if you're sure it's no bother for your folks and all."

"Bother? Nah, it's the least I can do after getting in your way all day. And it'll be nice," Jodie said, putting the glasses on the picnic table. Hal came back to find the two of them sipping their drinks and smiling at each other, which brought a smile to his face too.

Dinner with the Luckys that Friday night was like having dinner with family. Jodie wore the same smile and happy look on her face that he left her with after their fence building the weekend before. Her grandparents were just as friendly as Jodie, and it was no wonder where she learned that happy expression that simply radiated warmth—it was how Ben and Dina looked at their granddaughter every day. Whether laughing through his cooking lesson with Jodie and Dina, or swapping their childhood stories over dinner, it quickly felt very comfortable—like Christmas morning with his own grandparents.

That dinner was followed by lunch the next day in his woodshop, where Joe described his plans to go more and more into custom carpentry. Afterwards, he and Jodie wandered through the woods on their property while they chattered away. Jodie was back Sunday afternoon to watch Hal and Joe in the woodshop, and they coached her through some sanding and final prep work. Over an early supper before heading home that Sunday evening, Hal and Jessie became just as captivated by Jodie as their son already was. That smile and her easy way—they couldn't help catching some of that natural happiness that just flowed from her and that they could see lighting up Joe's eyes.

The rest of the summer followed this pattern. Joe spent Friday evening laughing and telling stories with the Luckys. Jodie spent Saturday and Sunday in the woodshop, either helping or sweeping up, either way "earning her keep" in her words, and then staying for supper with the Demings. Both families looked forward to their time together and were so tickled with their newly expanded circles that the new routine quickly felt normal.

The summer drifted by like a sleepy dream for Joe and Jodie.

Neither remembered when they first started holding hands while walking through the woods around the shop on weekends. Like their first kiss as Jodie was leaving one evening, it all just felt so natural—like it was the way they were meant to be.

In that same way, as the two of them sat one day on Jodie's favorite grassy spot in a clearing not far from the shop, Joe looked around with a smile and a sweep of his hand and said, "I can see our house right here. Three bedrooms, a couple of baths, all up on short pier and beams. Covered porch all the way around so you can sit and watch whatever you like, even in the rain."

Jodie could see in his eyes that he had a clear vision alright, but she wanted to make sure she wasn't missing something. "So, you're building *us* a house? I mean, it sounds perfect. But, uh, is this your lumberjack-proposal?" she asked sweetly with a tilt of her head.

Joe turned to her, still smiling, and squeezed her hand, "Well yeah. I guess I *should* ask and all, but I can't imagine life any other way. So why try? Let's get on with our life."

Jodie laughed as she kissed him, then said, "Good enough for me. It sounds like quite an adventure."

"Boy, it's gonna be," Joe said with a grin as he pulled her close. "I have a few things to take care of before we're off and running, but that won't take long. Couple weeks, maybe."

Jodie stood up and pulled Joe up by his hand. "Let's tell everyone now and get going."

Joe's parents and Jodie's grandparents were all thrilled and unsurprised. They'd seen what was happening in their kids' faces all summer. In both houses, it already just felt like family, and this would make it official.

Once again, Jodie saw that Joe was no one's idle dreamer. He had done more than just dream about this plan, and he started right into it. The next Saturday Joe and his dad pulled up towing a used Airstream travel trailer behind Hal's pickup. Jessie and Jodie, sitting outside still drinking coffee, watched as they drove well past the shop and set the trailer up at the left edge of their clearing near the trees.

The two women walked into the clearing as Joe and Hal finished leveling the trailer. Joe turned to Jodie and said, "Now, I know it ain't much, but it'll give us a place of our own, right in your favorite spot while we build the house. My folks got it for us as a wedding present. Have a look inside."

Jodie hugged him and said, "I don't need to look to know it's just great." She then quickly hugged Jessie and Hal, then stepped into the trailer and looked out the window, imagining the house that would be in that clearing one day.

Joe stood outside the door, beaming and said, "I know they haven't told you yet, but your folks are covering the first step on the house, the main plumbing hookups. One of the bubbas at the mill has a brother who's a plumber who works in construction. He's coming out in a couple of weekends to put in a new meter for us and get it connected to city water. He's also going to install a septic tank at the back of the clearing and connect it to the trailer. When the house is ready, we'll connect it right up. I was telling Ben my plan, and he wants to cover this part, which is just fine by me!

"I've got weekends and the next couple of weeks after work to lay in the water line from the meter at the road to the clearing for the trailer and the house. By then, the mill's electrician will be out to set up a power meter. Then we're off to the races. I'm telling you, I've got it all figured out," Joe said, nodding as he looked back and forth across their clearing.

The next couple of weeks' work went almost as he had it planned.

The day after setting up the trailer, Joe muscled a big rented trencher into place at the road and started digging. Jodie walked along watching, occasionally running to the shop for a shovel or an ax, with Joe explaining what he was doing, step-by-step. At the end of the day, he had covered half the distance to the clearing.

"Not bad," Joe told Jodie as they walked to the house. "I'll put in an hour or two every night after work until it gets too dark and then finish up next weekend." After dinner with Hal and Jessie, Jodie drove home as usual.

Monday, when Joe and Hal got home, Jodie's car was in the driveway and Joe found her sitting at the table behind the house. She was filthy—literally—covered in dirt, drenched in sweat, and wearing one of Joe's old baseball caps backwards on her head. She jumped up, gave Joe a sweaty peck on the cheek, took him by the hand, and pulled him towards the trench. "Just take a look before you say anything."

Joe saw a series of trenches extending from where he'd left it the day before, covering about a third of the distance they had to go until they reached the trailer. There were also several untrenched areas interspersed, making it look like a dotted line. He scratched his head and turned to Jodie, "You did this?"

She clenched her hands up like she was praying and said, "Don't be mad. I tried to make it match what you'd already done." Pointing at the untrenched stretches, she added quickly, "I got stuck in a few places so I skipped those spots. I figured I'd leave the ax-swinging to you and do the parts I could. What do you think?" Jodie asked, watching Joe nervously.

"What do I think?!" Joe grabbed his dirt-covered fiancée in a bear hug, lifting her off the ground as he swung her around, "It looks great! I'll get after whatever's getting in the way, and we'll finish those spots up too. Easy-peasy. Boy, we keep this up, and we'll have us a house before you know it!"

"Well, first things first," Jodie said with her usual smile. "We'll have a place to live once we get that trailer hooked up, and then we can get on with it, as you said. So, all hands on deck!" With that, she gave him another grimy kiss.

They ate a quick dinner with Hal and Jessie, outside, since Jodie was still covered in dirt, then Joe got to work finishing what Jodie had dug that day. She helped where she could and headed home after Joe had finished just as it was getting dark.

The rest of the week went the same way. Jodie made progress during the day, and Joe took care of some tricky parts after work. They had finished by Friday, allowing Joe and Hal to catch up on some cabinetry work over that weekend.

The lumber mill's electrician came out Monday to install the power meter at the trailer, and he explained to Jodie what they'd have to do to run conduit back up to the road for the main connection, and which connections to leave open for him to make. That evening when Joe got home, Jodie told him what the electrician had explained to her, and Joe

called in his new list of supplies to a wholesaler that did business with the lumber mill. The next day, Joe and Hal pulled into the driveway from work with a trailer loaded with PVC for the electrical conduit and large rolls of heavy wire. They then got to work running as much conduit and wire as they could for the evening.

The rest of the week went like the trenching had, with Jodie making progress during the day, and Joe making more in the evening. They finished over the weekend, and while they did, the plumber made it out, installing a meter at the road and putting in the septic system. He then walked them both through the details to lay the pipe back to the road.

Again, Joe and Hal came home Monday with a trailer full of PVC, and again, Joe and Jodie went to work laying their water line back to the main line at the road. Thursday morning, the electrician and plumber both came back out to make the final connections, arriving within minutes of each other. Jodie walked down the trench with them as they marveled at the work she and Joe had done. Before they started their work, the plumber tilted his hat back and said, "I know you two have a lot of work to go before this patch of ground is a house, but I ain't worried. Our boy Joe has really got something with you, little lady. You're the real deal. When we're all wrapped up, I'll call a buddy of mine at the city who will take care of the inspections and get you connected."

Not to be outdone, the electrician said sheepishly, "Well, hey, I'll call a buddy *I* know at Texas-New Mexico Power, and after the inspections are done, he'll get your power tied in. And he's right about you, alright. You're something else."

Jodie was beside herself and, smiling her usual smile, she hugged them both as she said, "Thanks, both of you. This means the world to us." She looked at the two of them and said, "I'm Jodie, by the way, and what are your names?"

The old electrician blushed for the first time in many years and stammered, "Oh, well, I'm Bud, like it says," as he tapped the patch on his shirt.

"Me too," blurted the plumber. "No, I mean my name's Emmitt, like mine says," as he tapped his shirt several times.

"Well, it's good to make two new friends, and thanks again to you both."

The two men turned separate directions to start their work, and both men now had smiles to match Jodie's, as was usually the case after people met her.

Friday afternoon the trailer had running water, and Monday afternoon, after Jodie paid a visit to the company office, the electricity was on. A month after Joe first told Jodie his plan in his roundabout attempt at a proposal, the trailer was all set up, and the utilities were in place for the house. They really were off and running.

A month later, on October 7, 1994, a hot and windy Saturday, Joe and Jodie were married in the middle of their clearing. They were just nineteen years old, but both were old souls who were mature beyond their years and absolutely committed to their simple and shared dream. They had a small ceremony. Jodie didn't really have anyone her age that she ran with, and Joe just had his boss and a few friends from the lumber mill there. Both sets of parents had a few friends attend. In all, there were fewer than two dozen people present, and they all felt the contagious joy that was evident on Joe's face as he watched Jodie and on hers as Ben walked her to the center of the clearing for their vows. Hal stood up with Joe. Jessie and Dina, clutching hands together and beaming, both stood with Jodie, thrilled to see their cherished young'uns taking this step together. Ben conducted the ceremony. If it hadn't been for Jodie's infectious joy, they'd have all been in tears. As it was, everyone who was present would remember it later as being one of the happiest moments they'd ever witnessed, although they couldn't really say why. Afterwards, right where the house would eventually sit, everyone gathered around picnic tables for barbecue, Shiner beer, and laughing into the night, not wanting the revelry to end.

Their honeymoon was just as low-key. Joe unhooked the trailer and drove them to the Bolivar Peninsula on the Gulf Coast. Ben's boss had an empty lot across the road from Crystal Beach, and Joe planned to park the trailer there for a week of walking the beach, cooking out, and living like new lovers. Like anything that Joe came up with, Jodie loved the idea. This little trailer was their home now, and she couldn't get too much time in it with Joe, wherever it was parked. How perfect that they could take it with them to spend their honeymoon in beautiful seclusion while still being "at home."

At the end of their fourth beach-day routine, Joe was lighting a cook fire, with Jodie sitting nearby on a folding chair. In her usual carefree way, Jodie said, "Hey, Husband, this week is as fun as it is beautiful. I wouldn't want anything to be any different. Really. It's perfect. I'm just wondering, though . . . Have you thought about any of the things we could be doing on the house if we weren't here?"

Joe flinched and chuckled, glancing over from the fire that was just starting to catch, "Now see? *That's* why we're perfect together! I was wondering the same thing. We've seen this beach now, and we could use the next few days to get on with the plan!"

"Well then, let's go home and do it. First thing in the morning, though. One more night listening to the waves," Jodie whispered into his ear as she padded past him through the sand and towards the trailer. Something in the smile she gave over her shoulder told Joe he could let the fire burn down for a while, and he was on his way into the trailer before the door had closed behind her.

The next year followed a familiar and comfortable pattern. Joe would lay out the details of the next step or two in the construction plan and arrange to buy materials through customers at the mill. When he ran across some work that was outside of his experience or required a certified journeyman, he was always able to find someone at the mill, or a friend of a friend, or sometimes on the recommendation of someone who had already done some work for them.

Little by little, the patch of ground in front of their clearing went from a skeleton of wooden bones, to a two-story tree house on eight-foot stilts. When the roof went on after their first Christmas, it really started to look like a house. And just like with their utilities, Joe would get some new chore started, often with Hal's help, and Ben would come out on weekends to help also. While Joe was at work during the week, Jodie would keep making progress on work that she had learned how to do while watching, and when she got stuck or needed help, she'd pause and wait for Joe to get home. Once the house was dried in, there was even more work that Jodie could tackle on her own during the day.

Joe and Jodie never seemed to tire of the endless list of jobs they kept taking on while making progress on the house. They didn't spend every spare moment working on the house, but it was a rare day that didn't include something they could show towards realizing their dream. They also managed to plan most big family dinners at their place, either around the picnic table beside the trailer when the weather was good enough, or inside Hal and Jessie's house. And who didn't want to have some family fun before a holiday dinner, like painting trim or floating drywall?

Many days, Jodie was just there to give guidance to one of the contractors who was there to do some part of the job. She'd hang around and watch them work, staying out of their way but close enough to pick up a trick or two and to offer them cold drinks when they paused in their work. All but one or two of the most surly tradesmen warmed up to her presence on the job, and the word got around the trades about the couple who was building their own home outside Grayton with the great young wife acting as a construction supervisor who was also able to pitch in and help.

Thirteen months after they'd started building and just after their first anniversary, Joe and Jodie finished the house with the last of the flooring finally in place. To celebrate, they invited back anyone who had sold them materials at a discount, delivered materials, or did any work on the house, either as friends or paid contractors. Truth was, most of the paid contractors had become friends, thanks to Jodie's "superpower" in winning people over. They were all happy to be included in celebrating this happy and industrious couple's good work, and a barbecue pit full of good, smoked meat and ice chests full of beer didn't hurt either.

Jodie was showing another group through the house when a familiar face walked through the front door, "Well hey there, if it isn't my favorite electrician! It's good to see you, Bud." With him was someone Jodie didn't recognize.

Bud gave her a bear hug and said, "Little miss, I told you that you were the real deal. That husband of yours too, by the looks of this place.Y'all did a fine job alright."

He nodded to his friend, "This fella here is Bill Arceneaux. He owns a company I do a lot of work for, and I told him all about this place and about your husband's work in that barn."

"Ma'am. If it's okay with you, even though I'm bargin' in on your party, could I look at some of your husband's handiwork? He is all I hear about from this old coot and most of the other trades who have been out here," said Arceneaux, quickly adding with a grin, "plus a word or two about his wife."

Jodie laughed and said, "Well, with an intro like that, I guess you can just help yourself and look around as you please. It's good to know people say good things if they're saying anything. You two should stay around and enjoy the fun with us. The more the merrier, you know."

"Darlin', you know we will," said the old electrician, patting her on the shoulder as they walked towards the kitchen.

An hour later the small crowd had settled into their barbecue and beer at tables set up in front of the house, when Joe and Jodie climbed up the front stairs to the porch and stood with their arms around each other, looking at the people who were there to help them celebrate. Joe waved and shouted, "Hey, everyone, look up here. Hey, can I have just a minute? I promise, just a minute, and then you can get back to it."

Conversations trailed off and Hal turned off the music that had been blasting from a boom box next to the trailer. "You all know what you're here for, and I hope you like how it turned out as much as we do. We sure couldn't have done it without a lot of help from all of you."

Some of Joe's buddies from the lumber mill were gathered in a group, and one shouted, "We're not out of beer, are we?" which got the crowd laughing.

Chuckling himself, Joe said, "No, no, and thanks for checking, Dave. Well, we have one more, little thing to drink to . . ." He turned to Jodie who was patting her belly with both hands.

"I guess this house isn't the only thing we made this year," Jodie said with a nervous smile towards her grandparents and Joe's parents.

Dina put her hand to her chest and smiled through tears, "Oh my! Honey, when?"

"They say I'm at ten weeks now, so it should be March sometime," all nervousness gone, Jodie was beaming, and so was Joe.

With all the clapping and some cheering, only Bill Arceneaux heard a misty-eyed electrician sniff and say, "Well how about that? I hope it's a girl just like that mama of hers!"

Like the rest of the crowd, Arceneaux thought he knew just what the old codger meant. *Boy, there* is *something about that gal,* and they all left the happy party just a little happier inside.

1995 was a big year for Joe and Jodie. They had just settled into their new home in the middle of their favorite patch of ground a stone's throw from Joe's parents. Bill Arceneaux hired Joe to build custom cabinets in a few of his expensive new homes, and then he made Joe an offer he couldn't refuse that found Joe quitting the lumber mill to do custom work for Arceneaux full-time.

And most importantly, their daughter was born. Neither of the young parents would budge on the name, both wanting to name her for the other, so Jodie settled the tug-of-war when she wrote the name: Jo Dee Deming. As Jodie saw it, everybody wins . . . although she won just a little more since they called their little person Jo.

The old electrician's wish came true: There was no doubting who Jo Deming's mother was. She not only looked like her mother, but she had the same natural and infectious smile and that difficult-to-explain joy that emanated from her like warmth from the sun.

From the start, Jo and her parents were all but inseparable, just as Joe and Jodie were before she was born. As a baby, Jodie would take her into the barn while Joe was working, with Jo either in a carrier on her mom's chest, or in a playpen where she could watch her parents working—Joe moving through several cabinet projects, and Jodie cleaning up behind him—and hear their voices. When Joe's work got noisy, Jodie put headphones on them both or moved the playpen outside under a tree by the barn.

Over time, Jodie took on more and more of Joe's business management. Not wanting to be stuck in the house away from Joe, she set up shop on a table in the corner of the barn with a laptop and a file cabinet. In his third year in business, Joe added on another section of barn and intended to add a small enclosed office to block the noise for Jodie and Jo, but Jodie vetoed the plan. Instead, she kept her office area on the shop floor and kept those headphones handy for her and Jo both.

True to form, when they took vacations, they were low-key and intimate affairs, almost always involving the old travel trailer and a campsite somewhere. Often they would take it to their old honeymoon spot across the county road from the beach on Bolivar, except now they owned that lot, having bought it from Ben's boss when Joe's business had made them some spare cash. Their days at Bolivar were simple and carefree: long walks hunting for seashells, swimming in the warm Gulf water, hide-and-seek in the bushes and short dunes along the waterline, and late nights watching a wood fire burn to coals and laughing through stories from their lives until it was time to sleep again to the sound of the waves.

Life at home was just as simple and carefree for Jo. Until she went to kindergarten as a five-year-old, except for the days when Joe went to a construction site to take measurements or install a finished project, Jo hadn't known a day when she and her parents didn't spend most of their time together. From work to the little things of everyday life, she absorbed indelible lessons about love, partnerships, sharing, giving, and enjoying the simple things every day, and she reflected them back at her parents. The same innate aura of joy that people so often felt with Jodie grew stronger and stronger within this little family and those closest to them, like trees all drinking from the same life-giving water.

When it was time for Jo to go to kindergarten, she took her first ride to school on her grandmother's bus, a happy morning for them both. Jo made new friends in her class and saw Gramma again every day at lunchtime, where Jessie was serving food behind the counter. She rode home again, perched on the seat behind Jessie as she drove, and Jo chirped away about each day's fun. Rain or shine, Jo would find Jodie waiting for her under the shade of the old oak tree by the driveway to their house, and, as they walked down the lane to the barn, Jo would tell Jodie all the same stories with the same enthusiasm she'd already shared with her grandmother. Never pausing in her chatter, Jo would throw her backpack down and climb up the chair to take a seat in the middle of Jodie's desk. There she'd sit cross-legged while she finished her "report," then say with an expectant smile, "Now *your* turn, Mommy. What did you do while I was gone?"

When Joe was in the shop, he'd slow down his work to watch and listen to his gals talk about their day. When he was out working, Jo would fill him in over dinner and then insist that he tell them about his day too.

Simple, carefree, and priceless, and Joe and Jodie treasured it all.

One fall afternoon in November 2001, Jo hopped off of her grandmother's school bus, ready to regale her mom with another first-grade day, but Jodie wasn't there. Jo turned to look at her grandmother, who was watching her, and Jessie asked, "Hey hon, are you okay to go down to the barn and see what your mom's up to while I finish the route?"

Jo nodded happily, waved and yelled, "Sure, Gramma. I bet I can run all the way there before Mom comes out!" Jo took off down the lane towards the barn, the *Monster's, Inc.* backpack that was almost as big as she was bouncing crazily on her back as she went. Concentrating on her new mission, she only barely heard the mild engine roar as the bus drove away. She was grinning excitedly. *I'm going to surprise her!*

Jo burst through the open door into the barn, anxious to share their days, but finding the shop empty, yelled, "Mom?! Mo-om!" She tossed her backpack in its usual spot next to Jodie's desk in the corner and stood looking around. Finding no sign of Jodie, she shrugged, curious and more than a little disappointed to have their news-sessions delayed.

Jo walked around the desk to sit in her mom's chair while she waited, but she stopped, confused by the sight of her mom laying on the shop floor next to her desk. Her first thought was, *Uh oh, she's getting sawdust all in her hair! Why is she sleeping on the floor!?* She knelt and shook Jodie's shoulder lightly, "Hey, Mo-om. Mom. Hey, wake up. Mom!"

When Jodie didn't respond, Jo shook more rapidly, now pleading, "Mommy! Wake up! I don't like this game!" Now Jo was crying as she tugged her mom's shoulder to roll her over. She knew something was very wrong. Jodie's arm flopped to her side, and her hair, matted with sawdust, splayed across her face. One eye was half-open but it stared, sightlessly.

Jo bent over Jodie, wrapping her arms around Jodie's neck as she buried her face in her mother's hair, sobbing and scared, "Mommy! Please talk to me. I'll let you go first this time, just please wake up and talk to me!"

When Jodie still didn't answer, Jo thought, *Daddy!*

When Joe heard Jo's voice on his cell phone, he couldn't make out what she was saying, but he knew it was bad. He looked at his watch and realized Jessie and Ben were both not home. As he bolted for his truck, he'd heard enough to know that Jodie was unconscious for some reason, and he told Jo, "Kiddo, I have to call someone right now to come help. So, I'm going to have to hang up to call them. Then I'll call you right back and talk to you until I get home, okay? So, keep the phone in your hand."

It took Joe forty minutes to make it home from the jobsite. After calling 911 for an ambulance, he was back on the phone with Jo, assuring her—and himself—that everything would be okay. He was on his way. Halfway home, he heard a siren over the phone that stopped abruptly at its loudest. *Probably pulling in, thank God! Hang on, babe!*

A few minutes later, he heard a man's voice in the room with Jo, "Hey, there, sweetheart. We're here to help. Is that your mommy? Yeah? Hey, who are you talking to there?"

Jo sniffed and said unsteadily into the phone, "My daddy."

"Can I talk to him? Yeah? Step over here with me, while my friend here looks after your mom for a minute. Okay . . . Uh, sir?"

"Yeah, I'm here. That's my wife and my daughter. How's my wife?" Joe asked, trying not to sound as scared as he felt.

"Well, sir, we just started examining her. All I can tell you so far is that she's unconscious, and we're going to do everything we can for her."

"Okay, okay, thanks. I'm only a few minutes away, and I'll be right there," Joe said as he realized his hand was shaking.

"Sir, you just be careful. I promise we'll look after your little girl until you get here."

Joe pulled in to find the ambulance backed up to the barn, slid to a stop next to it, and burst out the driver's door while the pickup was still rocking. He hurried inside to find Jo kneeling beside Jodie, who was now on the portable gurney, partially covered by a white sheet. Jo was slowly brushing her mom's hair, picking sawdust out of the brush, and talking soothingly, "It's okay, Mom, I can do it for you. Don't you worry. Daddy is coming." As she spoke, tears ran down her face, and her lips quivered.

One of the EMTs had been kneeling behind Jo, and he stood up and stepped aside as Joe knelt to take his place. Taking Jo and Jodie both into a hug with Jo sandwiched in the middle, Joe used his calmest

Dad-voice to say, "Hey, kiddo. I'm here, I'm here. You've done great," he kissed Jo's head then looked from Jodie to the EMT across from him.

"Um, sir, I'm sorry. This little sweetheart did great, but her mom must have had some serious event an hour or more before we arrived. We won't know for sure what it was until we get her to the hospital. But there was nothing . . ." the EMT trailed off. "Ah, we knew you were coming, so we waited. Thought it would be easier on this one to wait for you here."

Joe burst into tears, pulling Jo closer as he stroked Jodie's hair and face. "Oh, no, no, no, no, no. Jodie. Darlin'. You're my life . . ." His voice broke, and his body shook as he bowed his head, giving in to the grief as it poured through him, blanking out every thought. It was a few minutes before he spoke again with his hand resting on her cheek, "I won't let her forget anything about you, babe. I just don't . . ."

Joe was interrupted by a small voice that stunned him it sounded so much like Jodie, as Jo turned and hugged his neck while still crying, "I won't let you forget either, Daddy. Mommy says that when someone is gone, it's because God needs them more in heaven. Now he'll be happy like Mommy always makes us."

Although the EMTs had seen loss and suffering many times before, both men struggled to hold back tears as they listened to Jo and gently moved Jodie into the ambulance. They didn't talk about it as they drove away, both staring straight ahead and sniffling. The driver cleared his throat several times looking out his side window and thought, *Wow, I hope someone talks that way about me someday.*

Over the next several days, the hospital concluded Jodie had suffered a cerebral hemorrhage, most likely from a congenital defect in a vessel in her brain. There would have been no indication of the defect and nothing that could have been done to save her after the rupture.

After a private burial, the family hosted a celebration of Jodie's life in her favorite spot, the same patch of their clearing that seven years earlier was the scene of their wedding. This time, rather than the small gathering of friends and family, there were cars lining State Highway 1442 a half-mile in each direction from their driveway. The crowd was dominated by burly men from the construction trades, like Bud and Emmitt—men who had helped build their house and others who had met Jodie while doing business with Joe. For years, many of them had stopped by the barn as they were passing by going to or from a jobsite, just to say hello, have a glass of tea, and spend a few minutes absorbing her happy outlook on the world. Their wives brought so many plates and bowls that the tables around the yard were overflowing with food.

It fell to Joe's dad, Hal, to share a few words with them all, and he climbed slowly up to the porch to do it, just as Joe and Jodie had at their housewarming party. "Well, I don't have a long speech or anything for you. I don't think I could get through it if I tried talking about her too much anyway. But we—all of us, the Demings and the Luckys—want to tell you how great it is to see all of you here to remember this beautiful soul." Hal paused, looked down at his feet, and covered his face with one hand.

Jo, who had been standing in the yard huddled between Joe and his mother, holding their hands, stepped back, putting Joe's and Jessie's hands together. Biting her lip, she shot Joe a teary glance and forced smile and trotted up the stairs. When she reached Hal, she tucked her head under his arm and hugged him. "It's okay, Grampa. She still loves us all," Jo whispered as her tears streamed.

"Oh, Punkin," he said as he ran his hand over Jo's hair and smiled at her.

Hal lifted his granddaughter up to rest on his hip, took a deep breath, and continued, "If you knew Jodie at all, you know what a treasure she was. That way she had of helping you see the world through her happy eyes. Any time you spent with her, you couldn't help feeling better about your troubles, the world, life . . . everything. She made you glad just to share the world with her. That was her way of loving us, and it was just her. To really honor her, I hope you never forget *that* feeling, that *gift* she brought to each of us. I know I never will . . . we never will."

Watching his father and daughter, Joe was startled by how much Jo looked like Jodie in that moment. *No,* he thought, *it isn't just that she has her eyes or her whole face. It's how she smiles, that look in her eye like she can take away just a little of the pain and make us all smile. My God, she's Jodie in so many ways!* Joe looked down, memories of his wife flowing over him like the cool breeze on his face, and he shook his head slightly with a smile to himself. *I feel you, babe. I love you too.*

As Hal walked down the steps, the murmuring had already started from all around the crowd.

"Oh boy, she was really something."

"Did you ever know anyone else like her? I don't know how she did it."

"That little gal always put a smile on my face."

"I feel like I knew her, even though I only heard about her from Abe, and even just his stories about her cheered me up when I was down."

"I'm going to miss her, but I can't help feeling better just thinking about her . . ."

Hours later, as the gathering wound down, there were many tearful partings as people said their goodbyes to Joe, Jo, and the family. But most of them still felt that Jodie-glow as they walked to their cars, and as Hal had hoped, most would feel it for years to come.

Chapter 4

LOST IN THE DARK

Small wrong turns could change not only her path, but also the journeys of those she touched along her way, their destinations and her own.

Although literally born out of tragedy when her mother lost her life on the cusp of adulthood in a car wreck with three friends, Jodie Deming's almost twenty-seven years were happy ones. She lived every day with a profound joy in today's happiness and the opportunity it brought to take some next, positive step in life. It's not so much that she was full of hope as she was indifferent to the possibility of sadness. She took each day as it came and aspired for nothing more than making the most of the simple pleasures. She learned her remarkable worldview and approach to life from her grandparents who, after losing their only and beloved child, embraced their newborn granddaughter as a gift—a chance to pour that same love into her—and they did just that every day.

In contrast, the same twenty-seven years left no sign of the Ed and Margo from their younger days or the happy childhood memories with their parents. If losing Cy and Lois in that terrible accident hadn't irreparably crushed Ed and Margo's souls, the years that followed certainly did.

• • •

After the accident in 1974, when Margo's surgeries and inpatient recovery were complete, Ed took her home to the house they had shared with her parents. Everything was just as they'd left it two months before. Signs of Cy and Lois were everywhere, in the knickknacks and photos on the walls to the smells that had always formed the recognizable and comforting scent of home. Now, they had all become part of the stifling absence that Ed and Margo both felt, like weights they carried around the house.

Although Ed was still living primarily in their garage apartment, Margo elected to sleep in the bedroom where she had grown up, at least for a while as she finished her still-painful recovery from surgery. At the door of her parents' old room, rather than the comfort she had always found there, she was overwhelmed by the pain evoked with her memories from that room: her mom's jewelry on the dresser; her dad's shoes lined up under his side of the bed; and photos on every patch of wall, covering the dresser, Cy's bureau, and crammed into the edges of Lois' mirror. Eventually, she knew, she'd have to go through these things and do something with them, and, in the end, all of it had to go. Someday. Not today. She closed the door behind her and crossed the hall to her room.

She woke up to a still-darkened house the next morning. All the curtains were drawn, and no lights were on when she shuffled into the living room to find Ed sitting on the couch in front of a dark television. "You eat?" she asked in a monotone.

Ed looked up and shook his head, "No. There's coffee," he answered in the same flat tone.

A few minutes later he walked to the kitchen and leaned against the doorframe, watching as Margo finished a piece of bread with the open bread wrapper still on the counter. Seeing how Ed was dressed, Margo said, "You going to work?"

"Yeah, if you're alright."

"I'm alright," she said with a shrug. "Not supposed to go back to work for four more weeks."

Ed nodded and walked to the garage door, saying as he went, "There's other food if you want. Your prescriptions are on the table. Call me at the school if you need something."

After the door had closed, she sighed, stared at her reflection in the window. When she heard Ed's truck pulling away, she said to herself, "Yeah, whatever. I'm fine. I'm always fine."

Ed went about his day, keeping to himself, and moving robotically from one odd job at the school to the next. When the hall clock showed 5 P.M., he nodded to himself, put his tools away, and drove home. As he walked into the house, he almost said aloud, *This place feels like a tomb*, and it wasn't just the memories of Cy and Lois as he looked around. The place was dark, and it felt that much darker with the oppressive quiet. The life and soul were just as absent in the home as they were in Ed and Margo.

He found Margo sitting quietly on the couch in the clothes she had slept in the night before. The TV was on, but the sound was off as some excited guy in a striped suit appeared to be selling glass cleaner. Ed could see she wasn't watching it, just staring past it out the window. He stopped as he stepped into the room, "Everything alright?"

"Yeah, I'm fine. One day down, twenty-seven to go until I go back to work. Good times."

Ed pursed his lips and nodded, "Yeah, ok. Hungry? There's food."

"No. You eat. I'll get something later."

Nodding again, he turned to the kitchen. He was hungry, but he had no interest in cooking now. He grabbed a couple slices of bread out of the bag still sitting on the counter since the morning, put several slices of cheese between them, grabbed a beer, and walked back to the garage. Ed watched TV in their apartment but was more interested in the six-pack he drank than he was in any program. When the channels signed off for the night, he wandered out to find the still-soundless TV flickering in the otherwise dark living room. He stared down the dark hallway at the closed bedroom doors for a few seconds, sighed with a shrug of his shoulders, turned off the TV, and went back to the apartment for the night.

One day after another followed the same pattern. If Ed saw Margo, she was sitting in front of the TV, somewhere between sullen and dazed. He left coffee in the pot for her but stopped asking if she wanted to eat. Instead, he filled the freezer with frozen food, mostly single-serve packages like TV dinners and pot pies. *If she wants to eat, she can. Not like I can force her. And this way I don't have to cook for me either.*

During weekdays, he kept to himself at work, making whatever repairs came up. When he was home, he came out of the apartment only long enough to get food and beer or to shower. The rest of the time he was either watching TV or tinkering with a build-your-own color TV kit he and Cy had bought and not yet started. *May as well do something with the time. Not much to this compared to the repairs I used to make to motors in the yard. Bunch of soldering and eventually I'll be watching crappy shows in color instead of black and white.*

Margo slept fitfully most nights, often finding herself staring at the dark ceiling with the same question haunting her thoughts like the part of a song she couldn't stop hearing: *What's the point of any of this, of anything?* Most days, she waited to get out of bed after she heard Ed leave for work rather than risking another awkward moment and silence. It was easier this way, since she'd accepted that there wasn't anything left to say. After finally crawling from her bed, she went through the day with no thought of a goal beyond her new and simple routine: *Get up, trudge through another dull day, and repeat. The damned TV dinners suck, but whatever.*

As lifeless as the days were, they were still more tolerable than the nights, since the dusky daylight that filtered into the house through the closed curtains gave her just enough to look at to keep her mind distracted. Although seeing these reminders from her parents' lives also stirred a crushing sense of loss, they also evoked happier memories, however dim they seemed. But each night was more oppressive than the last, because in her dark and quiet room even those distractions were gone. There was nothing in the dark but emptiness. Her mind filled that emptiness with incapacitating grief, and it pounded in her head like an oppressive heartbeat: *Gone. Gone. Gone. Makes no sense. Why? Why them? Why me? Why always us?! Gone. Gone. Gone.*

This went on for almost four weeks until one Friday night she realized she had only two days until she went back to work. Then the emptiness took on a new edge and a growing anxiety. *Back out in the world?! Among all of those people, the ones going about their lives with no idea about what I've lost. The ones who don't care, and the ones responsible who paid no price at all! How am I going to do this?* Although even considering going back to her life felt like punishment, she knew it wasn't optional. They needed her pay to make ends meet.

She hardly slept that Sunday night, already agonizing over the next day. She could almost feel physical pain as she imagined resuming her life. Real, physical pain would have been so much easier to deal with. She could power through anything—mind over matter—especially after what she had gone through during and after the wreck. But *this?* This pain didn't fade away when she tried powering through. It simply thundered more loudly in her mind. The pain grew and grew, still beating out that ever-present reminder: *gone, gone, gone.* By leaving the house, it felt like she'd be taking the final step that made the nightmare and loss real and final—*no Mom, no Dad, no babies, and no life.* Along with these thoughts, she now imagined the faces of people who would see her in her suffering. Alone in her room through the night, she was desperate to hide from them all—all the people, the world, and her inescapable reality.

The next morning, Margo was up and dressed before Ed. She had intended to go in early, maybe miss seeing people and avoid any attention, but she sat on the couch staring again at the dark TV, dreading the day, and putting it off as long as she could. From the kitchen, Ed asked, "You riding with me?"

"No, I'll take Mom's car." She stood up with an effort like she was facing the Inquisition and added, "Guess I'm going." She hurried out the door without another word, hoping Ed would just let her go. Watching her as she went, he had nothing to say. He stared at the door for another moment after she'd gone, and then he went back to his own morning routine before driving to work.

As Margo drove through town, she could hear her heart beating and thought repeatedly, *What am I doing? No. I can do this, I think.* Her heart sank as she pulled into the almost-full faculty parking lot, realizing that getting in unobserved probably wasn't going to happen.

Once parked, she sat in the car for a few minutes, mustering the will to go in and face one person after another, these near-strangers who would see her at her most vulnerable. *Why can't they just leave me alone?! "Oh, look, there's poor Margo. Isn't she pathetic?" Instead of staring at me, when has anyone ever actually cared enough to do something about the world . . . the Jimmy Faisons, the murdering Mark Fricking Hammocks, the Mr. Fat Bald Bastard Thomases, and the rest in all walks of life?! They take and take, and they ruin other people's lives without remorse or consequences. Where were all these caring people, when they could have actually done something that mattered?*

These thoughts raced through her head until she could hear no other thought. Until that moment, she had been working her way into a full-blown panic attack—her pounding heart raising that helpless feeling like she was starting to drown; but now that panic was slowly giving way to anger. But now, through her anger, Margo felt the reawakening of her resolve. *Oh, the hell with it and the hell with all of them.* She stepped out of the car and began walking towards the entrance. As she went, one teacher after another in the parking lot got her attention.

"Oh Margo, I'm glad you're back. I'm so sorry about your parents."

"It is so good to see you, Margo. That's just so terrible about your mom and dad."

"Hey Margo. I wasn't sure when we'd get you back. Condolences about your folks. They were just way too young and will be missed."

As each spoke, at first Margo would turn her head towards them and mutter, "Yeah, thanks," feinting a half smile. After just a few of these, Margo stopped responding and only nodded with her half smile. All the while, the voice in her head was shouting, *Stop looking at me! Leave me alone!* After a few more, she dropped the pretense of a smile and only nodded. Once inside the noisy hallway and surrounded by high school students bustling around her on their way to their first class, she marched to the office, glaring at the floor in front of her and ignoring anyone else who spoke to her. Although Margo was grateful to the hallway noise for muffling the noise in her head, more than one teacher turned an indignant expression towards her as she stormed by without so much as a "How do you do?"

She finally reached sanctuary from them all as she stepped into the office, closing the door behind her, only to discover five potted plants and a large bouquet of flowers on her desk. Hovering above were several balloons tied to her chair, with bright and colorful pictures of clowns, kittens, smiley faces, and happy messages like, "Welcome back!" and "Welcome home!"

As she stood at her desk, taking this in with a grimace, she heard a chorus of young voices, "Hey Miss Schmutz. Welcome back!" The first period office-aides, two eleventh-grade girls, stood at the reception counter and were beaming at her.

"Yeah, okay, hey girls," Margo sighed without looking at them. "Great. What do I do with all this stuff?" She looked around the office and quickly stashed the plants and flowers in the back of the supply closet. Without pausing she snatched the balloons' ribbons in one hand, cut them all in one motion with scissors from her desk, and walked to the window. She opened the window and crammed the balloons through. As they floated up and out of sight, she sneered, "There you go. Be free. Smile at someone else."

The office aides, now wide-eyed, exchanged nervous looks and spun away to face the counter. Margo turned from the window to see Principal Clanton in his office, standing in front of his desk with his arms folded and watching her. "Um, hey there, Margo. You sure you're ready to be here? Not that I don't want you here, but we can get along if you need some time. I know you've been through a lot. It's okay to take all of this slow."

She stood at the window as he walked towards her. "No, I'm good. I could sit at home, or I could sit here."

Mr. Clanton put his hand on her shoulder and said in a supportive voice, "Hey, your folks were great people, salt of the earth. I mean it. I know that losing them is just terrible. It is for us too. I want you to know, if it wasn't for Ed, I don't know how we'd keep this old place going. Your dad was incredible—one of those old-school guys who could fix anything—and as much as the faculty liked him, most people had no idea about the miracles he pulled off for us all the time. I did. Thankfully, he brought in Ed as his alter ego, but I will miss your dad."

Margo looked out the window when she answered, "Yeah. I always knew too." She glared at him through narrowed eyes, "I guess you never got around to telling him though."

"Well, ahem. Yes, well I uh, um, I'm sure I didn't tell him enough, even if I did. So, look, get settled in and get your feet back on the ground, and we'll talk again after lunch. Hopefully we won't have messed things up too much for you to straighten out." After a nervous pat on her shoulder he went back into his office and closed the door.

Margo raised an eyebrow and watched him go. *Yeah, whatever.*

She spent the day sifting through her inbox and rummaging through files. She found a pile of paper the aides had screwed up and others that should have been processed but hadn't been. She sighed loudly, *Idiots*.

After the last bell and before Margo left for the day, Mr. Clanton pulled up a chair, "I hope it's all under control, Margo. I'm sure it will be, now that you're back." He smiled nervously.

The thaw he was looking for in her demeanor hadn't happened. She pushed away the stack of paper she had been flipping through with a sigh, "It's all good. Nothing I can't handle."

"Yes. Well, I thought I'd share some good news with you. I'm sure you remember our talk a couple of months ago about a new program here at the school. You know, the day care project?" She looked up at him, barely masking her lack of interest as he continued, "Yes, so anyway, after a few phone calls, it's all arranged. The junior college is ready to bring you into their program part-time, so that you can get our program up and running at the start of the next school year. We may even try it out during summer school. It took some doing, but the district is willing to let us give it a try. You can start when you're ready, something like two or three afternoons per week, all on the clock, of course. How does that sound?"

She turned back to face her desk, ignoring his imploring expression, "No, I don't think so. I have a job; I'll just do that. Thanks anyway."

He blinked and was clearly confused, "I thought this was something you wanted to do. You know, a growth path and a way to give back?"

She turned back towards him and narrowed her eyes again, "I'm not looking for growth, and 'give back'? I don't think you want me to 'give back' anything that's on my mind." As he started to respond, she held up a hand and shook her head curtly, "The answer is *no*. Find someone else."

"There isn't anyone else. The district is willing to give this a try because it's *you*. Because we can fill in for you with the office aides, we have the flexibility of trying it with you on a cost-neutral basis. Without you, no program, and girls we could have helped will be faced with other, bad decisions."

"Got it. So the baby I *wanted*, who I couldn't wait to meet, is ripped from me. Any chance of *ever* having a baby is ripped from me by this shit world, like everything else. But *me?* Oh, *I'm* supposed to make it easy for these mindless girls to do something careless and to have normal lives with babies they never wanted in the first place?!"

Margo stood up, still glaring at him, "Well, I can't save the world. Guess that makes us even. We done?" When he didn't answer, she took that for his answer and walked out.

Days like this turned into weeks and then months. Margo did her job—she kept the paperwork moving, ensured correspondence was read and answered, and made sure the school staff didn't miss any district and state due dates. She didn't attempt any kind of heroic process improvements or bother trying to make anything better or easier, and she certainly didn't permit herself any happy moments. She kept to herself except when the work left her no choice, rarely speaking to anyone around her except to answer direct questions, get direction from Mr. Clanton, or give direction to the office aides.

By the end of the school year, everyone at the school, faculty and students, had accepted her new normal. What had started out as sympathy for her loss and personal suffering led to some understanding for the awkward estrangement they all felt from her, and a teacher could occasionally be heard saying, "She just needs some time. She's been through a lot, bless her heart."

As the months wore on, however, those feelings gave way to less generous sentiments: "Hey, she ain't going to speak. She ain't even going to acknowledge you're there. She's just mean."

If she had been aware of it, that evolution would have suited Margo fine. The struggle she had felt that first day back at work stayed with her day after day for weeks, but the subtle transition from panic to anger deepened as well. Little by little, her heart hardened against the experience and, more importantly to Margo, against the pain, which felt oddly like a lifeline from that sense of drowning in anxiety. This was something she could make sense of, and it gave her a focus for all of the emotion that was churning inside. Rather than being incapacitated by unfillable loss and unresolvable grief, anger helped her get out of bed and out the door in the morning. It quieted the voice in her head, replacing it with a much lower buzz of general disdain for the people in her world.

Life at home continued as it had since she came home from the hospital, with Ed and Margo leading essentially separate lives. She settled into her old room, and Ed stayed put in the garage apartment that he and Margo had shared as newlyweds in what felt like a lifetime ago. They rarely saw each other in the morning on a school day, but they did eat their simple dinners together. One or the other of them took two frozen dinners out, heated them in the oven, and they ate them out of their foil trays. In the evenings and on weekends, they watched television separately with little real interest, and most nights Ed would take some next step, tinkering with the TV project.

One evening in May 1976, not quite two years after the accident, Ed answered the phone to hear, "Is this Ed Schmutz?"

"Yes."

"Ah, good. Okay, Ed, sorry to call like this. This is Harry Rezak, I did some business with your dad awhile back. You probably know that my company bought your dad's place with a contingency that he could live in the house. Anyway, the hotel manager went by there yesterday after seeing the place needed some work. And well, son, he found your dad inside. Uh, he's passed away, is what I mean. He was sitting in a recliner in front of the TV and just looked like he'd gone to sleep."

Ed sighed and grimaced, "Okay, I uh, I understand. Is there anything I need to do?"

"Well, no. I just wanted to let you know so you can make whatever arrangements you want and can come get his personal property and whatever papers you need. Because of the . . . *situation*, and that he'd already passed, I went ahead and had Blackburn's Mortuary pick him up. You'll need to call them to discuss a service and the rest. Again, I'm very sorry to have to tell you this. I'm sure you and your dad were very close."

"Sure. I'll take care of it tomorrow." Ed hung up before Rezak could reply.

The next morning, Ed pulled into the drive at the old house for the first time in almost two years. Although the house looked mostly the same, it was noticeably more shabby. It sat incongruently in the shadow of the Interstate Motel that Rezak had turned their junkyard into: an old, worn-down shack of a structure in a back corner of the modern building's parking lot, looking like someone had brought it along and abandoned it there.

Standing in the front doorway, the inside looked dark and gloomy, not unlike his and Margo's place now. It seemed like nothing had moved, frozen in time from the last time he was there: the old, stained recliner, with stuffing showing through on the arms where the upholstery had been worn off; a similarly well-used couch; and a small black-and-white TV, rabbit ears wrapped in foil. There was a thicker layer of grime on everything than he remembered, and it smelled like stale beer in a locker room.

Ed walked into the room slowly. It no longer felt like his home and he felt an urge to be quiet and not disturb anything, like he was trespassing. Behind the couch was Carl's desk, littered with mail. Ed fetched a brown paper grocery sack from the kitchen and scooped the mail and the contents of the file drawer into it. With the bag under his arm, he walked down the hall and looked into each room. A few early memories from these rooms went through his mind, but the sound of his own breathing in the empty old house quickly reminded him they were long gone, replaced by many more sad and lonely years. He thought of the way things could have been, and the future he once believed fleetingly they were going to have. He closed his eyes and shook his head to escape the memories. *Yeah, thanks, Dad. I guess you were right, "No happy endings."*

He strode toward the door and something caught his eye on the table next to his dad's chair. It was the only truly personal item in the room, and he instantly recognized the faded photo of himself at eight years old, grinning at his mom and dad who were holding hands above his head and laughing. There was the happy family memorialized in a picture taken at the gate into their junkyard the summer before Hildie died. He froze in place for a few seconds, staring at it. He blinked away a tear angrily, sighed, and put the photo in the sack with the rest of the pile from the desk and walked to the door. Turning for one last look, he said out loud to no one, "They can have the rest. There's nothing left that matters," and he walked out that door for the last time.

Over the next several weeks, Ed was reminded of Carl's death almost daily as he took care of the details that accompany a close relative's death: funeral arrangements, death certificate, and reconciling bank accounts and bills. Carl hadn't quite drunk up all the money he'd received for the property, and there was enough left to bury him with a little left over. Ed's final call was to Harry Rezak to tell that him the house and everything in it was his to do with as he pleased.

Since there were no signs of foul play, there was no police investigation and no autopsy. The funeral director explained to Ed that Carl appeared to have passed away in his sleep or watching television, although he was surprised that Carl was only sixty-five, given his older appearance. What appearances alone couldn't explain was Carl's life in the almost two years since the accident; neither could Ed, since he'd neither seen nor spoken to his father again after Carl told him he'd canceled their business deal and sold the property.

Having stoked his resentment for years since Hildie's death, it was an easy segue for Carl to close himself off from the world. He kept to himself, only going out for groceries, a large part of which was beer. He started his days late in the morning, usually nursing a hangover which he treated with a little hair of the dog at breakfast. He channel-surfed from his recliner, using up each day and some of the night in meaningless television programs and a case of beer. From time to time, he delayed his second beer of the day long enough to write a check for a bill or two.

His retreat from the world had been near-complete—Carl read no newspapers, watched no news programs, wrote no letters, and took and made no phone calls—including from and to Ed. But it hadn't really been Carl who had walked away from Ed, he simply let Ed walk away from him. Rather than harboring bad feelings towards his son, at least once a day Carl would look down at the photo of his once-happy but now-departed family, tap it with two fingers and smile slightly. *The boy's better off without me.* Some nights, when the beer hit him just right, a tear would roll down his face and he'd remind himself, *The best part of me of me died years ago anyway.*

Before closing himself off from the world, he had already been well on his way into depression, and he then added a touch of alcoholism to it. It was the combination of the two and his sedentary life that took such a heavy toll on his body, aging him years before his time. In an act of mercy, his heart gave out while he sat alone in his chair on his last lonely morning in his solitary world.

Three weeks after Carl died, Ed and Margo visited his grave in what had become a very rare moment of togetherness. Walking up to the grave, it wasn't Carl's headstone that first caught his eye but one next to it that read,

Hildie J. Schmutz
May 10, 1918 - August 4, 1962
Beautiful soul, light of the world, beloved wife and mother

Standing in front of his mother's grave, Ed hung his head and closed his eyes. He didn't wonder if she was disappointed in him, he knew it in his heart. Memories of her rushed through his mind like those that had haunted him when he walked through their old house.

Margo, however, wasn't brooding about memories and lost loved ones. Standing in Texas's early summer heat, she was thinking more about the sauna-like conditions and the sweat already running down her face. *How long do we have to drag this out?*

She read Carl's headstone, which was very simple,

Carl M. Schmutz
October 14, 1911 - May 4, 1976

It made sense to her that Ed hadn't added some touching epitaph to Carl. Not intending to say it out loud, Margo blurted out, "About right for him."

That snapped Ed out of his detached funk, "Huh? What'd you say?"

"He wouldn't expect anything more. Think about it. He always knew there were no happy endings. You live your life, then you leave it. Enough said." She pointed at the headstone, "So it doesn't need to say anything else. And he was *right*. I'll go one better—people in this world either actively try to take away your happy ending or don't care if someone else does."

Ed nodded. *Guess so.*

He looked towards her, but she had turned and started walking away, saying over her shoulder, "I'll be at the truck."

He turned back to the grave, but the memories and the moment were gone. Ed and Margo drove home in the same silence they lived with every day. They would never visit the cemetery again and may as well have buried their happy memories there with their parents.

With that, their path was set. This new course in their lives may have manifested itself differently in each of them, but it had the same overall effect on both. Margo embraced her anger at the world and settled into a permanent and contemptuous perspective about everyone and everything, and it had happened with the suddenness of a cannon shot. Ed's evolution built up more slowly, perhaps even reluctantly at first, but he gave in to a total disregard for the rest of the world and embraced his isolation from it. While his mindset may have felt less angry, it was still an active rejection of love and closeness of any kind. These changes in both Ed and Margo came to dominate their every judgment of the world, how they perceived and responded to everything and everyone in it, and who they were.

Thus, year after year, Ed and Margo continued down this same dark path. Naturally, their behavior alienated others, affecting—if not poisoning—other people's attitudes and behaviors towards them in return, which just as naturally reinforced Ed and Margo's negative judgments, perceptions, and behaviors into indelible habits. In time, these habits hardened into deep, inescapable personal ruts that left them unable to turn from this path, not that it would have occurred to either of them to make a change. This was fully transformational for them both, robbing them of any thought of joy and love in the world, and ultimately corrupting their identities and their souls into the meanness, bitterness, and anger that defined them for the rest of their lives.

Chapter 5

PATHS CROSS IN THE DARK

She knew there were things in the world to avoid and to fear.

Ed and Margo resigned themselves to living out their lonely and angry lives in their dull little East Texas town that was filled with dull and petty people who they despised. Although they had no love lost for Grayton, they had nowhere else to go, and that happenstance did nothing to endear their townspeople and neighbors to them. Nevertheless, they went on with their familiar, albeit lifeless daily routines.

They also never recovered from living apart. Ed stayed in what was now *his* garage apartment and workshop, and Margo remained in her bedroom at the opposite end of the house. If they happened to eat a meal together, it was just coincidental timing, with Ed retreating back to his rooms, and Margo to hers.

Ed plodded along in his job at the high school with very little interest. Since he had to do something to make a little money, he figured it might as well be something he knew. So, he fixed whatever broke without any of the zeal he and Cy had once shown in making things better and ensuring their fixes would last. *Hey, if things fall apart and break, that's the way it goes.. I'll fix it when I fix it. That's the job.*

The one thing in life he found some satisfaction in was his tinkering at home. After finishing Cy's build-your-own color television, he just happened to overhear two teachers talking in the hallway, "My husband has a computer he's trying to sell so that I won't complain about him buying a new one. I never knew why we needed the first one, and I sure don't know why we need a new one. I don't think they actually do anything."

A week later, Ed spent a happy evening opening and examining the inner workings of a three-year-old Apple 1 computer that he bought for next to nothing so that husband could save face with his wife. Maybe there wasn't anything obvious he could do with it, like the teacher had said, but he'd spend most evenings tinkering with it, eventually creating his own cassette recorder interface and programming the little computer to work as an alarm clock that played music and turned on a lamp every morning. Content with his experiments with this gadget, Ed pretty much kept to himself and wanted to be left alone.

Like Ed, Margo's approach to running the office at Grayton High School was unheroic—get things done that needed doing, make sure the paperwork is done on time, and take care of school mail. She always figured, *I'm a secretary, I'm not curing polio.*

Her approach to a hobby or pastime was a little different than Ed's, and she stumbled onto it in the rare but enjoyable opportunities for spite and meanness that life would occasionally provide. At first, they were trifling and petty, like that minute before the final, first-period bell rang, when a handful of kids would come running through the large, double doors. After that bell, the doors were locked, and everyone had to enter through the office entrance, meaning students were late—three tardies in a single nine-week reporting period meant after-school detention.

Most days would find the Principal, Edgar Clanton, in front of the doors, encouraging students to hurry inside before they were late, and he'd often hold the door open, grinning while chagrined stragglers ran past seconds after the bell. On days when Mr. Clanton was called away, Margo would mind the gates; but unlike him, a few minutes before the last bell, she'd allow the doors to close until they were almost latched. As panicked teenagers ran up the walk, she'd wait eagerly, hand on the door handle like a sprinter listening for the starter's gun. She'd snap the doors home at the first peal of the bell, delighting at the satisfying clang of the latches locking in place and the mortified faces peering through the windowpanes in the doors. *Gotcha!* Ignoring the desperate pleas and the pounding on the doors, Margo would turn away and walk into the office, where she'd wait behind the counter for the late, out-of-breath students to enter through the outer door.

Some would try justifiable anger to plead their case, "I was going to be on time, the doors were locked too early! That's not fair!" All but the hardest of the hard cases would end by begging for forgiveness, every now and then in tears, "Please, if I get another one, I'll get detention," or, "Coach will bench me for this! Don't do this to me!" The more desperate, the better for Margo, as she barely suppressed a thin smile every time she wrote out a tardy slip and wrote the student's name into the day's report.

Every now and then Margo added to her fun by managing to misplace a few students' class requests for the next year, dropping a pretentious rich kid from a dual-credit program at the junior college in Orange, or blocking another from participating in choir or the drama class or some other useless exercise in over-privilege. At home after those occasions, more times than not Margo would start a conversation of sorts with

Ed while they ate their frozen dinners, which was remarkable in itself, given their usual mutual silence. Between bites she'd say something like, "You know, some days what goes around really does come around. I like those days. Makes this place a little more tolerable."

Although Margo never explained what she meant, Ed always had the impression that somebody had probably gotten crosswise with Margo and hadn't fared too well in the experience. He'd happened along in the hallway more than once to see Margo locking students out and walking contentedly to the office, and he guessed there were more shenanigans like that in her bag of tricks. He'd answer simply with a half grin, "Yeah, well, it's good to take it where you can get it." They'd both nod, retreat back to silence, and finish their dinner, then they'd go back to their separate existences.

After nine more dreary years of this, a couple of new and unexpected items of interest came along. The first was in Ed's electronic tinkering. Since personal computers had become all the rage and were starting to advance, he finally broke down and bought another secondhand computer, a beat-up Apple IIe that the same teacher's husband had bought years before and had since given to his kids to abuse. Ed had squeezed just about as much customization as he could out of his now-vintage Apple 1 and was eager to do the same with a newer and more capable machine. Fortunately, he paid next to nothing for it, since newer and better computers were already flooding the market.

None of which, of course, was of any interest to Margo; but in April 1985, a man walked into the Grayton High School office who did provoke a rare interest. She paid no attention when he came in, leaving him to the aide at the front counter to deal with. When he spoke, she felt an old chill in the back of her mind, "These are homework assignments from David Thomas. He's out sick for a while, and he told me I could turn these in here."

Margo held her breath and froze, her mind racing and palms starting to sweat. *Thomas? That Thomas?*

"Yes sir. We'll take them to his teachers today. I have another folder for him with this week's assignments," said the helpful aide, trading folders with the visitor. "I hope he's feeling better."

"Yeah, he'll be fine. Just one of those things, but he's better off at home than he is here, where he could get all of you sick. I'll be back same time tomorrow. It's my off-period."

As he turned to leave, Margo unfroze and watched his back go through the door. Older, a little chubbier and balder, it could be *him*, but she couldn't really tell from the back. But that voice! She was all but sure, even though it had been twenty years since she'd heard that voice. After the door closed, she asked the aide, "Who did he say those papers are for?"

"Oh, just a ninth grader named Davey Thomas. He got mono and has to stay home for a while, remember? His teachers have been sending assignments home so he could keep up."

Margo looked down at her desk, folded her hands, and spoke quietly, "Leave his homework with me for now. I'll take care of it in a while." After the young girl set the folder down, Margo went to the file room behind the office, opened a drawer, and thumbed through several folders. She found the one she was looking for: *David D. Thomas, Class of 1989, freshman, Mrs. Walker's homeroom, blah, blah, blah.* As she read his file, she realized she didn't know what the kid looked like; in fact, she'd never even heard of him. She read the next line, and it didn't matter. *Ah, there you are . . . father—Donald Thomas, teacher at Grayton Middle School. Well, hello again, Mr. Thomas.*

Back at her desk, she thumbed through the folder of homework assignments. *English, science, and social studies. Boring, whatever, and pointless. And last but not least, geometry.* Margo couldn't suppress the smile now as she closed her eyes and wondered, *What am I going to do with you?*

• • •

When Margo had been suffering through Mr. Thomas's seventh grade math class years before, Don Thomas was a man with very little joy in his life, not unlike where she would one day find herself. Bookish and uncomfortable talking with people, he had difficulty making friends, and his tendency for sarcasm in almost any situation made him even less likable to many people. It was therefore against all of his and everyone else's expectations when he met and married a shy and thoughtful woman a few years after spiting Margo in his class for sport.

Although he would never be any woman's definition of an Adonis, Annie loved him just the same for his intellect and the kindness she found behind the bluster. Oh, what happiness he rediscovered in the world by the touch of her hand and the warmth of her smile! He felt reborn. The experience—and this good woman's patient acceptance of him as he was—pierced his heart and changed his view of the world, even if only subtly. No longer were his first tendencies to dislike anyone he met, to imagine some snide comment at another's expense, or to take random swipes at students "for sport."

His worldview and demeanor changed even more a year later when, at thirty-nine years old, he became the father of young David Donald Thomas. He may not have learned to understand people any more than he ever had, but, thanks to his wife and son, the world was again a happy place for Mr. Thomas. What hope he found in his son—the wonders he would discover, the dreams he would follow and live! Like with so many parents and their children, the sun rose and set on that boy, and there was nothing Mr. Thomas took for granted in Davey's life.

Yes, this was his perfect life. He went to sleep every night thankful and incredulous that he was so blessed.

When Davey was diagnosed with mononucleosis in the spring of his freshman year in high school, requiring him to stay home for several weeks under quarantine, Mr. Thomas was more than happy to be the courier for his assignments. Better yet, although he couldn't coach his son in sports, he could darn sure apply his experience as a teacher to get him through this without losing a step at school. Davey's teachers had made it pretty easy for them: Pick up a folder every week with new assignments, trade in the previous folder with finished homework. He could even use his off-period just after lunchtime to drive to the high school and back. And Mr. Thomas could see that Davey was doing great, since he was able to check his work every week before taking the folder back. *What a great world! Even if the boy was out the rest of the year, he'll sail right through his tests, and this won't even be much of a memory by next fall.*

• • •

At the end of the day, the aides were out the door before the final bell finished ringing, as usual. What was not usual was Margo still sitting at her desk when Mr. Clanton was walking out. He stopped at her desk, "That's another day, Margo. Ready to go?"

"Not just yet. I have some files I want to take care of this evening rather than leaving them for the girls in the morning. It'll make my day easier tomorrow if I just stay a little longer now. I can make sure the door is locked when I go. It won't be long."

"Okay, then. Thanks for taking care of things, as usual," and he went on his way. As he did, it struck him that he hadn't seen Margo visibly happy in longer than he could remember. *How about that? Miracles do happen!* He laughed to himself.

When he was gone, Margo opened Davey's folder and pulled out the geometry homework—several worksheets and pages of notebook paper, filled with drawings and equations. "Gotta think about this. Not too much and nothing too obvious." She decided to leave the drawings alone, they'd be too difficult to change and make look authentic. Better to change a few random numbers: an angle measurement here, a circumference and an area calculation there. She took her time to make clean erasures and to mimic Davey's scrawl as she "edited" his homework, making just two or three changes per assignment.

Satisfied with her handiwork, Margo put the papers back and dropped the folder in the office aides' inbox. One of the girls would deliver the papers to the teachers in the morning, and no one would be the wiser. On her way out, she was already in a good mood and smiling when she heard the familiar clank of the school door locking, just as it did whenever she locked some tardy student out. That thought made her laugh out loud, "Oh yeah, I crack me up! I needed that!"

The highlight of Margo's existence for the next three weeks was the anticipation of Mr. Thomas' next delivery and her ensuing venture in editing Davey's geometry homework. Every Monday after lunch, she found herself unable to get anything done as she waited for that all-too-familiar dad to bring in his beloved son's homework. She made sure to be at her desk and looking away when he came in, and each week one of the girls would put the folder on her desk to look through before taking it around to the teachers the next morning. And each week Mrs. Duke, the geometry teacher, was surprised to see Davey's homework grade dropped lower. He had done so well the rest of the year; perhaps his illness and being at home were distracting him. *What a pity.*

At lunchtime on the fourth Monday of Davey's homebound experience, Mrs. Duke brought a note to the office and asked Margo to put it in his folder for his dad to pick up. After the teacher walked out, Margo read it:

> *Davey,*
> *This week I'm sending home the nine-weeks' test. I want you to take your time on it. You've made some mistakes on your homework recently and stumbled on the last quiz, and it's pulled your grade down. I don't want to see you undo all of your hard work this year.*
> *Take your time on the test and get well soon.*
> *Mrs. Duke*

Another test, and a big one! Margo had added more and more mistakes to Davey's geometry homework each week, but this was the big-time! She could really sink the little devil with this one!

Every day felt like Monday for the rest of the week as the anticipation built for her *coup de grâce* when the folder came back with the completed test. Like always, the office aide put Davey's folder on Margo's desk when Mr. Thomas dropped it off. Also like always, Margo stayed at her desk until everyone had gone, then took her time going through Davey's geometry work, problem by problem, making numerous small changes and paying special care to match Davey's pencil strokes and handwriting. She put the folder in the aide's inbox and walked out of the school thinking she couldn't remember when she'd seen Grayton, Texas, look so good.

That evening at home, Ed and Margo had another of their rare meals together, with Ed more than a little surprised by how talkative Margo was about everything, from the weather to television shows she'd liked recently. For them, that amounted to giddy babbling.

Two days later, Mrs. Duke stuck her head in the principal's office to deliver the news that Margo had been waiting for, "Mr. Clanton, hey, I just wanted to let you know about Davey Thomas, the ninth grader who's been out with mono for a few weeks." Hearing that, Margo's ears perked right up.

The principal answered, "Oh sure, what's up?"

"Well, he definitely didn't do very well at home. He has made an A every nine weeks before now and was doing well until he got sick, but boy, did that change. You can see it in his homework grades right away, they went lower and lower. Then his test scores went the same way. He's ending up with a D. Could be worse. If he'd been out the entire nine weeks, I think he'd have failed. Anyway, I just wanted to let you know. I think I should call Davey's parents to let them know, rather than surprise them with the report card."

He nodded and asked, "What do you know about his other grades?"

"I asked his other teachers, and he's doing fine in everything else—pretty much like he had been before he went out sick. Not in my class though. By the way, he'd requested to move up to the advanced precalculus class next year, but the rules don't allow it with any single nine weeks lower than a C."

"Oh, great. Well, let me know how the phone call goes with the parents."

Margo hurried back to the supply closet before someone noticed her smiling like her face was going to burst. Laughing to herself, she thought, *Take that, Mr. Thomas! Too bad I didn't have time to flunk him, but you take what you can get!*

Mrs. Duke's phone call that evening didn't go very well at all. The very next day, the last day of class for students, an angry-looking Donald Thomas walked into the office for a conference with the principal. Margo, as usual, sat facing away from the counter and tried to look deep in thought while also not being noticed by her old teacher. Mr. Clanton came to his office door with a smile and waved to Mr. Thomas, "Hey there, Mr. Thomas. Good to see you. Come on in, Mrs. Duke is already here."

He went in without a word and Mr. Clanton closed the door behind him. Before the principal sat down, Mr. Thomas began laying out his complaint, "Look, I don't understand. How could Davey have gotten these grades? I checked his work. I *know* he did better than a D!"

Mrs. Duke pulled a stack of paper from a folder and spread it out on Mr. Clanton's desk. "Here they are, Mr. Thomas. I don't know what to tell you. I'm just as surprised as you are, but it has been an unusual time for Davey."

"Alright, fine, I'll look through them again." He flipped through the pages, and his expression became more confused as he did. "Seriously, I don't understand. Like I said, I checked these *myself.* He had done these right." Mrs. Duke and Mr. Clanton glanced at each other with raised eyebrows.

"Sixties and fifties? Where did these come from? And that final exam . . . a fifty? Are you kidding? This kid had all As before this!"

Mrs. Duke cringed a little, "I know, I know, Mr. Thomas. I feel bad, but you can see them right in front of you."

"Listen, I *know* he passed that test. I saw the bad marks on last week's homework, and I went over the final and corrected any mistakes myself. I would not have made these stupid errors. I've been teaching math for thirty years, and you don't think I can pass a damned geometry test?"

Mr. Clanton raised his hand, "Alright, Mr. Thomas, I know this is upsetting, but there's several weeks of a pattern here in these grades. You can see it for yourself. I don't know what to tell you about your efforts to fix his mistakes, after all, this was supposed to be *his* test and not yours. Be that as it may, *someone* missed a number of answers on this exam, and the resulting grade is a fifty. In the end, David's grade for the nine weeks is a D. It's a very high D, but it is a D. I'm very sorry. It is still a very good performance for the year, though. He'll still be able to take an advanced math class next year, just not the one he had hoped for."

"So there's nothing you can do? You're going to let this be the grade on his permanent report card, and block him from taking precalc next year?" Mr. Thomas was red in the face now.

Mrs. Duke answered, "I'm sorry, Mr. Thomas. It's a district rule, not ours. We only have the one section of that class and will already have to turn some students away. There's no way we could put Davey in there now, but he can still take Algebra II. That's a very good class."

Mr. Thomas stood up, glaring at the two of them, "So that's it? Screw this good kid, don't help him take as much as he can handle, even though he's been doing great all year? You know he can do it, but you're going to let this set him back an entire year in his math studies! It isn't fair to him. What's wrong with you people to be so uncaring, so, so . . . cavalier with a young person's future?"

Mr. Clanton started to answer, "Mr. Thomas, look—" but the angry father had had enough. He knew this wasn't going to change, and he opened the door and walked out, leaving the principal to talk to his back. Margo was still at her desk and had heard the entire conversation through the closed door, almost as clearly as if she'd been in the room with them.

When Mr. Thomas opened the door and walked through, Margo turned in her chair to face him with a *Mona Lisa* smile. Something about the expression on her face caught his eye as he walked by, and then she said, "You know, life doesn't always work out the way it should. Maybe this is just one of those *life lessons,"* making quotation marks with her hands. She added, "What goes around comes around, as someone once told me."

He had stopped in his tracks and stood staring at her in shock. The words stung like a slap in the face, and as his anger bubbled over inside him, so did the instant recognition: *Margaret Cormier!* In that instant, he didn't know how, but he knew that she had done something to pay him back for his callousness years before. Only, it wasn't him who would pay the price, it was Davey. He squinted his teary eyes and, for an instant, seriously considered grabbing Margo by the shoulders and shaking her until her neck snapped. Instead, he choked back a sob as he imagined the disappointed look on his treasured son's face. He walked out, feeling defeated and utterly useless to his family.

Margo's victory was short-lived, however. Two weeks later, Mrs. Duke offered to tutor Davey during the summer session and retest him over the material that he'd done so poorly on while sick at home. To the teacher's delight, Davey scored a 95. Although the school could not move Davey into the already-full precalc class he wanted, Mrs. Duke and Mr. Clanton worked with the district office to change his permanent grade from a D to an A.

Margo could live with it. After all, it was never about the kid. *He* didn't matter. But seeing Mr. Thomas at his lowest moment of despair? Oh yes, she'd have that image in her mind's eye forever, and with it, the delicious sensation that *she* had made it happen! It could only have been better if he had fully broken down emotionally or begged for help, but she didn't feel greedy about it. In fact, she could not remember feeling more vindicated and alive. It was spectacular! Her challenge now was to find more opportunities to stir those same feelings and to revel in some semblance of payback to an uncaring world.

• • •

While Ed and Margo had been getting on with their painfully altered lives, the Faisons also went on with theirs, blissfully unaware. Jimmy Sr. remained focused on building his business and power with his law practice, living the privileged life that wealth and status enable, and steering his oldest son into a preordained future in the family business.

Whether his son wanted to follow in his footsteps was never of interest to Jimmy Sr. He had grown up during the Depression, the son of a lumber mill worker, and had done his share of tough labor during summers at the mill while in high school. His father had watched his own father become an old man at an early age from the years of hard work, just as Jimmy Sr. then watched his father do the same. The old man had dragged him to the mill whenever he could, not to teach him the family trade but to let him learn for himself what that kind of bone-tiring work could do to a man. It worked.

As a kid, Jimmy Sr. had been determined not to follow his father, who had followed his father into the same work and the same life. He rode the Truman administration's post-World War II wave of financial aid into a small scholarship to the University of Texas that he supplemented by working part-time jobs around Austin. Knowing the life he had to go back to, he was motivated to work hard and rest little while working straight through a law degree. He returned triumphantly to East Texas, joined an established law practice in Beaumont, married his high school sweetheart, and started a family. As he gained experience, he also became known for his sharp and quick mind. In combination with the drive and work ethic that had become defining facets of who he was, this got him attention from senior partners, who promoted him ahead of the pack. By the time Jimmy Jr. was in middle school with Margo, Jimmy Sr. had gone from being just another senior partner to leading the firm as managing partner. In that time, the Faisons had moved from a modest home to a much nicer house in town and then to their mansion on the golf course, and their lifestyle had naturally moved up as well.

Along the way, Jimmy Sr. learned firsthand how an education and real and focused drive can change someone's life. However, he also knew that Jimmy Jr.'s easier upbringing had left him with less fire in the belly than growing up the son of a mill worker, so he kept his finger on the pulse of the boy's sense of direction. He let the boy enjoy the things that he couldn't have at that age—nice cars, money to spend with friends, being the cool kid—but he made sure Jimmy Jr. knew there was no real discussion about where his life was going and when he had to cut the crap and measure up.

Fortunately, the son had inherited his father's intellect, and school came easy. Even in college, Jimmy Jr. quickly learned how to balance his frat-boy party-life with his studies, earning a business degree at the University of Texas. He did well enough to get into UT's law school on his own, but Jimmy Sr. wasn't one to leave important steps to chance. He reached out through his alumni- and big-donor-mafia to ensure that his boy would be welcomed into the club.

Of course, those weren't the first or only strings Jimmy Sr. pulled, nor the only directions in which he pushed when it came to his son. He had already ensured his boy got into his alma mater, took the right pre-law curriculum, joined the right fraternity, mixed with the right scions of society, and *then* went to law school and joined "his" firm. There had been that distasteful business with a car wreck when Jimmy Jr. was still an undergraduate, but the father handled it, the boy did what he was told, and it wasn't even a speed bump in the larger plan. Jimmy Sr. even pushed his son towards a young marriage to a girl from a wealthy and influential local family, Jeannine Rezak, a combination that had been bound to open even more doors for the boy going forward.

Jimmy Jr. slid effortlessly into place at the firm, and he and Jeannine moved into their own mansion at the Liberty Pines Country Club. Although Jimmy Jr. had happily become accustomed to his family's more lavish lifestyle, he had some memories of their younger, leaner times as he was growing up. His and Jeannine's sons, Jimmy III and Teddy, however, knew only wealth and privilege, and without their grandfather orchestrating their lives as he had their father's, they had learned none of Jimmy Sr.'s focus, drive, and fire-in-the-belly. They were just another couple of rich kids who knew they were set for life and didn't need to make an effort.

• • •

After Margo's fun with Davey Thomas in 1985, things quieted down again for her for many years. There was still an occasional kid at home sick for an extended recovery, but going back to that well for just anybody bored her. She settled mostly for locking kids out in the morning from time to time, losing permission slips, and misplacing class requests.

It was eight years later, the first day of school in 1993, when Margo had her next inspired opportunity. With Mr. Clanton welcoming new students at the front of the school, Margo was glumly watching over the student parking lot entrance, when in roared a jacked-up and thundering Ford Bronco. This wasn't some redneck's rebuild; no, it was a brand-new, top-of-the-line Eddie Bauer edition with all the bells and whistles, monster tires, and an oversized chrome muffler that sounded like it amplified the noise coming out of the beast. Margo ordinarily wouldn't take any extra notice of a student, but there was something galling about a high school kid driving this outlandish vehicle that cost more than she made in a year.

With the deafening silence that ensued when the thing was parked, Margo shot an irritated look towards the students stepping out of both sides of the thing. She was shocked by what she saw and had to catch her breath, blurting out, "Oh my God!" For an instant, she just *knew* she was seeing Jimmy Faison, Jr. *No, that's wrong. And there's two of 'em! But those kids are his spitting image—same blue eyes and mop of curly blond hair on both! Still looking like Robert Plant wannabes.* Margo forgot everything around her as she watched Jimmy III and his freshman little brother, Teddy, make their grand entrance strutting through the parking lot. Just like their father had, as they passed small groups of students the two boys collected admirers like flies to a gut wagon, all of them anxious to be seen hanging out with the coolest of the cool. Margo took this in while old memories flew back into her head from having watched the same smug scene play out countless times when she was a teenager.

The bell rang a few minutes later, snapping her out of her near-daze, and she hurried into the office. Marching straight to the same file cabinet in which she had once looked up Davey Thomas's personal information, this time she flipped through the files until she found "Faison." And there *they* were, not one, but two! How she could have missed the older boy for two years she had no idea, but there he was: James D. Faison III, eleventh grade, father James, mother Jeannine. *Get outta town! That's gotta be the same Jeannine!* And next was Theodore E. Faison, ninth grade.

Staring at those files, she thought she might hyperventilate. *Oh, what to do, what to do?!*

That night, Margo took the Faison boys' school records home and learned everything she could about them. It didn't take a lot of study. In every grade so far, the story was the same for both of them and unremarkable in almost every way: barely C students, no advanced classes, no extracurricular activities of any kind. Glaringly average, which was the one thing that stood out as remarkable to Margo. She lay awake that night dwelling on the Faisons instead of sleeping. *Boy, the nuts sure fell far from the tree. Even their jerk-father looks like a go-getter compared to those two! This should be easy, but I need to think about it. Come up with something really good—better than the Thomas boy. There's gotta be something bigger.*

Margo couldn't have known just how far from the family tree this generation of Faison had fallen. If she could have been a fly on the wall, she would have had a better idea later that same week when during lunch one of Teddy's pals asked him what his plans were for college. He gave the same answer he'd heard his brother give to his buddies that summer, "Dude, I'm not worrying about it. I just want to be a dude and hang, ya know? My old man and grandfather will fix it without me having to kill myself. I'll do whatever and live the life."

Just two generations after their grandfather had created a new life for himself and his family out of sheer determination, the youngest Faisons had none of it. Although they still shared genes with their father and grandfather and undoubtedly were more intelligent than appearances would suggest, it didn't matter much. They had so thoroughly learned that they would have everything they needed—everything they *wanted*—without making any effort, they figured they'd be idiots to stick their necks out and do anything besides coast. Besides, they were the envy of their friends just as they were.

All of which made Margo's challenge that much tougher. How do you knock someone down who won't even stand up? Her answer came to her unexpectedly the next day when Principal Clanton walked in from a meeting with the superintendent, "Margo, will you make a note for the next staff meeting? The district wants us to get an early start planning for this year's TAAS tests. We'll need to look for volunteers to manage the process."

"Sure, got it. But before you go, I've been thinking that I could be of more use around here. How about I jump in?"

"Uh huh. Really? Why?" Mr. Clanton stopped in the doorway to his office and looked mildly confused. "I mean, great. But why all of a sudden? I thought you were settled in to doing what you do."

"Oh, I know. I guess I just have time on my hands, and you know what they say, 'Idle hands are the devil's workshop.' I wouldn't want to get into any mischief," Margo said with a conspiratorial smile.

"Well alrighty then. We'll bring it up with the staff. I can't imagine anyone will want to arm wrestle you over it. It's a thankless job, really, but someone has to do it."

Over the next several weeks, relief and disbelief rippled through the faculty. Relief that no one was going to be "volunteered" for the extra job and disbelief that, of all people, *Margo Schmutz* was pitching in. They were all more than happy to have her do it, however. The TAAS test was the set of standardized tests given annually to several different grade levels from elementary school through high school, the last of which was taken by eleventh graders and had to be passed in order to graduate. To protect against cheating, security procedures were somewhat complicated and the process of managing it all was restricted to state-trained staff and faculty. Anyone involved had to participate in many days of training, both to understand all of the accounting and security procedures and to demonstrate proficiency. And for all the extra trouble, they were then at risk for investigation and disciplinary action in the event of any irregularities.

Thus, while it didn't make sense to anyone, everyone was happy to have the ordinarily disagreeable and uncooperative office manager handle it. For her part, Margo hadn't been this cheerful in years. She and the guidance counselor, Ruthie Gray, conducted practice tests with ninth and eleventh grade English and math classes, and Ruthie coached Margo through the intricate paper handling, accounting, and packaging she'd have to carefully manage during the real tests in the spring. As Ruthie double-checked her understanding again and again, Margo suppressed angry outbursts like, *Yeah, yeah, yeah. No kidding. It ain't rocket science, Einstein. I've got it all figured out—and then some!* What she actually said was more like, "Oh yes, I see. It all makes perfect sense, thanks so much. I'll be sure to check with you if there's anything that isn't perfectly clear." All the while, she had her eye on the formal round of tests to come and the surprises she had in store for the Faison boys.

Jimmy III and Teddy both passed their practice tests that fall. Their scores weren't impressive, but they made the cut, which was all they were shooting for anyway. More importantly, Margo passed her evaluations from the state and from Ruthie Gray. Now she was all set to be the official campus coordinator for Grayton High's standardized tests, giving her full access and complete control of all test materials before and after they were given to students. Like a kid in June who was already anxiously counting the days until Christmas, it was all Margo could do to bide her time until her chance to make the most of her new power.

The months finally passed, and the April test day arrived. With the help of the office aides, Margo distributed test bundles to the ninth and eleventh grade English and math teachers in the morning before the first bell, collected the completed tests after each class, and locked them in a special file drawer in the office. At lunchtime, Ruthie Gray stopped by to check on her progress, "Now, are you sure you have it all under control? I can help after school if you need it. I know there's a lot to do in getting everything sealed and packaged the right way, with all the forms filled out and all."

"No, no. I had a good teacher. I can handle it." Cheerful Margo had made another appearance, and she was beaming, "I'll have it all ready to go to the district office in the morning if you'd like to check it, just to be on the safe side."

"Well okay then. I'll swing by in the morning, but I know it will all be just fine. Call if you need any help." Margo watched the counselor go and her smile shifted back to a conspiratorial smirk as she thought, *Help? No, I wouldn't want to share. This is all mine.*

At the end of the day Margo followed procedure, closing herself in the file room so she could audit all of the test packages from each class and fill out all of the tracking paperwork. After sorting it all, checking the count, and finishing the official procedures, she was more than ready to get on with it. She opened the filing room door and peeked into the office to make sure everyone had gone for the day. Then, just to be sure, she quietly turned the lock. "Now for the main event!" she announced with a clap of her hands.

She found Jimmy III's and Teddy's test packages and went to work changing random answers to every third or fourth problem throughout their English and math answer sheets. After all of the anticipation, it was surprisingly simple and somewhat anticlimactic—swipe a large, gummy eraser across several answers at a time and fill in the bubble for a different answer. *Oops, got that one wrong after all. Uh oh, there's another one.* All the while, Margo was giggling like a schoolgirl. When she had had enough, she slid the answer sheets back into their respective test booklets. She felt a pang of disappointment that she had no obvious way to mar the essay portion of the English tests. *Then again, it's lucky for me these two morons can't string together two coherent thoughts to save their souls. They did my work for me on those essays.* She then put the test booklets and answer sheets back into each class's envelopes and packaged them all up for delivery to the school district office in the morning after Ruthie checked them against the paperwork. She left all of it locked in the file cabinet for the night and was home by dinnertime, where Ed found himself again with an unusually talkative and jovial dinner partner for the evening.

The next morning, Ruthie was her usual chipper self as Margo watched her double-check everything. "I know I don't really have to check all of this. You did it all last fall, and it hasn't changed. But rules are rules," Ruthie laughed. "Anyway, it *is* important to the school to get it all right since it affects our ranking. Some schools have gotten in trouble for cheating to improve their state ranking." She whispered, wide-eyed, "Some people have gotten fired and even went to jail because of it. Neither of us needs any of that."

Ruthie noticed Margo looking suddenly pensive and quickly added, "Oh now, don't you worry. That's why I'm checking it. And it's all good. I can take it to the district office this morning if you like."

"Sure. That would be great, and thanks for checking it all." Margo smiled even more sweetly as she realized Ruthie's name was on the form as one of the faculty attesting to the veracity of Grayton High School's test materials and procedures.

The state reported the test scores two months later. Since Margo was managing the office during summer school, she was there for Ruthie to mention it, "All of your hard work paid off. The TAAS results are in, and everything was in order. Our school did about the same as previous years." The counselor spread the report out on Margo's desk, "You can see we'll have a few students to watch for the next couple of years to make sure they pass their eleventh-grade test, otherwise they won't be able to graduate. That would mean more work for them and doesn't make the school look so good either."

"Oh, I see one of the Faisons is on the list. That won't make that bigshot family happy," said Margo with concern in her voice.

"Yeah, especially the younger one . . . he's supposed to be in the tenth grade in the fall. The older one passed his eleventh-grade tests barely, so he's done. But Theodore didn't make it in English or math. He'll have to do a little better in two years, or he won't graduate. Funny, though, I checked his records, and he did better in middle school."

"Well, you know the old saying, life doesn't always work out the way it should. Maybe this is just another of those life lessons. Go figure," and Margo *was* figuring. *Guess I should have changed even more on the older one's just to be sure. Oh well, I know how to do it now, and that's a good thing. Whatever, the oldest isn't my problem now, but little Teddy . . . Oh yes, I'll see him again in two years for his last tests, and it's looking like he won't be as lucky as big brother.*

Walking away, Ruthie Gray was puzzled by Margo's comment and the dreamy smile on her face. *That's an "old saying"? Oh well, everyone processes stress differently, after all.*

The next couple of years veered further from the expected Faison path for Jimmy III and Teddy. Although Jimmy III graduated from high school, his mediocre grades and SAT scores didn't do him any favors. It was only because his father and grandfather still had stroke with influential alumni that he was admitted to college at all. He carried the minimum academic load and set about barely passing his way disinterestedly through a business degree at the University of Texas. It was going to take him at least six years to graduate, and it was clear from the start that law school was not in Jimmy III's future.

Teddy's path turned even more for the worse. With his already mediocre grades and poor showing on his ninth-grade state tests, he was moved down to remedial English and math classes where the curriculum was focused specifically on teaching and passing the TAAS tests. Several pressures now combined to drag Teddy down, starting at home where his father went into rages, like, "What the hell is wrong with you? You should be able to do better than this with your eyes closed! I did! For God's sake, it's basic grammar and arithmetic! And why the hell don't you do something besides playing video games and smoking with your redneck friends?"

During these yelling fits, Teddy had already learned it was best not to reply at all. Eventually his father would walk away in disgust, dropping the subject until another day. His grandfather rarely spoke directly to him at all anymore, preferring instead to scowl and shake his head at the complete lack of talent on display by the latest generation of his line. Teddy's mother, Jeannine, could always be relied on to defend her son, "Leave him alone, he's just a boy. He'll do fine, and he's no different than you were."

The last comment almost always generated a renewed rage from her husband. It also elicited a grin from her son, who thought, *Yeah, you tell him, but do it somewhere else. I don't need the drama, lady.*

Teddy also had to deal with the humiliation of being cast down with the kids he and his friends referred to as "the idiots and the retards." He may have been confident in the knowledge that he didn't really belong with these losers and wasn't one of them, but the stigma was there just the same. He saw the sneers and heard the snickers as he walked past people who had previously been part of his posse. *I guess my money isn't good enough for those losers anymore.*

For the final blow, Teddy surrounded himself with a rougher group of dedicated losers after the ninth grade, starting with a few kids in his remedial classes. Unlike Teddy, many of his new classmates were considered losers through no fault of their own, but from societal prejudices and the luck of birth. Most were poor, without either the resources or the family support that others take for granted, and many had legitimate learning disabilities. Nevertheless, some of these kids were still able to make good choices and not live out their lives as actual unproductive losers. Teddy, on the other hand, had the opposite problem. Despite all of the advantages of *his* birth—innate ability from his father and grandfather, wealth, and a privileged lifestyle—he frittered it all away through behaviors and bad choices and all but intentionally joined the ranks of the less fortunate losers. The kids who Teddy gravitated towards were some combination of apathetic, disruptive, and angry, and they introduced him to a larger circle of similarly unpleasant friends. Like him, they reveled in their status as outcasts and social rejects while at the same time raging against the world for ostracizing them, and their resulting behaviors ensured they'd meet the lowest expectations anyone had of them.

• • •

Two years later, in April 1996, Margo repeated her scheme in every detail and "helped" Teddy Faison by revising his final state exam answers at the end of his eleventh grade. Her effort two years earlier hadn't been quite enough to sink his brother, Jimmy III, who still managed to graduate and move on to college. She was keenly aware that this was her last shot at Jimmy Jr.'s boys, and she did not want to waste it. These being the tests he had to pass in order to graduate next year, she thought, *Oh no, this little Faison isn't getting by this time!*

Unbeknownst to Margo, she could have saved herself the effort. Teddy's academic ability had done nothing but deteriorate since his ninth-grade tests, and he would have failed this time on his own.

With that lifetime foundation from his exaggerated sense of entitlement, and despite all of the obvious advantages he could have leveraged, he was primed to settle into being a teenaged loser. It was then, at the critical point in his life as he was transitioning from boy to man, when—by some miracle of circumstance and guidance by just the right mentor—Teddy Faison may have yet come around, chosen differently, leveraged his advantages, and become a real contributor in life, he instead got Margo. He then did not simply learn to behave badly, he lost any *ability* to behave differently, to *be* better and to respond in any way other than self-pity and anger. Whatever advantages he had left were no longer in personal ability and intellect, all signs of which had permanently withered.

And fail he did, spectacularly.

In the ensuing parent conference with the high school's guidance counselor, Ruthie Gray, Teddy's parents were aghast at the implications about their youngest son. While his son sat sullenly next to him staring at his feet, Jimmy Jr. erupted, "That's enough! I don't know what you people have been doing here, pretending to teach these kids or whatever. You've screwed something up alright, and now my son is taking the fall for your inability to teach the basics! If you think for a second that we're sending him back here for another year of this, you'd have to be crazy. The hell with that and the hell with this school! We'll put him in a private program to get his diploma where teachers know what the hell they're doing!"

Teddy turned wide-eyed as his parents stood up, and his father said to him, "Let's go, Teddy. You're done in this place."

Teddy stood up slowly and sauntered through the door. He flashed a grin at the counselor and said, "Ta-ta, ya'll."

His father kept walking but said curtly, "Shut up, idiot, and come on."

That night, Teddy was in the mood to celebrate. He may not know what his old man had in mind for a "private program," but he was finished at Grayton High School. He rounded up his buddies and headed for Branson Pond just outside of town, where, like earlier generations of teenage boys, Teddy and his pals could often be found at the pond to smoke, drink beer when they could get it, play their music too loud, and act like hooligans. Teddy guffawed loudly as he parked and sneered at the other five guys crammed into his truck. "There he is. Damn, that dude is always here. Look at him, what a loser!"

Sure enough, there sat old Mark Hammock, right where you'd find him most nights, perched on his pickup's open tailgate. His beer belly was bigger, hair and beard were shaggier and graying, and his eyes circled in darker rings, but otherwise he was the same fixture he'd been in that spot for more than twenty years: unbuttoned work shirt, yellowing undershirt, grimy old blue jeans, and work boots with fraying toes and worn-down heels. Hammock had been the old dude at the pond since before these boys were born. Although he was the same age as the current generation's fathers, he had apparently had a tougher life that left him looking old enough to be their grandfather. Either way, he was now the de facto major domo of the pond's night life, but Hammock typically kept to himself, drinking as much as a case of beer through the night and watching the teenage shenanigans from a distance with a scowl.

Teddy knew that his dad and Hammock were running buddies back in the day until some car wreck screwed Hammock up, and they drifted apart. But like his brother, Jimmy III, Teddy had learned to use a familiar ease that the old guy seemed to extend to the Faison boys—probably left over from his time with Jimmy Jr.—and some nights Teddy could bum a six-pack or two from him. Usually by this time Hammock would already have a beer in his hand and several cans scattered on the ground at his feet, but not tonight. Fortunately, scoring beer from him wouldn't be necessary on this Friday night, now that Teddy's brother was home from UT for the summer. Jimmy III would be bringing tonight's refreshments as an early celebration to the end of their eleventh grade.

As if on cue, a BMW 325 skidded to a stop in a cloud of white dust beside Teddy's Bronco. The door swung open, and Jimmy III stepped out with a wide grin on his face, "Well boys, how's good ol' Grayton? You takin' care of my old truck, little brother?"

"Uh huh, whatever. Beer in the back?" Teddy's face went red as he opened the trunk and took out two ice chests full of beer. As glad as Teddy was for his brother to show up with beer, he seethed at the sight of the brand-spanking-new Beamer. It was just another case of his family screwing him over and gut-punching his ego. *Why does Jimmy get all the good stuff? What makes him any better than me? I deserve as good as anyone else in this family. And it makes me look bad to the dudes!*

The teenagers settled in around the coolers in front of the Bronco and Beamer, and Jimmy III headed over to sit with Hammock twenty yards away. Hammock nodded silently in greeting and turned his attention back to the pond.

Just after nightfall an hour later, three high school girls walked up the road to the edge of the pond, not far from where the boys were drinking beer. After giggling nervously, looking over at the boys and giggling more, the girls each lit a cigarette and almost immediately erupted into stifled coughs. Teddy wandered over, and the girls all held their cigarettes awkwardly, trying to look practiced and sophisticated, "Hey, I know you guys from school, right?"

After more nervous giggling, "Yeah, we know who you are, Teddy Faison," which, of course, elicited even more giggles.

"I don't think I've seen you out here before."

"We're sort of celebrating. Tina turned sixteen Tuesday, so we're getting out for her birthday," one of them said with a drag on her cigarette and a nod towards her shier friend.

Teddy smiled while looking from girl to girl, admiring the short skirts that had drawn him over in the first place. "Cool, happy birthday, *Tina*. Why don't ya'll come hang with us? Beer's good for a birthday, and this is my early graduation party," he said with a flourish of his hand.

Tina answered nervously, "I don't know. I don't really like beer, I don't think." Her friends looked crushed by her answer and shot pleading expressions at her.

"You don't *think?* Hey, aren't you guys tenth grade?" he asked. All three girls nodded. Teddy chuckled, "We were already drinking beer in *middle* school. Look, come on over and just try one. If you don't like it, one of us will drink the rest of it for sure."

Tina looked at her friends and rolled her eyes, "Okay, okay, but just a little. Don't forget, my mom's off at midnight, so I have to be home by then."

"Cool. Little over three hours from now. Come on, it'll be fun," Teddy said innocently.

Jimmy III had been watching and listening from his seat by Hammock. He watched the girls walk over to join the boys and, like his brother, took his time inspecting each of them from head to toe and appreciating that mini-skirts had come back into fashion. As the girls all tried sipping beers, the birthday girl turned her nose up and handed it back to Teddy with a shake of her head. Jimmy III ambled over and told her, "Hey, I have rum and Coke in the car too. It's what my girlfriend drinks. You can have that instead if you want."

Tina was mesmerized by the older boy's striking resemblance to his younger brother, both with the same surfer appearance and blue eyes. "Oh yeah, sure. That sounds much better," she said with no idea of whether it would be any better at all.

Teddy followed his brother to the car, "I'll take it to her, dude. Go on back to Hammock."

"Alright. And you're welcome, little brother."

Two hours later, the teenagers were all varying degrees of drunk. After four rum and Cokes, Tina was sitting on the ground next to Teddy, smiling dreamily. Her friends whispered to each other, then stood as one said, "T, we should probably go if you're going to get home before your mom."

Teddy flinched and put his arm around Tina, "Hey, hey! I can take her home if she wants to stay a little longer. No problem," smiling his most disarming smile.

Tina smiled back, "Sure, I guess I can stay a little while, if you're okay to get me home in an hour." She looked up at her friends and nodded.

"Okay then. See you tomorrow, T, and happy birthday again." The two turned and walked the way they had come earlier.

Teddy stood up, took Tina's hand, and helped her up. "How about you come with me to get one more?"

She shrugged, "Alright, but last one. I'm already woozy."

They staggered slightly to the back of Jimmy III's car, and Teddy poured two large rum and Cokes, heavy on the rum. As he handed Tina's back to her, she rocked backwards and almost fell, "Whoa. I should sit back down."

"Say, let's sit in my truck. It's more comfortable than the ground, and it's getting chilly anyway." Teddy guided her to the passenger side, opened the door and slid the front seat all the way forward. He took Tina's hand, steadying her as she climbed in to sit in the back seat, then he climbed in after her, closing the door behind him. They sat silently, sipping their drinks for a few minutes when Teddy jumped awake, realizing he had fallen asleep. He looked over at Tina, who was asleep herself, leaning against the window. He opened the door, fell out onto the ground, then picked himself up precariously and staggered over to his brother and Hammock.

"The chick's ashleep in the truck. I guessh you're going to hab to drive her home," Teddy slurred.

Jimmy III sighed, "Alright Mr. Big, let me go see how she is and find out where she lives. Give me your keys." When he reached the open door to the Bronco, he was met by Tina's bare legs and her skirt hiked up a little too far from getting into the back of the truck. *Well now, what do we have here?* As his eyes roamed upwards, he saw that she was still out like a light. He turned back towards the guys, waved and yelled, "She's good, dudes. I'll be back in a while." After climbing into the driver's seat, he turned the rearview mirror down towards those bare thighs. After a minute of thinking about the possibilities, he drove the Bronco slowly down the gravel road away from the pond, barely keeping his eyes on the road.

Less than thirty minutes later the Bronco pulled back up at the pond and parked in the same spot it had been in before. Jimmy III stepped out and strutted up to the boys with a goofy grin on his face, "Slight change of plans, fellas. We'll take her home in a while. She may be a little tired now and need a little more rest before going home to mama, heh, heh."

Teddy got to his feet and walked towards the Bronco. As he passed his brother he said, "What do you mean? Did you two do something?"

The older Faison kept walking towards Hammock's truck, "I showed her what it's like with a college man instead of a high school boy. She didn't seem to mind, heh, heh. She'll probably ask for more whenever she wakes up, heh, heh."

Teddy staggered slightly and yelled, ""You bastard! You knew she was with me! You were just supposed to take her home!" He looked in to see Tina still lying on the back seat, now with her knees pulled up to her chest and her skirt bunched above her waist. His drunk buddies, having heard the two brothers, had now appeared behind Teddy, straining to get a look at the girl. As he climbed in, Teddy shouted, "Hey, dudes, back off! If anyone's getting with her, it's me. My truck after all. The rest of you can draw straws or something and wait your turn!"

As Teddy jostled the seat sitting down, Tina looked at him groggily and slurred, "Uh oh. I'm in trouble now. Did we, uh . . . we didn't . . . did we? Oh, I'm in trouble." Her voice trailed off as she hugged her knees tighter, apparently still unaware of how exposed she was.

Teddy was very aware and couldn't take his eyes off her, "No, no one's in trouble. It's all cool. And no, *we* didn't do it yet, but we're going to. So, happy birthday to us both!" Although he was smiling, Teddy was angry. This was one time his older brother wasn't going to get the better deal! The girl sure didn't seem to be in any condition to say no anyway. Still ogling her, Teddy struggled to push his pants down in the cramped quarters in the back of the Bronco. He vaguely caught the sound of his brother's voice yelling angrily, but between the booze and his excitement over his luck with this girl, he couldn't really make out what all the ruckus was about.

His pulse now racing, he leaned over the helpless girl and pulled her arms away. As he reached towards her leg, Teddy heard the sound of something heavy hitting the truck, and someone behind him yelled, "Oww! What the hell, dude?!"

An instant later he was yanked backwards by his collar and flew out of the truck. Arms flailing, he arced through the air in what felt like slow motion, landing in the grass with a brain-rattling thud. Teddy thrashed around, trying to yank his pants back up and to make sense out of what had just happened. He was shocked to see Hammock backing out of the truck with the girl cradled in his arms. *Just what in the hell is he doing? She's mine!*

As Hammock turned to walk away, he was smoothing the girl's skirt down with one hand and concentrating on her face. Scattered around him were Teddy's buddies looking lost, two of them leaning against the truck holding their heads. One of them yelled, "Dude, what was that?!"

Hammock ignored them and carried the girl to his pickup, laying her down in the bed. Then he stood back, bowed his head and turned to shake his finger at the boys. He spoke in a low voice, "You boys get on out of here."

Jimmy III got unsteadily to his feet, still holding his face with one hand as blood ran down his arm, "Look what you did! What the hell?"

Hammock slowly looked from boy to boy. Teddy was on his feet and yelling, "You old bastard! You wait 'til our daddy hears about this! He'll fix you—you can bet on that! You know who our family is?!"

Nodding his head slowly, Hammock pursed his lips and said, "Uh huh. I've known your family longer than you have, *boy*. Now your daddy's gonna do whatever he's gonna do, alright. I know something else though, something *you ain't* gonna do." He turned to look at the girl in the bed of his pickup—hair and clothes in disarray, arms clenched tightly around herself—and shook his head, "The next time I have to come between you and this girl, it ain't gonna end so well for you. Believe me when I tell you, there's worse things than a bloody nose and a bruised ass."

After a pause, he turned and glared at the Faison brothers, "Now go on . . . all of you. I won't tell you again." He took a step toward the boys, and they all scattered, leaping into the two cars and tearing down the road away from Branson Pond in a hurry.

Hammock turned back and looked at the passed-out girl pensively with his hands on his hips. He noticed the young girl's still-bare legs and sighed loudly, "Hmm. Now what am I going to do with you, girl?"

Chapter 6

OTHER PATHS CROSS

She could also find beauty, goodness,
and sometimes salvation unsought.

Mark Hammock's life leading to that night at the pond with the youngest Faisons had not been a happy one. If the years after that terrible car accident in 1974 had already been destined to be unkind to him, he made them even worse at every turn. Before that dark day years ago, he had been attending junior college classes, but afterwards he dropped out and spent months hiding from the world in his room at his parents' house during the day and sitting by himself at Branson Pond late into every night. Not only had his dad's pal, the shyster-lawyer Jimmy Faison, pulled some fast ones to get him off, but he'd managed to lay the blame on some of the people who were killed in the accident. If this had been a story about someone else, the old Mark would have thought it a genius and hilarious outcome. Instead, the pain and

suffering he had caused, and the lives he had ruined, only to escape any consequence and push his sins onto others, crushed him under unbearable and inescapable guilt.

He couldn't turn to his closest friends for help, just the thought of which made him burst into tears. His buddies, guys he'd known his whole life—Jenks, Logan, Mallet, and Jimmy—were now just faces that were inseparable from this haunting and damning memory. And they didn't get it, any of it. If any of them might have been capable of understanding what Mark was feeling, it would have been Jimmy, he was the closest to being a thinker in their group. But when Mark had tried, Jimmy wouldn't hear it, "Dude, what's wrong with you? My dad fixed it. Why are you even thinking about it still? Who cares about those people? They were nobody going nowhere. Move on!"

Mark's own voice reverberated endlessly in his head after comments like that, screaming, "You killed them, and you got away with it! You don't deserve anything good in life. You don't deserve to live!" He hated himself all the more for lacking the courage to deliver what he knew would be a just punishment by ending his worthless life.

So he stayed away from his friends and everyone else. And that's when he started drinking—*really* drinking, enough to help him forget for a little while every night and have some peace before it began again the next day.

Several months after the accident in 1974, Mark's father, the esteemed County Commissioner, Ken Hammock, could no longer take it. Sitting in front of a television tuned to the nightly news as he read a newspaper, he looked up and stopped Mark who was going out the door for another night of beer at wherever it was he went, "Wait, Son. Where are you going again? Come on, you haven't been right for a while, and we need to get you past this."

Mark turned towards his father and took a deep breath. Tears started streaming as he spoke, "Sure Dad, okay, you want me to talk about it? Here goes: I keep seeing those people . . . those people I *killed*." Now sobbing and struggling to speak, he raised his voice, "And I feel like I'm lying every day. Like I stole their lives, and I'm getting away with it . . . every . . . damn . . . day. And, and I—"

His father slapped the newspaper down on the table next to him, cutting his son off, "No, stop. Just *stop!* Where's your head at, boy? What don't you get? This thing is done, over, taken care of. You better just wrap your mind around that and be damned glad your old man is somebody who can take care of business. Now it's time to put it behind all of us and move on!

"You're twenty-one years old now, you're a man! Act like one, dammit! You don't see Faison's boy ruining his life over this, do you? I hear Jimmy Jr.'s heading to law school in Austin next year. But you? Man, I don't know what to do with you. Hell, until last year, you at least could have been drafted, and maybe the Army would've made a man out of you serving your country in Vietnam, but that's over. So now what? You think you're going to drink your way through life living here? Oh, hell no! You trying to make me look bad in an election year, boy?!"

Mark stood there, head bowed and not answering. His father broke the silence after a painful two minutes, tossing a key and a piece of paper on the floor at Mark's feet, "I don't know what your problem is, but I can't let it be mine, not right now. So, here's what you're going to do. When you leave tonight, take your stuff with you. When you're done for the night, you go to that address. The key will get you in. It's a trailer over in the park down Highway 105. All paid for. It's better than it sounds and better than you've earned. Sit out your life there, not here."

Mark nodded, picked up the key and the address, stuffing them into his pocket. Without a look or word to his father, he made three trips from his bedroom to the beat-up pickup he was now driving. After three armloads of clothes, he left the front door open and drove away, stopping at the 7-Eleven for a case of beer on his way to Branson Pond. Late that night he made his way to his new home and resumed his routine—hiding out in the trailer during the day and drinking beer by himself while brooding at the pond at night.

A week later, he found a note stuck in his front door as he was leaving for an evening at the pond. It was typed on county letterhead and unsigned. *Nice family touch. Probably had a flunky bring it and didn't bother with it himself.* It was also the last contact the father and son ever had.

> Mark,
>
> It's time for you to do something. The trailer is paid for, but you need to pay your own bills now.
>
> I've made arrangements with a construction company we do business with who needs workers. It doesn't pay much, but it's better than nothing. A card with the number is attached. Use it. He's expecting the call.
>
> Your Father

Mark made the call. What else was he going to do? He was hired on as part of a framing crew building new houses. Having given up on any education, it seemed as good as anything else, and he considered himself decent enough with tools. He could handle the physical demands of that kind of work, and as he settled into it, he discovered that he had some talent in basic carpentry. Nevertheless, as the years went by, he bounced from job to job, rarely keeping one longer than a year, not because he couldn't do the work, but in time he simply stopped doing it. The cycle was always the same: hire on; get comfortable with the new crew; boss is impressed and compliments Mark's work; Mark starts showing up later and later, sometimes not at all; and he'd ultimately be fired.

The haunting memory and guilt were rarely far from his thoughts. When it felt like he was doing well on the job, and especially when the boss took notice and complimented his work, that guilt would become louder and louder as he brooded at the pond every night. *Why me? It ain't fair. Why can't you just leave me alone, and let me do my work? I don't deserve anything more.* He'd start drinking more and more and until later in the night, and he'd start showing up later and later for work—hungover to boot by the end.

Mark was stuck in this lonely and self-destructive cycle for the next twenty-two years, sometimes going for months without work, because he'd burned so many bridges. In time, there weren't any construction and framing companies left that he hadn't spent time with and whose bosses didn't know he'd burn out and stop working after a while. They wouldn't take another chance on him until they were really desperate for hands. Even so, he managed to stay employed just enough to make ends meet and put beer in his cooler every night, and that's as high as he was aiming anyway.

In late May 1996, Mark was wrapping up just over a year with Arceneaux Construction and was well into his eventual habit of coming in late and waiting to be fired, but for some reason Old Man Arceneaux had taken an interest in him. Driving to one of his construction sites

one afternoon, Bill Arceneaux was lost in thought about his perplexing employee. *I don't know, maybe I'm due for a charity case. I just can't figure this guy. Good work for months and then just peters out. Maybe I can get through to him. If not, he's a lost cause and won't ever work for me again, that's for sure.*

At a jobsite on the east side of Grayton, Mark heard a familiar voice yell from the front of the property, "Hey, Hammock. Come on out here." Mark was surprised to find his company's owner waiting for him. "I need you to ride with me to pick up some cabinets from the shop. My custom guy is on another job, and I told him I'd bring 'em to him to keep us on schedule. I can't lift them on my lonesome, so come on, and give me a hand."

Mark shrugged and climbed into the boss's pickup. They drove in silence for ten minutes while Arceneaux rehearsed in his head. He finally tapped the steering wheel with his right hand and said, "Okay, look, I've talked around about you. Everyone I talk to agrees you do top work, but we can't count on you. Some of 'em even told me the only reason their companies ever hired you was because your dad is Ken Hammock, and he could've given 'em trouble if they hadn't. Of course, he ain't County Commissioner any longer, so that won't cut it for you now, not that that would matter much to me anyway."

Arceneaux glanced at him, looking for any reaction, but Mark stared straight ahead, stone-faced. The older man sighed and cut to the chase, "Listen, I wish there was something we could talk through, maybe figure this out, because I don't want to be the next guy to fire you. But I durn sure will. Don't get me wrong, I like your work. Hell, I could see you learning to run our framing teams. That'd be a good ol' raise for you too, but I have to be able to count on you. And I *can't*, son. I want to, but I can't. There it is. The only thing holding you back is you." Arceneaux looked anxiously at Mark, "Help me out here, say something. What's going on in there?"

Mark just shrugged and kept looking through the windshield.

Arceneaux shook his head as he pulled into a gravel drive, passed an old house, and parked at a large barn. Before he could step out of the truck, a pretty girl who couldn't have been a day over twenty stepped out of the barn and waved them towards the back of the barn, where they pulled around just in time for the same pretty gal to slide open a large door, revealing some cabinet sections on the floor. Smiling like it was old home week, she said, "I thought that might be you, Bill Arceneaux. Joe told me you were coming by. You're going to spoil him—you know—by making *his* deliveries for him," she laughed and hugged him.

Arceneaux was beaming and answered, "Mmm, mmm. Pretty lady, just visiting with you is worth the trip. Besides, this way I can get more work out of that husband of yours."

Mark watched as these two friends caught up and laughed together, envying their easy way. He could tell that the old man thought the world of this girl and looked like the weight of the world had been lifted from his shoulders since he stepped out of the truck. Mark almost allowed himself a smile at the thought of it.

"And who might you be?" she asked, with her hand outstretched to Mark.

"Oh, I'm no one. Just here to lift stuff, I guess," Mark answered sheepishly.

"No, everyone's someone. I just don't know yet who *you* are," and there was that disarming laugh again. "I'm Jodie, Jodie Deming. This is my husband's shop. I just take care of the money and pretty much everything except the woodworking. That's all Joe."

Arceneaux put an arm around her shoulders and gave her a sideways hug, "This little gal and her husband are terrific. We've only been in business together a little while, but it was the best decision I ever made. Jodie, this fella here is Mark Hammock. He's been framing for me for a while, about a year now I'd guess. He ain't much of a talker though."

She was still smiling at Mark and said, "Well, not everyone is. It's good to meet you, Mr. Hammock. You're welcome here anytime." He nodded and smiled self-consciously while sizing up the cabinets. Arceneaux shot a glance at Jodie, rolled his eyes and shrugged, then he walked to the cabinets to help Mark.

When they had loaded the cabinets into the truck, they said goodbyes that were just as cheery as the welcome had been—like close family rather than business partners—and, again, Mark couldn't help noticing the visible effect the girl had on his boss. As they drove down the driveway, Arceneaux was still smiling and started talking about Jodie and her husband, how he met them, and how he came to admire Joe's work and bring him into the business. He may as well have been talking to himself, since he couldn't tell if Mark was even listening to him.

Still, he liked talking about that young gal as much as he did visiting with her, so he kept talking, "You know, everything about her seems special. Like this, for instance: I was at a barbecue at their place not too long ago when a couple of guys who knew them better than me at the time told me some of her personal story. It's one of those crazy stories. She was in this bad wreck years ago. Well, no, *she* wasn't, exactly. Her mama was, with some friends in a car, young people. Anyway, they got in a pileup out on 105. Killed a bunch of people in more than one car, I don't know how many. Except her mom lived long enough to have her at the hospital, and then she died too—but not until *that little gal, Jodie,* came into this world!"

Mark sat up straight and looked at Arceneaux for the first time, "What did you say?"

"I know, sounds crazy, but it's true. Makes sense to me too, 'cause that girl is *special*, and I don't think the Lord wanted us to miss out on her," Arceneaux said, still smiling and in his happy place thinking about Jodie Deming. Mark had gone white and looked like he was going to either be sick or burst into tears, or both. He bowed his head, turned towards the window, and didn't say another word. The old man thought to himself, *Huh, I thought for a second there that this guy had a heart after all, letting that story get to him. But maybe not, by the looks of him.*

After they dropped the cabinets off at Joe's jobsite, Arceneaux drove them back to the house where Mark's crew was still working. When they pulled up, Mark said quietly, "Hey, uh, Mr. Arceneaux, I'm not feeling very good now. If it's alright with you, I'm going to knock off for the day. I heard what you said earlier though, about not being able to count on me and all. I'll be here on time Monday; you can count on that. But I just have to go now, if that's okay."

"Yeah, alright. Go get yourself well. We'll see what we see on Monday and every other day. I do want you to think about what I said earlier, and I'm going to want to talk about this again, alright?" Mark nodded, went in to grab his tools, then drove off.

He hadn't paid too close attention to their route when Arceneaux had been driving, so Mark was looking for anything familiar to make sure he didn't miss it. And there it was, that barn behind the old house! He pulled into the gravel drive and parked before he reached the barn.

He was still sitting in the truck, wondering if he could do this, when the barn door opened and Jodie stuck her head out, hand over her eyes to shade them from the afternoon sun, "Hey there! You comin' in?"

Mark stepped out and walked slowly towards her, "Hey, I'm sorry about bothering you. I probably shouldn't even be here." He looked from side to side like he needed an exit.

"What? Nahhh, I told you, 'Come on anytime,' and I meant it. You'd be surprised how many visitors we get here every day." She put her hand down and cocked her head to the side, "You look like you have something on your mind. Is there something I can help you with?"

Mark opened his mouth to speak and nothing came out. He bowed his head again, surprised and embarrassed that tears were once again streaming down his face. *Oh hell, what am I doing here? Idiot.*

He felt the light touch of her hand on his arm and looked up to find her peering up at him, "Hey, hey now. Whatever it is, I'm sure there's a way through it. There always is if you keep looking, even though it's sometimes hard to look." He nodded and blinked away the tears, rubbing his forearm across his eyes. She pointed past the barn and said, "Tell you what, walk on up the drive past our house there. Have a seat in the grass behind it. I'll be there in a few minutes."

He was sitting in a pretty little grassy area beyond a house on stilts, still wondering why he was there, when Jodie walked up carrying a baby. She sat cross-legged next to him, looking at the woods as if for the first time, then looked down at the infant and said with a smile, "Mr. Hammock, this little one is Jo, our pride and joy. She's going to sit with us for a little while. Now, where were we? Oh yes, something's bothering you. You can talk about it if you like. Or you can just sit in this peaceful spot with us. Up to you, after all."

After a few minutes that felt like an eternity, he squinted and looked up at the sky through the trees, and said softly, "Well, I guess I was never really much use to anyone. Pretty much a good-for-nothin' kid, really. Not really a bad sort, but not worth much of a darn either, truthfully.

Then it caught up with me. I did something bad, not on purpose or anything, but I did it. It was no one's fault but mine."

Mark looked at her and saw a concerned look on her face. He spoke again, hoarsely, almost in a whisper, "See, I was the one who killed your mom, and those other people in that car wreck the day you were born. Since the moment it happened, all I wish is that it never happened. That it was *me* it happened to and not all of them—people who were worth something in this world and who deserved to live, to meet their daughters and their granddaughters." He looked from mother to daughter, felt like his breath was being squeezed from his chest, and stopped talking, staring at the ground beneath him.

"Oh, Mr. Hammock, you poor man," Jodie said quietly. "I can't imagine what it has been like, carrying that with you for all these years." A tear rolled down her face as she looked down at Jo and back up at her sad visitor, "I never knew my mother, you know, but I had this great life with my grandparents—*her* parents. As far back as I can remember, they talked about her: things that made her laugh, things she liked, how my eyes and smile were hers . . . They wanted me to know her as well as I could. But I think something changed for them in maybe an unexpected way after they lost her.

"She was really just a kid still when she had me, barely out of high school, three years younger than I am now, and unmarried. My grandparents were having the same struggles coping with that that most parents would have. After the accident, they took me home and saw her in me. They've always told me that I was God's gift to them, a second chance to love a little girl and to love *their* little girl, and they filled me with that idea every day. And I try to fill this little one with that same idea—with that love—every day. I want her to feel the things I did my whole life, to find joy in her life every day, and to see the goodness and the possibility for goodness in other people, every day."

Mark spoke again, still struggling to not fully break down, "I wish I could, but I could never ask you to forgive me. That's not really why I came back, I don't guess."

"I don't think it's up to me to forgive you, Mr. Hammock. But I think I can ask *you* to try. I can see how much you've suffered. It's been a long time, a lifetime for some of us. I know you would change what happened if you could. So, forgive yourself. That doesn't mean you forget that terrible day and the pain that came from it, but that young man also paid a heavy price. You're still paying it. I can see that. Forgive him . . . forgive *yourself*. Allow yourself to live again, to find joy again. For those people who lost their lives that day and can no longer look for themselves, look for the goodness around you and in other people. When you have the chance, help someone else find it too. I don't think the world has to be any more complicated than that."

They sat quietly for a few minutes, listening to and watching the wind in the trees. The infant started fidgeting and then fussing, and Jodie sighed, "Well, Mr. Hammock, I think this one is ready for something to eat, and when she gets like this, it's pretty much her world. I'm going to have to take her on upstairs. You're welcome to sit here as long as you like. It happens to be my favorite spot for thinking, you know."

The big man stood up, wiped his red eyes once more with his sleeve and managed half a smile, "No, I'd better get along too, little lady. It is a great spot though, and I sure appreciate you taking the time to talk with me. It ain't your job to make me feel better, but you sure did. It is a crazy world, I guess, but I am glad we met."

Jodie patted his arm, "I am too, Mr. Hammock, I am too. You come back whenever you like." She smiled at the baby she was carrying, "We're holding down the fort in the shop or out here somewhere most days."

As he walked back to the barn to get in his truck, Mark felt the smallest bit lighter and breathed a little easier than he had in years.

Pulling onto the drive to leave, he saw Jodie upstairs on the deck, holding her baby and waving. He grinned, waved back, and said to himself, "You're right, Mr. Arceneaux, that little gal really is something."

Mark passed the grocery store that evening as he drove to Branson Pond, skipping the night's beer-run on the way. He still needed his time at the pond, looking out over the water and into the trees to think about the glimmer of hope that Jodie had sparked in him. It was on this same fateful May 1996 night that Teddy drove up with his buddies and was met shortly thereafter by his brother Jimmy III. As Teddy's bunch piled out of the Bronco, Mark shook his head and sighed. *Really, tonight? Great. Can't they just leave me alone this one time?*

Just seeing the boisterous boys there clashed with his mental image of Jodie and her sweet outlook on the world. Sure enough, they were soon blaring their music and making the same nuisances of themselves that Mark and his friends had at their age. He then watched and was disappointed to see three teenage girls walk up after a while, only to end up mixing with these boys, a development that surely wouldn't have thrilled those girls' parents. *Girls, just keep walking. Ain't nothing good going to come from this bunch.*

Hours later, after the teenagers seemed to have had their fill and Jimmy walked toward the Bronco to drive the last of the girls home, Mark almost intervened. Something just didn't feel right to him. *Then again,* he thought to himself, *it ain't my business. That young girl doesn't appear to object, and I'm not her daddy.*

He thought nothing more about it until they came back less than an hour later. Hearing Jimmy's bragging as he strutted past the younger boys with a smirk, Mark felt a pang of regret that he hadn't listened to his own conscience earlier. He narrowed his eyes and asked the boy, "Something keep you from taking that girl home?"

Jimmy laughed, "Heh, heh. You could say that. Might as well start 'em young, right?"

Mark grimaced, "She's a little young for you, isn't she? Sixteen she said? What are you, twenty-one, twenty-two?"

"Hah, whatever, man. She's put together more like eighteen, and everything worked like she's eighteen," answered Jimmy, still grinning.

Mark shook his head, "Pretty sure that's not how the law sees it."

"That's the best part! She was so out of it on all that rum that she didn't know much of anything. She kept calling me Teddy: 'No, Teddy, stop. Don't, Teddy.'" Jimmy doubled over with laughter, "So she doesn't know *I* ever laid a hand on her. Oh man, it's beautiful! Besides, chick like that from the trailer park . . . Well, better me and not one of the losers she'll end up with someday."

Jimmy III looked up from his laughter just as Mark's fist connected with his nose, throwing him upright and lifting him off his feet. He landed on his back in the dirt, the ground punching the air out of him on impact. Gasping for air and still seeing stars, Jimmy grabbed his face with both hands, "Dude, what was that for?! What's the matter with you, are you crazy?!"

Mark stormed past him towards the Bronco with both hands clenched into fists. He didn't like what he was hearing the youngest Faison brother and his punk buddies talking about and was now wishing even more that he had stepped in earlier. *Can't do anything about that now, but* this *ain't gonna happen.*

When he reached the truck, Teddy had already climbed in with the passed-out girl and was fumbling to push his pants down, while the other four clowns were squeezing around the open door to watch. Mark grabbed the first two by the scruff of their necks, smacked their heads against the truck, and slung them aside as one of them yelled, "Oww! What the hell, dude?!"

The other two almost knocked each other down jumping away from Mark as he brushed past and reached inside. He was a bear of a man on autopilot as he grabbed Teddy's shirt collar in a bunch and, in a single motion, stepped backwards with a jerk, pulling the boy out of the truck and launching him through the air and out of his way. Mark then climbed in and, saw the state of the girl's clothes and her semi-lucid expression. *Damn it, son! You let this happen! Hammock, you loser!* He tucked an arm under the girl's back and another under her knees, then, as lightly as he could, he scooped her out of the Bronco and walked away.

The boys were yelling all around him, but Mark ignored them. *Alright, girlie, let's put this little skirt back down and find you someplace to wait until you come around.* He walked back to his pickup without so much as a glance at Jimmy, who was still kneeling in the dirt and holding his face, blood covering both hands. As Mark laid the girl down in the bed of his truck, he was lost in thought, *How would I tell that little gal, Jodie, about this? That I could have done something and didn't?! Damn, damn, damn it!*

It was only then that Mark became aware that the boys had followed him and might be looking for a little more trouble. *Oh yeah, that's just fine, boys. You want some more? You came to the right guy!* He shook his head, took a deep breath, and concentrated on being calm as he encouraged the boys to leave without any further unpleasantness, repeating over and over like a mantra in his mind, *Careful now, Mark. What would Jodie think?*

Even with that caution on his mind, Mark still put the fear of God into them when he ran them off, noticing with satisfaction that they looked like the Keystone Kops scurrying to leap into their vehicles and tear out of there. Watching them leave in such a hurry, he wasn't sure that he was glad that they took him up on his warning, but he turned his attention to the young girl sleeping in the back of his truck. Mark realized then that he didn't know the first thing about her—who she was, where she lived, and, rather importantly in this part of Texas, whether her daddy had a shotgun. Considering the condition that she was in—and all by herself with him in the middle of the night—that last one seemed like an important detail.

Something stirred in Mark as he brooded in the dark, only the sleeping girl's whispered breathing to remind him that he wasn't alone. The last twenty-two years of despair flooded through his mind mixed with glimpses of Jodie and the reassuring sound of her voice. He couldn't make sense of everything that was swirling around him as, mixed with his yearslong anguish, he felt a familiar panic welling up in his chest. But like an unlooked-for lifeline, Mark latched onto a desperate urge to live up to or at least try to do something to earn what Jodie had said to him. *Why? Why me? Why would she care?*

Not long after the boys had driven away, a jet-black Escalade roared up the gravel road and skidded to a stop where Mark still sat watching the young girl sleep. Jimmy Jr. was yelling as he leapt out, "Hammock! Who do you think you are, putting your hands on my boys?!"

Mark looked up at him without moving, "Maybe you should ask them."

"That her? That the little *tramp* this is all about?!" Jimmy Jr. asked as he stormed up to confront Mark. What he saw confirmed what he expected to find: an unconscious, pretty young girl, with an alarming amount of bare legs sticking out from under a jacket Mark had thrown over her.

"That's the *girl*, anyway. I wouldn't say this is about her though, not really," Mark said quietly with a slow shake of his head.

"I don't care much what you'd say. The boys told me you got this girl drunk and were messing around with her. When they stopped you, you freaked out. Hammock, I don't care what you do with *other* people's kids—this girl, those other boys, whoever—but no one touches *my sons*. Oh, hell no! You are going to rue the day you put your hands on them! You better believe that, you fat bastard!" Jimmy Jr. stood in front of him, red in the face and one provocation away from throwing a punch at his old running buddy.

Unfazed, Mark shrugged and nodded his head, "Yeah, well, like I told your boys, you're going to do what you're going to do. Before you do, though, you'd better think *real* hard about it and about those precious sons you keep going on about. What do think the chances are that they told you the truth about what happened here tonight? For starters, look around: I ain't been drinking. Don't even have a drop with me, and I surely didn't give any to this girl or anyone else. Just maybe it was your boys who gave her the alcohol. Maybe it was your oldest that did some things he shouldn't have with her. You know, your son who's *twenty-one* . . . with this *underage* girl who was so drunk on his booze that she didn't know what was happening to her. And then maybe the younger little prince thought it'd be okay to try and take his own turn and then pass her around to his punk buddies."

Jimmy Jr. glared at the girl, then back at Mark as he took his cell phone out of his pocket, "That's what you say. They've got witnesses that will say otherwise, and they're damn sure going to when we press charges!"

Mark's face tightened into a thin smile, "I tell you what, Junior. When this little girl comes around, you and I will take her together to the Orange ER for a little test, the kind where they can figure out who, uh, 'did the deed.' And you can press charges then, if you like. I'll even willingly confess the story, exactly the way it happened—to the police, to her parents, to anyone you want. We'll see what all charges are filed *then*."

He could see in Jimmy Jr.'s unsure expression that the gears were now turning. Mark sniffed and looked at the ground, "Jimmy, a long time ago your daddy pulled some strings and got me off when I had done something bad-wrong. We had a bunch of witnesses back then too. Those people in that wreck hadn't done anything to deserve what happened to them—what *I did* to them. I had never done anything that justified getting away with something like that, and all I cared about back then was not getting into the trouble that I deserved. And I got off. Thanks to your dad and you, I got off scot-free, and it's eaten me up every day since.

"But something's changed in me. I can't really explain it—I won't to you anyway. I can't stand aside again and let bad happen, not to this young girl who didn't do anything to deserve it, not when I can do something about it. I know you can try to do something like your daddy did a long time ago after that wreck. Maybe this time it won't go so well for me, but it does for your boys . . . *maybe*. But maybe not.

"So what's it gonna be, Junior? Leave your punk sons with a rough lesson that they can't just do whatever they want to people, or do we have a visit with the ER and the police? You decide. Of course, no telling what this girl's folks will want to do, but that's not my business," Mark smiled innocently at Jimmy Jr. and shrugged.

Jimmy glared at his old friend and stuffed his phone back in his pocket, "You stay away from my boys, you got that? You'd better remember they're still Faisons."

"Oh yeah, you might ruin my life or something, right? Oh, wait, too late, I already did." Mark waved dismissively, "Go home, Junior." Jimmy Jr. deflated a little, turned slowly and walked back to his car. He drove out without another word or a look at Mark.

Two hours later, the girl sat up, still groggy from the booze and confused about what she saw. Mark, hearing her stir, looked over his shoulder at her and nodded. She looked down at the jacket that was over her, her eyes widening as her gaze moved to her legs and snippets of memory rushed through her mind, "Oh no. No, no, no!" She looked up at Mark, covered her eyes, and through her tears asked, "What did we . . . ? Did *we* . . . ?"

Mark looked away and spoke softly, "No, girl, *we* didn't. You're safe with me."

She put her hands down and stared at her legs, "I . . . I think I remember Teddy. It's like a fog, but I know—I know that we . . ." She clenched her arms around herself and closed her eyes.

"Yeah, you got mixed up with those Faison boys. It got a little outta hand before I put a stop to it."

"Wait. Did I . . . with *both* of them?"

"No, just the older one, and I'm sorry about that. I shoulda seen it coming and done something sooner. I wish I had. I really do."

She was crying uncontrollably now, "I've ruined everything, my whole life!"

Mark turned and patted her foot timidly, "Look here, I'm not trying to be your daddy or anything like that, but you have to know this could have gone even worse. Be glad it didn't. Now, you're going to feel bad about whatever you're going to feel bad about, I know. But you don't have to let it beat you or let *them* beat you. Turn it around, learn from it. I know that sounds hard, but remember tonight, and next time you'll know. You'll make a better choice. But you know, when you hang out with hoodlums and jerks—when you do the stupid things they do—it can go all kinds of ways, most of 'em not so good. Be better than that, be better than *them*. It's always up to you."

She nodded her head, and her crying slowed down. Mark stood up and said, "Now maybe we should get you home, young lady."

Driving away from Branson Pond, Mark was surprised to learn that Tina lived with her mother in the same trailer park he did, only a little farther back in #22. She reluctantly admitted that she and her friends knew him as the angry redneck hermit in #15 and someone to avoid. He chuckled at that and thought, *Yeah, I guess that's about right.*

He parked at his place then walked Tina down to her trailer. She gave him a shy look and turned away, "Well, thanks for being there and watching over me."

He patted her on the shoulder and smiled, "Anytime. Remember, learn, and be better—every day. It's all any of us can do."

When she opened the door, Mark heard a woman's loud voice, "Where have you been?! Do you know what time it is?! I've been worried to death!" He saw a woman grab Tina into a bear hug as the door closed, and he walked away with a sigh and smile.

When Mark went to bed that night, it was the first night he hadn't been drunk or had a single drink since he could remember. He woke up the next morning with an idea from nowhere and spent the weekend building a deck along the front of his trailer and wrapped around the end. Most evenings from that Sunday on, he could be found sipping coffee in a rocking chair at the end of his deck where he could watch the sunset through the trees and look down the lane at Tina and her mom's place.

Mark Hammock never took another drink and was never seen at Branson Pond again. He also showed up for work early on Monday.

• • •

Life's lessons are often near misses, those experiences that get our attention and teach us something before it's too late, before the cost would have been unpayable if we hadn't been so lucky as to learn the lesson first. Sometimes the lesson isn't a near miss and comes at a terrible cost. Tina Davis learned the hard lesson that sometimes it only takes once. In January 1997, as a sixteen-year-old eleventh grader, she gave birth to her daughter, Nancilee Davis.

The summer before had gone uneventfully after Tina's awful experience in May. By August, her fear was growing that her prayers would not be answered, and a month later it was clear for all to see as her young body began changing with the growing life inside. When they were sure, Tina and her mom, Jenny, cried together. Tina's were the tears of a terrified young woman, still really a girl, faced with responsibilities and public judgments she was nowhere near prepared to handle. Jenny's were for her daughter, the hardships she knew all too well that were ahead of her now, and her own failure to help her daughter break a cycle that she herself had passed on to the next-generation teenage mother.

Then mother and daughter talked about the challenges and what they needed to do. Jenny set the tone, "This is your child, so it's your decision, but you're mine too, you know. So, in case you're wondering, I think you should keep it—*we* should keep it. It will be tough, but we'll figure it out." Tina hugged her and nodded. Her mom continued, "The next hard thing is, you need to stay in school. Your life and this baby's life are going to be hard enough as it is. That diploma will make a difference. The surest way to get there isn't dropping out and maybe getting a GED someday, it's staying right where you are, in school and ignoring what some people are going to think or say. Some of that will be hard, but it's less than two years."

Tina took a deep breath and nodded again, "I know. It's okay. I don't care what they say anyway."

Fortunately, Walmart had come to Orange ten years earlier, and Jenny had worked her way through a series of cashier and sales jobs until she had been promoted last year into the first-level management ranks. It didn't take much convincing of the others to allow her to take a night shift permanently so she could stay home during the day with Nancilee while Tina was in school. Tina took over baby duty and studied when she could in the evenings, and she started working part-time on weekends at the same Walmart to help make ends meet.

From outward appearances, Mark's life hadn't changed much in those same months. He was still on Bill Arceneaux's framing crew, and, when he wasn't working, he kept to himself at his mobile home in the trailer park. Although he was often still lost in serious thought, his focus was rarely his old, dark brooding about his unworthiness in the world, but instead it was about how he wanted to be different and truly take Jodie's advice to heart. From his seat on his deck, he often saw Jenny and Tina coming and going in the evenings and during weekends. Like everyone else, Mark could see Tina's physical changes as her pregnancy progressed. Of all people, he didn't have to wonder what those changes meant, but when he saw her walking past his place, he'd simply say, "Hello, young lady. How are you today?"

She'd look up nervously with a faint smile, "I'm fine, thanks," unable to look him in the eye. Although she didn't care what anyone thought at school, she couldn't help being embarrassed in front of someone who had borne witness to her shame and was the only reason it hadn't ended much worse. Not being someone to come up with any words to break through that kind of awkwardness, Mark only nodded and smiled in reply as she walked by.

In late January 1997, after having not seen Tina out for a few weeks, Mark saw the young new mother pushing a stroller. He stood up and leaned over the deck rail to get a glimpse of the baby's face almost buried by blankets, "Well now, would you look at that? So, is everybody healthy?"

Tina blushed, "Yes, we're all fine. I go back to school next week, but I don't know how I'll do it on three or four hours of sleep a night. If I'm not holding her or pushing her in a stroller, she fusses. So here we are . . ." She reached down and lifted the infant out of the stroller, "Want to see her?"

"Ah, sure. I guess," and he stepped down from his deck to peek at the baby's face through the blanket she was wrapped in.

Tina smiled, "This is Nancilee Genevieve. The Genevieve is after my mom. Here, hold her if you want," as she deposited the tiny girl into the crook of his arm.

"Whoa, I don't want to break her or anything. But look at her, pretty like her mama and grandmama."

Tina laughed, glad they were finally having a real conversation. She pointed at his deck and said, "I've been meaning to tell you, we sure like what you did here. What a great idea."

"You think so? Tell you what, if your mom likes it and you ladies would like one, I'll build one onto your place." He looked at the infant he was holding, "Call it a birthday present from me for this little one."

"No, we couldn't let you do that. That's too much," Tina said as she took her daughter back.

"Consider it a favor to me. I'd be able to do something for y'all, and it's good advertising for me. I was thinking I could convince some other folks to hire me to build one for them, and having another one and some satisfied customers might help."

"I'll talk to my mom about it. It's very nice of you to offer, though. Guess I'd better get this one out of this cold, so bye for now," Tina quickly stepped up and gave Mark a brief hug, then walked away pushing the stroller. For both of them, that hurried gesture was about more than his deck idea, but neither of them could talk about the previous summer and its aftermath. Mark stood like he was made of stone as he watched Tina walking away, and he didn't move from where he stood until she reached her front door. He was blinking back tears when he settled back into his chair on the deck.

Jenny wasn't sure at first how to take Mark's offer. She knew about and appreciated what he had done for her daughter last summer, but she wasn't sure they knew him well enough to accept such a gift, especially from the trailer park's mean-looking curmudgeon. In the end, Tina convinced her it would be alright. Mark spent several evenings in the next week tweaking his working design, bought the materials one evening after work, and set the posts for the deck the next evening. With his experience in construction, he then built them a wrap-around deck in a single weekend. He took it a step further than his own, topping it with a roof attached to the mobile home and adding a ramp to help with the stroller.

Jenny and Tina were thrilled, and Jenny caught Mark as he finished up, "Mr. Hammock, this is way more than a simple deck. It's beautiful. Surely you'll let us pay you for it."

He shook his head and waved his hands, "No, no. This was the deal, and it's what I had in mind all along. That little one needs a place outside, out of the Texas heat and out of the rain, and here it is. I'm just glad you like it," he added with a smile.

"Well, the least we can do is let us give you dinner. Please stay. It isn't fancy, but it'll be good." Seeing his reluctance, she took him by the arm, "I mean it. Please. We'd both like you to." And that was that. From then on, at least one Sunday each month and most holidays found Mark eating dinner with Jenny, Tina, and Nancilee, sometimes with him grilling the meat. Rather than just looking down the street at their place, he now felt like he was watching over a small family that was becoming like family to him, and they had taken a liking to him, gruff shyness and all.

Six months later and a year after his visit with Jodie Deming and that night at Branson Pond, Mark found himself once again riding along with his boss, Bill Arceneaux, for a visit with Jodie at the Demings' shop. This time they were both welcomed like old friends by Jodie and her two-year-old "assistant" and daughter, Jo. Mother and daughter both wore the same happy and welcoming expression, and when Jodie hugged both men, Jo insisted on giving her own with a giggle.

Jodie looked at Mark thoughtfully and said, "It's been too long, but you've changed some—for the better. I can see it, and it's good to see. How have you been?"

Mark turned red and chuckled, "Well, I know it's been a year now. I thought about coming to see you many times, but I wasn't sure I had enough to say." The big man turned more serious, "I know I do now though. You saved me, you know. That short talk we had a year ago—I can't tell you how much it affected me. It changed how I look at a lot of things and kinda woke me up again after a lot of years in a bad dream."

Jo had settled into playing with pine cones in the grass, so Jodie motioned to Mark and Arceneaux to have a seat at the picnic table and said, "It's so good to hear you talk that way. I've worried about you some, but Bill here has told me some news about you from time to time."

Mark nodded at his boss, "Yeah, he's another one who did more for me than he probably knows and more than I deserved." Arceneaux smiled and shook his head briefly, but Mark went on, "The crazy thing is, I'm still just me working the same job I was working a year ago, but I bet Mr. Arceneaux would tell you he can count on me now. He couldn't a year ago—even told me so back then. And I stopped the drinking. And, get this, I kinda have a hobby now building decks for my neighbors. In fact, I have a waiting list and just sort of hired two high school guys to help me. It doesn't even feel like work. It's more like therapy or something. Heck, I'm just glad I can help out, and these people like my work.

"The *really* crazy part is I kinda adopted—or have been adopted by, not sure which—the three sweetest gals you can ever meet . . . uh, present company excepted, of course." He then regaled them with stories about Tina, Nancilee, and Jenny, and was moving so fast from one detail to another that he didn't notice Arceneaux and Jodie smiling at each other.

When he finally ran out of stories about the Davis women, Arceneaux cleared his throat and patted Mark on the back, "Son, you have had yourself a year alright. I've seen it too, just like Jodie said. And you're right, I *can* count on you. If you're up for it, I'm gonna count on you some more and put you in charge of my framing crews. I figured I'd tell you here, since I've thought for some time that your talk with her helped more than your talk with me."

As Arceneaux shook his hand, Mark smiled and said, "I'm up for it, and thanks, Mr. Arceneaux. I won't let you down. Boy, that's good news! I gotta come here more often!"

A teary Jodie came around the table to hug both men, and said, "I told you, you're always welcome, Mr. Hammock."

Chapter 7

EPIPHANIES

She did not understand how desperately some wanted her to fear them or why.

After Margo had her fun scuttling Teddy Faison's state literacy tests in 1996, she and Ed kept up their habit of watching the evening news and eating dinner together, although her improved mood and the occasional conversations quickly faded away. She sometimes thought about the irony that it was her intentionally spiteful and hurtful antics that led to these brief times together and her moments of vague happiness. It was a familiar notion, and she remembered feeling some of that same admittedly maniacal joy after her Davie Thomas fun almost a decade earlier, only to eventually find herself back in her same dreary, Grayton existence.

One evening in February 1998, she was again brooding about her apparently inescapable and joyless life when a droning voice on the television broke her train of thought:

> And from Mexico tonight, gloomy news and warnings about humanity's impact on nature. Scientists studying monarch butterflies estimate that their population plummeted by 80 percent this winter. This is based on a survey conducted in the Central Mexico region where almost all North American monarchs spend the cold season, as they wait for the next migration northward. Just this year, the total population is estimated to have plummeted from just under a billion butterflies to under 300 million.
>
> Scientists from across the country have speculated on a wide range of contributing factors. There appears to be strong agreement that mankind's influence is a primary cause, and it could only be worse if we were attacking the butterflies intentionally. Biology researcher, Dr. Sam Waterston, tells us that although the total population of monarch butterflies seems enormous to most people, it's only a few subtle changes that could cause permanent devastation and even extinction of these majestic creatures. Let's go to Cerro Pelon, Mexico, for more from Dr. Waterston . . .

Margo was no longer listening to the reporter, instead she was deep in thought. *We can make things worse on a large scale with subtle and intentional acts? Permanent devastation? Oh, I like the sound of that! I just need to be a touch more strategic in my intentions!*

Ed saw a familiar look emerge on his wife's face, like a cloud's shadow suddenly rolling across the landscape. He didn't think of the expression as happiness, necessarily, but one that suggested satisfaction and resolve. Rarely did she talk about what was on her mind in those moments, but over the years he'd pieced together enough to speculate that someone had just gotten crosswise with Margo and was destined to come out the worse for it. *Whatever it takes, I guess*, he thought with a sigh as he left her there and headed back to the garage and his own distractions and tinkering.

Margo wasted no time. The next morning, she visited the guidance counselor in her office to get the ball rolling, "Hey Ruthie, I've been thinking. I have the system down for coordinating all the state tests, and I could easily do the same on the other big tests—you know, the SAT and ACT. That's only a few more tests each year, so it wouldn't really take that much more of my time, just a couple of days now and then. I wouldn't mind doing a little more, since it's pretty much the same stuff. What do you think?"

An astonished Ruthie grinned and answered, "Well, good morning to you too, Margo! Uh, wow. I don't even need to think about that one. Sure! That's great for me if you have the time and Mr. Clanton is okay with it. But if you keep this up, I won't have anything left to do."

Margo laughed, "Oh, it's not that much. Besides, this will help me with an idea I have to have a much bigger—ahh—*impact*."

"Okay then. Boy, if only the rest of the faculty knew how much you're really up to for the school," Ruthie gushed with a shake of her head.

Margo shrugged as she turned to walk back to the office, already deep in thought and oblivious to anyone else. *Yeah, if only they knew, they might not like what I'm* really *up to! Enough of this onesie-twosie stuff. Messing with Davey Thomas to get back at his dad, or with the Faison boys, that's fine. It was better than locking a few kids outside after the bell*

every now and then, but it still leaves the rest of the preening little rich kids and takers to go on with their lives literally fat, dumb, and happy, without paying the price that's taken from some of us.

Oh, and it's not just the takers who are guilty. It's everyone else who just sit by and let wrong things happen—who let other people take and take—people who could have helped but chose not to, because nothing matters to them but them! And why do they do nothing? Because it doesn't hurt them. *So why should they care enough to do something? Why should they care at all?!*

Well, I'll give 'em something to care about. I'll just do some taking myself, and give 'em a taste of how it feels. How it feels to have people take things away from you—take your life away from you—and then have no one even try to help.

Margo closed her eyes and shook her head. *Whoa, Margo, deep breaths, and step away from the bazooka . . .*

After taking her own advice and taking a deep breath, she reminded herself, *It's all good. I'm on it now! Between the state tests and these college tests, things are about to change. I just need some time to see what's what, and I'll be able to knock more of them down a few pegs—and maybe one or two to the ground to boot! I just gotta get through the door and get control. Once I have all of their precious little tests literally at my fingertips, I'll figure the rest out.*

"Margo? Hey Margo," she was jolted back to the present by the principal's voice. "Earth to Margo. There you are. I just said, 'Good morning,' and you walked right on by in a trance like you couldn't hear me. Must be something good, 'cause you sure look happy."

Margo chuckled, "Oh, right. Sorry. Mornin'. I'm a little lost in thought thinking through the next steps in my evil plan."

"Oh, is that all? Well then, good luck with that, and I hope that *I'm* not on your list. I know better than to get on your bad side," he laughed as he went into his office.

Her smile widened and she thought, *No, you're not on the list, Edgar. No promises, though.*

That evening, Margo felt a calm she had not known since her last hours with her parents, when her future, hers and Ed's, theirs and her parents', and theirs as a family had been so clear and joyous. She found her way back to this peaceful state through a series of emotions that started yesterday when she realized, *Oh yes, I can do this!* That led to a sense of purpose she had not felt in almost twenty-five years—most of her adult life—*I get it, this is how I can make a difference. This matters—I matter!* From that purpose came resolve, *I will do this, whatever it takes.*

And thus, she found peace. She was no longer consumed by her anger and the empty existence she felt she had been left with by an uncaring, if not malicious, world. Instead, she focused on all of the possibilities within her reach to gradually accomplish something much further-reaching than her own loss, and that focus dulled her pain and masked her anguish. The calm that she now embraced was seen by those around her. At work, while they couldn't explain what exactly was different about her, people took notice of a rounded edge to her cynicism and overall demeanor. Ed noticed as well, unsure of the larger implications to her improved mood but glad to have the more frequent company when they were home.

For Margo, this calm meant patience. She knew where she was going and simply needed to take her time. Avoiding missteps and overreach was more important than short-term victories, and she was definitely looking towards the long game and widespread devastation.

• • •

Joe Deming came home one Saturday that same spring in 1996 after installing some cabinets in a new home across town. It was early enough that the sun was still up, and he marveled at the unusually pleasant East Texas weather as he walked up the stairs and into the house. He yelled for his gals, "Hey, anyone home? You two should be outside enjoying this before the darn mosquitoes come back!"

Hearing no response, Joe walked out the back door and onto the deck, and they were nowhere in sight. He listened for a few seconds and there they were, the unmistakable sounds of his daughter's voice squealing with delight. The young father smiled and trotted down the back steps and towards the sound of Jo's voice coming from the woods. As he got closer, Jodie looked wide-eyed at her three-year-old daughter, "What's that noise? Is that a bear? What is that?"

Jo's eyes grew large, but not in fear. She was excited by the mystery and looked like she'd be just as happy if a big ol' bear really did crash right out of the woods. As she watched, she giggled and screamed, "Daddy!" The little girl tripped through the leaves and hugged her father like she hadn't seen him in weeks.

Joe picked her up and kissed her, "Now that's what I call a welcome home!" He was still beaming as he hugged his wife with their little girl sandwiched between them. He put the little girl down, and the three of them walked through the woods toward the house with Jo in the middle, leaning forward and pulling both of her parents by the hand. He chuckled and said to Jodie, "You know, I think I need to change some things in my life."

She raised her eyebrows, "Huh. And just what do you have in mind, cowboy?"

"Maybe my priorities are screwed up, and I need to stop working weekends, at least outside the shop. I mean, look at her. She's going to grow up all of a sudden, and I'm going to miss too much of it."

"Well, I don't think it's as bad as all that. I know you have to do what you have to do to make the business work. But you're home every night, and we spend time with you in the shop some during the day," Jodie gave him her best sympathetic look.

Joe shrugged, "Still, I want to bring someone on to take some of the load, especially the weekend installation work. Maybe I can shift my work around to be here earlier in the evenings during the week and all day on weekends. Thanks to Bill Arceneaux's backlog, we've got the business—we can afford a part-time guy. I just need to find someone I can trust who does good enough work."

"Try asking Bill. He may have someone who fits the bill perfectly."

Joe narrowed his eyes when he answered, "Hey, you have someone in mind already, don't you? I should have thought of that. It's one of your groupies, isn't it? Come on, who is it?"

Jodie leaned over Jo to kiss her husband on the cheek, "I won't jinx it. Just talk to him and see who he recommends."

A week later, at Bill Arceneaux's urging, and as Jodie hoped and predicted, Mark Hammock started working with Joe and his dad, Hal, on Saturdays and sometimes part of Sunday learning the ropes on their cabinet installation. By the end of the summer, it was all Hal and Mark on weekends, with Joe staying close to home and his gals.

Everyone involved came out of that summer feeling good about this small turn of events. It just felt right. Arceneaux loved this feeling that he had helped pull someone back from the brink who was showing every sign that he had been right to listen to his heart, and if that helped the Demings, then so much the better. Mark had taken another step in helping people who meant something to him and finding that he meant something to anyone else, leading him imperceptibly towards following Jodie's advice and forgiving himself. Joe was glad to have a helping hand who was a natural at their work and appeared to want nothing more than to be helpful. And Jodie, well, it simply warmed her heart to see Mark slowly allowing himself to come back to life.

Chapter 8

BATTLE PLANS

Those who saw her knew only the moment,
not the journey.

Margo took a logical and businesslike approach to her new project. She first needed to increase her access to all students' educational metrics—the metrics she had every intention to corrupt. If she was going to take advantage of that access, she also needed to cultivate trust from stakeholders at the school and in the district office in order to gain freedom from scrutiny. Then she could slowly increase the damage to the students' performance until she had bled as much opportunity as she could from Grayton's aspiring youth. If she did it right, the change should be imperceptible at first. When she thought about her plan, which was often, Margo always chuckled to herself, *What's not to like? It's just about life lessons, right? And they'll never know it's happening!*

She already had that kind of control of the school's state literacy tests and had used it several times in dealing with the Faison brothers. By adding the college entrance exams to her arsenal, she could chip away at student performance from two sides: access to advanced classes and the ability to graduate from high school; and access to college.

After the principal had thought about Margo's idea for a day, he stopped to talk with her about it, "Margo, I'm a little worried about you getting spread too thin since you're already coordinating much of our annual testing. So, before we go 'all in,' I've asked Ms. Gray to set you up as an SAT and ACT proctor first. She'll still do the rest of the test coordination, you know, the paperwork, packaging, and that kind of thing. That way we can kinda see how it goes for you for the rest of the school year. If you're able to handle proctoring those tests, and managing the state tests, *plus* the rest of your regular workload, *then* we'll get you into the test coordinator training for those tests too. We'll still get you there, but a step at a time. Sound alright?"

Irritated but not surprised, Margo nodded, and smiled sweetly, "Sure, Mr. Clanton. One step at a time. There's no rush. It will all come in its time."

"Good, good. I wasn't sure you'd see it that way, because I know this is something you really want to do. I'm sure it will all be fine, and you'll be running it all before we know it." He turned and laughed over his shoulder as he walked away, "All according to your evil plan, of course." Still smiling, Margo nodded. *You got that right, Buddy-Reaux!* Although this would delay her chance to affect the SAT and ACT results, it gave her time to build up more trust with Ruthie Gray and Edgar Clanton, before she really dropped the hammer. All the better for her handiwork to go unnoticed when that chance came along.

The rest of that school year and the next went just as Mr. Clanton had predicted. Margo coordinated several more rounds of state tests and proctored the SAT and ACT at Grayton High School twice. All the while, there were no hiccups in managing the school's office. So, at the end of the 1998 - 1999 school year and at his recommendation, the school district sent her to Lamar University in Beaumont for a day, where she received the formal training that was required to manage the SAT and ACT exam process at the high school. In the fall of 1999, Margo was finally in position to take the reins as the coordinator for all standardized tests at Grayton High School.

A week after school started that fall things had settled into the usual rhythm. Mr. Clanton called Margo into his office after the morning announcements, where she found Ruthie Gray sitting in front of his desk. With a happy expression, Mr. Clanton motioned for Margo to sit, "Well Margo, first of all, I wanted to tell you how impressed we are with the effort you've made in the last couple of years, stepping up to help with all of the testing. This stuff is very important for the students and the school—I should say it's *critical* for the school, since the state uses the results to grade us and the district on how well we're doing. With you jumping in like this, you not only made Ruthie's job easier, you gave her time to work on other things that are also important, and we don't need to worry about how all of the testing is being handled."

He paused and the counselor nodded happily in agreement. "Anyhoo, what we really wanted to do is not just say, 'Thanks, keep up the good work.' We want to make it easier for you to 'get 'er done'—you know, to do what you need to do. So, we're going to remodel the file room a little and add better office space in there for you. That way, when you have to take care of the various paper shuffling and packaging all the confidential exam materials, you'll have a place to do it that's private and all yours. What do you think?"

Margo was almost speechless. She chuckled and said, "I think it's great, and thanks. That will definitely make it easier for me to 'get 'er done' alright."

"Hey, it's the least we can do. Now you two put your heads together on workspace and storage, and we'll take care of it. I should say, 'Ed will take care of it,' since he's probably going to do most of the work. Then you can wreak havoc without interruption."

"Ha, you can count on it, Mr. Clanton," said Margo as she and Ruthie stood up. They headed down the hall to scout the file room and sketch out a plan to make it work for Margo's test coordination.

An hour later, Ed walked into the school's office after being summoned by one of the office aides. Margo showed him how they wanted the file cabinets rearranged and where she wanted a large worktable. She pointed at a large metal door in the middle of the back wall, "Tell me about this thing."

Ed shrugged, "It's the old trash chute. Used to lead down to a dumpster outside that wall, but it was bricked up way before my time here. You can see it on the outside wall if you look closely at the bricks." He walked across the room and pulled down the chute door which creaked loudly as it swung open. He reached in and knocked on the chute with a low, hollow thud, "Huh, I figured. The old metal chute is still there, probably goes all the way down. Feels like it's built like a durn battleship. It'll still be standing when they demolish this old building."

Her face clouded like she was lost in thought, and she said distractedly, "Okay, that could come in handy." She brightened, refocused on Ed and asked, "Can you cover it with a large cabinet on the wall? I have to lock my test materials in something, but I can't mix them with the other files since a bunch of other people have access to the regular file cabinets."

"Sure, it'll have to stick out from the wall a few extra inches, for the back of the cabinet to cover up that chute though."

Margo shook her head, "No, leave the back of the cabinet open, so I can get to it. Leave enough room in the cabinet opening to open the chute door if we ever need to, but I want the cabinet doors to lock over it. Sort of secure and camouflaged, in case we ever need to use it for something. You never know."

"Yeah, right. Okay, whatever you want. I'll take some measurements and can have something up in a week or so."

"I'm sure it will be great," and she hugged him quickly as she walked past him on her way back to the office.

Dumbfounded, he turned to watch her go and thought, *Now what the heck has gotten into her?*

Two weeks later, Margo sat at the worktable in her somewhat private test coordinator room. It was only somewhat private since, when she wasn't behind a locked door to process test materials, this was still the file and records room and housed one of the office's copy machines. So other members of the staff and faculty wandered through from time to time. But when it was test time, the room became her secure sanctuary.

Ed had outdone himself by attaching two large cabinets to the wall, one of which covered the old trash chute door, which could still be opened when the cabinet door was fully open, just as Margo had asked. Although there were many keys to the room, only Margo and Ruthie Gray had keys to the cabinet that housed the test materials. Relying on Margo for all of the test coordination and trusting her implicitly to take care of it without supervision, Ruthie never had a reason to use her own cabinet key.

The room was ready just in time, since the stacks of test materials and instructions were trickling in for the first round of tests this year, and that was going to take up a lot of time for the next month. The process was essentially the same for every round of tests, whether from the state or one of the college boards. Instructions and test materials would arrive the week before the test, and Margo would prepare the faculty and staff to administer the test and collect the materials. When the exams were complete, the proctors would bring the completed materials to Margo's coordinator room where she locked them in the cabinet until after school. All that remained of her *official* duties that evening would be some audit and accounting paperwork to certify proper handling and security of the test materials throughout the process, and then packaging for return to either the district or the college board the next morning for scoring. Before the package was sealed and shipped, Margo would lay it all out on the worktable, and Ruthie Gray would make a separate audit and co-sign that everything was in order.

Of course, there was one more *unofficial* step that Margo would add the evening before Ruthie inspected everything. She'd select a handful of the students' test packages for one of Mr. Thomas's "little life lessons," and then she'd set to work randomly changing some of the answers. Thanks to Mr. Clanton, she could now do that work securely behind a locked door in a windowless room and could take her time without fear of discovery.

First up was the SAT on October 9. A little over half of the seniors turned out for the test and a quarter of the juniors, for a total of 180 Grayton High School students. Once the tests were underway, Margo went back to her office and scanned their class records to pick out a few top performers. Paging through the printouts, she thought, *Alright, go slow. Too much too soon will attract attention I don't need, so let's pick just a few and make sure I can make this work. How about three? Yes,*

I'll go with the top two seniors and the top junior, whoever they are based on their class standing. Hmmm, here we are: Akers, Thorne, and, for my junior, A. J. Miller. Looks like you're the lucky winners. Now we wait.

Hours later when the tests were finished, the proctors brought the test packages to the office. Locked in her coordinator's room, she pulled the three students' tests from the stacks, then carefully laid the first answer sheet on the table. *Don't forget, easy does it. There will be time to build up to more damage.* That thought made her smile as she started randomly erasing answers and penciling in different ones. In "keeping it small," she decided to change only 10 percent of the answers in each section of the test for the three students she had selected, which meant only 14 changed answers out of 141 in each student's package. In her mind, since this was equivalent to only a single letter grade in regular schoolwork, and although it may still disappoint these three students, the relatively limited impact to their individual scores and to the overall results for the larger group should escape additional scrutiny. *I mean, everyone has a bad day now and then, right? This is only three kids. Not so unusual, is it?*

Margo made all of the changes and reassembled the three "updated" test packages in only ten minutes. She then filled out the paperwork certifying all test materials had been assembled and controlled according to the security procedures. *Ten minutes? Now that's a good bang for the "life lesson" buck!*

The following Monday morning, Ruthie made a perfunctory inspection. As she cosigned the paperwork she laughed and said, "Margo, you sure have all of this under control. My signature doesn't mean a thing after everything you've done."

"Well, it's good to have someone else look it over to keep me honest and to share the blame," and Margo sealed the tests for shipping. They went out later that day to the College Board for scoring.

Margo was still waiting for confirmation that she had gotten away with her scheme on the SAT when the first round of the ninth-grade tests, the PSAT, came along the following Wednesday. Although the PSAT scores were not used directly for college admission, they did result in a number of scholarship opportunities and were therefore still important to the college-bound students. She followed the same strategy for the PSAT, choosing only three of the almost 200 freshmen and randomly changing only 10 percent of their answers in each section. Ruthie cosigned the next morning, and these tests were also sent off for scoring.

On Saturday less than two weeks later, Margo was at it again, this time with the ACT, and she stuck with her strategy—three students and only 10 percent of the answers changed. The very next week brought four days in a row of Texas state literacy tests for the ninth graders. True to form, Margo drew the tests for the same three freshmen that she had "helped" on the PSAT and changed 10 percent of the answers on their tests each day.

In that single month, October 1999, Margo had tried out her plan on top-performing students taking the SAT, PSAT, ACT, and the state literacy tests. Looking back on the month, she thought, *So far, so good. Not found out yet.*

The real proof came a month later when the scores trickled in from the various agencies, and not only were no alarms raised, but she didn't hear a word about the very small number of students whose test scores could have looked suspiciously lower than some may have expected. No one gave it a second thought, since she had changed the answers for so few students; the scores went down instead of up; and all had scores that were still adequate for college admission, just not competitive for the top-tier schools—a not-unprecedented outcome, even for top-ranked students. Similarly, the freshmen whose PSAT and state test scores she had dropped were still in a respectable range, albeit not especially impressive.

The following spring, Margo used the same strategy across the board for the SAT, ACT, and junior literacy tests, the latter of which required passing in order to graduate the following year. In each case, she was able to make all of the changes to the students' tests in ten minutes or less. Except for the few students who were surprised by lower scores than they'd hoped for, her efforts were again almost fully unnoticed. The one exception in not taking notice was Ed, who always knew when his wife had been up to something when her disposition turned friendly and they spent more time together at home. But he had become accustomed to these periodic stretches and simply took them without question as they came along, knowing things would go back to their estranged norm before long.

Despite her apparent success in the first year, Margo was still afraid to overreach, so she only went a little further. Thus, in the 2000 - 2001 school year, she doubled the number of the "lucky" recipients of her attentions to six during each test, but she again limited the changes to only 10 percent of all answers. She was still able to make all of the changes in no more than twenty minutes. And once again, the limited number of affected students and the relatively small change to their outcomes drew no undesirable attention to Margo or the school.

Margo no longer thought of the affected students as people, only cogs in the wheel of her plan. She gave not a thought to how her mild blurring of their test results might ripple into their lives, intent instead on how far she dared reach in each next step. Had she looked a little more closely, she would have seen very real consequences already, even with the light touch with her very first three. One of her first seniors, Bobby Akers, who was heralded as his family's genius and first to have a real shot at college, fell out of eligibility for admission into Texas A&M

and the scholarships he needed to attend any school after two lackluster SAT results in a row. Believing he had let his family down, he enlisted in the Navy with a hope to try his hand in college in a few years with the help of veteran financial assistance. In similar circumstances the other senior, Ricky Thorne, stayed home, took a job at the Chevron plant in Port Arthur, and started taking night classes at a community college. Her third target, Annie Miller, took it harder. As a junior when this started, the poorer performance was reflected in her eleventh grade SAT scores and state literacy tests, and in two more rounds of SATs in the twelfth grade. She lost confidence in her aspirations to get into and through medical school and took a "gap year" from school while she searched her soul for what else she wanted to do with her life.

In the fall of 2001, Margo doubled the number of targeted students again to twelve per test. Since this was such a small sample out of the total of 150 - 200 students taking any given test, their somewhat lower scores would hopefully still not draw attention. However, with more than two years of this behind her, Margo was growing impatient with her plan and ready to go after more students and drag them down even further. She was pondering her next steps to increase the damage when, just after Thanksgiving, Ruthie Gray and Edgar Clanton called her into the principal's office again.

Ruthie spoke first, "The scores are in for all the tests from last month. Guess you're thinking you pulled it off again. Proud of yourself?"

Margo felt her heartbeat pick up, and she looked from Ruthie to Mr. Clanton and back, "Ah, I don't know. Is there some problem?"

Mr. Clanton answered, "Actually, Margo, that's what we wanted to ask you."

Margo raised her eyebrows and thought, *Uh oh. Well, that didn't take long. Damn it! What was I thinking? There's no way they can prove anything, can they? Damn, damn, damn!* Mr. Clanton and Ruthie both stared at Margo stoically, and she flushed and felt her hands turn clammy.

Mr. Clanton smiled and broke the silence, "No, seriously, how'd it all go? I know test times are busy months for you, but from where I sit, you always seem to take it in stride." Ruthie smiled and nodded her head in agreement.

Margo blinked, "Oh, is *that* all? Geesh, that's a relief!" She looked a little sheepish and said, "I mean to say, it was all fine, as always. Not really much more work, and the aides were able to fill in for me some. So, uh, it's all good, *right?*"

"Just what I thought you'd say, but it's good to hear it from you. By the way, I've been talking with the superintendent, and he's finally approved a promotion for you to the next level on the admin scale, thanks to the extra responsibility you've taken on. I wish we could have done it sooner, but you'll see it in your January paycheck. Look, we're all lucky to have you, and I know it. Please keep doing whatever you're doing," and he patted her on the shoulder with a grin.

Margo looked from him to Ruthie and back, "Ok, well that's good news, thanks. I'll definitely try even harder from now on! I can promise you that."

• • •

Just outside of town on that same day, Mark Hammock had been working part-time for Joe Deming for just under four years. In that time, Jodie had also worked her usual natural magic, and in so doing, Mark had become a regular fixture around their place, almost like family. He couldn't remember exactly when, but it started with a casual request at the end of one of those first Saturdays several years ago as he was putting tools away to wrap up another day. Jodie called out to him on his way out the door, "Hey there, big fella, if you're not running off to something else, why don't you stay and eat with us? Joe's grilling, and he always cooks too much, so it's no imposition at all." He turned towards her and felt his neck flush as the question struck him almost as intimately as if she had kissed him on the cheek. There was never any doubt that he'd take her up on the offer, but he hoped he didn't look either as happy or as embarrassed as he felt.

From then on, it was always clear that it was a standing invitation and an expectation from Jodie that he had a place at the family table Saturday night. It was never anything fancy, just plenty of home-cooked food, warm conversation, and a touch of belonging surrounded by the three generations of Demings and the Luckys, Jodie's grandparents. He'd have been there on holidays too, but his gals at the trailer park—Jenny, Tina, and Nancilee—already had dibs on his time for those occasions and most Sunday dinners, and he felt some of that same belonging with them too.

Looking back in November 2001, things had certainly taken a warm and family-like turn for Mark, considering the self-imposed exile in which he had lived in for so many years. That he had come so far also accentuated his anguish on this November afternoon as he sat in silence at a picnic table with Jodie's family after her memorial service.

Around them, at a dozen folding tables overflowing with food and standing in small groups throughout the clearing, were several hundred friends and admirers who were here to pay their respects and seek some relief from their grief in losing Jodie without warning at such a young age. Although he was with Jodie's family—people he knew well and felt at home with—he could only stare down at the table. Whenever he looked at their faces, he could only imagine the emptiness and pain they had to be feeling, and he felt his own grief boiling up inside. He quickly looked down each time to avoid losing control, telling himself, *No, no, no. Don't do it. Don't you lose it!*

When he thought he could keep it inside no longer, he stood up with a nod to Joe and a half smile to Jodie's grandmother, and he wandered away, still chastising himself, *It ain't your place to fall apart in front of these poor people—her family—who just lost such a special part of themselves. You're lucky to even be here at all, you lunkhead!* He slowly threaded his way through the clusters of people, many of whom he recognized from their visits to the shop or from construction sites. Without a destination in mind as he walked, he found himself at the spot of his first quiet conversation with Jodie where she lit the way for his climb back out of his abyss.

The memory made him smile, as did the dancing rays of sunlight peeking through the trees right on Jodie's spot. *Yep, just like it should be. Maybe that's her reminding me that she's still watching.* He closed his eyes and faced up towards the light, memories of her filling his thoughts as the sun warmed his face and a whisper of a breeze stirred up the scent of pine and wet leaves from the woods. It felt like East Texas goodness and a Jodie hug all wrapped up together.

As he stood there, pieces of the quiet conversations all around him mixed with his memories.

"You know, she really was the sweetest thing."

"Was there anything she couldn't do?"

"Boy, how could someone so young have so much wisdom? That little gal had something about her when she was twenty-nothing."

"That girl was good people."

"Well, she sure made me want to be a better man just by talking to me."

"Hell, that girl made me want to *be* as good as she made me feel."

Mark agreed with everything he overheard and then some. *In that simple way you had, you made me see that I could matter to someone, to anyone, that I had something to give, and that there was still a place for me in this world.* With that thought, Mark realized he now had tears streaming down his face, and they felt cool on his sun-warmed cheeks. He wiped both eyes with his shirt sleeves and chuckled to himself, *There you go, tough guy.* He glanced back to see Jo standing on the picnic-table bench with her arm draped over her dad's shoulder while she regaled him and her grandparents with a story. He then looked up at the light streaming through the leaves and said out loud, "Yeah, yeah, I guess you're still right, little lady. I know it's okay for me too." He took a deep breath, then found his way back to the table where he sat and listened to happy stories about Jodie, shed a few more tears, and shared some hugs with the family.

Joe had asked everyone to stay as long as they could, swap happy stories, and celebrate Jodie's life just as she had lived it. Since it meant both showing support for the family and putting off a more final goodbye to Jodie, a large part of the crowd was happy to oblige, and the last of them were leaving just as darkness fell a few hours later.

The next six months until the end of Jo's school year were a blur for Joe. Of course, he had immense grief to contend with after losing the love of his life, the mother of his child, and the center of his universe. He ended most days in private agony, reeling from the hole in his heart, and he began each next day praying for God and Jodie to help him get out of bed and face the day. But he still had to take care of business, some of it being actual business in order to pay the bills and put food on the table. Most importantly was Jo. Joe knew he wouldn't be doing his daughter any good at all by giving in to his grief. He ended many nights on their deck, brooding about their loss and their way forward.

Each night, he'd bring himself back around by thinking about his wife and imagining the soothing words she'd surely have for him. He could almost hear her voice. Then he'd remind himself, *That kid's hurting just as much as me, losing not just any mom, but Jodie. No one knows better than I do what that means!*

Jodie's was a huge presence to make up for, starting with just keeping everything covered, and, for that, the young father thanked God for the grandparents. Joe's mom, Jessie, was still Jo's chauffeur to and from school in her Orange ISD school bus and could even check in with her in the cafeteria while she was serving lunch. Jodie's grandparents (and Jo's great-grandparents), Dina and Ben, came over every afternoon during the week so the first-grader didn't walk into an empty house after school while Joe was working. Joe then did the best he could to keep churning out the custom cabinets during the week, but it often kept him working later into the evening when he knew he should be spending time with Jo instead.

Now, more than ever, Joe was thankful he had Mark's help on weekends. He was barely keeping his head above water trying to do all of his work and Jodie's, the latter of which sometimes seemed like rocket science to him. Still, although he was back to working longer hours during the week, he was able to take off every other Saturday. He and Jo often drove down to the beach and spent the weekend camping out in the old trailer and reliving the happy pleasures the three of them had always found on the beach.

When summer rolled around, Joe realized he hadn't thought enough about how to keep her occupied and looked-after when she wasn't in school. For the first week, she could usually be found in the shop, sitting at her mom's old desk and goofing around on the internet or following Joe around, asking questions about his current projects. Saturday morning he looked up from his work to see her sitting there.

He walked around the desk, sat on the corner and said, "I think I may have missed you hiring-on for the summer, young lady. Don't you have something you'd rather be doing? Like watching TV, or exploring in the woods, or something?"

Without looking up from the computer, she answered, "No, I like being here."

He hooked a foot under her chair and pulled her toward him, "Hey, I'm serious, young'un. You don't need to be sitting in here with us just because I have work to do. You can go see what Gramma Jessie's doing in her house, or I'm sure Gramma and Grampa Lucky'd be happy to have you over rather than you just sittin' around here watching me and Mark turn boards into sawdust."

She looked down at her lap when she answered quietly, "Mom always let me keep her company in here. She said we were partners." She looked up with tears in her eyes and her lower lip puffed out as she tried not to cry, "I don't want to be anywhere else."

Joe looked at his daughter and saw her mother's eyes. Seeing those eyes filled with sadness gave him a chill, and he hoisted her out of the chair and into a hug, "Hey, hey, kiddo. It's okay. Sure, you can stay. You don't have to go anywhere. We'll figure it out, just you and me. You know you'll always be my partner too." He saw something move out of the corner of his eye and looked up in time to see Mark wipe a sleeve across his eyes and turn away.

That night after their big family dinner, Joe asked Mark to stay awhile to talk a little shop. They were sitting on the deck behind the house, looking into the woods when Joe said, "I need you to think about something. You've been helping out for four years now, and it's been great having you here on weekends. It feels like you've been part of the business and part of the family for much longer than that. Really, it's been great. I never thought I could bring someone in who could do the work like my dad and me, but you're a natural."

Mark shrugged and smiled, "Hey, thanks. It's been fun for me, the work and being around your family both." His face became serious, "Uh oh, is this our 'thanks for playing, time to go' conversation?"

"Oh, hell no! This is our 'how'd you like to come on full-time so I can spend more time with Jo' conversation." Mark looked stunned, and before he could respond, Joe went on talking quickly, "I haven't talked with Bill Arceneaux about this, and I don't want to leave him in a bad place. That'll be something we'll need to do pronto, if you're interested. But if we can work it out, I'm betting we can increase our output enough to cover your pay and still give me the time I need with Jo.

"The thing is, I can't just be there for her at dinner and the occasional weekend. I owe it to her and Jodie both to do more than that. I don't know any other way to make sure she remembers every beautiful detail about her mom. I don't know who else to turn to. You know the work, you have the skills, you know *us* . . . Anyway, look, before dinner I scribbled down some notes with ideas about projects, revenue, and pay. Just ideas, but—"

Without waiting for Joe to finish, Mark stood up and shook his hand while nodding and said, "Deal. Whatever it is, it's a deal. I'll talk with Bill on Monday, but I have a couple of guys who are ready to step up and replace me. So, he should be fine. Besides, I know he'd always want to help you guys just as much as I would." He turned away to look towards the woods and after a pause said, "I want you to know how much I appreciate . . . everything. You know, giving me the job, and . . ." he trailed off, then added in a husky voice, "I'd better get going now. See ya." He was down the back stairs before Joe was out of his chair. The last Joe saw of him as he turned the corner towards the driveway, Mark was wiping his eyes with his sleeve, but at least he was smiling.

Chapter 9

SETTING OUT

She recognized some threats on sight
and tried to steer clear of the ones that did not avoid her.

CERRO PELON, Mexico (World News)—After what appeared to be a steady recovery since 1998's surprising decline, scientists this winter report another record-setting drop in the world's monarch butterfly population. Although experts agree that some part of the problem is likely caused by human activity, they remain unsure about steps that could be taken to protect this fragile and important species.

Margo went into the spring of 2002 with more than just renewed confidence in her plan; she was now convinced she could get away with it. She had slowly increased the number of students whose scores she set back on every test from three to twelve, and she wasn't just getting away with it. She was being rewarded for doing such a great job! First, they rewarded her with a private workroom where she could literally lock herself away to do whatever she wanted with no fear of being seen or interrupted, and then a pay raise. She realized the most important facet of these rewards wasn't the privacy or the money, it was that she had won over the right people. That is, people like Edgar Clanton and Ruthie Gray, who were in the position to give her the access and responsibility she needed to bring her plan to fruition, were in position to watch over her and the testing process at the school, and who now trusted her implicitly. Her "watchers" knew that she had it all under control and needed no watching. Better yet, they had convinced the senior managers at the school district to extend the same trust. Margo would use that trust to keep inquiring eyes out of her business, and now no one was watching the henhouse.

The freedom that bought her meant Margo could now really turn up the heat, which she was as impatient to do as ever, even as she still cautioned herself to take it slowly. It occurred to her that she needed to be much more deliberate as she cast her net wider. *Don't forget, this is about having maximum impact. Don't blow it by jumping the gun or taking potshots. It is all about knocking down the students who are the highest achievers with the greatest potential for even more, and then keeping them down—lowering the expectation for their realistic, long-term potential.*

For starters, she needed continuity in her efforts for each year group. This spring would bring her first three ninth graders all the way through her process—every state or college board exam they'd taken would have her mark on them. She looked back and saw that if she ensured that the kids that made it onto her lists stayed there for every state and college board test at Grayton High School, not only was she hurting the same students' scores on successive efforts, but the similar outcome would help mask her efforts. Better yet, if she changed the answers on their tests from year to year, the track record itself would become even less remarkable. One or two surprising and lower test scores than usual may raise an eyebrow for some previously high-achieving kid, but a series of low scores only confirms past—and now *expected*—performance. The faculty, the family, and the student have that message reinforced: "This kid's not a good test taker," or "This kid's not destined for the highest academic achievement, look at their record." Either way, it isn't the test or the *test-coordinator* who is suspect, it is the *student* who can't cut it. *Okay, once on the team, always on the team. Got it. Who says continuity in education isn't a goal?!*

However, as the "target" list size grew from year to year, there was no way Margo would be able to remember all of the names. She needed to save the record system printouts she scoured each test season, but that was a huge risk—it was evidence. In this case, it would be evidence of an actual crime, since tampering with any of these tests in any way was a felony. If Ruthie or anyone stumbled onto them, they would raise a number of questions that Margo wouldn't have convincing answers to, and further review could lead someone clever enough to the right conclusions. Those conclusions wouldn't bode well for Margo.

Locked in her workroom with three years of class listings spread out on the table, Margo mulled that problem over while she double-checked her target list before the next round of exams began. She needed them someplace close but also secure. Secure meant no one else could have access, so just locking them in the cabinet wasn't enough, since Ruthie also had a key. *The chute! I knew that crazy thing might come in handy! What if . . . ?* Margo emptied the bottom shelf inside the cabinet and pulled the metal chute door down with a loud creak. She couldn't reach down to the bottom of the chute, and anything she put on the chute door would slide into the wide black hole when she closed it. As she stared into the chute, she noticed a series of quarter-inch holes at the back edge of the chute door where it formed a curved lip upward. *I don't know what you're there for, but if I can hook something through those holes, I bet I can hang these papers inside this thing.*

That evening after school, she stopped at Walmart on the way home and picked up a locking, three-ring binder. She then stopped at the hardware store and picked up a couple of two-foot sections of light chain. The next afternoon Margo was back in her workroom where she secured one end of each chain to a hole at the base of the chute door and the other end of each chain to separate rings on the binder. Using these chains, she could lower the binder down into the chute, where they'd hang, suspended from the holes at the bottom of the chute door. She could have used a single chain, but better safe than sorry. This way, if one of the rings popped open, the other chain would still hold the binder and her paper trail, rather than losing them down the chute. She punched holes in her printouts, popped them into the binder, and then lowered it again into the chute, out of sight. After closing the chute door, she moved some blank practice tests back to the lower shelf in the cabinet to hide the chute door from view, then she closed and locked the cabinet. Satisfied, she unlocked the office door and went back to work with a smile. *Boom, that'll work! Glad that's settled!*

• • •

Hanging around Joe's shop when she wasn't in school was not an adjustment for Jo. She was simply doing what she remembered always doing with her mom. She may not be with her mom in the shop anymore, but she was right where she knew her mom would be if she could.

Jodie had loved being right in the middle of Joe's business because that wrapped her even more in his life, and—Jo was right—it was the only place her mom wanted *them* to be. So, Jo's days hadn't changed that much. Gramma took her to school and back on the same school bus as always, and Jo then spent most of her time at home in the shop watching her dad and Mark work.

Joe was happy to have her underfoot, partly because she was such a punkin, and also in no small part because she helped fill the hole that still lingered in his heart from her mom's absence. Beyond how much Jo looked like her mom, he could see and hear Jodie in everything the little girl did, from the way she rolled her eyes at the men's bad jokes to the easy laugh that could take the sting out of just about any bad day. He often caught himself standing in a daze, watching mesmerized as Jo exuded her mom in so many ways, especially in her innate happiness—an apparently unquenchable joie de vivre. Like her mom, Jo saw something to smile about in everything and in everyone, and most people who interacted with her, even casually, came away feeling re-energized from it, just as they did with her mom. Seeing so much of her mother in his daughter, the young father couldn't help feeling his wife's presence all around them, almost as perceptible as the inevitable soft brush of Jodie's hand on his arm when she walked by while he worked. It was that feeling that carried him past the grief in moments when he could have easily given in to it, and instead he was reminded of the blessing he had in his time with Jodie and still had with Jo.

With Mark in the business full-time, he and Joe were able to plan most of their jobsite work during the school day so that when he still had work to do, Joe could be in the shop with his daughter after school. From time to time when they had no choice, Joe took her along to the jobsite, where she would watch them work. Like her mom, Jo was like a sponge, rarely asking the same question twice and often anticipating help or a tool the two men needed before they asked for it. Also like her mom, Jo would always talk with whatever other workers happened to be at the job, men who would often be amused at first by the precocious seven-year-old. Before long, even the most curmudgeonly tradesmen were delighted by her presence and were not shy about expressing their disappointment to Joe when she wasn't with him.

Life went along like this until the summer of 2003, their second since losing Jodie; and having just finished second grade, Jo was again in the shop or at a jobsite with her dad and Mark on most days. One afternoon while installing cabinets in a new house, Joe watched through the kitchen window as his daughter talked to an electrician who was clearly captivated by the youngster. He gestured towards her to Mark, "I think I might not be paying enough attention to her development or something. I'm pretty sure her friends are all guys like us, a bunch of construction workers. That can't be the best idea. None of us can teach her any girl-stuff."

Mark looked past Joe at the little girl, "Oh, I don't know. It sure looks to me like you're doing just fine. She's a happy little thing anyway, and that counts for a lot. I'm sure she has girl friends at school, and she has her grandmothers still."

"Yeah, I know, but she's around us and guys like us most of the time. And now that you mention it, I don't think I've ever heard her say the name of any kids from school." Joe shook his head, "Jodie would know. She'd know what to do, what to say to her, who her friends at school are, *how to brush her hair the right way!*" The thought that he might be letting down Jo—and therefore Jodie—was one of the few that brought on the rare moments when the sadness would sink back into his heart, and his eyes teared up.

Mark patted him on the shoulder, "Hey there, Dad, don't be too hard on yourself. Seriously. Look at her, she's great. But if it's really bothering you, I think I could bring over my little gal, Nancilee, on Saturday while we're working. I mean, she's not *mine*, but I know the family real well. She's a year younger than Jo, but I bet they'd get along great. I've thought about asking about it for a while, but I didn't want to act like it was my place to bring kids over to the shop."

Joe looked out the window at Jo and smiled as he wiped a tear from the corner of one eye, "Hey man, mi casa, su casa. Bring her this weekend. I'd say, 'We'll see how they get along,' but this is Jodie-Junior we're talking about. Of course they'll get along."

After graduating from high school five years earlier, Tina Davis started working evenings at Walmart in addition to her weekend shifts. This gave her mother, Jenny, the chance to go back to day shifts while still allowing one of them to always be at home with Nancilee. When the little girl started first grade, Tina was able to switch to weekdays during the school year but had to switch back to evenings and weekends during the summer. Therefore, Mark was lucky to have caught them both at home when he walked over to talk about taking their youngster to the shop.

He knocked on the door and heard little feet scurrying across the trailer floor like a hollow drumbeat. The door was yanked open and there stood a grinning Nancilee, with her bushy mane of curly blonde hair and big blue eyes. She yelled over her shoulder, "It's Uncle Ma-ark!"

The seven-year-old leapt up so Mark could catch her under the arms and swing her onto his hip, where she gave him a tight hug. He flushed every time the little girl greeted him like that, and he loved it. He walked in to find her mother and grandmother talking quickly as Tina was ready to rush out the door for work. Both women smiled brightly, and Jenny spoke first, "Hey there, Mr. Man. What's up?"

Mark explained Joe's concern about Jo and the idea he'd suggested for the girls to spend time together. "Look, I know she's not mine to make decisions about, but I hope you know I'll watch out for her. And I'd trust these people with my life, or I wouldn't even have mentioned it. But maybe you could think about it and let me know if you think it'd be okay?"

Jenny looked at her daughter and said, "You know, we've been talking about the same thing for Little Miss here. About the only people she'll talk to are you, me, and Mark. You said her teacher told you she's still shy with the kids in her class. Maybe this'll help?"

Tina looked at her daughter, who had her head on Mark's shoulder and was smiling back at her, "Hmm, we haven't really let her go places without one of us yet. I don't know, maybe you're right. Since I'm off during the day, how about we go with you tomorrow morning instead of Saturday, unless that's too soon? I'll be home and could meet the dad and help introduce Nancilee to his daughter. We'll see how it goes?"

Mark set Nancilee on her feet and tousled her hair, "Sure, whatever you'd like to do, Mom. Alright, now you need to go to work, and I'm going home. See you gals in the morning." Walking home, he understood Tina's reluctance. Jenny and Tina had both lived through some rough experiences and learned to take care of their own. Those experiences and their modest means led them to keep Nancilee close at home, protected by their maternal umbrella. *Who knows? It's probably why the little gal is so shy around other people. There's worse problems to have.*

The next morning, an unsure-looking Nancilee walked into Joe's shop between her mom and Mark, holding both of their hands. Joe was sitting next to the desk reading a newspaper and sipping a cup of coffee, and Jo was sitting cross-legged on the desk reading the comics. Jo

looked up expectantly and smiled at the visitors. Joe stood and greeted them, "Well hey there! Big crew for work today, I see. It's good to finally meet Mark's other family. I'm Joe, and the boss here is also Jo."

Tina shook Joe's hand, "Hi Joe and Jo, I'm Tina." She reached up and hugged Joe, "We've heard so much about your family for so long, I feel like we know you already."

Mark was beaming when he pointed to the little girl, "And this little mop-top is Nancilee. She's a little shy at first, but she's a pistol." She looked down at his feet, looking every bit as shy as he said she was.

Jo patted the desk next to her and said, "You can sit up here with me if you want. I'll give you half."

Nancilee looked at Jo hesitantly and then to her mom, who smiled and said, "Go ahead, I'll be right here for a while."

Jo motioned behind her with her thumb, "I use the chair to climb up. It's easier that way." Nancilee walked around the desk, clambered up the chair, and sat cross-legged next to Jo, who slid a page of the comics in front of her.

The three adults walked farther into the shop as Mark and Joe showed Tina their work. Jo said to Nancilee, "I'm going into third grade this year, what about you?"

The younger girl held up two fingers and smiled.

Jo nodded, "Cool. I liked second grade. I kinda follow my dad around in his work when I'm not in school though. We also have a camper on the beach we go to sometimes. That's pretty fun. What do you do?"

Still smiling, Nancilee shrugged.

Jo knitted her brow briefly, "You don't talk much, do you? That's okay. Hey, we have a big deck where you can almost see over the trees. Wanna go see?"

Nancilee shrugged again and turned to look for her mom.

"It'll be alright. We'll tell 'em before we go. Besides, it's like ten feet away," and Jo climbed down and held her hand out to the younger girl. Nancilee took her hand, slid off the desk, and was quickly pulled around the machines and cabinets until they found the others to ask permission to wander off.

Hearing what Jo had in mind, Joe told her, "It's okay with me if it's okay with Nancilee's mom."

Tina smiled and ruffled her daughter's hair, "Sure, sounds fun."

"Just don't wander off our property, kiddo," Joe told Jo. He turned to Tina and said in a low voice, "It's only five acres. Don't worry. They won't go far."

"Okay!" Jo yelled as she pulled Nancilee toward the door. Outside, they were still walking hand in hand, with Jo serving as tour guide and talking nonstop. "That house in front of the shop is Gramma and Grampa Deming's house. They're both working right now. This one is our house. My mom and dad built it. My mom always said Dad was a genius with tools, but my dad says Mom was the brains of the outfit."

While Jo chattered away, the younger girl nodded seriously and watched her wide-eyed. They went up the stairs and through the house, picking up a couple of juice boxes on the way, then sat on the bench swing on the back deck. "See, told you you could almost see over the trees. I like it back here 'cause of that. Our woods go a long ways back. Hey, I know, let's go exploring in the woods, and then we can come back to my mom's spot down there for a picnic. Wanna do that?"

Nancilee nodded and smiled.

"Alright! Let me call my dad to make sure it's okay. Do you like peanut butter?" Nancilee nodded again and followed Jo into the house.

After talking to her dad on the phone, Jo said, "He said yes. So, let's make a lunch, then we're off." She spread everything out on the kitchen counter, and the younger girl mimicked what the older girl did, step by

step, from making her first peanut butter and jelly sandwich to stuffing potato chips and grapes into baggies. They put it all into Jo's backpack with a couple more juice boxes, and she pulled it on. "Let's go!"

Back in the shop, Joe was still chatting with Mark and Tina, "You know, you're welcome to hang around here as long as you like, but it's okay for you to leave her with us. We can check in on them from time to time while we're working. No problem. And Jo's reliable, she won't let them get into any trouble."

"I guess so, if you're sure it's okay. I can pick her up after their picnic, so you don't feel like you're babysitting instead of working."

"Why don't we see how it goes? If they're doing alright, we can call you later."

"Okay, if you're sure you know what you're getting yourself into with two little girls. I'm just a phone call away if you change your mind. I'll see you later, and thanks." Tina hugged them both and left.

As the door closed, the two men smiled to each other and Mark said, "See? She's a sweetie, isn't she? All three of them are, actually."

They lost track of time after they'd gotten to work, when Joe realized it had been almost three hours already and went to check on the girls. He heard their voices first and followed the sound into the clearing behind the house. They were lying in the shade under an oak tree, what was left of their picnic scattered around them. Joe started to call their names but stopped when he heard them laughing and pointing at the sky, Nancilee saying, "No, that's not a clown, it's Santa!"

"What? No way. Santa doesn't even go out this time of year!" Both girls busted out laughing again.

Joe snuck back the way he came and whispered to himself, "Remember Joe, if it ain't broke, don't fix it. Guess they ain't broke." He was still smiling when he walked back into the shop and told Mark how the girls were getting along.

Mark chuckled, “Hey, if it’s alright with you, I’ll call Tina now and let her know Nancilee can stay until I go home. Unless you think that’s too much for Jo.”

“Fine with me. They both sound happy to me. I’m just glad Jo has someone to spend time with who’s close to her own age and a *girl!*”

Mark was still smiling after he phoned Tina, who was as thrilled as Joe for her daughter to have made a friend who wasn’t her mom or grandmother. He went about his afternoon work feeling good about the world and imagining Jodie in the room with them smiling back at him.

The girls spent the day darting from place to place—from the woods, to Jo’s grandparents’ house, Jo’s room, and back to the deck where they watched the wind rustle through the trees—talking incessantly about school, their families, favorite movies, favorite food, and more. As the day wore on, Nancilee began feeling unusually at home at this place, and just as unusually had taken a great liking to Jo, who at only a year older, seemed to her to be much older and wiser. There was something about the older girl that she found calming and reassuring. In addition to the awe she had for Jo, Nancilee imagined that the Demings must be the richest people in town with their own woods, two whole houses, and a barn-workshop, especially compared to Nancilee’s trailer-park life!

Jo took to Nancilee right away. Although shy and quiet at first, as the younger girl warmed up she had an easy and happy way about her that felt familiar, like family. She had never felt like she was missing anything, but Jo found herself talking with Nancilee about thoughts and ideas in ways she hadn’t since her gab sessions with her mom. And she liked how it felt again, after missing her mom for more than a year.

At 4:00 P.M., the two girls went back to the shop. Jo grabbed the chair at the worktable her dad usually worked at and wheeled it around her desk to sit adjacent to her own. She climbed into her chair, patted the other, and said to Nancilee, “This one’s yours.” Jo leaned back and propped her feet on the desk with her hands clasped behind her head, and Nancilee did the same.

Joe and Mark had stopped working when they walked in, and Joe rolled his eyes and said to Mark, "Well, I guess I need to find another chair. The boss has spoken." Mark winked at Nancilee and went back to his work. Joe said to the girls, "How about we knock off early so Mark can get Nancilee home? No need wearing her out on her first day on the job."

"I don't think she's tired, Dad," Jo answered, "we've just been walking around and stuff." Nancilee shrugged, smiled, and nodded at Joe.

"It's probably a good idea anyway. Get you home, and you can tell your mama all about your day. You can come back here anytime, young lady. Uncle Mark, we'll have to make sure we're going to be in the shop for the day if she comes along during the week. We probably shouldn't have them both on a jobsite."

Mark finished clamping a cabinet joint, set it aside and said, "Makes sense to me. I'll talk with her mom and see how she feels about it, but I'm happy to bring her along anytime."

Jo and Nancilee hopped down and followed Mark out the door. After climbing into Mark's truck and before closing the door, Nancilee waved and said, "Bye, Jo! Thanks for showing me everything."

Jo ran to the door and handed her a scrap of paper, "I almost forgot. Here's our phone numbers—one's the house and the other is my desk in the shop. You can call me and give me yours when you get home. Bye, and tell Mark to bring you with him from now on!" Jo waved with a grin as she walked back to the shop door.

As they drove away, Mark looked sideways at Nancilee and asked, "So, did you have a good day with my buddy Jo?"

"Oh yeah, it was fun. She's pretty cool."

"Yeah, I hoped you'd like her too. She's a good kiddo, like someone else I know."

"Can I come back tomorrow?"

Mark said, "Hmmm, well, it's fine by me, but we need to talk with your mom."

At home, before Mark could say anything, Nancilee started talking about her day in a long, unbroken rush. Jenny and Tina stood grinning as the little girl gushed about one detail after the next and how cool her new friend was. She ended with, "They said I can come back anytime. Uncle Mark said he had to ask you. Can I?"

"Sure you can, sweetheart. I'll talk with Uncle Mark to make sure we're not taking up too much of their time or anything. And you know, on days when they're busy at work, maybe we could invite her over here?"

Nancilee hugged her mom's legs, "Thanks mom! I'm going to call Jo and tell her!" She ran into the kitchen, threw the piece of paper Jo had given her on the table and picked up the phone.

Tina stood on her toes and kissed Mark on the cheek. She had tears in her eyes when she said, "Thanks, Uncle Mark. I love to see her like this. You let me know whenever you'd like to take her along, and if it's okay with Jo's dad, it's always okay with me."

She looked over at her mom who had the same smiling but teary expression. Tina said, "Oh boy, I'd better go on to work before we all get all weepy." She looked into the kitchen where she could hear her daughter talking excitedly and yelled, "Bye Nancilee! I'm off to work and will be home late."

The little girl stopped talking mid-sentence and yelled, "Bye Mom!" The last Tina heard as she stepped outside was her daughter's happy voice chattering away.

• • •

With Margo's system in place to track her targeted students from year to year, she began incrementally increasing the size of the group. The spring of 2003 she went from twelve to twenty students per test, and in the fall grew the list again to thirty and kept it there for the full school year. Other than a few more disappointed kids, no one took notice. In the fall of 2004, she notched it up again to forty—more than ten times the number she'd started with—and still nothing.

In the five years since she'd started her project, the amount of time it took for Margo to change the answers after each exam had grown and was going to get worse as the project grew. What had been a ten-minute exercise to affect three students' test scores in 1999, now took over an hour for some exams, two hours for the ACT, and that was while still changing only 10 percent of the answers. She planned to go after more students and change even more answers for each of them. On some exams this would eventually grow to just over fifty changes per student and take more than five hours for each group.

She knew she needed some kind of shortcut, both to help manage the time and to easily ensure she was changing the right number of answers on each answer sheet. She found her answer when she saw a Scantron answer key a teacher was carrying in the office. She asked her, "How'd you punch the holes in the middle of the page like that?"

"Oh this? I have a long-handled hole punch just for that. It's a heck of a lot easier than trying to read each line the hard way. I just look to see if the right dots are filled in," the teacher said matter-of-factly.

"Well that's a great idea," Margo said as she went to look in the supply cabinet. Sure enough, she found one.

That night she took it home with another she used to punch slots into the top of new visitor badges. She showed them to Ed at dinner and asked, "Do you think you can take the long slot off of this one and replace the regular hole punch on the long-handled punch? I need to be able to punch slots across the middle of a page, if that makes sense."

"I'm sure I could. Let me take 'em to work tomorrow. I'll take 'em apart and monkey with some ideas. No promises on how it'll look though. You never know with this kind of thing."

Margo smiled, "I'm sure you'll figure it out, and it will work just fine, as usual."

Two days later, Ed set the long-handled punch on her desk in the school office, "Told you they might not look great. I ended up spot-welding the head from one onto the other. Ain't pretty, but it works." He punched a few slots into some paper from the trash can, "See?"

"Oh yeah, that's perfect." She gave him a hug and hustled off to her workroom to give it a try. After taping a PSAT practice answer sheet over a piece of card stock, she punched across the answer-ovals for five random questions. She then laid the card over another answer sheet, where it showed each of the answer-ovals for the five she had punched out. "Bingo," she said to herself as she put her new gadget in the cabinet for safe keeping.

A month later, while the ninth grade was taking the PSAT, Margo made her "answer key" card using an extra answer sheet, punching out the answers for 14 of the 139 questions. When completed test packages had all been returned to her, she pulled her forty target students' packages out and, one-by-one, used her template to erase all answers in the punched holes then filled in some other answer in each opening. When she was finished, she put her card-template in the binder with the student records and stashed them down the chute. When she finished the rest of the paperwork, she locked it all up as usual. She smiled to herself as she unlocked the room on her way out and thought, *Like I*

said, "Bingo." She used the same process on the exams for the rest of the year without a hitch.

Margo had made her process simpler just in time. That spring she bumped the size of her groups up to fifty students per exam, which was approximately the top quarter of each year group. In the fall of 2005, she finally upped the percentage of answers she changed from 10 to 15 percent of the entire exam for each student on her list. She was incredulous when the final scores again raised no significant alarm.

At the end of the school year, Margo mulled over her next steps. She wasn't willing yet to increase the percentage of changed answers, wanting the 15 percent to have some shelf life to make the final ramp-up less noticeable. She also didn't really want to increase the total number of students whose college board exams she changed; at fifty it already took her three to four hours after each exam and was affecting almost the entire top half of the highest-achieving, college-bound kids. There wasn't a lot to be gained by driving down the answers of the already lower-scoring students. The state literacy tests, however, were broken into five smaller tests on different days, and those individual tests were much shorter than the college board exams.

It occurred to Margo that she could double the number of students whose answers she changed on the state tests and still make all changes in less than four hours. And if she wanted to really make a splash by hurting the school's state test scores, that's what she should do. At one hundred students, she would be reducing the state literacy scores of the top half of every year group. That would be taking a swipe at a lot more kids and have real ramifications for the school as a whole. The state ranked individual schools and school districts based on how their student bodies did on those tests. *That's settled. I'll keep the board exam groups at fifty students but start ramping up the literacy test groups until I get to a hundred in each year group. Either way, I'll be knocking down the top half of all students in both types of tests, and the school will feel the pain too. Giddy up!*

• • •

Jo and Nancilee's first visit that summer had been the start of their years as inseparable pals. Joe and Tina originally thought Nancilee would repeat her first visit on the occasional weekday that Joe and Mark thought they'd be in the shop all day, and sometimes Jo would come over to the trailer park to visit when the guys were at a jobsite. Instead, the two girls made plans every day, either while they were hanging out or later in the evening on the phone, and rarely went a day without spending time together. Sometimes that involved Joe or Mark dropping the girls back at Tina's trailer while they were on the way to a job. Other times Tina brought Nancilee to the shop later in the day instead of having her ride over with Mark, or they picked up Jo to spend the day at their place. By mid-summer, at least a couple of nights each week found one of them spending the night at one or the other's house, often switching from one to the other the next night.

Joe and Jo had several weekend trips planned to their trailer on Crystal Beach before school started. Nancilee was nervous about going on such a new adventure as swimming in an ocean she had never even seen, so she didn't go along. After that weekend apart, the two friends decided she just needed to get over that and go. Two Sundays later she did get over it, and when she came back from her first beach trip, a sunburned and elated Nancilee regaled her mom, grandmother, and Uncle Mark with long stories about their adventures while eating barbecue on Mark's deck. After that trip, it was simply a done deal—Nancilee was always a part of the plan.

School started in late August, ending summer as it does for all schoolkids and especially for Jo and Nancilee, who attended different schools and would now not spend almost every day together. During the week, they settled for talking every morning on the phone before school and again at least once after school. They kept up their visits on weekends, however, and would have been appalled by any other plan. By then, Jenny, Tina, and Nancilee had become part of the Demings' Saturday dinners, and Joe and Jo were at Mark's or Jenny's place for Sunday dinner, sometimes with some or all of Jo's grandparents too. It was therefore a natural progression that their now even-more-extended family also gathered for all holiday dinners and birthday celebrations.

Chapter 10

KNOW THY FRIENDS AND ENEMIES

Like a late freeze, some things could not be seen coming.

The next several years became a familiar and comfortable blur for Jo, Nancilee, and their families, just as that first summer had. The girls spent as much time together as they could during the school year and almost every day during each summer, whether at the shop and Jo's woods, the trailer park, Jo's grandparents' homes, or the trailer at Crystal Beach. While there may not have been a lot of variation in their routines, it was warm, real, and treasured by them all.

The families couldn't have been happier to see the girls together, albeit often oblivious to the rest of the world, and they all enjoyed both girls' company. Although the parents and grandparents often wondered if the year difference in their age would become a problem, the girls never seemed to tire of each other. For Jo and Nancilee it was never awkward. At only one year, the age separation wasn't so great as to be a gulf between them, even if it was also a full grade in school, and they each found something they needed in the other. Nancilee felt an ease and trust with Jo in a way she had not with anyone else except her mom, gramma, and Uncle Mark, and she definitely looked up to Jo as a slightly older big sister. Jo treasured the joy she felt when they were together or simply talking on the phone and loved Nancilee like a sister.

That they were best friends was an understatement. They hung on each other's words when they were talking, never failed to laugh at the other's jokes, preferred to do everything together, and when that wasn't possible, the experience was never complete until the two of them talked about every little detail. They liked and loved each other thoroughly and without reservation in the way that children often can, and adults just as often forget how. The warmth they felt from each other stayed with them when they were apart and helped them deal with life's daily trials and tribulations in much the same way that Jodie had affected people around her.

Nancilee's relationship with Jo was certainly having an effect on the younger girl who, although still shy, was showing subtle but noticeable gains in confidence, ease with others, and overall demeanor. It wasn't just her family that noticed Jo was rubbing off on her, and that she was coming out of her shell. Near the end of the third grade and after almost two years of palling around with Jo, Nancilee was walking down her elementary school hallway at the end of the school day without a care in the world and thinking about their next adventure. Her first-grade teacher, Miss Mallet, stepped in front of her with her hands on her hips, "Well hey there, Miss Nancilee! And just where are you going with that big smile on your face?"

Nancilee looked up from her reverie and said, "Oh, I'm just going to catch the bus and go home."

"I've been hearing about you from Miss Thomas. She says you're one of her best students, *and* you're even talking in class. How about that? It made me feel good to hear a teacher talking so nicely about one of my special girls. I'm sure glad I saw you so I could tell you that. Now you'd better give me a hug and get on out to your bus."

Nancilee hugged her old teacher and said, "I sure hope I get a teacher as nice as you and Miss Thomas in fourth grade!" She smiled all the way home, as did Miss Mallet.

The rest of Jo's grade school experience was surprisingly not much different than Nancilee's. Although the more naturally outgoing of the two, Jo was content to go through each year in class without attracting much attention. She was friendly and not disliked by anyone, of course, as her mother's daughter. She laughed at other kids' jokes and joined in conversations, but she drifted away when groups became cliquey. She stayed out of the all-girl conversations about boys or clothes or whatever else some of them seemed so distracted by, and although she found the boys' conversation less strange, she was often perplexed by the stereotypical male behaviors many of them were growing into. As her class fell into their routine each year, outside of the classroom at recess and lunch Jo tended to find herself with a number of quieter kids—sometimes more serious, other times just more shy than the others, or someone who had been singled out for teasing. She always found something interesting in them, and most of them warmed to her just as Nancilee had. Likewise, Jo's teachers all took a liking to her as a good student who had a calming influence on the class and was always a pleasure to talk to.

In 2007 when Jo moved up to sixth grade at Grayton Intermediate School, things began to change, starting with the social dynamic. Like so many generations before them, eleven-year-old sixth grade girls saw seventh and eighth graders dressing like high school girls and behaving much differently than what they'd left behind in elementary school. Not just little girls anymore, these older girls had redefined cool and were becoming women, and there was a rush to emulate them and be cool—dress right, wear the right makeup, talk right, read the right magazines, and talk to the right boys. The boys mostly became more strange than they already were, trying to act cooler and older. Jo found it all more perplexing than ever, not that she had ever tried to fit into any group, but she definitely found herself now clearly on the outside with the rest of the obviously uncool kids. Simply being likable was no longer enough to many of the kids in her classes.

By Halloween, comments began circulating in numerous circles of girls about her: *What's with that hair? Why does she dress like a boy? It's like she doesn't care that she's so uncool. She doesn't even wear makeup, maybe she wants to be a boy.* One girl she had known since the first grade made it clear one day when Jo tried to sit with her at lunch, "You probably shouldn't sit at this table anymore. A lot of the cool kids like to sit here, and you don't really fit in with them. I mean, you know, it's bad enough that your mommy still makes your lunch, but no one our age carries a Shrek lunch box, and . . . and . . . and stuff like that. It's just better if you sit somewhere else."

Jo looked at her like she was speaking a foreign language but shrugged and said, "Okay, sure." She picked up her lunch box, wandered over to another table with only two people, and began eating her lunch in silence. After a few minutes she looked down the table at them and smiled.

They both looked at her suspiciously, and the boy nodded towards the other table and asked with a mild sneer, "Banished from Cool Island?" That made the girl snicker.

Jo laughed, "Yeah, I guess so. Whatever. I hope you don't mind me sitting here."

"It's a free country. Even if some people don't think so." That got another laugh out of the other apparent social reject, and then they went back to talking to each other and ignoring everyone else, including Jo.

It was clear from that day that Jo was not going to be one of the cool and popular kids in middle school. The whole idea baffled her, but it didn't really faze her. After a few days of tolerating her presence in what had been their spot, the two kids at the end of her new lunch table gradually started speaking to her, first just short greetings, then actual conversation. By then, Jo was no longer sitting at the far end of the table, and they had become her friends, Will Jackson and Rennie Castle. Will was an endless stream of bad jokes and observations about the goofy games the "cool kids" busied themselves over. Rennie was quiet and almost painfully introverted, but she was quick to laugh at Will's antics and gradually became comfortable talking to Jo. In time, their conversations grew into more than just snarky observations about the "cool kids" and more about their interests, from movies to books, music, and life. Over the next few months, others trickled in one or two at a time, and by the end of the year they had a full table of formerly misfit friends, all very uncaringly uncool and all very glad to know Jo Deming, as she was of them.

Jo and Nancilee had eagerly awaited the next year. After years of attending different elementary schools, in 2008 they were finally in the same middle school, with Jo in the seventh grade and Nancilee in sixth. They laid out a plan over the summer that would take the fullest advantage of the opportunity, which they explained to Joe and Mark one afternoon. With their work interrupted by the two happy girls, the two men feigned serious expressions and listened attentively as Jo started, "Well first, we'll both ride our regular buses to school, but Nancilee will ride home with me on Gramma's bus. Uncle Mark can take her home when he leaves after work."

Mark raised his eyebrows, and the men glanced at each other. Before either spoke, Nancilee jumped in, "Don't say no yet. It's a good idea. That way Mom and Gramma don't have to worry about one of them being home or something, and I can still do homework here with Jo. If I need help, she'll be here. It's perfect."

Mark cocked his head and said, "Sure, but—"

Jo interrupted him, "Wait, there's more. We'll each have our own locker, but we're going to split them and each put half our stuff in both lockers, depending on where our classes are. Even if we don't have the same lunch periods, we'll be able to catch up between classes and at our lockers. It's brilliant!"

Mark's eyebrows were still raised when Joe spoke up, "Okay generals, sounds like you've got it all figured out. Why don't we start with seeing how Nancilee's mom feels about it? And I guess it wouldn't do any good to say that maybe you should—I don't know—*ask* Mark?"

"What? No!" A grinning Nancilee ran to Mark and put an arm around his waist and looked up at him, "*He* doesn't care. He *likes* my company, *don't* you? And I already talked to my mom and gramma. They both said it was fine with them if we could talk you guys into it."

Mark looked down at Nancilee, "Hey, it's okay by *me,*" then glanced at Joe, "but it's up to the boss to say if he wants you two troublemakers around every afternoon."

Nancilee looked indignant but Joe laughed, "Alright, alright. I'll talk to your mom just to be sure, but it sounds like you've outmaneuvered us. You two will have to make sure you can actually get your homework done though, and not blow the time . . . being you two." That elicited a laugh from Jo, who high-fived Nancilee and hugged her dad.

Their first year in school together went almost as well as they'd hoped. The plan went like clockwork, with the two of them meeting up before school every morning and between classes either at one of the lockers or in the hallway. Jo waited for Nancilee at the back door to the bus line every afternoon, and the two of them sat together behind Jo's grandmother for their ride to Jo's house, either talking about the day or taking care of homework. The girls even managed to make good use of their hour together in the shop to finish any remaining assignments and study, to Joe and Mark's great surprise.

Watching them together one afternoon, Mark mentioned it to Joe, "I think Jo is rubbing off on Nancilee. I don't think she's ever been all that interested in school, but she sure is now. I think it's because she can tell Jo takes it seriously, so she does too now. Her mom told me her grades are better now than ever. I'm sure it's because of Jodie Junior there."

"You think?" Joe grinned, liking the sound of that. He went back to his work, saying, "They're definitely good for each other, that's for sure."

Not quite everything went as well as the girls had imagined, and like Jo, Nancilee discovered some of the less pleasant aspects of middle school social dynamics. Although she had come out of her shell to some degree after several years as Jo's sidekick, in a new school, every class being a different mix of kids—many of whom she did not know—and without her older pal around, Nancilee tended to revert back to her quiet and shy natural tendencies. She preferred to sit as far back and to the side in each class as she could and rarely spoke up unless specifically called on by the teacher. At lunch, she sat by herself and read a book or worked on homework. Although she didn't attract much attention, neither did she make many friends.

As the year went on, however, classmates took notice that Nancilee's test scores were always good, which broke the ice with some who were impressed by the quiet, smart kid. One who noticed but was not impressed was Jamie Faison—James Faison IV. He was in Nancilee's

sixth grade math and science classes, and by Christmas Jamie had heard enough about her, "For God's sake! Who does that mouse think she is anyway? *Ewwww, she got another A*, she must be a real brain!"

Like his grandfather, Jimmy Jr., Jamie sat in the back of the class surrounded by boys who were easily amused by his antics during class. This time was no exception as they all laughed and parroted him with a loud chorus of, "Ewwww!"

"Who cares? This stuff doesn't matter. My family already owns this town, and it's all going to be mine. Just like my old man always says, 'We're Faisons.' Let other people waste their time on tests that don't matter. What's it going to get her? She's a weird little mouse with no friends and always will be."

That elicited guffaws from Jamie's boys, prompting the teacher to say sternly, "That's enough back there. Quiet down, all of you!"

The youngest Faison was partly right: As an eleven-year-old he was already known as a rich kid, from an important family, and a ringleader of the cool kids. There was a long line of kids who wanted to be his friend and to be known to be in his circle, good grades or not. Unfortunately for Jamie, besides the family wealth and influence, the only other attribute he shared with his grandfather was his looks, and Jamie had the standard Faison blue eyes and curly blond hair. Everything else he learned from his father, Jimmy III, and his Uncle Teddy, especially his sense of entitlement and the resulting nonexistent work ethic. Also like his Uncle Teddy, Jamie's poor grades reflected his attitude but at a much younger age and without Margo's "help." The more Jamie heard about Nancilee's grades while he fell behind, the more he showered her with abuse.

Nancilee learned that if she could ignore him long enough, he'd lose interest and move on to haranguing someone else or heckling the teacher. She also knew she'd escape him when the bell rang, and she'd meet Jo for a few minutes at one of the lockers where her friend was always able to make her smile. At the end of the sixth grade, Nancilee's grades got her moved into the advanced classes in the seventh grade, just as Jo's had, which also separated Nancilee from Jamie Faison, since he was already working his way towards remedial classes.

For someone who also wasn't interested in attracting attention, Jo had a growing group of quiet admirers, in part because of her good grades, but mostly for her easygoing and accepting way with anyone she came across. The more kids got to know her, the more they liked her, and many of them were happily surprised that she liked them as well. Her lunch group had grown from Will and Rennie into several tables of regulars, mostly other bookish and non-conforming kids who found common ground with each other. After breaking the ice during lunch, these kids grew into friends who sat together in class and never failed to acknowledge each other in the hallways, from head nods and grins to high fives on their way past each other. Like Jo and Nancilee, many of them now got together outside of school—for some of them, the first friends they'd had since they were in elementary school. Coming at an age when cliques and social dynamics were becoming unnaturally prominent, they found themselves rarely fitting in, leading to strong bonds and loyalties between the fellow outcasts.

Outside of school, Jo and Nancilee's life went on in their familiar and comfortable pattern. After five years, it would have seemed wrong otherwise, since all of the parents and grandparents had become close friends as well.

In the last week of their second year in middle school together, Jo was finishing the eighth grade and Nancilee was wrapping up the seventh grade. Each was anxious to share her news with the other when they met at Jo's locker after the last period. Jo started talking excitedly first, "It's official, I'm in ninth grade geometry next year! Hah! Just found out."

Nancilee was beaming when she answered, "Well yeah, you are! Big surprise for the math genius! But that now makes two of us. *I'm* in eighth grade algebra next year!" The two pals were both so happy they didn't know what else to say and gave each other a congratulatory hug.

"Well looky here, will you?" The girls turned to see Jamie Faison standing across the hall with several of his troublemaker admirers. He pointed at Jo and sneered, "Little Nanci-loser and her nerdy guy-girlfriend finally go public."

Nancilee let go of Jo and looked crushed. Jo looked quizzically at Jamie, then put a hand on Nancilee's shoulder, looked her in the eyes, and said, "Hey, ignore that guy. If anyone cares what he thinks, then we don't care what they think, either. They don't matter to us or to our lives, and we don't need to give him or them a second thought."

Nancilee smiled and stood a little taller. She started to speak but was cut off by Jamie, who had stomped across the hall and shoved both girls against the lockers, "Hey, who do you think you're talking to? I don't have to take that from a couple of losers like you!"

Before he said another word, two hulking shapes in black sweatshirts and black jeans stepped between Jamie and his entourage. One of them stepped between him and the girls, and the other dragged Jamie away by the collar and swung him into the lockers with a loud, reverberating clang. A red-faced Jamie whipped around, "Oh, that's it. You're dead," but as he said it, the much larger boy stepped up and pressed him against the lockers with Jamie looking into this chest. The other big fellow turned to glare at Jamie's astonished entourage, none of whom had the courage to speak or step up and, for once, neither did Jamie.

Jo smiled at the two brutish looking boys, "Oh hey, guys. Nancilee, I don't know if you know my friends. Don't worry, they're nicer than they seem," she said with a laugh. She gave a quick hug to the one closest to her, "This one is Timmy, and Little Big Mouth's new friend over there is Matt. We sometimes call them Wolf and Lion because their names are Tim *Wolf* and Matt *Lyons*. Get it?"

Nancilee nodded. Still holding Jamie by the collar, Matt laughed, "Yeah, Jo, that's a hard one to figure out."

Jo smirked at Matt and said, "Anyway, she's my best friend Nancilee. And thanks for the intervention."

"So, you okay? You want me to put this one *in* this locker?" Matt bounced Jamie lightly against the locker with another clang.

Nancilee smiled widely and looked at Jo, who shook her head, "No, don't do anything that will get you in trouble. Just send him on his way."

A now-embarrassed Jamie Faison was regaining his composure, "You better get your hands off me, or—"

He stopped when Matt gathered his shirt more tightly into his fist, gave him a stronger bounce against the locker, and leaned towards him menacingly. "Careful what you say, little fella. I don't think your homies over there want any of this." A serious-looking Tim took a step towards the other boys, who scattered and hustled down the hall. Matt shoved Jamie in their direction and said, "Now you go on and don't make me disappoint my friend Jo. Mess with them again, though . . ." slowly nodding his head knowingly.

Jamie backed away, then turned and hustled out the door, yelling over his shoulder, "You better watch yourselves, *fat boys!*"

A grinning Matt shook his head, turned and high-fived with Tim. Jo hugged Matt, "Oh, look at you two tough guys. Thanks though. He's a pest."

"S'alright. That's what friends are for, ain't they, Wolf?" Tim's serious face eased into a broad smile as he nodded his agreement. "Alright, see you, Jo. You too, Nancilee."

As the girls walked to the bus, Jo explained, "Most people see Wolf and Lion the same way Jamie does: a couple of big, quiet weirdos. I guess they seem weirder because they're usually so quiet. Funny thing is, they're the sweetest guys if you just talk to them. I got to know them at lunch in sixth grade: two chubby kids that didn't have many friends. I think I was taller than both of them then. Anyway, Matt—that's Lion—knew Will in fourth or fifth grade and started sitting with us. Sometime after that, Timmy came along—he used to be called Timmy, now it's just Tim or Wolf. The two of them got along, I guess because they were both chubby, but they've been buddies ever since. Last year, both of them just *grew*. All of a sudden after the seventh grade they turn into these six-foot-tall, gentle giants. They started goofing around and challenging each other with arm wrestling, and push-ups, and stuff like that. That led to weightlifting, and the next thing you know . . . Wolf and Lion, these giant eighth graders. Most people don't realize they're not really fat under those baggy clothes, and they don't really want people to know. They just want people to leave them alone, and they're kind of touchy about bullies."

"They seem nice to me," Nancilee said. "And I'm sure glad they were there. I thought I was done being around that Jamie Faison."

"Like Lion said, 'That's what friends are for.'"

A few minutes later on the bus, Nancilee asked Jo, "How do you do that? How do you always know what to say or how to make stuff like the hurtful things Jamie said seem like no big deal?"

Jo shrugged and looked into the distance, "Oh, my mom. I remember her telling me things like that all the time. I can still hear her voice saying, 'Don't pay attention to what other people think or how they want you to live your life. You know who loves you, love them back. Find the goodness and love in other people. Most people have it. And the ones who just don't, well, feel bad for them, but don't let them make you feel bad about yourself. Be you. Be love. Be happy.'" Jo looked back at Nancilee with a smile, "I mean, my dad too, but it's like I have my mom in my head. So that's how."

The bus door creaked closed and the engine revved to pull away as Nancilee said, "Cool. Your mom sounds like you." Neither girl noticed Jo's grandmother smiling and the tear rolling down her face as she pulled the bus away for the ride home.

• • •

Margo was still churning along with her malicious grand plan. In every college board exam session, she was still changing 15 percent of the answers on the top fifty students' answer sheets. By the spring of 2010 she had finally increased the target size in the state literacy tests to one hundred students—half of every class—and 25 percent of their answers. This effort now took four to five hours after most tests and seven hours for the ACT. As much work as it was, she never tired of it, and she relished each new test day as another meaningful step along her way. And as she had from the beginning, after each test day Margo would come home in uncharacteristically good spirits, having taken some next mean step. Ed would then get his hopes up, *Maybe this time, maybe she's coming back from all of this*, only to have things go back to their normal dreary and solitary lifestyle within a day or two. And each time, he'd lose a little more hope and sink a little more into the personal darkness of his lonely life.

Ed still found his own sense of purpose, if not refuge, in what had become his electronics workshop in the garage. His years of experimenting and customizing old Apple 1 and Apple IIe computers had prepared him well for the rapid improvements that were now becoming possible. Years earlier in 2000, as Margo was just starting her project at school, Ed bought a barely used iMac from another teacher's husband who had decided he needed something a little more powerful. This crazy-looking, bright-blue computer had one-upped the industry again, and, most importantly for Ed, these new machines were loaded with internal gadgets, including a built-in network card and Wi-Fi antenna. Added to his existing menagerie of older Franken-computers, he then had several years of experimenting with surplus networking gear, both to connect the older computers to the new one and to try different upgrade schemes on the iMac.

He still had no real goal in mind; ideas and what-ifs would come to him, and he'd start with some new modification that he thought would enable each computer to exceed its design specifications—more memory, faster processors, additional hard drives, faster communication, and more. His hobby became more complicated when he ran across limitations in the computer's operating system and software. Since he had nothing but time, he picked up some books and started dabbling with his own code that would allow him to work around each limitation that got in his way.

By 2007, after much trial and error, Ed had become quite adept both in dismantling and repairing the hardware and in creating software patches to push his creations along, and he had added two more newer-model iMacs to his collection. When the iPhone came out that year, he was not initially interested; after all, who was he going to call? But a year later, Apple got his attention by opening an online store to buy applications. He realized, belatedly, *These darn things really are like miniature iMacs, not just cell phones. They have processors, storage, and Wi-Fi! Oh, the things I could do with them if they just weren't so expensive!* Ed's mind was reeling as he considered the possibilities of connecting these new devices to his crazy network of gadgets at home.

Fortunately, rich high school kids were there for him, and he was able to buy broken iPhones for $10 to $20 from kids whose parents simply bought them new phones as quickly as they broke them. After buying several, he had enough parts to reassemble a fully functional iPhone. In less than a year, he had a steady side business repairing iPhones for kids at school and jailbreaking them for other kids who wanted to install unauthorized software. Both efforts helped pay for his hobby. As he had with computers, Ed started experimenting with the iPhones, creating Franken-phones like his Franken-computers and learning to write his own code to run on the phones. His projects then became more complex as he experimented with different methods to send data between devices and to control different devices from a Mac or iPhone on his network. Some worked, some didn't, and occasionally some device didn't survive the experiment. But by 2010, all of his tinkering had resulted in Ed becoming a true and self-taught guru in customizing computer and smartphone hardware and software, and there weren't many ideas he couldn't make work when he set his mind to them.

One evening in April 2010, after months of failures, Ed managed to move files from one of his Macs to an iPhone and then to another Mac, all controlled by another iPhone and using his own custom applications to manage the data transfers across the other devices. Elated, he stood up and congratulated himself, "Yes, now we're talking! Who's the man?!"

Happier than he had been in some time after that success, he walked into the kitchen to grab dinner and found Margo already there. She smiled and said cheerily, "Just in time. Pick out what you want, and I'll heat 'em up."

Grabbing a frozen dinner, Ed glanced at her guardedly and thought, *Hmm, looks like this was one of her good days. Wonder how long this one will last?*

It had certainly been a good day already for Margo. She had wrapped up another school year of standardized test changes the day before,

which was always good for a warm feeling of accomplishment for a day or two. But this day was different. After everyone else had left for the day, Edgar Clanton stopped at her desk on his way out and pulled up a chair. The principal looked tired and sounded worse, speaking in a low, hoarse voice, "Margo, you ever have one of those days when you just don't know what's going on anymore? Things you thought you had all figured out that don't work the way they should—the way they always have?"

She looked at him with wide eyes, "Uh, sure. It happens to all of us sometime or another."

"Well, mine is now. Actually, it's been the last few years." Mr. Clanton looked around the office like he was seeing it for the first time, then went on, "Something's been going on with our test performance." Margo rocked back in her chair and took a breath. "No, no, it's not you. The administrative stuff is all good. It's the only thing that is, actually. Of course *you're* getting it all done. But the district has been following a trend in our state exam scores. Small town like this, our scores were never going to be the highest, but they're going down and have been for a few years. It's hard to tell when it started, but it's really clear when you look at the last few years. *Something's* going on, and it ain't good."

"The superintendent's been breathing down my neck about it for almost three years, but darned if I can figure out what we're doing wrong. When we look at grades for the same years, they don't show the same trend. The kids that came in with good grades are still getting them, just not on the state tests. If that wasn't bad enough, we've done some looking and found a similar trend in SAT and ACT results. Did you know that in the last three years we haven't had a single student qualify for a top-tier school and not a single merit-based scholarship?"

Margo shook her head. Not really expecting an answer, Mr. Clanton continued, "Oh, Dr. Williams did. That's how *I* found out, and let me tell you, *that* was not a fun conversation." He sighed and looked down at his hands, "Crazy thing is, it's just like the state tests. The kids we'd expect to do well are still making good grades, but it isn't reflected in those college board exam results. I'll be damned if I know what to do with that! Have we all of a sudden forgotten how to teach?!"

It took all of Margo's concentration to keep an empathetic expression pasted on her face. All the while she could almost her own voice screaming in her head, *You mean it's working?!* Instead, she said in as soothing a voice she could muster, "I'm sure you and the superintendent will figure something out. It would be terrible to let the kids down and all."

He looked up at her with sad and pained eyes and said, "Yeah, I guess that is what I'm doing . . . letting them down." He looked away again, "I've had a lot of meetings with the department heads, and they're just as clueless as I am. We'd better get on with figuring that 'something' out though."

He turned to her again, "Aw listen to me. Sorry for the cheery talk at the end of the day. Forget about it. Go home to your happy life. I'll see you tomorrow." He patted her desk and stood up like he could hardly carry his own weight, then he walked slowly out.

Margo sat quietly at her desk, staring at the door after he walked out. She was stunned by his news and still trying to process it all. *I guess it has been ten years since I started this craziness! Whoa! Really, no scholarships or top colleges?! A serious schoolwide downturn in the state tests?!* She had been so focused on each incremental step of her plan and not raising suspicions, that she hadn't done any kind of reckoning on the total number of students she'd affected nor the overall efficacy of the entire campaign. Had she kept up with her "body count" since 1999, she'd have realized that she had lowered the SAT and ACT scores for more than 350 Grayton students and the state tests for over 500, and she was adding 100 to the total from each new freshman class every year. By targeting the top half in every exam, she had quite literally eliminated the "A team." Although making A's in their classes, by every outside and standardized measure there were no longer any top percentile performers; some 350 kids who did not get a shot at one of the big-league colleges, many of whom lost the courage to try college anywhere.

Driving home, it was all Margo could think about, *Some days there really is justice! Thank God it wasn't all a waste of time!*

It was Margo's afterglow from this news and the accompanying twisted self-affirmation that Ed had walked into that evening after his successful electronics and networking project. The two of them were eating dinner quietly, both lost in their own happy thoughts and ignoring the reporter droning away on the evening news. Margo's ears perked up when she heard:

> Scientists in the US and in Mexico continued to be alarmed and puzzled by the decade-long decline of the monarch butterfly. Dr. Sam Waterston leads a renowned team of experts at UC Santa Cruz who have been studying this crisis since it began in the late '90s. Here he is on location in the mountains of Central Mexico just this week:
>
> "We still don't know what is causing the annual decline. But when we review the data, we can see evidence of the phenomenon as early as the mid-1990s. Then there was a well-known spike in their total numbers in 1997 and 1998. This only got worse in the years that followed. The winter die-off last year was the worse we've seen by far. They bounced

> back this year, but we don't really know how or how long they can keep coming back.
>
> "To give you an idea for how little we know, we're now losing more of these critical pollinators than we knew *even existed* twenty years ago. We worry now about what this means to the monarch as a species, not to mention all of the species that depend on them throughout the continent.
>
> "Although we have theories about the causes, we're really no closer to definitively identifying the real culprits today than when this started. But we're looking. We know we have to solve this riddle and help these little creatures."

Margo smirked and said out loud in a mocking tone, "Oh, what could *possibly* be happening? Gee, what if they never figure it out?" She started laughing and then progressed to near hysteria, finally turning away from the table to catch her breath.

When she turned back, she saw Ed looking at her with an expression that was somewhere between, "That ain't that funny," and "I think you have a screw loose!" She picked up her fork and said, "What?"

"Nothing. I guess you can laugh at whatever misery you like," and he focused on his frozen dinner.

She shrugged, "It just tickles me, I guess." She rolled her eyes in exaggerated concern and waved her hands, "I mean, 'Oh *noooooo*, there's something going on that we don't understand!'" She started howling again as she waved her hands in mock concern, "How will anyone ever catch the 'culprit'?! Oh, what could be causing it, and how do we think it could end?"

That thought stopped her laughing, and Ed found her satisfied expression more disturbing than the weird laughing.

Six weeks later, the week after school was out for the summer, Edgar Clanton cleaned out his office. Instead of moving up to serve as an executive in the school district as he had hoped, he had been "encouraged to retire in honor of his years of service" rather than face the action the superintendent would otherwise take in light of his failure to lead the school successfully.

Chapter 11

PREPARING THE FIELD

Dark storms sometimes veiled unseen malice.

The week before school started in August 2010, Margo was in the Grayton High School cafeteria for a welcome-back faculty meeting, trying not to look bored. She had been brought up to speed the week before and now sat at a computer on the left edge of the low stage, waiting to click through some presentation slides. The teachers and staff were spread around the room, sitting sullenly at the lunch tables. Having heard rumors about Mr. Clanton's departure on the heels of disturbing results in student testing, they were waiting for whatever bad news was sure to come and looked every bit like a group of kids in detention waiting for the details of their punishment.

A surprised murmur and the sounds of chairs scooting on the tile floor filled the room when the school district superintendent stepped out from behind the closed curtain and onto the stage. He waited for

them to settle down then said, "For those who don't know me, I'm Steve Williams, Orange ISD Superintendent. I thought it best for you to hear this from me, and to give me a chance to reassure you that the district believes in this faculty and in this school."

He paused to provide an opportunity for grateful applause but heard only silence as the teachers waited for the real point of his appearance. He scanned the room looking for any positive response, grimaced slightly, then sighed and continued, "But we have to face the tough reality: Grayton High School has some real performance issues, and when I say that, I mean that the data suggests we may be failing our students somehow."

The murmuring started again and got louder and more agitated. From the back of the room, a voice sounding very much like Coach Jackson stood out, "And it's the faculty's fault, right?!"

Dr. Williams, looking even more pensive, shook his head and raised a hand to quiet them down, "Alright now, just hang on! I know no one wants to hear this. Believe me, I don't like saying it, but we'll share some data with you in a few minutes to help you understand. Before we get to that, let me just assure you all of the seriousness of this concern. We've been watching this for some time at the district and had worked with your principal and his staff for a couple of years to better understand and do something to turn the trends around. Not only has the problem gotten worse, but now the state Board of Education has become concerned. It's now up to us to take some additional action before the state takes it off our hands, and we'll have to live with whatever we're given. None of us want that.

"So, the first step was a change in leadership. Now, Edgar Clanton is an old friend of mine, so this isn't any kind of an indictment of him or his decades of service. He's done great work here, but he was out of ideas, and he knew it. And since our first priority has to be our students, we needed to bring someone in who had experience in exactly this kind of situation. For that, we've turned to a real rock star, Dr. Theodore Markus, your new principal." Dr. Williams pointed to the side of the stage and waved, "Come on out here, Dr. Markus."

Out walked a younger man than most expected, dressed rather formally in coat and tie. Although in his mid-forties, genetics and a near-obsession with running had served him well, and he looked more like a new teacher than a hotshot principal. He waved and nodded to the silent and serious-looking faculty as Dr. Williams finished his introduction, "We're lucky to have landed Theo. For starters, his doctoral internships and thesis focused on leveraging successful charter school practices in public schools to improve student outcomes. He then worked for several years in charter school settings in Washington, DC, and in Arizona, and he comes highly recommended for the exact challenge Grayton High School now faces. With that, I turn your team over to you, Dr. Markus. Everyone please give him a warm welcome."

Dr. Williams shook the principal's hand and walked off the stage to sit at a table near the stage. Dr. Markus stood at center stage, put his hands on his hips and smiled as he looked around the room, listening to scattered, half-hearted applause. "Yeah, well, thanks, all of you for being here, and thanks, Dr. Williams. I'm excited to join the team and help turn some things around. I want you to know that I want what you want: for Grayton's students to reflect your great work in their outcomes, and for those outcomes to open doors for them. That's what brought me into the field. And I know that all of you have to really want to be here and do this work while also putting up with everything that can get in your way year after year, from parents to some of the more challenging kids, and state and federal rules that seem to exist only to make your jobs more difficult than they already are."

"Yeah, I get it. And if it wasn't for the big bucks, you'd have moved on from teaching long ago." He looked around the room expectantly, but there were only one or two muffled, half-hearted laughs. Most of the audience looked uninterested, and they were fading fast.

"Look, this doesn't feel like a fun time to you. I get that too. And now I come along from God-knows-where to tell you how to do your jobs. Before you tune out though, I ask you all to indulge me for the next hour or two. Let's see if we can't all get on the same page for what kind of problem it is that we're trying to solve. You'll then get your chance to conclude if I'm able to help solve it. All I can say is, I've studied and been part of programs that had much tougher problems, including community and family factors that made them appear impossible to change, but things did change. And they improved beyond our wildest dreams and anyone's reasonable expectations. When this happens, it's never some crazy new educational theory. It's always after tough and sober review of the problems and a willingness to be accountable—us, the students, and their families."

"Let's take this a step at a time. Each of you will have a packet waiting for you on your desk when we finish this morning. It will include summaries of everything we're going to talk about, including some case studies of other programs for comparison. For now, though, let me take you through some things. Margo, let's switch it on, please." For the next two hours, Margo advanced through a presentation on a computer as Dr. Markus described the increasingly poor test scores across all year groups at Grayton High School, which stood in contrast to the students' grades in regular school curriculum.

Page after page of grades and test scores for every year group painted the picture that Mr. Clanton had described only briefly in May. It was clear to see that something wasn't working the way it should, and it had been getting worse for years. The last ten years of data reflected the expected "bell curves" for classroom grades in every year group—with the majority falling in the B and C range, a respectable number with A averages, and not as many in the D and F range. The same ten years also showed similarly normal bell curves for the state and college board exam scores in the first few years, but by 2006 a slight shift to the left is evident in the data as the top scores began falling into the equivalent of the B and C range with many fewer top scores. By 2008, the trend in the data was more pronounced; and regardless of how strongly the faculty felt about their teaching and what their students' class grades showed, standardized test results showed that Grayton High School was not preparing their students adequately to score well in literacy tests or to gain acceptance to the best schools, including the students with the highest A-averages.

This had gone from curious to crisis in 2009 when Grayton High fell from the state's second-highest rating of "recognized" to "academically acceptable," which was only one level above a failing rating of "academically unacceptable - low-performing campus." As a result, the entire district was now at risk of also being downgraded from "recognized," thus garnering the concern and attention of officials in the district and state hierarchies.

Dr. Markus wrapped up the data and shifted into his action plan, "Like I said, we're going to take this one step at a time, with all the focus on student outcomes. Some of the changes we're going to make will take effect across all four grade levels, but there will be an increased focus on incoming ninth graders, with a goal to replicate some charter school approaches for this class throughout their Grayton experience, and do the same for each next class. The goal over the next four years will be to see a complete reversal in the data we've just been through, and then push our student performance even higher.

"Dr. Williams has worked with the district and state to add faculty, which we'll need for the revised curriculum and study teaming we're going to shift to. We've also brought in two interim assistant principals who will help us for the first year, and then take some of the changes to both of Grayton's middle schools. You'll meet them when we finish."

This was met with rapid chatter throughout the room, and the teachers were again rustling in their seats. When Dr. Markus was presenting the historical data, the faculty's demeanor had appeared to shift from distrust to concern; but as he described the curriculum and teaching style changes they would be expected to implement, the faculty again became pensive and distrustful. If they had been watching Margo, they would have noticed a different emotional evolution. The more Dr. Markus illustrated the problem with his facts and figures, the more relaxed and even happy Margo became. Looking at the angry teachers' faces scattered around the room as they listened to this outsider full of ideas who was going to change everything about how they did their jobs, she couldn't help but smile, tuning out most of the dialogue and reveling in an almost overpowering sense of affirmation.

As the new principal explained the first steps he had in mind for them to solve the problem—shifting faculty around; revised and mandated curriculum focused on reading, writing, and math; eliminating extracurricular activity during school hours; standardized dress; and more like it to come—Margo stifled a laugh and thought, *That's it, pull out all the stops, Dr. Smart Guy! Rub the faculty's noses in what they've let happen. I have a funny feeling it won't help, and it may even hurt. It sure doesn't look like it's going to be good for morale!*

• • •

With Jo now in the ninth grade and Nancilee in the eighth, they were separated for school again and weren't able to ride the bus together to Jo's house every day. Although this disrupted their grand strategy from the previous two years, it wasn't as bad as they'd feared. Nancilee met some younger friends of Jo's "misfit" lunch group. They formed their own eighth grade lunch group, and a few of them were in some of Nancilee's classes, which helped make up for Jo's absence during the day. After school, she still rode Jo's gramma's bus to Jo's house, where they studied together and caught up on their days for an hour or two until it was time to ride home with Mark.

From time to time, Nancilee ran across Jamie Faison and his pack of hoodlum wannabes in the hallways or the cafeteria. When she didn't see them soon enough to avoid them, she had to put up with more "Nanci-loser" razzing. She'd duck her head and plow past without engaging with them, but despite her best efforts to not let them get to her, she often had to wipe tears from her eyes before she walked into her next class. As she did, she'd imagine Jo's concerned face and Nancilee would think, *I know, I know. They don't matter, and I shouldn't let them get to me. I can't help it sometimes though. I'm working on it!* That was always enough to put a smile on her face. Fortunately, given Jamie's poor efforts in school, Nancilee did not have to worry about spending time in any classes with him, as she was still following in Jo's footsteps into classes he couldn't have gotten into now even if he had aspired to.

Jo's group of misfit and nonconformist friends were with her at Grayton High School, and many who weren't in her classes were again in her lunch group, including Will, Rennie, Wolf, and Lion. The other thing that followed her to high school was that she was still not accepted by the in-crowd. Like her friends, Jo was still not cool enough, and the girls who knew her in middle school made comments like, "Look at her. She doesn't even try to look pretty for the boys. What is it with her?" Also like in middle school, Jo couldn't bring herself to care about things like that, preferring instead the company of her uncool and unpretentious friends.

Jo's first few weeks in school were a little confused, in part because she had moved up to high school and advanced classes, but also because the faculty had not yet come to terms with their new curriculum and a new study-group approach. Although this subject had not been discussed with the students, rumors were rampant that all of the changes were related to educational problems at the school, and it was Jo's class that would be the first guinea pigs as the teachers tried to turn things around. Not knowing what else to expect in high school anyway, Jo took it all in stride, completed all of her assignments, and had faith that the confusion would work itself out. In contrast to her calm, her teachers often seemed exasperated with what they were supposed to do next and not understanding what was wrong with the way they had taught for as long as they could remember.

In October, two months into the school year, Jo was sitting between a bored Tim Wolf and Matt Lyons in the crowded gymnasium bleachers for an assembly with the rest of the school during the last period of the day. The new principal had arranged a series of lectures from professors at local junior colleges and from Lamar University for what he called "Big Ideas by Big Thinkers." He had explained that the lectures were intended to stimulate an interest in learning among the student body by showing how their high school learning connected to the real world. If not all of the student body made that connection, the lectures definitely succeeded in stimulating interest in sitting in the gym instead of in class.

Today's speaker was Dr. Tom Baker, Professor of Ecology and Biology from Orange Junior College. After the lights were turned down, he talked his way through a long series of graphs and pictures as he described evolution, species interdependence, the life of monarch butterflies, and a growing concern that monarchs were a critical but threatened species at great risk of becoming extinct. Jo found everything the professor showed them interesting, but she was intrigued when she heard him say:

> . . . it isn't likely we can do much to protect any particular species forever. But we can definitely hasten their demise. Man-made pressures contribute to the environment change that affect species around the world, including our friend the monarch. Whether it's our contribution to climate change, habitat destruction, or simply making the environment more hostile through our use of pesticides and herbicides, people have increased pressure on this wondrous and fragile species.
>
> How terrible—and terribly easy—it would be, with just the "right" carelessness, to hasten their extinction.
>
> And when the last butterfly is gone, with it go all of their contributions in the world, the wondrous and enriching uniqueness they are in creation, and the simple joy of their existence.

As she listened, Jo's mind jumped from one profound observation to the next: that all life on our planet is fragile and fleeting; that not only *can we* make it worse, but *we do*, and sometimes *on purpose*; and the world loses in ways we may not understand for each loss. She sat back and bowed her head slightly. Although still listening to Dr. Baker, her own thoughts were running away. *"Right" carelessness? How is that ever "right"? Why would we do it if we knew what we were doing? Oh, that's the thing, isn't it? We don't always know when our carelessness hurts someone or something. Maybe we can't even always know when some things we do are careless. Whoa!*

Her face became more serious with that thought, and then she could almost hear mom's voice in her head: *But . . . we can care, Jo-Jo. If we try to always care, then maybe we'll cause fewer careless hurts, maybe the "right" carelessnesses then are the hurtful ones we avoid or catch before it's too late, and we undo the hurt.*

Jo felt an elbow jab her left arm and looked up to see Matt's concerned face, "Jo, whatsa matter? Are you into butterflies or something?" Matt looked over her head, and she followed his gaze to see Tim watching her from her other side with the same concern.

As she watched her friends watching her, she realized she had a tear running down her face. She chuckled and said, "No, I'm good. Just thinking about my mom." She wiped her cheek and thought, *Yes, I still hear you, Mom.* She then hooked arms with her big escorts and leaned into Matt with a lighthearted nudge. She looked up at him with a reassuring smile and turned her attention back to the professor as the door across the gym from her opened, briefly casting a bright beam of light across the darkened gym floor until it swung closed with a heavy metallic thunk after someone walked out.

• • •

Standing across the gym from Jo and listening to the lecture, Ed had heard enough and left early to beat the mob of students who would soon be making their way towards the buses and their carpools. He was distracted as he walked back to the main building, squinting in the bright sunlight as his mind raced. *Oh yeah, Mr. Professor, you're right! It does sound like it would be terribly easy to finish the job if someone really wanted to. So many ways to skin the cat though, which ones would work best? Oh yeah, that's the important question: How to get the most bang for the butterfly-buck?*

That made him laugh out loud and say to no one as he reached for the door to go inside, "Nothing personal, butterflies. I just like a good challenge. Besides, it was his idea, not mine, and I'm just *thinking*. It ain't like I'm going to *do* it!" Instead of going back to his shop down the hall, Ed stayed just inside the front doors, pointlessly sweeping the same few feet of the tile floor while he watched the visitors' parking spots through the windows.

Fifteen minutes later, the students crowded giddily down the sidewalk like they had been paroled from prison. As the kids piled into their parents' cars, somber-looking teachers straggled into the building and passed Ed without a glance. It was another fifteen minutes before he saw the professor step off the sidewalk towards the parking lot. He leaned his broom against the corner beside one of the doors and rushed out to head off the visitor. Ed caught up with him as the professor opened the back door of his car and set a worn leather satchel on the back seat, "Say, Professor, would it be okay if I asked you a few questions about your lecture? I found it fascinating, and I want to make sure I understand it all."

Dr. Baker looked surprised and then grinned, "Well sure, that's fine with me. I'm glad you liked it. Ask me whatever you like. And call me Tom, the professor thing is for students."

"Great, thanks. So, anyway, what I've been thinking about is what I think you called 'the right carelessness.' There's all those different ways monarch butterflies are at risk, but surely some are worse than others—or at least some man-made causes have worse effects on them overall, right? Like pesticides, maybe?"

"Well, we're pretty sure they all contribute, but we're not sure how much any one cause is hurting monarchs. Take pesticides, for example, neonicotinoids being just one type that is a concern for butterflies and honeybees both. Now, we know that these are extremely dangerous for the monarchs when they're exposed to them, and deadly in high enough concentrations, of course. But we also know that the entire population isn't exposed to those high concentrations, or none of them would make it back to Mexico for winter to start the next year's cycle. They'd all just be gone. One obvious reason that doesn't happen is the huge area all of the monarchs spread out through during their migration. They don't just go to one area or follow just a few paths; they fly throughout North America, all the way into Canada through countless routes. Because of that, some are lucky enough to not get sprayed, others aren't so lucky.

"So, whether it's pesticides that kill them directly, or the use of herbicides that kill milkweed in gardens depriving monarchs of their food, or other climate-related or man-made changes to the environment, every year it's kind of a mixed bag of some or all of these challenges that affect every one of them as they travel through North America during their short lives. And the challenges stack up such that it's the combination of all of these threats that take the toll on the population as a whole, but many monarchs still make it back to Mexico every year. That way, so far at least, the species lives to fight another day.

"What we do know though, is that just in the last two years, the total area of the monarchs' home in Central Mexico has shrunk by two-thirds, down to a total of less than five acres providing the winter home to pretty much the entire species! Think about that."

Ed was nodding slowly with a slight smile, "No, I see what you mean. And that very small area is key, isn't it? I mean, if all of the ones that survive have to be on that patch of ground for the winter, then *that's* where 'the right carelessness' could really hurt them—like game over."

Dr. Baker nodded, "You're absolutely right. That's ground zero for the monarch. Again, whether it's climate-related impacts to the habitat, or something we do there, like logging or causing forest fires—hoo boy, the list just goes on and on for how we could wreak havoc on them. That's why we can't just leave it all up to chance, and there are a number of studies looking into that very thing."

Ed looked surprised, "Are there now? I was thinking about that myself after hearing your lecture."

Dr. Baker nodded again, "Let me grab some data sheets and a pamphlet out of my bag for you. They have some good summary information and even some websites you can check out if you want to learn more." He reached into the car, thumbed through a stack of paper in the leather bag and handed several to Ed, "Here you go, my email and phone number are on the data sheets. Reach out anytime if you have more questions. Happy to answer what I can."

Ed took the papers and was beaming, "Well thanks, Professor Tom. I'll definitely do my homework with these. I'll have a real head start thinking all of this through now."

"It's my pleasure, Ed, really. I always like helping interested students, and it does me some good to know that I gave you something to think about. Good talking with you, Ed." Dr. Baker shook Ed's hand and got into his car. Ed watched the professor drive away then walked happily into the building to put his broom away and lock up for the night.

Driving home, he thought about the different strategies one could use in unleashing the "right carelessness" on the monarch's winter home. Like Jo, he was intrigued by the picture Dr. Baker had painted for him. Ed grinned still as he played back their conversation and the lecture, and as he thought about how easy it would be to be do something so monumental, even if it was pointless. As he drove and the closer he came to home, his amused sense of intrigue slowly gave way to dark resolve. Unlike Jo, the inner voice in Ed's head that came to him along with the professor's wasn't Jodie's, it was Carl and Margo, just as it had been for a very long and lonely time. He could no longer remember who said what, but he could hear their voices in all of it, *Because that's just how it is. We get what we can get, when we can get it, and we wait for life to take it all. There is no happy ending. There is no justice, no meaning, no reward for goodness. There is just this life until there isn't.*

He could almost hear Margo whispering in his ear, *Nothing really matters.*

• • •

Margo now had all kinds of extra eyes lurking around the office every day, between the state and district visitors and Dr. Markus's new staff, all looking for any facet of their daily routine that needed to change. She was constantly answering questions about student records, class assignments, and her process for managing all of the standardized tests. But as relentlessly curious as they all were, even though this was the first test week of the year, for whatever reason, so far they hadn't shown any interest in watching her package the tests up at the end of each day. Sitting in her kitchen at home, she thought with a wry smile, *I guess they figure whatever the problem is, it can't be me. Who cheats to lower scores?* Still, she was being very careful not to get sloppy and leave anything unsecured, especially her cabinet and the chute where it was all tucked away.

When Ed walked in from work, he looked like a man on a mission and walked past Margo with barely a nod and a mumbled hello. After he went into the garage and closed the door, she said to herself with a shake of her head, "I wonder what's up his craw?" She didn't dwell on it long, though, and went right back to brooding about her own problems. She ate dinner and watched television alone for the rest of the night.

Ed sat down at his computer and went to work trying to learn more about the scope of his puzzle: What what were the best ways to skin this cat if someone actually took it on? He was amazed at the things he could find on the internet about lethal compounds and ways to ignite fires. Some were more complex than others, but not only was there plenty of information available to formulate plans, a surprising majority of the materials could be bought online and delivered right to the house! *No wonder terrorists are able to figure this stuff out, it's all out there for anyone and everyone!*

He spent the next several weeks scouring the web for more detailed information about his candidate materials, which would be most effective, and what it would take to use each one. Ed learned right away that there was no use pursuing any homemade pesticides or herbicides; they all required complicated chemical processing and sounded terrifying to have around. *And why bother? Someone else has already made them. If I go that route, I just need to spray them over the butterflies' winter home, but boy that'd be a ton of stuff to cart in and spray. It'd be a tricky one to make work, except maybe by plane, and even then I'm not sure you could saturate the whole area enough. Besides, there's so many places for the little buggers to hide from it, even just under leaves, branches, and rocks.*

Ed filed the chemical ideas away in the back of his head as something to consider revisiting later, and he went back to the other obvious threat, *Fire. Now that's a-whole-nuther beasty. If you did it right, it's the gift that just keeps giving, spreading all around, wiping out both bug and habitat. If you miss some spot, it'll spread anyway. Now think, boy, there's got to be easy ways to start fires in the woods.*

Not wanting to reinvent the wheel, Ed searched next for information about explosives, firebombs, and incendiary grenades that were made for and used by the military, since they seemed the obvious major users for such things. Right away, white phosphorous stood out as a prime fire starter, with the wonderful trait that once ignited it kept right on burning and igniting everything it touched. Known as Willie Pete to the military, he found several recipes for producing it at home, all of which were almost as complicated as refining his own pesticides would have been. The combination of this complexity, the relatively high quantity he'd need to produce and then handle while building whatever devices he came up with—*without* blowing himself up at every step—all led him to backburner Willie Pete, just as he had the chemicals.

Then Ed came across thermite, another interesting fire starter used in military incendiaries. Unlike chemicals and Willie Pete, thermite was not dangerous to handle until it was ignited, and it wasn't difficult to make in bulk. However, it was safe to handle because it was also damned difficult to ignite. The more he read, the more he liked it. *If I could come up with some kind of reliable igniter though, this stuff would be perfect. Once it's lit, it burns until it's gone, even underwater, and it can burn its way through most metals! Better yet, this stuff is sold for fireworks, and I can buy as much of it as I want. Oh yeah, this stuff is the ticket!*

Just in time for his Thanksgiving holiday and thanks to an online fireworks supply store, Ed received two build-your-own firework kits that came with everything he needed to mix eight pounds of red iron oxide thermite and a box of sparklers to use for fuses. The directions were simpler than making cookies: He sifted the iron oxide and some aluminum powder together, packed it into some casings he made from cardboard wrapping paper tubes wrapped with duct tape, and capped the ends with more duct tape. He cut the sparklers into two-inch sections, which he jammed through one end of each of his "fireworks."

For his first test, he started with only three tubes of thermite, each a different length. *No need to rush this thing. I better make sure I can light this stuff at all and get an idea for how long it burns. Then we'll see where we go from there. Should be a neat show anyway.*

Not wanting to burn the house down, Ed created a test area in the middle of the backyard. It was a four-by-four-foot square with a simple low wall on all sides that he made by stacking two rows of cinderblocks. He put another cinderblock in the center to lay across his first "firework," just to make sure the crazy thing didn't take flight when it lit. Ed lit the sparkler with a long butane lighter and stepped back halfway to the house to watch with an expectant grin. He wasn't disappointed; five seconds later the sparkler had burned into the tube, and the center of his low burn pad burst into a two-foot-diameter white ball of light and fire that burned for less than a minute. It was like looking into the sun, and the intensity made him flinch, clench his eyes shut, and shake his head to clear the starbursts etched onto his retinas. He repeated the experiment with his other two small improvised fireworks, but this time with sunglasses he retrieved from his truck.

After the third test, Ed stood beside the firepit mulling over the results. *Well that was cool. Now what? Well, clearly, I need to figure out how to sustain the burn as long as I can to make sure it has time to light the surrounding area. So, is that long and thin, or is it more like a big bucket or ball? Guess I better plan this out. Looks like it's going to be a fireworks kinda year. This oughta be fun.* He chuckled and went back into the house.

Margo, who had seen the first flash and watched through the window for Ed's next two tries, now watched him walk by and head towards his shop with his serious "project-in-progress" look, something she hadn't seen in a while. *Who knows what he's up to now? Long as it gives him something to do and he doesn't burn the place down.* Having made it through her fall testing series at school without incident, still managing to change a quarter of all the answers on the top half of all students, Margo was looking forward to some quiet time. So, she was happy for him to have a project to keep himself busy.

In an irony that was lost on Ed and Margo, after ten years of scheming and executing her grand plan, Margo was no longer as excited

about her efforts to lower Grayton test scores, because she had hit her stride and was just turning the proverbial crank. The thrill of discovery and chasing the expanding idea was pretty well spent for her, whereas Ed was just getting going and still enjoying all the open and unsolved questions. That meant all kinds of possibilities for where his ideas would take him, and it was that pursuit that gave him some respite from his colorless routine and breathed new life into him.

• • •

The only really dark spot in Jo's first year of high school came just before Christmas when she saw her crazy-low scores on the state literacy tests—and it wasn't just her, several of her friends had the same wake-up call. After school she was still in shock and rushed into her dad's shop to show him her test results. After he flipped through them, he looked at her with an understanding smile and said, "Hey, you passed. Yeah, okay, you've done better before, but you are at a higher level now, kiddo. Besides, aren't you getting all A's still?"

Jo shook her head, "No, Dad, this stuff was all easy, basic stuff. I could have done well on these tests in *middle* school. And yeah, my grades *are* as good as ever. That just makes me not get it even more!"

"Well, just do what you always do. Get back on your studying thing, and you'll get the scores you want. Remember, you're half your mom, and she was the one with the brains in this outfit."

Jo sniffed and looked down, "I know. I just feel like I'm letting her and you down—and me too!"

Joe pulled his daughter into a hug, "Hey, it'll be fine. You've got a few years to go before it matters. And your mom's in there somewhere helping you. Between the two of you, you'll figure this out."

At the back of the shop, Mark was inspecting a set of cabinets to ensure they were ready for delivery. Like he had so many times over the last several years as he tried not to eavesdrop, he smiled to himself, listening to the young father and daughter. He took it on well-earned faith that Joe was right, Jo *would* figure it out, just like her mom would have. His thoughts were interrupted when he realized Jo had walked back to give him a hug and say, "Hey Mark, that looks good, as always!"

He beamed at her, and she bounced back the way she came on her way out. He brushed a sleeve quickly across his face to wipe a tear when Jo stood on her toes to kiss her dad's cheek as she left. Joe looked back at his partner with a mildly puzzled look, and Mark shrugged a smile at him and went back to work.

The 2010-2011 school year ended festively with a family party at Joe and Jo's house which, of course, included Mark, Jenny, Tina, and Nancilee, who had long since been part of the family. Although the occasion was officially about Nancilee's "graduation" from middle school, the girls were celebrating their reunion, first during the following summer, and then when Nancilee joined Jo at Grayton High School. The group was squeezed into two picnic tables that were pushed together and overflowing with food. The two girls sat across from each other in the middle, surrounded by the chattering and laughing adults.

Nancilee's mom, Tina, got up and stood behind Jenny and Mark. "Hey everyone, I have another little announcement. There's another super-achiever at the table with us." She leaned over Jenny's shoulder and kissed her on the cheek.

"No, don't do this. It's not a big deal," Jenny flushed.

"Sure it is. Well, most of you know that Mom's been taking some night and weekend classes for what seems like forever."

Jenny threw both hands up in feigned offense, "Hey, it's only been three years, and some of us who work for a living have to do things like this part-time!"

"Anyway . . . Mom wasn't going to tell anyone, but she has enough credits at Orange Junior College for an associate degree in management." Tina paused until the cheering eased up, then went on, "And I think I have her convinced to transfer to Lamar University to get a bachelor's degree!"

Dina and Jessie both jumped up to hug Jenny, with Dina gushing, "Oh, we're all so proud of you. You should be proud of yourself too, look at everything you've done for you and yours!"

Jenny looked sheepishly at Mark, who simply grinned and yelled, "Let's have a speech from the pretty college girl!"

She stood up and said, "I don't know what kind of college girl I am at forty-nine years old, but I guess I'm going to do this. Who needs to sleep? Anyway, I figure I have the time to give this a try now. I mean, what with the young-un able to do for herself mostly, not to mention all the time she spends with everyone around this table. And my company is willing to pay for the next part of the tuition as long as I pass every class, and after I graduate they're going to move me up to the next level of management training. In other words, this is the way to way-better pay, and all it takes is a few more years of classes. So, might as well, huh?"

She turned and cocked her head towards Jo and Nancilee with a smile, "I have to say, it was you two that got me thinking about this several years ago. I watched how you studied together and built each other up, and you made me think maybe I could do it too. So, thanks to you two hellions, here I go! I may even finish about the time little Miss Nancilee here gets out of high school."

There was loud cheering and clapping all around. Mark was still grinning and reached an arm around Jenny's waist to give her a firm hug. Dina nudged Jessie and nodded slyly toward Jenny's hand resting casually on Mark's shoulder while his arm hung easily still on her waist. The grandmothers shared a smile and looked down to see Tina turn a puzzled look from them to her mother and then to Mark. After a moment, Tina's eyes widened, and she quickly suppressed a smile. She looked down at the table, wondering if this was really nothing and heard Nancilee ask, "Mom, what's wrong?"

Tina wiped a tear from her eye, looked up, and answered, "Nothing at all, kid. It's just a happy day and a long time coming." Although she could see Nancilee was oblivious, Tina caught Jo looking from her to Mark and Jenny with the same sly smile that the grandmothers had shared. *Boy, nothing gets by you, does it, Jo?*

• • •

Ed had spent his Christmas break and spare time through the spring of 2011 experimenting for better ways to build his fire starters. Week after week he experimented with different shapes and sizes, mostly built out of an armload of cardboard shipping tubes that he bought at the office supply store in Orange. He filled long ones, short ones, fat ones and skinny ones. For good measure, Ed also filled and tested large Tupperware bowls full of thermite and three foot-long sections of PVC pipe.

His fireworks starter kits ran out before he had gotten very far, but by then Ed had a better idea for what he was doing and ordered 30-lb. bags of red iron oxide and 20-lb. bags of aluminum powder. *Man, it really is incredible what you can buy on the internet, and they bring it right to the house! Now I really can just roll my own. Who needs their little kits?* While he was waiting for his refill of thermite ingredients, he visited the fireworks stand out on Orangefield Road to bulk up on sparklers for test fuses.

All of his trial and error was zeroing-in on the design that would burn for the longest amount of time, therefore giving him the most bang for the buck and his devices the longest time possible to ignite whatever was around them. Ed would have loved nothing more than to spend all of his time in an endless series of experiments, but he had a backlog of student phones to repair or to jailbreak. Since the phone work paid for his experimenting in the first place, he could only work on his project a little at a time. By April he had finally burned enough different designs to have concluded what flare-makers already knew: Long and thin tubes of thick-walled cardboard gave him the longest burn time (even if the large bowls of thermite did produce much more impressive but much shorter duration blasts of light).

As he surveyed the sooty mess after his last test and wondered how long it would take the acrid funk to clear, he heard the back door creak open and looked back to see Margo glaring from the house. Ed shrugged and gave her a silent, *What?!*

Margo tilted her head to the side and raised her eyebrows like she was talking to one of the juvenile delinquents at school, "Really? You don't know what's on my mind? Your little fireworks hobby is all well and good until you burn the house down or have the fire marshal show up for doing whatever it is you're doing. And for God's sake, can you make it stink even more?" She didn't wait for an answer and had slammed the door closed before Ed could think of anything to say anyway.

"Boy, no scientific curiosity there," Ed laughed, looking into his blackened test-pit and seeing nothing but success.

That night, Ed had his feet up on his desk thinking through his test results. "Cool. I know what the thing needs to look like. Now how would you light 'em? You can't really stand around holding a lighter to a bunch of sparklers, now can you, Eddie Boy?"

That was no simple task since the stuff was notoriously difficult to light, which is why his fireworks kits used sparklers for igniters in the first place. But even lighting a sparkler could take many seconds, and it was more difficult outdoors with wind or rain. Once again, commercial fireworks and suppliers pointed the way to "electric matches," which are commonly used in large fireworks shows to remotely light large banks of rockets. After a little more web-searching, Ed had a pretty good idea how to create his own electric match using wooden match heads, some bare copper wire, and a lantern battery.

Ed gathered the materials more easily for this phase of his experimenting, since the only new parts he needed were a 6V battery and a large capacitor, the latter of which he picked up on a tip from an amateur fireworks buff's website. He already had all kinds of copper wire and matches in the bins above his workbench, and assembling the electric match couldn't have been easier. He wrapped a match head with the middle of a copper wire, attached both ends to the capacitor, then touched the leads from the capacitor to the battery terminals, and poof! The match head burst into flame. After he'd successfully lit half a dozen in a row, he thought, *Okay, now what? That still ain't hot enough to ignite thermite. I need another step.*

As he kept looking for information about thermite's ignition temperature, Ed ran across an explanation of different metals used to produce thermite, some with lower ignition temperatures than aluminum powder. And, yet again, web searches led him to another thermite mix as the basis for his igniter, this one using copper powder mixed with sulfur. Although this mixture burned at half the temperature of his red iron oxide and aluminum thermite, it was easily lit by a single match and burned much hotter even than his sparklers. *Eureka!*

Two weeks later he received ten pounds of copper powder and sulfur, mixed equal amounts, and then substituted them for the aluminum in his thermite mixture. Sure enough, when he held a match to a small tube of it in his test pit, it flashed instantly into bright life. He then

filled several cardboard tubes almost full of his original mix, then added a top layer of his copper-thermite starter, pressing one of his electric matches into the copper layer. He touched the leads from the electric match to his lantern battery and his fire starter flashed instantly, and after three seconds flashed more brightly to life as the copper ignited his core thermite charge. Ed slapped his leg and sat back in the grass with a grin. *Giddy up! Now we're talking! I could definitely do this, and it would be a piece of cake!*

However, once Ed had satisfied himself that he could build a workable incendiary from readily available materials, he lost interest in pursuing the idea any further. For him, it had always been about solving the basic problem—proving to himself that he could come up with something to start a fire if he chose to, and now he had. *The rest is just details. A little more tinkering here and there, and we could light however much fire we needed. Why bother with it anymore? It's not like I'm going to actually do it! May as well get back to fixing my box of smartphones. They ain't gonna fix themselves.*

And that is exactly what he spent his time doing for the rest of the summer—fixing phones and stepping back into the lonely rut that was his life.

• • •

Jo and Nancilee spent the summer back in their old routine, with most of their time together at either girl's home and several weekend trips to the trailer on Bolivar Beach with Joe. When school started in the fall, the two couldn't have been happier to be reunited in high school—as much as possible for two kids separated by a full grade level—and once again riding to Jo's house on her grandmother's bus at the end of every day. Even better, they now shared a lunch period, and not only could the two best friends eat together, but their group of friends merged easily. By October, their group of ninth and tenth grade "misfits" often filled as many as four tables in a corner of the school cafeteria. Life was simple and good.

Will Jackson, who Jo had first befriended at lunch in middle school, noticed Rennie's discomfort with their sometimes-boisterous bunch one day. He leaned over and said dramatically, "I'm not so sure we're comfortably ensconced with the losers and misfits anymore, kid. We can repair to quieter locales if you want."

Rennie smiled and looked sideways at Will, "Nah, it's all good. Long as I can just watch from the sidelines and don't have to participate, I'm cool. You know, I don't mind having peeps, *these* peeps anyway," she said, looking around the table with a relaxed smile. As she looked from face to face, she caught Jo's eye, who smiled back and waved from the far end of the table. That was enough for Rennie to blush, snap her gaze back to the table in front of her, and go back to minding her own business.

Nancilee settled happily into the same awareness as Rennie and Will. She felt at home at Grayton High School in a good group of friends who didn't mind her being herself. She had steadily grown confidence in the last several years and now thought nothing of taking difficult and advanced classes and looked forward to them. That included the occasional special project, like the large posterboard she painted of the periodic table for her science class during the Thanksgiving holiday. After telling Mark about it during Sunday dinner, she sighed, "Now I have to carry the big ol' thing on the bus tomorrow. That'll be a trick."

Mark shrugged, "Why bother with it? Ride with me. I have to go right by the school on my way to work anyway, and you can put that thing in the back seat of the truck instead of getting it messed up on the bus."

Tina, who was sitting next to Mark, elbowed him good naturedly, "One of these days the Davis girls are going to wear out their welcome with Uncle Mark."

He smiled across the table at Jenny, who smiled back when he answered, "I can't imagine that ever happening."

The next morning, Mark drove Nancilee and her posterboard to school, just like he said he would. She loved the change of pace from the bus and riding with Mark, which he sensed from the way she chattered all the way there. He drove along, not really paying much attention to what she said but loving the carefree tone of her voice. When they pulled up to the front of the school, Nancilee leaned over and hugged Mark before hopping out to grab her posterboard from the back seat. She nudged the door closed with her hip and started walking toward the large double doors. He paused to watch with a smile, then started pulling away as she stopped and turned, chirping loudly with a wave, "Bye, Uncle Mark. Thanks for the ride!"

She was so taken with the happy start to her day that she took no notice of the ominous-looking, black Dodge Challenger that pulled up a few car lengths behind them rumbling obnoxiously. Jamie Faison, who had been slouched down in the passenger seat and sullenly waiting to be dropped off, sat up and glared at her back as she walked inside.

His Uncle Teddy was almost as sullen, "Well, are you goin'? It's bad enough that your *actual* parents stick me with being your taxi. Don't make me wait all day."

"Yeah, I'm going, I'm going. That girl just bugs me." He shouted behind the rolled-up windows, "Nanci-loser! Oooh, bye Uncle Mark!"

As Jamie opened the door, Teddy watched the pickup pull away and did a double-take pointing with his thumb, "*That* guy? You think *he's* her Uncle Mark? Wrongo, punky dude, that's Mark Hammock. Man, I haven't seen him in a long time, but I'm pretty sure he ain't anyone's uncle. That guy hung out with my dad back in the day until he got some people killed in a big car wreck, and then he kinda drifted away. He was an old dude still hanging out at the pond when *I* was in school. Man, once a loser . . . Your old man and me had a run-in with him in those days, over some girl."

Teddy cocked his head and closed his eyes as old memories came back to him, then he grinned and said, "Oh man, I forgot all about *that*. The story that went around was that Hammock got this girl drunk and knocked her up. She was like tenth grade or something. All I remember is she was drunk as a skunk and coming on to me. But before we got very far, Hammock literally carries her off and puts her in his truck. Really! And that was *after* he kicked your daddy's butt into the dirt. Then he ran me and my boys off, so he could do whatever he wanted with her, I guess."

Teddy shook his head and muttered to himself, "Huh, I hadn't thought about that in forever."

Jamie got out of the car and said over his shoulder, "Yeah, dude, that old guy *is* a loser. It would make sense if he is her uncle, though; she *is Nanci-loser,* you know." Jamie snorted a laugh, slammed the door, and slouched up the walk into the school. By the time he was inside, Nancilee was nowhere in sight, and he had forgotten all about her and Teddy's story.

That night at home, Jamie's memory was jogged when his father walked in from work, "Dad, Uncle Teddy told me about some dude you were in high school with, and we saw him today."

Jimmy Faison III was rarely interested in his underachieving son's thoughts, and tonight was no exception. Still, he had to indulge his wife and pretend to care, so he asked without paying real attention, "Oh, and who might that be?"

"He said it was some loser named Mark something. Something about a car wreck."

Jimmy III rolled his eyes, "Ah yes, that must be Mark Hammock. Haven't heard that name in a long time. He was a friend of my dad's a long time ago."

"Uncle Teddy said something about him beating you up over some drunk girl."

His father, turned to look at him, "Is that what Teddy said? Well that's not exactly what happened, not that it really matters. Ancient history, after all."

"Well, I know this girl that he was dropping off at school, and she called him 'Uncle Mark.'"

Jimmy looked thoughtful, "*Uncle* Mark? What's her name?"

"Nanci-loser . . . no, Nancilee. Hah, I crack me up! Her last name's Davis, Nancilee Davis. She's in the ninth grade like me. I knew her back in middle school too."

Jamie's father turned white and his eyes went wide, "Davis, huh? What else did your Uncle Teddy have to say?"

"I don't know. Something like the old dude got the girl drunk and fooled around with her. Then she ended up having a kid while she was in high school."

Jimmy III looked out the window, cleared his throat, and then regained his disinterested tone, "Yeah, I guess that's the story. Maybe this girl you know is that kid after all—*his* kid, I mean. Good ol' Mark Hammock's one and only with a drunk high school girl. Who knows?"

Jamie watched his dad refill his drink and walk outside to sit in the dark on the patio. The boy stared at the closed door and said, "Well, *I* know now. Bet we can have some fun with this."

• • •

As the next fall semester dragged on, Ed's bored mind wandered back to his project. Although it hadn't been very long since he considered it solved, it now occurred to him that he hadn't fully developed the idea, not really. Sitting alone in his shop at school, his thoughts kept going back to his unfinished work, and he said to himself, "I know I could figure the rest out. I know it. I'd just need to flesh out a few little details, and there's a couple of things I'd need to know about 'ground zero.'" He fished around in his desk drawer and found the professor's brochure, which didn't answer his questions. *Guess I could go right to the horse's mouth, huh? Hey, he said I could call anytime I had a question. So here goes . . .*

The phone picked up on the first ring, "Tom Baker."

Startled, Ed almost hung up but said after a moment's hesitation, "Uh, Dr. Baker. You probably don't remember me; my name is Ed Schmutz. I had some questions for you after a lecture at Grayton High last year."

"Oh, sure I remember you, Ed. The maintenance fellow from the parking lot who was interested in butterfly studies. Ask away."

"Yeah, that was me. So I was wondering about how many acres the butterflies fill during the winter and where exactly that would be."

The professor sounded more professorial, "Well, the truth is the monarchs have bounced back some compared to a couple of years ago, doubling their winter home in Central Mexico to ten acres. Although that was good news, it's still a far cry from the forty-five acres they occupied less than twenty years ago. And, sadly, early indications are that this winter is seeing another reduction—it's going to be much less than ten acres again.

"As for where, well, the great majority of all monarchs make their winter home in the same small area in Mexico outside a little place called Cerro Pelon. It's in the middle part of the country, somewhat rugged and remote, resembling the Big Bend region in Texas. That's one of the reasons we still know so little about what's happening to them. We really need better data about the environment, even something as simple as hourly temperature measurements."

While Ed listened, his mental gears were turning, and an idea came to him right away. As Dr. Baker finished, Ed was lost in his own thoughts and had half-forgotten he was on the phone when he said out loud, "Oh yeah, that could work. I could spread 'em out across all those acres and control 'em using iPhones. It shouldn't be too tough to map out how many it would take to cover the whole area."

The professor stopped and asked, "What's that, Ed? What will work?"

Ed silently cursed himself for having said that out loud and stammered an answer, "Oh, uh, I mean . . . Well, I mean if you wanted to connect some kind of monitoring device or something, I bet I could network some iPhones together to record everything, that's all."

"Say, that's an interesting idea, if it could be done. Might be relatively cheap too. Have you done something like that before?"

Ed was back to his problem-solving mode now, "Not exactly, but I have done a lot of computer and smartphone repair and modification, including a little programming. It's been kind of a hobby of mine for a while. I call 'em my Franken-computers and Franken-phones. And using some smartphones for something like this wouldn't be too hard at all. Probably use the existing sync-cable connection on the phone to connect an external battery and a temperature sensor or whatever you wanted to measure. The phones would record the information and could even send it to a central location once a day if you wanted. All pretty easy stuff, even the little bit of programming you'd need for the data part." Now Ed was primarily thinking out loud for himself again, "Oh yeah, I could do it alright."

Dr. Davis was as enthusiastic as Ed when he answered, "Boy, I'm sure glad you reached out today, Ed. The thing is, I have a friend at a university in California who is leading a study in Mexico, and he's been looking for inexpensive ways to collect data like this without having to measure it in person all winter. I'm going to mention your idea to him. Hey, you never know, maybe this will be a way for you to leave another mark on the world."

Ed chuckled at that thought, "Well now, that would be something, wouldn't it?"

He gave the professor his phone number and email address, but he was quickly off the phone and continuing his train of thought on his design. Again thinking out loud, Ed said to himself, "I bet I could build a little converter that could charge the phone with the same kind of battery I used for the electric match. A little bit of extra wiring and the phone could turn on the electric match to ignite the thermite; I'd just need to transmit some kind of message to the phone so that it will light the match."

He closed his eyes and thought about that for a moment, then said, "Yeah, yeah, piece of cake. I bet I could use a small number of phones as masters that have cell service, and they'd relay the message to other phones over Wi-Fi.

"Oh wait," he clenched his eyes as he thought. "That's beautiful . . . the same app I use to collect the temperatures from each phone could be used to relay the message *to* each one to light its thermite! The code to manage all of that wouldn't be too hard either."

Ed leaned back in his chair, ran his hands through his hair, and smiled, "Oh yeah, I could do it." Now that he had new ideas buzzing around in his head, he knew he'd have to follow through and prove he could make them work. He got busy working out the details that night.

Before Christmas, Ed had the parts he needed from the surplus store in Orange to build a simple power supply that would charge a phone from his 6V lantern battery. It didn't take much: a small voltage converter, a couple of capacitors, a diode, and a small inductor, all mounted on a small circuit board, and the circuit design itself was readily available online. Any kid with a soldering iron and a little experience with a Mr. Science circuit board kit could make one, and Ed had been way past that since before he was in middle school repairing equipment in his dad's junkyard.

After building his power supply, Ed connected the input wires to his battery and the output wires to a USB cable. He held his breath when he plugged the USB cable into an iPhone and said jubilantly, "Well looky here! We have power, first try! That's a good omen!"

Ed's next step was trickier, but he knew he could find a way to modify a phone to control his igniter. His experience jailbreaking and programming iPhones now came in handy, giving him a better than normal, firsthand appreciation for what was possible and how to make the already-ingenious gadgets do things they weren't originally built to do. After stewing on the problem for days, an idea came to Ed from nowhere as he was driving home from work, "Oh yeah, that's it! Hell yeah, that can work! I just have to find the right wire and output to send a pulse down it."

It was another month before he was able to program a phone to reliably send an electric signal from an iPhone through the audio-out wire in the sync cable to a switch that he had connected to his electric match. Half a dozen blown transistors later he finally got the circuit right and his electric match burst into glorious flame, right on cue, "Yeah baby, another domino tumbles!"

Reveling in the familiar feeling of another problem solved, Ed kicked back again and smiled as he counted on his fingers, "So let's see, I have power to keep the phone charged from the lantern battery, and with just a little adjustment the same USB cable gives me control of the switch, which can then use the same battery to ignite the electric match and the thermite."

Ed raised both fists in triumph, "Boom! Nothing left now except a little bit of code to send the "go" message from one phone to another, and there's nothing to that. Like I said, this whole crazy idea is *so* doable. Good one, Eddie Boy."

• • •

Jo and Nancilee's spring went about the same as their fall had, which is to say they remained comfortably and happily in their old routine. Whether at home with family, or finding time to be together at school, the girls wanted nothing more than the warm contentedness they felt in their simple life surrounded by family and friends, mostly enjoying their schoolwork, and treasuring each other every day.

Although both girls were still making good grades in advanced classes, they also were both dumbfounded with uncharacteristically low scores in the state literacy tests—and Nancilee now had a poor showing on the PSAT—like most of the previously high-performing kids in their school, thanks to Margo. As long as their grades stayed up, they would still move up to the next year's advanced classes, but the girls knew they had college applications to submit before long. If they didn't turn the corner on the simpler literacy tests, their college board exams had all the promise of following the growing trend for Grayton students, and that wasn't good.

On the other hand, thanks to one of Dr. Markus's efforts, Jo and Nancilee now found themselves in a new kind of study hall every day.

Only this one combined grade years and grouped the kids into study and mentoring groups based on common course loads. For the girls that meant the school had now arranged for them to not only share a class, but also to do much of their usual team-studying while they were still at school. Their study group quickly expanded to include some of their lunch group with many of the same, "less cool" kids warming up to Jo and Nancilee's easy and open way of helping each other without judgment.

By the end of the school year, a normal study hall session started with any one of the kids who was struggling with an assignment speaking up with a question like, "Hey, is anyone else stuck trying to solve these equations with more than one variable?"

In answer to which a few would reluctantly nod their heads, but almost always someone else would answer, "I get those. Want me to show you?"

Day by day, small sessions like this helped many of the kids in the group to better understand some things they may not have grasped as well on their own. Little by little, the effort was reflected in their class grades. Just as subtly, many in the group saw small boosts in their self-confidence in school and even larger boosts in friendships among the group.

• • •

In May, just before the end of the school year, Ed answered his phone and was surprised to hear a serious and official-sounding voice, "Hello, my name is Sam Waterston, from UC Santa Cruz. Am I speaking with Ed Schmutz?"

Ed blinked, "Uh, yeah."

"Ah, good, good. Listen, Mr. Schmutz, I've been talking with Tom Baker out at Orange Junior College about some ideas you gave him.

My little program here has recently received a grant to study conditions in the monarch butterfly wintering grounds, and I wanted to get a better idea about your invention and how we might use it, if that's okay with you."

Ed pulled his phone away from his ear momentarily and stared at it like the caller was speaking Greek, then he said, "Alright. What would you like to know?"

"Why don't you just give me an idea for how you could build a stand-alone device for measuring temperature and humidity that we could deploy in remote areas but collect the data here at home? As I understand it, you think you could modify iPhones to do this?"

Ed scratched his head and answered, "Well, yes and no. It really wouldn't take much modification except a little code for the data collection. Most of the inventing so far is the power supply, which I've already built from a lantern battery and a custom converter. You'd still want to put it in a weatherproof enclosure, of course. Depending on cell coverage in your area, you could even add an external antenna for better signal. Not all the phones would need that though. The newer iPhones can use Wi-Fi to talk to each other and to share cell service, so only a few of them would need to have the external antenna; the rest would communicate through them."

Dr. Waterston asked, "You think your power supply could last through a five- to six-month season?"

"Well, we can do some things for really low power usage on the phones to make sure they last, and we'd calculate the amps we'd need compared to what the batteries start out with. At worst, maybe we end up with a larger battery?"

Seeing it assembled in his mind's eye, Ed added, "Really, this thing is very doable," which almost made him laugh out loud.

"Look, I hate to drop this on you on such short notice, but in two weeks I'm flying into Mexico City for a weeklong surveying project in Cerro Pelon, right in the heart of the area we want to monitor. How much would you have ready to bring down for a feasibility test, and could you come with us? The center here would pick up your expenses, of course."

"Whoa! Yeah, I'll be off for a few weeks before the school reopens for summer classes. Hmm, I definitely have the power supply and could bring a couple of extra batteries. I could also grab an external antenna, although I have to look around for that. I'd want to have something to make sure we get some signal if the place is as remote as you say," Ed paused as his mind settled into his problem-solving mode.

Dr. Waterston added, "That'd be a good idea. They officially advertise no cell coverage in the canyon, but we've had it intermittently before, although with like a single bar. It isn't great or reliable."

Still thinking out loud, Ed said, "Also, I won't have any code ready for the data collection, and I have some homework to do for the sensors themselves. None of that is hard though. In two weeks, we'd definitely be able to use the power supply, test the cell coverage with the external antenna, and even test Wi-Fi connection to a couple of other iPhones if you want."

Dr. Waterson was now enthusiastic, "Yes, yes! Let's do it. If we play our cards right, maybe we could put together even one full demo unit to deploy this fall as a test. First things first though. I'll have my research assistant contact you right away to make the travel arrangements, and we'll find out if we can make your devices work at all."

Ed spent the next two weeks building and testing a second power supply as a spare. He also scoured electronics supply stores from Orange to Beaumont for cell antennas, finally settling on a three-foot whip antenna and iPhone cradle that were intended for truckers to boost their reception on rural highways.

Thus, in early June, Grayton, Texas's own Ed Schmutz found himself almost inexplicably tromping through the Cerro Pelon monarch butterfly reserve with Dr. Sam Waterston and three tanned college boys who looked more like surfers than scientists. After hiking to a high spot in the middle of the reserve, one of the college boys shinnied up a tree and strapped the whip antenna to the trunk with a bungee, running the cable back to the ground.

As Dr. Waterston had said weeks earlier, the iPhone showed only a single bar, then it flipped to "no signal." "Damn it! See what I mean?"

Ed slipped the phone into the cradle and attached the antenna cable. Cell strength jumped to two bars, intermittently switching between one and two bars while they huddled around watching. They then placed two phones fifty yards away in different directions, each at the base of a tree, and each connected by Wi-Fi to the first phone, which was set up to share its cell connection as a hot spot. Ed typed a test email to himself and pressed send. Moments later the two research assistants yelled and waved, having received Ed's message through Wi-Fi.

They then sent the third college boy back up the trail to the base camp, where cell coverage was better. An hour later, that student sent an email from the base camp. In just a few seconds, all three of the test phones in the butterfly reserve sounded the familiar chime of an incoming email, as that message was received via the external antenna, and the hot spot again relayed it to the other phones by Wi-Fi.

A jubilant Ed raised his arms in victory, "Boom, fellas! I'd say that's another win! This is our data connection. I told you it was doable!"

Dr. Waterston was grinning and patted Ed on the back, "Wow, that's great. Now we just need the rest of the device. Think you could have something ready to test by August? We'll cover all of the materials, of course."

Ed nodded, "I don't see why not. The rest of this ain't the hard part."

Dr. Waterston, still smiling, looked around and said, "You just never know where you'll find inspiration, do you? I mean, look where technology has taken us. It's amazing what even a *janitor* can come up with these days!"

Ed turned slightly away. His smile faded as he felt a familiar dark feeling closing around him, and he said evenly, "Yeah, I guess you just never know what people are really thinking."

Chapter 12

SCORCHED EARTH

Night comes for all at the end of their day.

Even with the frequent whirring of power tools from Joe's shop, the girls' favorite spot in the clearing behind Jo's house was still a peaceful place to listen to the wind in the trees, smell the Texas pine and wet leaves, and watch the clouds while contemplating the good things in life. Jo and Nancilee had been lying in the grass, staring at the sky for a while, talking about their summer and avoiding the subject of the school year that would start the next day. Neither girl was ready for another carefree summer to end, and the conversation petered out after they had talked about anything else they could imagine. After a few minutes of silence, Nancilee sighed, "I just wish things didn't have to change."

Jo turned toward her with an understanding smile, "Me too, but it's not that big of a change, really. I know that working as an office aide means I won't be in study group with you, but we'll still have lunch, our ride home on the bus, and studying at home before dinner. Plus weekends, of course. So it's just one period difference. We'll hardly even notice."

Not wanting real tears to fall, Nancilee kept studying the clouds. She answered in almost a whisper, "Yeah, I know. *This* year . . ."

Jo reached over and gave her friend's hand a reassuring squeeze, "Hey, it's going to be a good year, and there are good changes too. My gramma is going to let us borrow her car some evenings and on weekends when we want to do stuff. We'll be able to hang out more with Matt and Tim and our friends, like going to movies. It'll be good. You'll see."

Nancilee took a breath and asked, "But who's going to keep everyone on track in study group without you?"

"You will, of course, just like you already do for me all the time. Just talk to them like you talk to me. That's all I do."

Nancilee closed her eyes, patted Jo's hand, and thought, *She always does that—reminds me of how easy it is to see the happy things. That's why we're always going to be best friends. Now, don't cry!*

• • •

Ed knew he was right when he told Dr. Waterston in May that the rest of the work to build prototypes wouldn't be difficult, since he'd already done most of the work. Looking for ideas, he stumbled right away onto a plastic, wall-mounted cable box to use for a weatherproof case. It was just large enough to fit two lantern batteries, his controller, and an iPhone, and the cell-antenna wire fit through a grommet on the bottom. He was even fortunate enough to find temperature and humidity sensors that plugged into the iPhone's antenna connector. The only real effort was the several weeks it took him to write and test a program that collected the sensor measurements every fifteen minutes and sent them automatically by Wi-Fi to the hot-spot phone, which then sent the data hourly via its cell connection.

Before school started in August, Ed visited Dr. Baker's lab in Orange and set up his three upgraded prototypes for a demonstration on the lawn, with Dr. Waterston watching by video from California. After panning the video to show the two Wi-Fi boxes sitting a hundred yards apart and the box with the cell antenna between them, Dr. Baker focused on Ed, who explained the setup: "The distance between them that you see here is about what we'll need to use in Mexico. It's close to the limit of the Wi-Fi range, but it definitely works and will give us the most coverage with the fewest devices. I mapped it out, and we'll need something like nine cells, each with six more Wi-Fi boxes slaved to them. The Wi-Fis send the data to the cell boxes, and the cell boxes then send it all to you. Watch," and he touched the screen of an iPhone in his hand.

In less than a minute, Ed's phone chimed and he turned a knowing grin toward the camera. Dr. Waterston turned to look off-screen then exclaimed, "Hey, the test phones emailed me! First data take in Orange, Texas is complete! Well that was easy!"

Ed nodded, "I was thinking I'd leave them running at my house for a week so you can see them continuing to report in over time. Also, we can set them up to send the data to wherever you want." Ed waved the phone in his hand, "I'll also have some control over them from home with *my* phone as sort of a master controller, but that's really just for me to start the data collection and for a little troubleshooting. I tried to keep it all pretty minimal in order to keep the phones powered down as much as possible and make those batteries last. In fact, there are a few other custom changes I made to the operating system to keep power usage down, but they're not important. So, what do you think?"

Dr. Waterston gave Ed a thumbs-up and said, "I think you need to send me another materials list for everything you'll need to build the full set. We'll get the prototypes set up in Mexico this fall for a better field demo and make sure there's nothing we need to tweak in the design. That will give you next spring and summer to build the sixty or seventy we'll need to cover the whole reserve next year. Will you be able to get them done, or should we build them at my lab here in Santa Cruz?"

Ed shook his head, "Nah, I'll be able to get them done, no problem. I'd rather do it myself and make sure they're built my way."

"Alright, mad inventor. Send me that list with enough for spares, and I'll get back to you with some dates we're looking at for going down to set up these first three for this winter. While you're at it, send me your coverage mapping, and we'll double-check your plan just to be sure."

After signing off and saying his goodbyes to Dr. Baker, Ed was driving home and deep in thought. *Mad inventor now, huh? Well, the "janitor" has one more idea to finish up for the final design. We'll call that an "extra feature"—a little surprise with purchase.* That made him laugh, but he then turned serious again as he thought through the final step in his design.

• • •

Not long into the new school year, Nancilee saw that Jo was right once again. Nancilee had segued easily into her friend's role as the unofficial leader of their study group and added a table full of freshmen, many of them younger friends of one or more of the misfits. And as Jo had predicted, she and Nancilee spent as much time together as ever.

It was Jo who had her hands full working in the school's office. It wasn't that the work was especially difficult: answering the phone, checking kids and visitors in and out, copying, filing, running papers to classrooms, etc. But the guidance counselor, Ruthie Gray, asked her for a little bit more after the first month, "Jo, you picked up all of the office stuff very quickly and make it look easy. Ms. Schmutz is also going to need someone to help her get things together for standardized tests in the fall and spring, kind of an assistant. Some girls find her a little intimidating, but I get the impression that won't be a problem for you, will it?"

Jo shrugged with a smile, "No, no problem for me at all. I'll do whatever I can to help her."

"Great, I'll let her know, and she'll let you know what she needs you to do."

After days with no word, Jo caught up with Margo as she was going into the file room, "Ms. Schmutz, Ms. Gray said I'd be helping you when test-time rolls around. Just let me know if you need anything."

Margo stopped in the doorway, glanced at Jo with a skeptical expression and answered, "Yeah, I'll let you know. For now, I have some private work to do in here and don't need any help," and she closed and locked the door without waiting for Jo's response. Over the next three weeks, Jo would watch Margo close herself in several more times, and each time Jo would wonder if today was the day that she'd need help. On many of those days, she'd also hear an odd, metallic sound like an old rusty gate slowly swinging open.

Finally, the day before the PSAT, Margo summoned Jo into the file room with a wave of her hand. "Tomorrow, I'll have all of the tests packaged for each ninth-grade homeroom. All you need to do is load them into the cart and deliver them to the teachers. Afterwards, take the cart back to get them, bring them back here, and leave the cart by the table in my room. Got it?"

"Sure thing, Ms. Schmutz."

The next day went as easy as Jo had expected, and she chuckled to herself as she pushed the cart down the hallway. *Deliver some packages, then bring them back. Not exactly rocket science.*

Margo followed Jo into the file room and stood by the door for her to leave. On her way out, Jo asked casually, "Oh hey, Ms. Schmutz, I was wondering what that screechy sound is that I hear coming from in here sometimes?"

Narrowing her eyes, Margo snapped, "Don't you worry about sounds or anything else that's none of your concern. Now why don't you just go on back out front? We're done here," and she hurried Jo out with the closing door, which she then locked. Jo stood and frowned at the closed door in confusion, then shrugged and walked to the front of the office.

Alone in her the file room, Margo muttered to herself as she turned to the stack of tests, "There's more going on in here than creaky hinges, young lady. You should be careful you don't get some of my personal attention for sticking your nose into my business."

• • •

Ed filled his spare time in the fall with his favorite hobby—more experimenting—this time creating a Franken-battery as the final piece in his plan's puzzle. Along the way, he destroyed twelve lantern batteries, three shirts, a pair of pants, and several patches of skin on his hands with battery acid; but he was finally able to replace the inside of a 6V battery with two thermite charges that were wired to the terminal posts and then reseal the battery without leaving signs of any tampering. When finished, it looked just like any other battery, right off the shelf.

It only took three tests in his burn pit to convince him that his Franken-batteries would work, with the thermite burning its way through each battery casing within two seconds after ignition. Even so, something bothered him, and he wasn't sure the problem was fully solved. He talked his way through it, as he sat down at his computer to follow a hunch, "They burn great, but they sure burn up fast. If the point is to catch the surroundings on fire, I think these things need something more than just the thermite, they need something that burns longer."

Once again, Ed found what he was looking for online, and the next evening he mixed a napalm-like gel from gasoline and Styrofoam cups. He lit several small puddles of the gel in his burn pit, nodding his head at the results. *Once again, the internet got it right—this stuff burns much longer than thermite and keeps burning wherever it's spread, even on cinderblocks!*

He then filled two travel-sized shampoo bottles with the gel, stuffed them into a Franken-battery with the thermite charges, resealed it, and marched back to his burn pit for another test. The thermite ignited immediately, just as before, and by the time the white-hot thermite flame died down, the small bottles full of his concoction had melted and the burning gel had created a large puddle of fire around what was left of the battery casing and was still burning. Ed clapped his hands and was ecstatic, "Whoo-hoo, now you've got it, Eddie Boy! Look at that stuff burn, even after the thermite has burned out! If that doesn't light a fire in the woods, nothing will."

When the Thanksgiving holiday came around, Ed met Dr. Waterston and one of his research assistants again in Mexico, where they deployed Ed's original three test units in the monarch butterfly reserve, almost in the same spots they had tested in May. These all had normal batteries, not Franken-batteries with their fiery surprise, since he'd need months to build up enough units to cover the full reserve next year.

After the cases were each strapped to a tree and the Wi-Fi connections were confirmed, the professor and his assistant left Ed to monitor the hub-phone's cell-signal strength, while they walked through the reserve's core forty-five acres to survey the year's butterfly population. When they returned two hours later, Ed explained what he had seen while watching the cell signal, "Just like we thought, service is almost non-existent without the external antenna. So my regular phone was lucky to have a single bar of service for a few minutes at a time, and then it had a lot of nothing. But the hub-phone with that antenna was good, bouncing between one and two bars the whole time."

Ed handed his phone to the professor, "Here Doc, you can have the honors. Push the picture of the butterfly to start the data collection."

"Don't mind if I do," the professor said with a smile as he pushed the button. "Since it doesn't have coverage now, how will we know if it's working?"

"The program on my phone will keep trying to send the start-code until the hub replies. When it replies, the hub will also send the first measurements it collected from the others. We'll receive the data at the email addresses you sent me and on my phone. Since we're out here with lousy coverage, it may take a little while until my phone has solid-enough service to get through, but it'll get there eventually. I bet we'll get a message within an hour though, based on what I've seen the signal doing."

They waited under the tree, and twenty minutes later Ed's phone chimed to confirm it had received the reply from the hub with measurements from all three devices. When he heard it, the professor craned his neck to look over Ed's shoulder and said, "I guess that's that. Once again, you made it look easy, Ed."

The three men high-fived and started their walk out of the reserve. As they walked, Dr. Waterston added, "Now we'll just watch how they do over the next several months. If all goes well, we'll have seventy phones shipped to you after New Years, and you can invoice us for the rest of the materials when you get started on next year's batch."

Ed was distracted and hadn't caught Dr. Waterston's comment at first, "Oh, yeah, sure," Ed said, "I'll get right to work on them." He had been so focused earlier when they walked into the reserve to set up the devices that he hadn't paid attention to his surroundings. Now he was seeing them and was astounded by the rippling blankets of orange and black that covered many of the trees and bushes in every direction he looked. Many of the branches were so heavy with monarch butterflies that they bent to the ground. "Wow, it doesn't look real. Look at them all. It's incredible."

The professor laughed, "Yeah, they're real, alright. And within the next month the rest of them will arrive, and this place will then be home to almost every monarch in the Americas, at least until spring. It *is* pretty incredible."

They walked the rest of the way in silence. Ed remained quiet for the rest of the night and the trip home the next day.

By the time Ed pulled into the driveway the next evening after his flight home, he had been brooding about his plan for almost twenty-four hours. The same thoughts were going round and round in his mind: *Yes, this would work. It's all too easy. Piney woods with dry brush lying all around like a tinderbox. And all of those butterflies are just right there—easy pickings. But all those butterflies were so cool . . .*

He walked in the house and called out, "Hey, Margo! You in here?" He thought absently with a smirk, *Where else would she be, Eddie Boy?*

She answered without budging from her spot in front of the television where she had been doing some brooding of her own, "Of course I'm here. Where would I go? You're the world traveler now, not me."

He dropped his suitcase and stood in front of her, "You should have seen them, Margo. There were butterflies everywhere, and I mean everywhere! It was crazy! I know I haven't been to many places, but this was a sight to see. We put up three of those boxes I built to monitor weather over the winter, and they want me to build a bunch more for next year if these three make it. It's pretty cool when you think about it," and he trailed off, realizing from the blank look on her face that she wasn't really listening.

Margo looked up, "Huh? Oh yeah, butterflies, sounds cool."

He shrugged, "Not interested, I guess."

"I just have my own stuff going on at school with all these auditors and extra faculty snooping around everything we do. Not that they're doing any good, based on test results," she chuckled.

Ed sighed and stooped to pick up his suitcase, "Anyway, I'm back. Next trip shouldn't be until next fall." He turned and started walking toward the garage.

Margo answered to his back as he walked away, "Hey, I'm sure it was great. I'm just thinking some things through, trying to make sure I don't get caught up in any trouble, alright?"

This time it was Ed who barely heard her, and he didn't bother to answer. As he walked away, old familiar walls were going back up in his mind, and his fascination with what he had seen in Mexico was fading as darkness crept back around him. *God, I hate this place. It just sucks the soul right out of you. I keep forgetting that Dad and Margo are right, nothing really matters.*

Ed focused his free time and his aggravation for the next several weeks on an additional phone app. Using some of the same code as the app that collected data from the phones, this one would send the start-code to ignite the Franken-batteries. This was a more complicated problem, since he wanted to ensure every hub and Wi-Fi phone ignited the thermite in their Franken-batteries at the same time, while spread out in a large area with the spotty cell signal they'd have in the Mexican high country.

He came up with a scheme that set the ignition time to one hour after he pushed the button, then sent that time to every cell-hub that was powered on. Each hub then relayed the start time to the Wi-Fi devices that were using it as a hot spot. The hubs received and counted confirmations from each of their Wi-Fi devices and then sent their count back to Ed's phone. When all devices confirmed receipt, Ed's phone automatically sent a final go-message back to the hubs, without which they would clear their timers and no devices would ignite. Knowing how complex he'd made it, Ed spent every evening for a week testing the app to ensure he had caught and fixed any oversight that could result in either an accidental ignition or cause some devices to not ignite at all. Once he was sure, he built three more devices just like the prototypes that were in Mexico, but this time each box contained one real battery and one Franken-battery.

On the first Saturday of Christmas break, Margo watched Ed carry three gray boxes out back. He had been particularly sullen since his return from Mexico, but this morning he had some of his bounce back. Curious, she stepped to the back door to see what he was doing. She could see Ed standing just outside the door fiddling with his phone, but then he put the phone in his shirt pocket and sat in a folding chair, still facing the yard. She shrugged, sat back down and said, "I thought he was going to do one of his firework things again. Guess this one didn't work."

An hour later Margo heard several muffled bangs like firecrackers going off inside a cardboard box, and she immediately heard Ed hollering outside. She opened the door to a backyard engulfed in black-and-gray smoke that smelled like burning tires, "Oh great, I guess you got some new fireworks to work after all?"

He whipped around with a huge grin and said, "Something like that. I hadn't thought about the *regular* batteries going off like that, but I guess that makes sense! All that heat made 'em pop. Once the smoke clears, I'll have to see if the thermite took care of the evidence."

Margo was puzzled, "Evidence?"

Ed shook his head briefly, "Oh you know, I don't want to leave a bunch of trash around is all." He walked to the burn pit and looked in, "Nope, all gone. Damn, it worked like a charm!"

Margo heard him laughing and still talking to himself as she closed the door and shut the putrid smell out. She said to herself, "And what the heck is thermite?"

Outside, Ed was still thinking about "evidence" and decided to make one more change, "The app is pretty foolproof, Eddie Boy. They either all get the same start time and go off at exactly the time, or none of them go off. But just in case the thermite doesn't burn everything up, I'll add one last command for the app to initiate a full memory erase one second after ignition. Then boom, zap, gone. Not bad, Eddie Boy."

During his Christmas break, Ed sent Dr. Waterston his materials list. By February he had everything he needed and started the slow work of assembling the sixty-three devices they'd need to cover the entire 45-acre reserve next winter and another six backups—each comprising a weatherproof case with a phone, temperature and humidity sensors, one real battery, and one Franken-battery.

With some of his time taken by his day job and the occasional iPhone repair, Ed would only be able to build two or three devices per week and would need all the time he had to finish by the end of the summer. As tedious and repetitive as the work was, Ed was content and often smiled at his own dark humor while building yet another device, "Hey, at least I'm doing something. Idle hands are the devil's workshop . . . right, Eddie Boy?"

• • •

Tina had just walked in from work when Nancilee bounded out of her room towards the door, "Hi Mom, bye Mom!" Her daughter kissed her on the cheek as she went by.

"Bye? Where are you off to, and are you going to be here for dinner?" Tina asked.

"Jo's about to be here. We're going to hang out with Tim and Matt. I think we're going to stop at Dairy Queen on the way to a movie in Orange, so no dinner for me tonight."

Tina walked outside with Nancilee as Jo pulled up in her grandmother's Ford Explorer. She hugged her daughter while waving at Jo, "Alright then. I guess your poor ol' mom will have to eat alone since Gramma won't be home until late again."

"I won't be too late, Mom, before midnight for sure," and Nancilee hugged her mom again and jumped down the steps to get in the car.

Jo passed Nancilee on the steps as she ran up to hug Tina, "Hi Mom, bye Mom!"

Tina laughed as she answered, "You two might as well be twins. Have fun but be smart." She attempted a stern look at her daughter through the closed car window and raised her voice, "Hey, I mean it, you two! Be smart. You're in charge of you, and you two watch out for each other."

Nancilee rolled her window down and answered with an eye roll, "Okay, Mom, we know."

Jo shouted through the open window as she pulled away, "We know, Mom! Don't worry, we'll watch out for each other!"

Tina sat down on a rocking chair on the deck and watched the girls drive away and said to herself, "Don't worry? Yeah, right. Well, at least they'll be together." *And boys! Oh great, here we go. I guess they're good boys, if there is such a thing, or these two wouldn't have them around.* Her thoughts turned from the girls to her mom, Jenny, which brought a nostalgic smile to her face. It had been almost three years since Jenny had started working part-time on a business degree at Lamar University, and she had less than a year to go. *I don't know how she does it, but, like always, she gets it done. And a year from now, a Davis girl will have a bachelor's degree! I don't think that will be the only surprise around here, though.*

Tina looked up the lane at Mark's trailer and her smile became more tender. In the last year, Jenny had come home later and later after her evening classes. After a late trip to the grocery store a few months back, Tina had seen her mom's car parked at Mark's place as she drove past. When Jenny walked in an hour later, she looked happy and relaxed. Tina was sitting on a recliner by the window, and Nancilee was sprawled out on the couch watching TV. Tina asked Jenny, "Late again, huh, Mom? Did your class run long? Want me to heat something up for you?"

"Oh sorry, no," answered Jenny as she walked through the room to the hallway. "Mark was outside when I pulled in, so I stopped to visit with him. I ended up eating at his place, and we lost track of time talking, I guess. You know how it is talking with him. I'll be back in my room doing some homework for a while before bed. Night, girls," and she walked down the hall looking like she didn't have a care in the world.

Nancilee answered distractedly without looking away from the TV, "Night, Gramma."

Tina thought, *You're still oblivious aren't you, kid? Well I'm pretty sure I know what's going on. Wonder when your gramma is going to let us in on it?*

The rest of the school year was more of the carefree-same for Jo and Nancilee, which was just how they liked it. But along with sailing through their schoolwork and spending most of their waking moments with each other and family, they had also begun spending more time with Matt and Tim. It had started with Matt and Jo finally becoming official boyfriend and girlfriend over the Christmas break, something their friends had anticipated for a very long time. While Matt had had a crush on her since the eighth grade, Jo took longer to realize how much she looked forward to seeing her big pal and that maybe there was something more to it. It was only then that she saw the way he looked at her when he didn't think she was looking.

One Friday night the four of them had gone to a movie together, and when the lights went down, Jo leaned against Matt and whispered, "I think you should kiss me."

He looked at her with wide-open eyes, not knowing what to do. Her face relaxed into an innocent smile, "No, really," and she leaned toward him, leaving him no choice.

From that day forward, they were an item. Since the two boys were just as close friends as the girls were, it was a package deal from the start. Where Jo went, Nancilee almost always went, and Tim was usually with Matt. It was a natural progression over time for Tim to first put an arm around Nancilee and then to eventually kiss her, both of which were fine with her.

By then, however, Matt and Tim had become obsessed with computer programming and spent much of their time working on projects through a programming club at the Orange Junior College. That had the dual benefit of giving them something productive to do and to limit the time they had to spend with the girls, a complication that both the girls' parents were fine with.

One more thing that hadn't changed for Jo was the creaking sound she heard from behind the locked door when Margo was working on standardized test packages that spring. Remembering Margo's response the first time she asked, Jo knew better than to bring it up again, but she still wondered, *What is that? And why is she so touchy about it? Guess that's just her, touchy about everything.*

• • •

At the end of August 2013, after seven months of tedious work, Ed finished assembling sixty-nine of his devices. He shipped sixty-three of them and nine cell-antenna kits to Dr. Waterston's lab, where his research assistants took care of the packaging to get them through customs in Mexico as research equipment. Ed kept all of the phones at home to ensure they were fully charged and not draining the batteries in each box. He reminded the team that the goal was to conserve the large, external batteries until they were absolutely necessary so that they would make it through the winter. Had he used two real batteries in each box, Ed's calculations showed they would have easily had enough power to keep the reduced-power phones going through the winter. However, since one battery in each box was a resealed Franken-battery, they needed to conserve every amp the other battery had.

After he sent the reminder by email, Ed told himself, "I don't need them to have any reason to go mucking around inside those boxes, just in case my battery seals aren't all perfect. And, this way, *I'll* be the one to hook them up in Mexico."

The week before Halloween, Ed flew to Mexico City with the phones and drove out to the butterfly reserve in a bouncy work van with the professor and two of his assistants to set up the full array. Riding in the van, Ed and Dr. Waterston looked over Ed's diagram showing the overlapping Wi-Fi coverage. The professor nodded with a grin, "It looks good, Ed. As long as we get the coverage you're predicting and all of the cell-antennas do their jobs, this should do it."

"I'm thinking we should start in the center," Ed said, "and then we can lay them out one hub at a time, making sure we have good signal to each hub and to their Wi-Fi boxes. Then we'll just move over and deploy another one, and then another one, and so on. We can mark up the map as we go in order to make sure we cover it all, sort of a patch at a time."

"Sounds good to me. Looks like you've thought of everything," and the professor sat back in his chair with a satisfied expression.

Ed looked out the window at the Mexican desert going by in a blur. *Have I thought of everything? I thought I had. Now I don't know. This is crazy.*

Over the next two days in the reserve, the team clamored over rocks and pushed their way through thick undergrowth to lash all sixty-three boxes to trees throughout the 45-acre reserve. Ed connected the phones and ensured they each had a signal. Every time he opened a box to finish the installation, he thought, *This is it. Something's going to look wrong with one of these darn batteries, and these college boys are going to see something ain't right.* But he was wrong. It couldn't have gone more smoothly. Every device activated without a hitch, and no one was the wiser about the extra "feature" he had built into each of them.

Once they were all in place, the team sat in the shade under the same oyamel tree they had used during their test the year before. Ed pulled out his phone and announced, "Here goes nothing, guys," and pushed the button to start data collection. Ten minutes later the cell-hub phone mounted on the tree above them chimed to announce it had received the message. Ed's phone chimed repeatedly two minutes later as all of the hub phones answered with the first temperature and humidity measurements. "There you have it. You should all have the messages in your inboxes whenever you're able to check them. I have them set now to collect hourly and transmit every six hours. Now they just do what they do."

Dr. Waterston shook Ed's hand vigorously, "Well, that sure made it look easy. Great job! How do you want to handle the spares?"

"Oh, I'll hang on to them," Ed answered. "If anything needs to be tweaked, I'll have 'em and can take care of it right away in my shop. Besides, if we need to replace anything inside a box here, I'd like to do that myself." *I sure don't need any of you guys mucking around in there.*

"Fine with me," said Dr. Waterston with a shrug. "Well, I guess we're done here for this trip. Get a good look, gentlemen. The next time we see this place should be in the spring when we come back to take everything down after the monarchs have headed north again." The professor stood looking around fondly before starting up the trail with his assistants following him and Ed coming last.

As they hiked out of the reserve, Ed walked like he was in a daze. *Yeah, take a good look, fellas. This place probably won't look like this the next time you see it, if our little handiwork here goes as planned.*

Marching along, though, Ed's thoughts bounced back and forth from finishing his spiteful plan to the beauty and wonder he saw all around him—the rippling yellow and orange blankets completely covering many of the trees and the crisp country air filled with the clean scent of the woods. He sighed and thought, *Maybe the old saying is right, and I am just turning into my father—another angry old man just like him. It's no real wonder why, Eddie Boy. What has the world ever done for you?* He shook his head to stop the thoughts from buzzing around in his brain, but he couldn't keep his mind from going right back to it.

Like his last trip, he couldn't turn the brooding off. It haunted him as he traveled home, and also like the last time, he found no relief there. Margo was right where he expected her to be, sitting in the dimly lit living room in front of the television, watching without interest. She showed only slightly more interest when Ed walked in, giving a faint smile and saying without getting up, "Good trip?"

He walked by with his duffle bag and sighed, "Yeah, it was fine. We did what we went to do," and he retreated to the garage. *Back to the real world now. Great.*

With that thought, Ed's brooding quieted down finally, giving way to, *Oh yeah, nothing really matters.*

• • •

When school started earlier that fall, Jo had recruited Nancilee into the office staff during third period. As Jo explained it to her, "The work's easy, and it will give us some time to hang out during the day. This is our last year together in high school, so we might as well make the most of it."

Always ready to take Jo's lead, Nancilee hadn't needed any convincing. She nodded and held up two fingers in a peace sign, "Cool."

Guidance Counselor Ruthie Gray was just as easily convinced and told Jo, "Well, if she's a friend of yours, I'm sure she'll be great to have with us. I'll put her on the schedule with you." After Jo left her office, the counselor was still beaming and thinking, *I don't know what it is, but that girl always puts me in a good mood.*

In the office one morning a few weeks into the semester, Nancilee rushed over to stand close to Jo at the front desk and whispered, "I finally heard your noise. You're right, it's weird, especially since Ms. Schmutz is so weird about it."

Jo looked relieved, "See? I told you. Now it's a quest." She hunched over with an exaggerated conspiratorial expression, "It's the 'quest to find the creepy noise.' Mwahahaha!"

Both girls were still giggling about it when Margo came down the hall from the file room and shot them a judgmental scowl with a raised eyebrow. They went back to other and quieter work and tried to not make eye contact with each other for fear of laughing again.

As the weeks went by, when Jo or Nancilee needed something from the file room, they'd open and close an extra drawer or cabinet in search of that creaking sound. Nothing came even remotely close to it. With Margo's chute locked away in her cabinet, the girls had no chance of finding it, which was just as well for them, since Margo may have heard the sound too and would then be on to them.

During the fall test weeks when Margo was locked in the file room preparing the exam materials, every time the girls heard that sound it made them more determined to find it. More than once, Jo whispered, "We're going to find it. Even if it's just so I can stop wondering what it is. We know it's in there somewhere!"

• • •

One evening in late January, Dr. Waterston called Ed, "Master Inventor, I have good news and bad news. Good news first: The data has come in steadily since we set everything up in October. That's great. Now the bad news: My research assistants have been plotting battery charges, and it doesn't look like the cell-hubs are going to last until spring."

Ed took a breath, "Damn. I was afraid I might have cut it too close with those units, since they're at a little higher power level than the Wi-Fi boxes. I bet it was the cold weather in the high country down there. I didn't account for that, and it would definitely reduce battery amps. I think I got fooled by a couple of spares that I had running here in my shop for comparison, and they're doing fine. 'Course, they're in warmer conditions than the ones in Mexico. Damn it!"

"Yeah, you're probably right about the cold, but we still need to do something. I can send one of my guys down to—"

"No!" Ed said, cutting the professor off. "Ah . . . look, it's my mistake, I should fix it. Plus, I need to fiddle with the spares for the easiest way to do it without breaking anything, like the charge controllers." He added to himself, *Or setting off the thermite while I'm at it! I may be planning on setting them off before long anyway, but I sure don't need to be there when I do!*

"That's fine too, Ed," answered Dr. Waterston. "Take a day or two if you need it, then let us know. We'll set everything up and send you the travel details. We should even be able to get you the same driver in Mexico City."

After the call, Ed was thinking about his game plan as he wandered into the kitchen to gather some dinner. Turning to carry his plate back to his desk where he planned to work while eating, he noticed Margo watching him and explained, "What do you know? I have to replace some batteries in those phone charger things I took to Mexico for the professor in California. No one's perfect. I have some tinkering to do first but will probably fly down in a few days. I shouldn't be down there more than two days."

"Okay. I'm sure you'll figure it out. You always do," and Margo watched him walk out with his food.

Ed set his box of spare devices on the crate next to his desk. His two active spares were on top, and he opened one to use as his guinea pig. After disconnecting the phone, he carefully lifted the batteries out and inspected the wiring and the Franken-battery seal while he ate his dinner. It didn't take long for him to announce the verdict, "Well, dummy, this isn't that hard. Just disconnect the real battery terminals and connect the new battery. If you're having second thoughts about leaving the Franken-Batteries connected, you should have thought of that before you put them in there in the first place. There's no taking them out now without rewiring the controllers, which you don't want to do in the darn Mexican wilderness."

He heard his wife's voice right behind him, "What's a Franken-battery?"

Ed leapt to his feet, knocking over his chair, "Holy cow! You almost gave me a heart attack, Margo!"

She took a step backwards and was now startled herself.

He explained, "Uh, Franken-battery is just what I call part of my gadget here. Let's just say it's part of a phone charger in these thingamajigs I built."

Margo looked past him, "Phone charger? Aren't those the crazy fireworks you were messing with all last year? That's some kind of phone charger."

"I guess you could call those 'safety tests,' you know, the kind of things not to do," he said. He pointed at the parts spread out on his desk, "These batteries are connected to the phone to keep it charged for months. The phone is connected to a couple of sensors. All of that stuff goes inside the box and gets strapped to a tree, and every so often the phone sends the data back to us from Mexico. Pretty cool, really, even if it isn't that sophisticated."

"Sure, just don't do whatever you do to make them go off!"

Ed laughed nervously as he put the batteries back in their weatherproof shell and set it back in the larger box, "Well, yeah, that'd be nuts."

Three days later, Ed flew to Mexico City again with nine new batteries to replace the dying batteries in the cell-hubs and ensure the professor received the full season's data. On his way out of the house that morning to drive to the airport in Houston, he and Margo nodded to each other and neither said a word.

• • •

Ed left for Mexico just as Margo was preparing for the spring tests. At school that morning, an uncharacteristically tired-looking Dr. Markus pulled a chair up to her desk, "Margo, you probably know as well as anyone else that something is still not right. Four years after we started attacking this thing, we have less than half the number of kids taking college boards every year, and the scores for those who do are worse than ever, just like on the state tests. It makes no sense when you look at the grades. I'm at my wit's end. Like I said, you know this better than anyone, since you're the one who has to handle all of the tests."

"Yeah, I guess I do. Maybe it's just one of those things. People, right?" She looked at the principal innocently as if they were discussing the weather.

He shook his head and walked into his office. Standing at the front desk, Jo elbowed Nancilee and motioned toward the hallway. The girls walked into the hall and Jo whispered excitedly, "Did you hear that? Ms. Schmutz is the only person who deals with every standardized test in the school."

"Ah, okay. Yeah, I guess I heard it. So?" answered Nancilee, who wasn't following Jo's point.

Jo waved her hands, "I bet it's all connected. The weird noises, the test stuff that doesn't make sense, and all of it comes back to her. Oh yeah, the quest is on!"

Nancilee's eyes widened, "Shh, there she goes," and Margo hurried out of the office and down the hall. Both girls giggled and ran back inside the office before Margo turned to glare at them.

Before they had caught their breath from laughing about their conspiracy, Ruthie Gray walked in with two men, "Jo, is Ms. Schmutz here?"

"She's at school today, but she just walked out. You literally just missed her," Jo explained.

"Darn. I need some materials out of her test cabinet." The guidance counselor looked at the men who were with her and back at Jo, "Tell you what, can you run across the hall to my office and grab the key ring in my middle drawer? You can't miss it. It has several keys on it."

Jo nodded, "Sure, Ms. Gray. I'll be right back," and she trotted out the door. She found the keys, right where Ruthie had said she would. When she got back to the office, Ruthie had taken the visitors down to the file room and Jo took the keys to her.

"There she is. Thanks, Jo." Ruthie took the keys and fumbled with them until she was able to unlock the cabinet. "I just realized this is the first time I've ever opened the super-secret cabinet. Ms. Schmutz has always done it herself. Maybe we should just keep this to ourselves, how 'bout?" She looked at several of the shelves and said, "Ah, here they are," as she pulled a stack of thick manila envelopes down and put them on the table.

While the counselor and the men inspected the envelopes, Jo noticed something peculiar in the cabinet and walked around the table to get a better look. "Ms. Gray, what's that behind the shelves?"

Ruthie answered distractedly while still looking at the envelopes, "Oh, I don't know. Let me finish with this, and I'll have a look."

Jo raised her eyebrows, squinted an eye as she looked at the silver plate and saw a handle at the top and announced, "Oh, it's a door or something." She reached over the stacks of paper on the shelf and pulled the handle. It rotated down an inch before it was blocked by the papers, and as it did, there was a short screechy sound.

"Just what do you think you're doing in there?!" Margo charged through the door, obviously furious. Jo released the handle and the drawer creaked closed with a heavy thump as she backed away.

"Oh, hey Margo, just in time," Ruthie said cheerfully. "These gentlemen are from the state, and they're here for a spot inspection of our sensitive test materials. Since you weren't in the office, I used my key so we wouldn't hold them up."

Margo looked from Ruthie to Jo, who was staring at her wide-eyed, "Is that so? Well, I don't like other people getting into this cabinet without me. I'm responsible for it, you know." She pointed at Jo, "And, and, and . . . that student should not be in here at all when it is open!"

Ruthie held her hands up, "Now, now. No offense, Margo. I think we're done here, and we'll leave you to lock things back up." The counselor led the two visitors and Jo out of the room. Still curious, Jo turned to look back at the cabinet as she walked through the door and saw Margo standing with her hands on her hips, still glaring at her.

When Jo reached the front office, she grabbed Nancilee by the arm and pulled her into the hall, where she hurriedly whispered how she'd stumbled onto it after Ms. Gray had unlocked the cabinet, "I found it—the creepy sound. I found it! It's in Ms. Schmutz's locked cabinet, and it's some kind of drawer or something."

Nancilee was stunned, "Wow! So what was in it? Why all the secrecy?"

"I don't know. I had barely opened it when she came in and yelled at everyone. So we all left." Jo grinned, "But I think we ought to have another look to see what she's hiding."

"What? Are you crazy? You don't want her to go mental on you!"

Jo shook her head, "No, not now. I was thinking we could come up here tonight after dinner. It'll be dark, so no one will see us. And we can use these to get in," Jo said as she jingled a set of keys in front of Nancilee. "Ms. Gray put these on the table and forgot all about them when Ms. Schmutz got so mad. We'll just come in quietly, have a little look in that metal drawer, then lock everything back up, and leave the keys in Ms. Gray's desk. No one will ever know."

"Oh, is *that* all? Right. You *are* crazy," answered Nancilee matter-of-factly. She sighed, "But I'm crazy enough to go with you, as always."

After her trespassing visitors had left, Margo locked the door and turned quickly toward the chute. *Damn it! I don't think they got in there, but that stuff has got to go now!* After marching across the room, Margo yanked the chute open and tugged angrily on one of the chains to pull up the binder, almost hyperventilating as her temper boiled over. Heavy and crammed with years of old lists, the binder popped open. She heard a rustling *whoosh* as the chain suddenly felt much lighter, and the binder flew up and out of the chute.

"Noooo! Damn it!" Margo yelled, as she threw the now-almost-empty binder on the table. She craned her neck to look down but saw only darkness. She tried reaching in but was unable to get her arm more than a few inches past the chute door. Margo dragged a chair over and stood on it, adding another foot to her reach into the cavity, but the papers were still too far down. She then grabbed a yardstick that was leaning against a file cabinet and tried to stick it through the chute opening to reach to the bottom. Again, no luck. The back of the chute door blocked anything long and straight from reaching through the opening and down to the bottom of the chute.

After racking her brains, Margo realized there was no way she'd be able to reach down and pull the papers out. Although only five to six feet down, it may as well have been a mile. She gave up, put everything back in its place, and locked the cabinet. She sat at the table staring at the cabinet for the rest of the day, anger replaced by desperation and then fear. *After all this time, now I'm screwed! How'd they find it? What am I going to do? If someone finds those papers, they could put two-and-two together! Damn, damn, damn!*

Her anxiety grew for the rest of the day and threatened to bubble up to a full panic by the time the last bell rang. She was the first person out the door, desperate to escape and think. Back at home and still barely able to keep the panic at bay, the empty house felt darker and more joyless than ever, and for the first time since Margo could remember she felt Ed's absence. She took a deep breath and thought of her current predicament. *I wonder what he'd think of all this? I wonder what he'd do?*

As she thought, she wandered back through the kitchen and stood in the doorway, looking into his garage apartment and workshop. Her eyes locked onto the open box beside Ed's desk. There sat two of his phone-charger "thingamajigs." She remembered him saying after one of his tests in the backyard, something about "taking care of the evidence" and "not leaving a bunch of trash." The hint of a solution appeared in her mind, and she said to herself, "So, what do we have here?"

She pulled one of the devices out of the big box and opened it, "Yep, that's it. Some batteries and a bunch of wires, but no phone in this one." She spotted a phone sitting on the desk and said, "That one must go with this box. What about that one?" She reached into the big box and pulled another of Ed's weatherproof units out and opened it. Sure enough, this one had a phone inside and attached.

Margo sat at Ed's desk, her mind racing. *This is crazy. Crazy! How else are you going to fix this? Well not this way! Damn, damn, damn.*

Her eyes narrowed and she talked her way through it, "It's only a matter of time now. But I remember him saying it, 'No evidence—nothing left.' If that's right, then this thing can take care of the papers and destroy evidence of itself at the same time. That chute is metal, so it should be fireproof and not catch the school on fire. Then there's just be a bunch of smoke, and how the heck should I know where it came from?" She looked at her watch and urged herself on, "The place is empty now. Better get on with it. I've got to get in there now while I can. I know Ed does something with a phone to make it go off like fireworks. I'll figure that out later."

She closed the device, tucked it under her arm like a football, and grabbed the phone from the desk. Margo then hurried out the door, and fifteen minutes later she was back at the now-deserted school. Already nervous about what she planned to do, the unnatural quiet and solitude in this usually bustling place only made it worse. She had her own keys to get into the school and office and was quickly locked in the file room. After opening the cabinet, she pulled the remaining files up using the chains that suspended them, unhooked them, and tossed the files down the chute with the rest of the papers. She checked Ed's device and confirmed the phone that was inside was turned on, then hooked the chain to the latch on the box, and lowered it slowly into the chute. Once it was dangling from the chute door above the discarded papers, Margo closed the chute, put everything else back on the shelves where they had been, and sat on the edge of the table staring at it all, now unsure that she had thought this through.

After a few minutes that felt like an hour, Margo stood, took a deep breath, and said, "In or out, which is it?" She closed her eyes and pursed her lips, hoping for some idea that had not yet occurred to her, then sighed, "Fine . . . in. What else am I going to do?" She locked the cabinet and hurried out of the office and the school.

Before she started her car for the drive home, she thought, *Ed!* With it came a compelling urge to call him, so she reluctantly pulled the phone from her pocket. *What will I say? Why would he care?*

When she touched the screen, it asked for a passcode. "Well, I guess that's the end of that," but she tried 1-2-3-4 as a futile gesture. It worked. There on the screen were two buttons, one with a picture of a butterfly and the other simply labeled "Ed." Margo laughed, "Thanks, Ed. That makes it easy," and she pushed the "Ed" button to call him.

Nothing happened. No call, no error message. The icon flashed then went back to normal. "Oh, forget it, I gotta get out of here," and she drove home just as the sun was setting.

The ride home with her mind still racing led her back to thoughts of Ed. Once inside, she decided to try the call again and saw a message on the screen. "Ready?"

She snapped while pushing the "Ed" button again, "Yes, damn it, I'm ready!" The icon pulsed again, then nothing. "Great. Maybe it's for the best."

Margo set the phone on the kitchen table while she rummaged through the refrigerator for something to eat. She didn't notice the message that appeared briefly on the phone, "Timer set," then the display went dark again.

Unbeknownst to Margo, she had stumbled onto an oversight in Ed's system: He hadn't considered the possibility that someone else would use one of his phones. So, when he loaded the data-recording and thermite-lighting applications on them, he made them all the same. That meant that not only would the "Ed" button on his *personal* phone initiate the sequence on every active phone, but *any* of the cell-enabled phones could do the same, including the spare that Margo had picked up earlier from his desk.

• • •

During Ed's travels back to the butterfly reserve in Mexico, his mind was in a fog and wracked with doubt about his plan, which, after all of this time and effort, he now couldn't reconcile as anything other than stupid and pointless. Walking through the reserve alone, again mesmerized by one of nature's curious miracles as he gave witness to an entire species congregated in one place, his misgivings settled around him like a heavy blanket he couldn't kick off. Hiking from one cell-hub to the next, as he replaced each 6V battery with a new one, those feelings became a conviction.

At the end of the day, as the sun was getting low, he sat under the same tree he had sat under on the last trip. "Look at this place. It's incredible. How did some 'janitor'—to use the professor's word—get to be here and to be part of this?"

He sat, marveling at the unspoiled forest, listening to the wind rustling through the trees. *For how long has this happened? A thousand years? Ten thousand years? What did Dr. Baker say? Oh, I should have listened better.* He made up his mind, "Yeah, you're not doing this, Eddie Boy. Nice job figuring out your great master plan, but you can't do this."

Ed leaned back against the tree, closed his eyes, and realized he could hear his heart beating and the shallow rhythm of his breathing. He felt a peace he hadn't felt in more years than he knew.

• • •

Jo and Nancilee rode Jessie's bus to Jo's house after school, as usual. In the shop, Jo told her dad, "Nancilee's going to stay and eat dinner with us, then we're going to her house to study, if that's okay."

Joe kept working and said, "Okay by me. We'll be done here shortly and see about an early dinner if you want." He looked toward the back of the shop, "Hey Mark, wanna stay and eat with us? We can talk some business afterwards?"

Mark looked up and smiled at the three of them, "Okay but you're buying." He laughed and went back to work.

Less than two hours later, the girls were in a hurry to leave. On their way out the door they took turns kissing Joe and Mark on the cheek, and each girl said, "Bye, Dad" or "Bye, Uncle Mark" to them as they did. They then giggled and hustled each other out.

Joe chuckled and said to Mark, "Those two. What would we do without 'em?"

Mark smiled broadly and nodded his head.

Twenty minutes later, Jo parked in the empty Grayton High School parking lot. After turning off the car, she looked at Nancilee and whispered, "Are we really going to do this?"

Nancilee rolled her eyes and whispered back, "*Now* you're asking me?"

"What? I don't want to get into any trouble or anything. And why are you whispering?"

"I am because you are. You're freaking me out, quit it!"

Both girls giggled nervously, then Jo said, "Let's wait a little while and let it get darker. Maybe that will make it safer," and she slid down lower in the seat as if to hide.

"Sure, Miss Burglar, whatever you say," answered Nancilee as she slid down too, and both girls giggled again.

Another twenty minutes went by and Jo could wait no longer, "Let's just get on with it," and she jingled Ruthie Gray's keys between them to start their adventure. At the school's entrance, Jo realized she didn't know which key would open the front door. After trying what seemed like every key on the ring, she finally got the door open.

Inside the dark school, Nancilee said, "Geez, I thought it was creepy in the daytime," which started them giggling once again.

"Shhh. This is serious. Focus," hissed Jo, still giggling as she crept along in exaggerated caution.

Joe and Mark had finished cleaning up from dinner and were sitting on the back deck sipping coffee when Mark's phone rang. He glanced at it, and told Joe, "Hey, it's Jenny. Let me just make sure she doesn't need something."

Joe frowned in mock understanding, "Oh yeah, sure. Good neighbor and all."

On the phone, Jenny told Mark, "Hey, I didn't have class tonight. The prof had some kind of schedule conflict, and they gave us a walk. How about that? So . . . earlier dinner tonight? I can cook for you for a change."

"I'll definitely come on home, young lady, but I already ate with Joe and the girls. If you're at home already, didn't they tell you?"

"What? No, they told Tina they're studying at Jo's this evening, so they're not here. Aren't they *there?*"

Mark could hear the concern in Jenny's voice and he tried to reassure her, "Oh, I'm sure there's a good explanation. Come on, it's Jo and Nancilee. They're fine." He noticed Joe looking at him with a concerned expression, so Mark added, "Tell you what, I'll leave now and head that way, just to make sure they're not broken down on the road or something. Why don't you try calling Nancilee, and Joe will call Jo. It'll all be good."

Jenny said, "Okay, I'll call her now. Let me know when you're home . . . *Uncle Mark*. Are you gonna say it before you hang up? Come on, say it."

The big man glanced nervously at Joe and blushed, "Yeah, okay, I'll let you know. And, uh . . . me too. Okay now, bye."

Joe raised his eyebrows and said, "'Me too?' I bet 'Me too' won't be good enough for much longer. Besides, it's just me. You can say it in front of me. You've already let me in on your little secret, so don't worry about it."

Still red-faced, Mark said awkwardly, "Aw, I know. It's just strange for me still, and we've been trying to keep it under wraps for so long that it's kind of a habit. It won't be for long though, and you're the only other person who knows." He looked up at the night sky, then closed his eyes and smiled, "I'd better get going so she doesn't worry. Let me know when you hear from little miss."

Joe watched Mark take the outside stairs two at a time on his way down, then looked up into the same night sky. After Mark had driven away, Joe dropped his gaze to the clearing behind the house and said, "I guess you knew this too, didn't you?" A tear rolled down one cheek, but he was smiling. *I can almost feel you here, Jodie.*

Between the night and being windowless, the file room was pitch-black, so Jo turned on the overhead light. She told Nancilee, "We're going to need the light to see in here, but push the door closed so no one will see."

After fumbling with the keys again, Jo managed to open the cabinet. The girls then methodically moved the stacks of papers and envelopes from the shelves inside to the table in the center of the room. They were careful to arrange everything on the table just as it had been in the cabinet, so they could put it all right back where Margo had them.

Once cleared, Jo grabbed the chute handle and grinned at Nancilee, "Here goes," and she tugged it open with the signature screeching sound of the rusty hinge. The girls crammed themselves together trying to look into the dark chute, but, like Margo, they couldn't see anything.

Nancilee stood on a chair to look into the chute and couldn't reach past the chute door. "I see something though. I don't know what it is, but I can't reach it anyway."

"Let me try, my arms are longer," and Jo hopped onto the chair. She looked, then swept her arm inside, "I see it. I don't know what it is either. There's some kind of line or something hanging from this metal thing. I can . . . almost . . . get . . . Got it!" Jo reached in with her other hand and pulled, but the top of Ed's box hit the bottom of the chute and wouldn't budge.

She tried three more times, then stood up. "My arms are hurting, it's a weird reach. Give me a minute, and I'll try again. I know I can get it."

• • •

Margo couldn't stand her anxiety or the quiet in the empty house. Recognizing her growing panic, she thought, *Ed, where are you?*

She picked up the phone again, noticed it was almost out of charge, and decided to try calling him again anyway. Instead of pushing the apparently useless "Ed" button again, she punched his number in manually, made more difficult by her shaking hands. *Be there. Come on, Ed!*

Ed was still leaning against his tree in the butterfly reserve, almost asleep when his cell phone vibrated. He started, surprised that it rang at all. He didn't recognize the number, but answered tentatively, "Hello?"

Margo started to cry, "Oh, Ed!"

He sat up straight and asked incredulously, "Margo?"

She didn't know if she was having a complete emotional breakdown or finally waking up from a terrible dream. She couldn't explain and didn't understand the rush of feelings as she became intensely aware that the cold emptiness in her heart had once been filled with meaning and love from a sweet young Ed. Like a mist clearing after sunrise, Margo saw clearly what had always been there and said in an anguished whisper, "Ed. I . . . I . . . I have ruined everything, for so long. I was a fool."

"Oh my God . . . Margo," Ed said, as tears started to run down his face. He wasn't hearing the Margo he had just left at home; he heard his beautiful and happy wife before she had descended into a grief from which he had never been able to help her recover. "It's you, Margo, it's you," and he covered his face with one hand as he wept quietly.

No longer thinking about anything except him and all of their lost years, Margo said, "I need you here, Ed. Come home as soon as you can. There's so much we need to talk about. So much that . . ." and Ed's phone went silent. He looked at his phone and saw the signal was bouncing between one signal bar and none.

At home, Margo noticed the sound coming from her phone changed when the sound of the Cerro Pelon wind in the background stopped. She looked at the phone and saw that the battery had finally run out, and the screen was black. She burst into tears again, "No!"

She hurried back to Ed's shop to find a charger. Not seeing one, she opened the box that she had looked into earlier. Sure enough, there was a phone-charging cable. She sniffed and wiped her eyes as she plugged the phone into the connector in Ed's box, "He said this was a phone charger. Just what I need!"

The phone responded right away and began charging, but it would not allow her to do anything until it had charged for a few minutes. While she waited, Margo wandered to the back of his shop. *This is where he took refuge all this time, when I wasn't there for him. How could we have lived like this all this time? What have I done?* She sat on his bed and heard the phone chime that it was waking up. Lost in thought about Ed and all of their squandered years, she stroked the bed tenderly as though she was touching some part of him that was still there.

When the phone finished restarting, it also resumed the applications that were active when it lost power, one of which was the code that Margo had inadvertently started and then given a final "go" by pressing the "Ed" button twice. Margo heard a second chime but didn't see the message that appeared on the screen: "T-0."

Two seconds later a bright light flashed beside Ed's desk as a huge ball of white sparks appeared to be shooting out of the large box and into the ceiling. Margo rocked backwards on the bed, grabbed a handful of Ed's blanket in each balled-up fist, and clutched them to her chest. She gasped, terrified by the sight.

Inside the large box, although the other phones were turned off, the thermite from the device on top—that Margo had plugged her phone into—had ignited and in seconds had burned through the other cases and ignited their Franken-batteries too. In only a few seconds more, the white-hot fire penetrated the bottom of the box and the crate beneath it, inside which was sixty pounds of leftover thermite ingredients and two gallons of gasoline-gel. Before Margo took another breath, the crate exploded, filling the garage with white fire, hot enough to melt steel. It swarmed around and consumed everything in the room in seconds, including Margo.

In Mexico, Ed sat looking at his phone, tears still flowing as his heart poured out a lifetime of lonely sadness. But he also felt a sudden hope. This place that had brought him unexpected peace and long-forgotten clarity, could it perhaps bring even greater redemption, maybe finally bringing him and Margo back to life together? In that moment, nothing mattered but Margo. Laughing and crying at the same time, Ed stammered happily to the wind, "Margo . . . I . . . we . . ."

He was interrupted by a familiar hissing sound and was instantly surrounded by what looked like white fireflies as the device strapped to the tree above him lit, with the other sixty-two devices scattered throughout the reserve. He was still smiling as he had his last thought, *Margo!* And then the flames took him as they roared through his beautiful forest.

• • •

Mark almost hadn't seen Jessie's Explorer as he drove past the high school, but it caught his eye sitting in the empty lot. He pulled in and parked next to the Explorer, but when he didn't see the girls inside it, he decided on a whim to check the school. Finding the door unlocked but the school clearly closed for the night, he was reluctant to go inside. Standing just outside the open door, he thought he could vaguely hear laughing. *That's gotta be them!* He shook his head and followed the sound into the office, which was even darker than the hallway. Just as he was going to give up and chalk it up to hearing things, he noticed a thin line of light under a doorway down an inner hall. Hearing voices again, he walked down the hall and slowly opened the door.

Nancilee was standing beside the chair as Jo was reaching into the chute again, trying to pull up whatever was hanging from it, "I've almost got it!"

Mark opened the door wider and said, "And just what do you two think you're doing?"

Nancilee spun toward him, startled, and Jo jerked upright but still hung on to the chain, desperate to solve her mystery. Jo recognized his voice and answered without looking, "Uncle Mark, this isn't what it looks like. We're not stealing or anything."

He walked into the room and around the table toward them as he said impatiently, "Yes, that all sounds fascinating. What do you say you tell me about it at home before we all get arrested?"

Nancilee looked up at him and pleaded, "Don't be mad. We can explain!"

Mark's stern expression melted as he looked in the young girl's face, "Hey, kid, who's mad? I'm just looking out for you." He put a hand on her shoulder and looked at Jo, "Both of you. Come on now, come with me, and let's talk about this somewhere else," and he reached up to put a hand on Jo's back.

Jo, still hanging on to the chain with both hands, sighed and started to loosen her grip and let the device slide back down. She turned a defeated smile to Mark, "Okay, okay. We're going."

As she turned to look back into the chute, Mark saw her flinch backward from the cabinet opening. In one motion, he pulled Nancilee away and behind him with one arm as he caught Jo with his other arm behind her back. In that same instant, he saw bright white light shoot up through the chute opening and wheeled his body reflexively between it and Jo.

The blast that poured out of the chute lifted him off of his feet, and his sense of time compressed as adrenaline flooded his brain. In the two seconds that followed, Mark pulled Jo to his chest, wrapping her in a bear hug. He could hear the voice in his head screaming, *Protect her!* He did his best to wrap himself around her as he and Jo flew together away from the cabinet and across the table in the middle of the room.

As Mark pulled her to him, Jo's focus was first on Nancilee, who was stumbling backwards away from Jo. The two had locked onto each other's eyes, and Jo thought fleetingly, *You're good, thank goodness!*

Still arcing through the air over the table and not comprehending what was happening, Jo looked into Mark's wide and anxious eyes and thought, *I'm glad he's here, Mom.*

At the same time, Mark looked into Jo's eyes and saw her mother's eyes looking up at him, and he felt inexplicably calm. Jo pressed her face against him, and he pulled her closer, *I've got her, Jodie!*

Mark and Jo closed their eyes, and even in that terrifying moment, they were both imagining—and could almost feel—her there, hugging them, when time caught up with them again. In the blink of an eye, the blast shattered their bodies against the wall across the room, and life left them both.

Chapter 13

ASHES AND DESPAIR

Had she anticipated the storm,
she would have journeyed just the same.

MEXICO CITY (World News): Experts fear the worst for monarch butterflies in the aftermath of a catastrophic fire that swept through their winter home. With a total population now at its lowest in history, the endangered species is considered to be well below levels required to prevent extinction.

GRAYTON, TEXAS (Beaumont Enterprise): Investigators suspect arson in a fire at Grayton High School. Although two people were killed and a third person was injured, severe damage was contained to a file room with smoke damage throughout the school's front offices.

Nancilee's world had turned upside down.

That she was alive at all was only because the right conditions were aligned to contain the fire, rather than allowing it to engulf the file room, as it had in Ed and Margo's garage. When the device ignited at the school, Jo had been holding it near the open chute-door, and since the chute was sealed shut at the bottom, the air pressure spike from the small explosion blew almost all of the thermite and gasoline-gel out through the open chute door. There, instead of filling the room with a fireball, the cauldron of still-burning materials was funneled through the opening like water spraying from a hose, with almost all of it striking Mark in the back as it tossed him and Jo across the room.

Nancilee woke up the next morning in a hospital bed to find Tina, Jenny, and Joe sitting at the foot of her bed. When she stirred, all three of them stood up, and her mother and grandmother stepped quickly to opposite sides of the bed where they leaned over to hug her desperately. She could see the fatigue in the women's faces and their red eyes, swollen from crying. Joe didn't look much better.

She croaked out some words, "How are Jo and Uncle Mark?"

Tina bit her lip, and her eyes filled with tears, as Jenny swallowed and said, "Try not to talk too much. The doctor said you might have some respiratory damage from the smoke."

Nancilee looked down at her bandaged hands and held them up with a confused expression. Jenny stroked her granddaughter's arms tenderly and said, "They think you must have patted some flames out or burned your hands rolling Mark over to put them out." Jenny began crying.

The young girl looked from Jenny to Tina, and then to Joe and asked, "How are they?"

Tina glanced at Joe and nodded slowly. The expression on his face before he spoke was enough to start Nancilee crying. After a long pause, Joe said softly, "There was nothing more you could have done, kiddo. They were both hurt too badly, and we might have lost you too if you hadn't done whatever you did putting out the fire. As it was, when the firemen found you lying next to Jo with your burned arms around her, they thought you were gone too."

Joe hung his head and covered his eyes as the tears rolled down. Tina walked to the foot of the bed and wrapped her arms around him. Jenny cleared her throat and said, "The docs are worried about how much smoke you might have inhaled, so you're going to be here at least until tomorrow. And we're going to have to keep an eye on your hands until they're healed."

Nancilee didn't hear her grandmother. She held her bandaged hands over her face and cried so hard she was gasping for breath. She felt someone's arms around her and heard Joe speaking softly in her ear, his voice cracking, "Hey, I know how hard this is. It's going to be hard for a long while still. Just remember how much she loved you—how much both of them loved you."

Tina sat on the side of the bed next to Joe and waited for Nancilee's immediate grief to settle down. She then said, "Nance, we need you to tell us what happened. What were you doing at the school and what caused the fire?"

Blinking away tears, Nancilee explained, "It was just this crazy idea. We called it a quest to find where this crazy noise was coming from . . ." she trailed off into a few, light sobs before she explained Jo's idea to sneak in and open the cabinet to find whatever was hidden behind the metal door.

Her mom asked, "Hon, why didn't you just ask someone? Why go up there at night by yourselves?"

"We did ask, or at least Jo did, and Ms. Schmutz bit her head off just for asking. After that, we thought we could look for ourselves. That's all we were trying to do . . . *look*. What could happen?"

Jenny patted Nancilee's leg, "What about the fire, Nance, what *did* happen?"

The young girl sniffed and swung a bewildered look to Joe and Tina then back to Jenny, "I don't know. Jo was pulling something heavy out of this dark hole in the wall when Uncle Mark came in. I don't even know how he knew we were there. He got onto us for being there, and we were going to leave with him. But before you know it, this crazy, white fire shot out of the wall, and . . ." Crying again, Nancilee closed her eyes and pictured Mark and Jo flying across the room like they didn't weigh anything. She remembered Jo looking at her with what she could only describe as a peaceful expression as she clung to Mark mid-flight. It didn't make sense to her last night, and it stood out in her recollection now because it was so surreal, like everything else about that moment. Her last memory was feeling a blow to her head and chest as the pressure wave blasted out of the chute and into the room, slamming her against the wall.

Her chest hurting and now out of breath, Nancilee's crying slowly tapered off. After a few minutes she looked up at Jenny and said, "I don't remember anything else until I woke up here. I don't know what that fire was, but it wasn't anything we did. All we did was look."

It was then that Nancilee noticed a man in a dark suit standing in the doorway, and everyone else turned to look at the sound of his voice, "Young lady, if it's alright with your folks, I'm going to need you tell me that story again, and I'll have a few more questions for you." He showed Joe a badge and handed him a business card, "I'm Bobby

Powers, Orange County Sheriff's Office. I know this is a tough time, but we have to do this right away while the memories are fresh."

Joe stood aside as the deputy walked to the edge of the bed, "I need to start with something you may have heard on TV, it's called your Miranda rights. It's where I tell you all the things you have a right to do, including not answering my questions if you don't want to. Do you understand?"

Nancilee nodded, and Joe leaned towards the deputy, "Miranda rights? Why?"

"Sir, right now we have three people who were present during this fire, and the facts so far aren't so clear. As I said . . ." he turned to Nancilee and recited her rights.

Joe looked puzzled, "Officer, you don't think our girls did this, do you?"

"Sir, we haven't ruled anyone or anything out, and I'm just trying to sort it all out for now." The sheriff turned again to Nancilee, "If you and your parents understand what I've told you about your rights, are you willing to answer some questions?" He looked at the adults in the room, "Or would you prefer to have your lawyer present?"

Tina answered first with a wave of her hand, "That won't be necessary, Officer. She doesn't have anything to hide. Nance, you go ahead and tell him whatever he needs to know."

Nancilee nodded again, and the deputy said, "Alright, then, why don't you start from the beginning—why were you at the school after hours and how did you get inside?"

Nancilee explained it all again. When she finished, the deputy said, "Tell me again, what were you looking for in there?"

"We were really just trying to find where this weird noise was coming from that we heard every time Ms. Schmutz was in that room. Jo got it in her head that maybe Ms. Schmutz had something to do with the bad test scores at our school, so we were just trying to see whatever was there."

The deputy nodded and looked thoughtful, "And did you use something to look inside the chute, something that might have gotten away from you and caught fire by accident?"

"No!" Nancilee said as she started to cry. "We didn't have anything. We just looked, and when Jo tried pulling something up by some kind of chain, the fire just started. We didn't do anything but look!"

"Yes, you said that," the deputy answered. "And how about Mr. Hammock, perhaps he put something in there, not meaning to start a fire?"

"No, I told you, he just walked in by surprise. I don't know why he was there, but he wouldn't even look in the cabinet. He just wanted us to leave."

The deputy nodded, "Just what do you suppose he was doing there, if he wasn't there with you?"

"I can answer that," Joe interrupted, sounding impatient. "We were worried about where the girls were, when we thought they were already at home with Tina and Jenny. Mark left my house to go home and look for them on his way home. He must have seen them or the car and gone in to round them up. The rest of us had no idea what had happened until your office called my mom two hours later after tracing her license plates."

The deputy closed the notebook he had been writing in and said, "That's enough for now. I appreciate you speaking with me, all of you. I know this isn't a good time, and I'm very sorry for your loss. For a serious incident like this, especially with the loss of life, I expect I'll be back to see you before long, as will a few other investigators." He looked at the doorway and motioned to another large man in a dark suit standing there quietly, "And here's one now. So I will just get out of everyone's way. You have my card, if you think of something, please give me a call."

The new visitor walked in the room as the deputy was leaving. "Good morning, everyone. I'm Lieutenant Mason Bourgeois, from the Texas Rangers, and we're participating in the investigation. I listened to most of what you said to the deputy, but I'm going to have to go over the same things with you again. It's procedure. I know he went over your Miranda rights with you, and they still apply if you'd rather have an attorney present when you answer."

Tina bristled and snapped, "Just get on with it so she can rest."

Bourgeois nodded. "Yes, ma'am." He walked to the foot of the bed and spoke to Nancilee. "Now, young lady, I want to be clear on something you said before, then we can get on with the sequence of events. The person who you and Miss Deming were suspicious about, who did you say that was?"

"Ms. Schmutz?" Nancilee answered.

He leaned forward. "Schmutz. That's what I thought you said. Was it *Margaret* Schmutz?"

"I think so. Some people called her Margo. We never did," she said.

Still leaning forward, Bourgeois cocked his head and asked, "And what specifically were you suspicious enough about that you'd go into the school after hours and risk getting into a lot of trouble just for being there?"

Nancilee shrugged. "I guess it sounds dumb, but we thought maybe she was doing something that was messing up all of the test scores. We didn't think that just because she was mean or anything—which she *is*, and everyone is scared of her—but Jo heard her and Dr. Markus talking about Ms. Schmutz being the only person who handled all of the tests. And she *is* the only person who has done that for like a million years. So, Jo thought, maybe it was *her*. Maybe she was doing something—I don't know what—and if we looked inside that locked cabinet, maybe we'd find something."

She covered her face again with her bandaged hands as the tears started to flow, "I wish we had never started looking for that sound, and I wish we didn't go to the school last night. Now they're both gone . . ."

The Ranger stepped back and looked out the window, deep in thought. When Nancilee's crying had stopped, he faced her, took a deep breath, and said, "I'll try to keep this short now. Please just start at the top and tell me things like: Why you were there, how you got in, what you did inside the school, and what you remember from the fire."

Nancilee then told him the story just like she had told the deputy.

Three days later, Nancilee was recuperating at home when two cars pulled up to the mobile home. Lieutenant Bourgeois had called and asked for another visit, and he and a severe-looking man—obviously another cop in a suit—were there to follow up. Jenny let them in and led them to the kitchen table where Nancilee and Tina were waiting.

"Good afternoon, ladies," the Ranger said, "This fella is Wayne Meyer. He's from the ATF. That's the Bureau of Alcohol, Tobacco, Firearms and Explosives, a federal agency that gets involved in certain kinds of serious crimes. I need to remind you that this is a criminal investigation, your Miranda rights are still valid, and that anything you say can and will be used against you in a court of law. Do you still agree to answer our questions?"

Nancilee looked wide-eyed at her mother, who nodded slowly.

The other man spoke up, "I know you've already given statements to the sheriff and the Texas Rangers, but I'll first need you to tell me the events of five nights ago."

Looking down at the table, Nancilee recited the story. When she finished, the ATF agent folded his hands on the table and squinted his eyes, "I'd like you to tell me more about Margaret Schmutz and how much you and Miss Deming disliked her."

"Ms. Schmutz? I mean, she's kind of unfriendly—rude, really. But it's not like we hate her or anything," Nancilee answered, looking confused.

"Is it possible that you and your friend were playing a prank on her that got out of control that night? You can save a lot of people a lot of work by telling us," the agent said sternly, glaring at the girl.

Jenny slapped the table and raised her voice, "Now wait just a minute, Mr. Agent-man. She just told you—"

Meyer cut her off by holding up a hand, "Ma'am, I'm going to have to ask you to be quiet and let the girl answer. Otherwise, we'll have to have her come down to the police station for a formal interrogation." Still glaring at Nancilee, he went on, "Well, is it possible that a prank got out of control that night?"

Nancilee shook her head, "No. All we did was look inside the cabinet."

"Uh huh," he answered, tapping the table impatiently. "You said you had keys to get into the school. Is that also how you got into Ms. Schmutz's house that evening? Did you have keys to her house?"

"What? I've never been to her house. I don't even know where she lives and wouldn't go there if I did!" Nancilee answered, now even more confused.

Meyer nodded and raised his eyebrows, "*Lived.* You mean, *lived.* We're just getting started sifting through the evidence at the house, but we'll get there. It's going to take awhile though; *that* fire wasn't contained like the one at the school. It burned that house to the ground. But even so, we're seeing some similar residue in both incidents. So, I'll ask you again, how did this prank go so badly?"

She burst into tears, "What do you mean?"

The ATF agent, indifferent to Nancilee's tears, said curtly, "I want to know what was put in the school and in Ms. Schmutz's home, where they came from, and why they were used. And since you're the last person alive who was present, I'd like *you* to tell me right now."

Nancilee, still distraught, looked from Tina to Jenny, shaking her head, and said, "You know that isn't something Jo would ever do."

Jenny took her hand in both of hers and told Agent Meyers, "Alright, I think that's enough! Any more questions will have to wait until another day." All three women glared defiantly at the agent.

Meyers sighed and stood up, still staring at Nancilee, "Fine. I'll see you again soon, Ms. Davis." To Tina and Jenny he added, "My office and some others will be calling to schedule follow-ups, probably with a warrant. Before then, I suggest you have some frank discussions about the seriousness of giving false statements to federal investigators. It's one thing to be a person of interest or a suspect to a crime that included three deaths," he looked back at Nancilee, "don't make it any worse than it already is."

The women, taken aback, all sat wide-eyed and blinking.

As the agent walked to the door, Lieutenant Bourgeois nodded solemnly and said, "Ladies. And young lady, I hope you're healing up fine." He then turned and followed Agent Meyer out.

Jenny watched through the window as the two men stood next to their cars and talked. She told the others, "I don't know what the problem is, but that Texas Ranger is giving the ATF guy what-for about something." With all three women now peeking from behind curtains, an angry-looking Agent Meyer got in his car and drove away. Lieutenant Bourgeois stood by his car for a few minutes more, again looking deep in thought, before he also drove away.

• • •

Miguel Gallego had worked as a groundskeeper at the butterfly reserve in Cerro Pelon for more than twenty years. He knew every trail, rock, and tree throughout his woods, but he didn't recognize the black and dead-looking wasteland that he had just walked through in his first foray through the place since the fire had run its devastating course. Back at the park office near the entrance, he sat at a table outside and kicked soot off of his boots, unable to escape the charred smell saturating everything around him. With the destruction he'd just seen, Miguel wondered how the monarchs would ever recover.

His thoughts were interrupted when his phone rang. "Miguel, boy am I glad I finally reached you. This is Sam Waterston. I saw the news and have been calling for days. How bad is it?"

Miguel grimaced and looked up at the blue sky, "How bad? Oh Dr. Sam, it's crazy. It's all burned, everything. The groves in the heart of the reserve where most of the monarchs were, they're all burned. The fire spread through another thousand acres but burned itself out before the forestry commission guys even got here. They told me that it was just luck from the rocky terrain and wet conditions from rain the day before the fire, otherwise it could have kept burning and been worse. Worse! I don't know how that could be! You wouldn't believe it!"

"Oh my God, Miguel." After a pause, Dr. Waterston asked, "Hey, have you seen Ed—Señor Schmutz? He was there repairing some of our equipment. I had an email from him that he had finished his work, but I haven't heard from him since. His driver said he didn't show up for the ride to the airport."

"No, I haven't seen him, Dr. Sam. But he left a bag here, so I don't know . . . maybe he didn't come out? Dios mio."

Dr. Waterston said, "Oh no, that's what I'm afraid of. I'll keep trying to reach him, but I haven't been able to get through to his home number either. Let me know if he shows up there."

"Oh yes, of course I will," Miguel said.

"What are you seeing of the monarchs?" the professor asked hopefully.

Miguel shook his head and looked toward the blackened landscape, "I only saw a few small patches of them today. All the ones I saw wouldn't cover two trees if they were all in one place. I don't know how they ever come back from this. There's just not enough left, I don't think."

"I talked with Jorge Osorio at the university in Mexico City, and he's bringing a team up tomorrow," the professor said. "We'll see what they find, but keep your fingers crossed. I'll talk to you soon, Miguel."

As soon as he'd hung up, Dr. Waterston called Tom Baker in Orange, Texas, "Tom, I know this is a strange request, but could you go by Ed's house? I haven't heard from in several days, and the last I heard was an email the day of the fire in Mexico."

"Sure I will, Sam. I know I have his address somewhere from all our work together last year. I'll go as soon as we hang up," Dr. Baker said. "What are you hearing about the conditions in the reserve?"

"Not good, Tom, not good, at least according to one of the guys who takes care of the grounds," Dr. Waterston replied. "Just based on what he said, this may be it for the species, and that's going to ripple out and hurt many, many more, as you know."

Thirty minutes later, a stunned Tom Baker was standing on the street looking at the burned remnants of Ed and Margo's house. He stopped a neighbor who was walking by and asked what had happened.

The woman shook her head, "Who knows? It just went up in flames a few days ago. We don't know for sure, but we think one of them might have been inside. There was an ambulance here early the next morning, but they had all these curtain-things up, so we couldn't see what they were doing. All kinds of cops were here after the fire was out, and some have been here a few times since, which doesn't surprise me."

"You mean it doesn't surprise you because there was a fire?"

She looked surprised, "No, because they were always doing something out back that made all kinds of noise and smoke. Like they were playing with fireworks or something. I always wondered if that was legal, even if we are just outside the city limits. I guess they really did it this time, though."

"Yeah, I guess so. Wow," Dr. Baker said, still stunned. "Did you know the Schmutzes pretty well?"

"Not really. I don't know anyone who did. They kept to themselves, kinda curmudgeonly types, you know. Between that and whatever they were doing out there, some of us figured they'd burn down the whole neighborhood one of these days, just out of spite."

The professor gave a faint smile, nodded his goodbye, and got back in his car. On a whim, he stopped at the sheriff's office on his way back to the junior college in Orange to report Ed being missing.

• • •

Demands for action at Grayton High School were skyrocketing. Dr. Williams, the Orange ISD Superintendent, was inundated with calls from the school board, the County Commissioner's office, and the mayor. Many of the calls were of the understandable, "What the hell is going on in that school?" nature. He did his best to deflect them with variations of, "Yes, yes. We're very concerned, and we have been giving Grayton High direct attention for some time. This incident is a reminder that there is still work to do."

There was now a heightened level of energetic interest from the governor's office and the Chamber of Commerce. Hanging up from the last in a series of those calls, he said to his deputy superintendent who had just walked into his office, "Well, now it's at an all-new level. There are several corporate partnerships the state has been pursuing with Walmart, Amazon, and the like—all about luring big, high-profile investments and jobs—and they're now at risk. CEOs are suggesting they might have to look harder at other states' offers and are not in any hurry to be anywhere near East Texas unless this is resolved."

The deputy superintendent looked shell-shocked, "Yeah, that's what I came to talk to you about. The dang Chamber of Commerce is raising hell with the mayor, and he wants us to know that it's *our* problem to fix. Seems they're also seeing several companies slow-rolling some development plans. The mayor wants us to understand what that means in property and corporate tax revenue, not to mention the trickle-down commerce hit if the county loses one of these big-time distribution centers—because of 'our mismanagement.'"

"Exactly. Money. Forget what's going on in education . . ." Dr. Williams scratched his head and looked pained. "Doesn't matter. We're going to have to get out in front of this now. Lousy politics or not, it's the nature of the game. Someone's gotta take the blame when the politicians get ahold of this. Close the door, and I'll tell you about some calls I've already made."

Two weeks after the fire, Dr. Williams met with the Orange ISD School Board to take his beating and to quell the insurrection. He sat alone at a table in front of them, as they sat at a long table arcing around him. With an election in the coming fall, all of the board members were interested in being on the record with their dissatisfaction in the state of Grayton High School. One of the most outspoken was Lanita Westchase, "Dr. Williams, I want to be clear in my concern for the continued mismanagement of the education of Grayton's youngest generation, and now their personal safety! If you aren't able to do something about it, perhaps it's time for more assistance from the state."

The superintendent sat expressionless until the clapping died down and then said calmly, "Well, Lanita—ah, Ms. Westchase—I hope you believe that I share your concerns about Grayton High School. As for more state assistance, I recall that only three months ago, in this very room, you criticized the school district for enabling so much outside and state-level interference."

"Now just wait a minute, Dr. Williams! It is this board's job to evaluate the school system's performance and set policy! It is *your* job to get it done!" Ms. Westchase said indignantly.

Dr. Williams held up both hands in surrender, "Yes, yes, Ms. Westchase. I agree completely. What I meant to say is that the situation at Grayton High School has been a complicated problem for a long time, and we've been reaching out for more help to resolve it. You all know that we brought in a specialist team with some new ideas to reverse the downward trend we've seen in test scores—a trend that started years before Dr. Markus and his team arrived. Part of our goal was also to try to fend off more intervention from the state so we can manage our community's education to meet this board's expectations."

Ms. Westchase nodded but was still glaring at the superintendent as he went on, "You've all seen the data. Whatever is causing the Grayton students' test scores to plummet has only gotten worse in the last few years. We're seeing student enrollment in advanced classes drop, although grades in course work have gone up. It's baffling. We're also now seeing less than half the number of students taking college board exams compared to a decade ago, and those who do aren't performing as well as they once did. Again, it's baffling. To make it worse, we've seen a spike in faculty retirement and many others seeking transfers, and the recurring theme is about the new curriculum and teaming they have been forced to adopt, when they believe they've been doing everything right all along."

He took a deep breath and scanned all of the board members' faces. *This ain't going well, pretty much like I thought it would go. Here goes nothing* . . . "All things considered, the district must accept that our strategy is not working, and things are still amiss at Grayton High School. Effective immediately, we are replacing Dr. Markus and the staff he brought in from other programs. We are transferring an experienced principal from our college-prep school, West Orange High, and bringing in assistants from Port Arthur and Beaumont."

"So you're finally firing Dr. Markus with all his charter-school ideas?" Ms. Westchase asked.

"Ah, well yes. And we're suspending the new programs and curriculum indefinitely. The new administration at the school will need some time to shift things back to something you may recognize and be more comfortable with. We can also expect to have state auditors participating in the district's management processes for some time," Dr. Williams said.

Ms. Westchase turned an expectant look to the board chairman, sitting to her right. He cleared his throat, looked in Dr. Williams's direction without making eye contact, and said, "That brings us to our last order of business. We have been notified that the state has formally reduced Grayton High School's rating to "academically unacceptable," and Orange ISD has been stripped of our "recognized" rating. Which means, now we're *really* going to get "help" from the state board of education. Given the district's continued struggle to straighten things out, the board has no choice but to invoke a performance clause in the superintendent's contract to remove him for cause and replace the district staff with a team that has our confidence going forward. We thank you for your service, Dr. Williams, and wish you well in your endeavors elsewhere. With that, I think that brings our meeting to an end. Thank you, everyone," and the chairman banged a gavel, and the entire board immediately stood and walked out, leaving Dr. Williams stunned and alone at the front of the room.

• • •

The day after reporting Ed's disappearance to the Orange County Sheriff, Tom Baker was visited and interviewed in his office by Deputy Sheriff Bobby Powers. Afterwards, Powers was intrigued by something the professor told him and called Texas Ranger Bourgeois to pass it on, "I know this ain't TV, Lieutenant, but it feels funny. Mrs. Schmutz dies in a suspicious fire that appears connected to another suspicious fire the same night at the high school. And now we hear that not only is *Mr.* Schmutz missing, but on the same day as our fires here, there was a fire somewhere in Mexico where this guy went missing! I don't have all the answers, but, like I said, it sure feels funny."

"Yeah, I see what you mean. I'll give Meyer a call at ATF and let him know. And I think I'll have a chat with this Dr. Baker myself," Bourgeois said. "Hey, thanks. I'll let you know if we connect more dots."

Two days later, Bourgeois and Meyer visited Tom Baker, where he told him everything that he had shared with Deputy Sheriff Powers. Agent Meyer then said, "I'm going to have to make some calls, first to this professor in California, and then to some of our counterparts in Mexico. We have a couple of joint task forces we work with on some things on both sides of the border, maybe they can help clear this up."

"Good idea," Bourgeois replied. "I'm going to run back to the office to go through the evidence list and photos from both scenes. Something's bugging me about these gadgets Dr. Baker said good ol' Mr. Schmutz built. Could be nothing, I know. It'll be good to see the lab reports when your folks are finished too."

Both men were busy chasing leads for the next several weeks. After Agent Meyer interviewed Dr. Waterston, he was able to pull a few strings and contact investigators who had been in Cerro Pelon. Over the ensuing months, that put a number of other inquiries in motion, the first outcome of which was a short, unsigned letter Dr. Waterston received from Mexico City:

> Dr. Samuel J. Waterston:
>
> This is to inform you that, pending the investigation into the fire at the Santuario del Cerro Pelón, your program's and your personal visitation privileges at the Reserva de Biosfera de la Mariposa Monarca and all teaching privileges at Universidad Nacional Autónoma de México are revoked. Also, my program at UNAM will cease all collaboration and affiliation with you and your laboratory. I am directed to inform you that any further correspondence must be sent through the Policía Federal Ministerial.
>
> Jorge Alfredo Osorio
> UNAM, Director Ejecutivo de Estudios y Preservación de Mariposas

• • •

Joe had been at home for the two weeks since the fire. He found himself unable to work, with too many memories in his shop of people he loved and had now lost. His only visitors had been family, including Jenny, Tina, and Nancilee, who had joined him every night for dinner at his or his parents' house. As comforting as it was to have them all around, he couldn't bring himself to talk about Jo and Mark. The pain he felt was all too fresh and overwhelming. He still wasn't sure he had it in him to heal the missing part of his heart and move past the grief.

Stopping by for an unannounced visit, Bill Arceneaux found Joe where he now spent most of his time, on his back deck, staring listlessly at the treetops. The older man said hesitantly, "I hope you don't mind me stopping by, son. I just thought you might need some company." He sat in the wooden rocker beside Joe and patted his arm.

Joe gave a half smile, then turned back to look at the trees. After they had sat quietly for a while, listening to the wind rustling through the pines, he said, "I always feel her here, you know. So much about this place is all about her. That spot right down there was her favorite place to sit and think about life. She called it *her* spot. Remember, we had that old trailer right over there against the woods next to it?" Joe's voice cracked and tears filled his already-red eyes. "Losing her . . . it was like a part of me died. I don't think I could have survived it without Jo. She needed me, needed me to be Dad, to help her be strong and live her life the way her mom would want her to, so I couldn't just give up. But now, I don't know how to take the next step or why I would even try with *both* of them gone."

He looked at his old friend then turned back to the woods, "I don't know how Ben and Dina survived this years ago. They lost their own daughter, then raised *her* daughter—Jodie—only to lose her at a young age too. But *they* never lost their way, never lost that light in their eyes. I don't know if I can do that now. I feel . . . broken," and the younger man covered his face as his tears fell.

Arceneaux squeezed his shoulder and said, "I know it hurts, son, I do. It broke a lot of people's hearts when you lost that wife of yours, mine included." Struggling to stay composed, he went on, "This old man still gets misty sometimes when I think of her. But, you know, as special as she was, and even though it hurt to lose her—hell, it still hurts—I smile when I think of her too. She had a way about her, and I know you know that better than anybody. She had this way of sharing some light with other people, without really trying. It was just how she was . . . *who* she was, really.

"I don't understand why things happen the way they do sometimes, but I do know that's how her grandparents got through it when she passed," Arceneaux said, now looking at Jodie's spot. "They still felt that light, as you called it, from that wonderful little gal of theirs, and they knew they were better for it, for having had her as long as they did. They saw how she affected other people, especially those who loved her, and most especially you and your precious young'un. I know they also had your daughter as a reminder to help them move on again from the loss, but it wasn't just that. And it wasn't just that for you back then, either. Part of it was *her*," Arceneaux's voice dropped for a moment to a whisper, "that sweet little Jodie—and that gift she gave you, and her gramma and grampa, and all of us. It was that light, that happy way of seeing the world and going through every day. And like the rest of us who knew her, you know she'd want you to keep that in your heart.

"Since I'm giving you bits of old-man wisdom, I'll give you one more: You know, in some ways, she shared that light of hers with your daughter more than anyone. That little gal was her mama to a tee, especially in that way—she had the same effect on people. I could see it, and I don't mind admitting that this is one old man who liked coming around for a visit because she was like a fountain of youth and happiness, just like her mama," Arceneaux chuckled. "Don't you forget that. When you look out there in that clearing where they both spent so much time, you remember that light. The light they both had, and the light they both shared with the rest of us."

Arceneaux stopped talking and bowed his head, wiping his eyes with his sleeve. Joe patted the older man's arm, and Arceneaux laughed again through tears, "Oh hell, now ain't this great? I didn't come over here for you to make me feel better, young fella!"

After a few minutes, Joe looked sideways at Arceneaux, cleared his throat, and spoke softly trying to keep his voice from cracking again, "You're right, Bill, about the two of them, that is. They did both have something about them—all from Jodie of course," and now he laughed through tears. "I do still feel it, feel *them*."

Joe paused, looking at his girls' spot like he was studying it, "I know what they'd want for me, but it's just so hard to see through all of this right now. One thing I have to remember is, it isn't just me. I mean, yes, I know I've lost a lot, and it's breaking my heart. But other people loved Jo too, like you said, and some—like the family—maybe as much as me. And Mark. He was like a father to Nancilee and Tina both. And he was head-over-heels about Jenny, which I didn't think would ever happen for him."

Arceneaux chuckled again, "Yeah, people do come around sometimes. And don't you forget it was your wife who pulled him back from the abyss years ago. Just think about how his life changed starting on that day."

Joe smiled, "Yep, she was a wonder." He sat quietly for a few minutes, and then said, "Speaking of Mark, that reminds me, I hope some of his good fortune rubs off on his gals now. There's been some talk by the police about Nancilee being a *suspect* in that fire and some other fire in town. We may have to lawyer-up, and I don't know where to start for something like that, even if the whole thing is crazy. I'm not sure yet when they'll release their bodies because of the investigation."

"Now that ain't right at all, none of it," Arceneaux said, dumbfounded. He sat there thinking for minutes, then stood abruptly and said, "Tell you what, I had better move along. I just remembered I have some calls I need to make."

Joe stood and shook his hand, "Okay, life doesn't wait for us, does it? I'm glad you came, Bill. Come on by anytime, whether it's to share more old-man wisdom or just to have a beer. And you didn't say anything about work, but I know I've been leaving you high and dry on the job. I just don't know how to go back into the shop yet."

Arceneaux shook his head, "Don't you worry about it or anything else. I figured you would have your hands full for a while, so I pulled in a couple of other outfits to fill in for you for now. They're guys you like, don't worry. You take whatever time you need, and we'll talk when you're ready. Take care, boy."

The first call that Bill Arceneaux made once he was in his pickup was to Ken Hammock, Mark's father. They were old acquaintances but certainly not friends, and Arceneaux wasn't looking forward to the call. When Hammock answered, Arceneaux took a breath and started talking, "Ken, I know this is a bad time, and I'm very sorry about your boy. Now, this ain't really my business, but I think there's some things you should know about. You do whatever you want after that, 'cause, like I said, it ain't my business." He explained Mark's connection to Joe and Jodie Deming and to Jenny, Tina, and Nancilee, and the predicament they now found themselves in.

Hammock snorted, "And you think it's my job to bail these people out somehow? Didn't you say he worked for the guy? Why can't he bail them out?"

"He isn't connected in this county like you are," Arceneaux said, trying to sound neutral. "I figured you might want to hook them up with someone who has some stroke, with your boy being so close to them and all."

"Alright, you said what you wanted to say," Hammock said. "You were right, this ain't your business," and he hung up.

• • •

The next week, after missing two weeks of school, Nancilee reluctantly returned to school to finish the eleventh grade. However, because of the fire and on-going criminal investigation, the school district reassigned her to the troubled-youth program at Lee High School on the east side of Orange. Tina was now working evenings and weekends at Walmart, which gave her the time to drive her daughter the forty-five minutes to school and back every day.

Dropping her off the first day, Tina told a stoic Nancilee, "Hey, hang in there. It's only a few months until summer, and it's still better than repeating the whole year, right?" Seeing the tears welling in her daughter's eyes, she pulled her into a hug, "Hey now, I know it's hard, kid, but it's going to go by fast. You'll see. Now don't let them see you cry; you don't want to have to shank anyone on your first day in the yard!"

Nancilee wiped her eyes, "Oh great, Mom, so it *is* like prison!" She laughed and said, "Don't worry, I'll be okay."

Tina was beaming as Nancilee got out of the car, "Damn, I'm good at this pep-talk stuff. I'll have to use that 'shanking' bit more often!" Nancilee rolled her eyes and went inside.

After enduring her first four classes filled with kids she didn't know but who pointed at her and whispered, Nancilee found a vacant corner in the cafeteria to wait out lunch while reading. She looked up when she noticed several people standing around her and saw the familiar face of Jamie Faison, who had been sent to the same school last year after failing the tenth grade and being expelled for threatening teachers.

"Well looky, looky here! One of the prissy little smart girls is now in the juvie school," Jamie said in a loud voice. He hadn't changed much, although he now had an almost-invisible mustache and a longer, unkempt mop of curly blond hair. True to form, the boys with him appeared to be his entourage and laughed like he had just said the most hilarious thing they'd ever heard as they crowded around him.

Nancilee sighed and said to herself, "Now it's perfect," and she put her book into her backpack and started to stand up.

Jamie stepped behind her and planted a foot on the bench next to her, blocking her way. "No, don't go yet, you should let me introduce you to everyone. Dudes, meet Nanci-loser." He paused with an annoying and evil grin, and then said, "She's always been soooo smart, her and the other guy-girl who she hung out with all the time. What's her name? Jo, right? Of course, and that makes sense too! She had a guy's name so she must have been the *guy* of your little couple, right?!"

Nancilee's face turned red as Jamie and his friends howled. "Do you guys know why she's Nanci-loser . . . I mean besides the guy-girl thing? It's 'cause she's trailer-trash, *real* trailer-trash living in a little house with wheels and everything! And get this, her trailer-trash mom got knocked up in high school by this murderer—another trailer-trash loser named Hammock or something, and he's like my *grampa's* age! Now they're all just a big, happy, loser, trailer-trash family."

Jamie turned a sad-clown face toward Nancilee, stuck his lower lip out and said in a sad voice, "Uh oh, wait. It's not such a big and happy family of losers now is it? Guy-girl and grampa got burned up in the school, didn't they? What were y'all doing there? Did he get tired of your mommy and trade her in for you two losers?"

He was laughing and looking at his friends and didn't see Nancilee's fist before it landed as hard a blow as she could on his mouth. When he stumbled backward, she made her getaway, putting her head down as she hurried out of the cafeteria before her sobs came. Behind her, Jamie yelled, "If that's how you want it, Nanci-loser! You better have eyes on the back of your head now!"

One of his pals asked him, "Dude, why do you hate her so much? It's weird that she looks just like you, except she doesn't have a busted lip from a girl punching her." That set them all laughing again, except for Jamie who tackled his pal with a shriek, and the two of them rolled on the floor swinging wildly. Fortunately for Nancilee, the fight was broken up by a football coach who had been monitoring the cafeteria, but he hadn't seen any part of her interaction with Jamie. He also wasn't interested in hearing Jamie's side of any story, otherwise that might have been her last day in any school for the year.

That Sunday night, the whole family gathered for dinner at Joe's parents' house. After dinner and sitting next to each other at the table, Jenny and Tina began arguing in hushed tones, eventually stopping conversation as everyone looked at them. Jenny sighed and explained, "Listen, I know this may sound sudden or rash, but I've withdrawn from college for the rest of the semester. Right now, I'm not sure if I'm going back."

Tina grabbed her mother's hands, "No, Mom, you're so close to finishing! You'll graduate in August if you don't give up—that's only five months! You know that's what we all want you to do. You know that's what *he* would want too." She looked around the table to see the family's sad faces nodding in agreement.

Jenny's head dropped as tears rolled down her face. After a few minutes she said, "You don't understand. I know we are all hurting, and I'm not saying my loss is any more than anyone else's. God knows, I loved Jo like she was my own." She covered her eyes with one hand, "but Mark and I . . . we were going to be married after I graduated." She trailed off and started to sob, and Tina burst into tears. Joe's mother, Jessie, jumped up, hurried around the table and sat next to Jenny, putting an arm around her. Jo's great-grandmother, Dina Lucky, reached across the table to take Jenny and Tina's hands in her own. Ben Lucky, who was sitting next to Dina, put a hand on her shoulder and stroked her arm.

After a few minutes, Jenny continued in a broken voice, "He didn't want to tell you all yet, because he thought it should be about me until I was done. And he wanted to ask Tina and Nance for their permission." Jenny and Tina burst into fresh tears, and Nancilee leaned against her mom, hugging her tightly as she cried too.

When everyone was breathing a little easier, Joe said, "I don't want to upset anyone, but maybe now would be a good time to tell you some things about Uncle Mark. You all know, he had his demons. Well, he did a long time ago anyway. The way he said it, he went from being a troublemaker as a kid, to a loser as an adult, and then turned himself into the Uncle Mark we all knew and loved."

He then explained Mark's troubled past, as Mark had explained it first to Jodie on that fateful day in her clearing, and as Mark had told Joe through their years of working together and becoming family. While he talked, the others would shake their heads and from time to time mutter, "No," or "Oh, wow!"

When he had finished, most of them sat back, letting Mark's story sink in. Joe wiped his eyes and said, "It's incredible, really. This guy who had given up on life meets someone who just happens to be the daughter of a woman whose death he was responsible for, only to have that daughter reach something in him that brings him back to life. And he becomes this important part of her life, *her daughter's* life, and our family."

He looked at Jenny who was smiling and asked, "You knew all of this, didn't you?"

She just nodded her head, and Joe came around the table and kissed her forehead.

After a few minutes of quiet, Tina spoke, tentatively at first, "Since we're telling Uncle Mark stories, I'll tell one more. Maybe you'll see another reason why he was so important to us." Jenny raised her eyebrows, and Tina smiled bravely, "It's okay, Mom. I want them to know." She told them *most* of the story from that night at Branson Pond, her savior appearing as if from nowhere, and how he had watched over her—and then watched over *them*—from then on. "We called him Uncle Mark, but he was really like a father to me, and I couldn't have loved him more."

After several more minutes of hushed crying around the table, Nancilee asked, "So, he wasn't really my father?"

Tina looked startled, "Nance! No! Of course not. Why would you ask that?"

Nancilee looked down at the table and she fought back tears as she explained her years of taunting from Jamie Faison, ending with that week's encounter in the cafeteria at school. When she finished, she had tears running down her face, and she looked furtively at her mom, "Sorry, Mom. I know I could have gotten in even bigger trouble, but I couldn't take any more of him talking about them."

Tina hugged her as all of the grammas came around to hug them both, and Tina told her, "Don't you worry, punkin. I know from experience that he'd have gotten a lot worse from Uncle Mark for messing with you." She added in a conspiratorial tone, "I just hope you broke some teeth," which set them all to laughing.

Two days later and almost a month after the fire, the coroner released Mark and Jo to their next of kin. The family was surprised to learn that Mark had been claimed by his father, of whom they had never heard him utter a word. Disappointment turned to heartache when Jenny learned Mark had been buried right away without ceremony.

That weekend, on an unusually temperate East Texas March afternoon, a crowd gathered around Joe's house, much like it had twelve years earlier. Once again, cars lined both sides of the state highway out front for more than half a mile in both directions. This time, rather than Jodie, this large group of family and friends came to remember Jo and Mark. Most of the people who were there had also been there for Jo's mother, and there were more still, including young people who knew Jo from school. The misfits and outcasts were there, of course, and many more.

After talking about it for a while over dinner earlier in the week, the family had settled on Nancilee speaking for them all, partly because they were all still struggling to speak at length about Jo and Mark, and also because Nancilee was adamant that *she* do it. When it came time, Nancilee asked everyone to gather into the clearing behind the house, leaving Jodie and Jo's spot open for her and the family. Nancilee took a breath and thought, *Help me do this, sister.*

Then she lifted her head and spoke from her heart, "I'm not going to tell you everything about Jo and Uncle Mark. There's so much to tell, and I wouldn't be able to say it all without breaking down, which I probably will anyway. But I do want to tell you who they were. Who they were to *us*. Who they were to *me*. I want you to know who we all lost and who you should remember.

"Jo . . . there's too much about her," she paused and wiped her eyes. "Jo was my friend. We were best friends since we met when I had just finished the first grade. Back then, I thought she would be my only friend forever, but she wasn't. She taught me how to be friends with other people too, taught me that I *could* be and could let them be friends. That may sound silly to most of you, but it was so real—it was just the kind of thing she did all of the time." Heads nodded and quiet agreement murmured throughout the crowd around her.

"She was so much more. She was my sister. I always knew that she loved me and would for the rest of our lives," she paused to cry briefly and then gathered herself. "J-J-Just as I loved her. I still do, and I know she does too. I miss her and wish she was still here with me, with us. She even gave me her wonderful family. She brought my family into hers, and we're just one big family now—a *real* family that loves each other and is there for each other. You see? She *was* my sister.

"And Uncle Mark—that's what we called him, Uncle Mark—he's been there literally my entire life. He was there for my mom when she was my age, and he has been a guardian angel for her, and me, and my grandmother for my whole life. I can't imagine a better or kinder guardian angel to have.

"Not only was he good to us every day, but he brought us into this family. He found his way to them first, and then he brought us with him. We have this family, and I have my sister, because of Uncle Mark. And just like her, I loved him, and I know he loved me."

After another pause, "We're here to remember them today because they're gone. I've heard people talk about things like this, when bad things happen and when we lose people we love. Things like God's plan, or karma, or fate. I read once about something called the 'benevolent universe' and that there's an arc of history that bends towards goodness.

"I don't know about any of that. Bad things happen, and I think they can happen to anyone, no matter how special and loved they are," she said, bowing her head to wipe away more tears. "Otherwise . . . I'm going to wake up from this bad dream to find that two of the best people I've ever known are still with us, that my *sister* is still with me.

"Jo told me something that she learned from her mom. It was, 'Look for the goodness around you and in other people. When you have the chance, help someone else find it too.' Jo's mom did that for Uncle Mark, and he did that for me, my mom, and my grandmother."

"I used to tell Jo that I wish I had known her mom. I realize now that I did know her, in Jo. And as hard as it is to remember most days, I know that in that same way, Jo is still with me. She'll always be with me and a part of me. And so will Uncle Mark," and she burst again into tears.

Nancilee looked toward the family and smiled as they all surrounded her in a group hug. She looked up to see Joe beaming at her. He bent towards her and tried to say something, started to cry, and simply laughed and grabbed her into a bear hug.

Someone weaving their way through all of the people that afternoon would have heard the same comments that were said about Jo's mother twelve years ago, and like that earlier group, they were all themes along the line of, "Yeah, wow, she really was something."

An eighty-five-year-old man stood unnoticed at the back of the crowd. Ken Hammock, Mark's father, felt like an intruder standing in a crowd who all seemed to know and love his son. He thought, *Who are these people? And who are these women that he "watched over" in a trailer park? Uncle Mark? I don't know these people from Adam!* He realized unhappily that having had no contact with Mark in almost forty years and hearing what these strangers said about him, he didn't know his own son from Adam, either.

He turned and hobbled unsteadily away, his cane barely keeping him on his feet. He looked over his shoulder and asked himself, "These are the people he turned to and who turned to him?" He suddenly felt very small, like the world had passed him by over the years. *My son and this girl who died with him, it doesn't seem like life passed them by.* With all of his money and connections, at the end of his life he had to hear the good things his boy had done with his life from strangers. Strangers who mattered to Mark when his own father had turned him away!

Sitting in his car, he recognized a familiar dull pain growing in his left arm and fished out a nitro pill from the bottle in his pocket. *Not today, I have things to do first.*

He pulled out his cell phone and called a number he hadn't used in a long time and was surprised when he heard a familiar voice answer, "Faison? Hammock. I need your boy to take care of something right away. It's about some women who knew my son. When can I see you?"

Three weeks later, Ken Hammock died alone at home, a broken and lonely old man.

Chapter 14

BUTTERFLIES

She would never know all the lives she touched, and most never knew how much she gave them.

For weeks after his and the ATF agent's visit with Jenny, Tina, and Nancilee at their home, Texas Ranger Mason Bourgeois scoured photos and revisited the file room at Grayton High School and what was left of the Schmutz house. If he took Nancilee Davis at her word, then the facts as he knew them still didn't make sense. The ATF's forensic analysis conclusively showed coarse red iron oxide, aluminum powder, and a petroleum-based residue at both sites. There was definitely a connection, but what and why?

Rather than wrack his brains to no effect, he scheduled another fact-finding session with the high school and district staff to dig a little deeper. Hopeful to make the public relations nightmare go away as quickly as possible, the school district was happy to oblige and was joined by officious representatives from Grayton City Hall and the Orange County Commissioners' Office. Rather than simply asking them questions, this time Bourgeois spread a large box of papers on several large conference tables, some of the papers obviously charred. He turned to the various civil servants and the high school staff who were there and explained, "I'd like you all to have a look at these, and maybe give me an idea what they are. Don't touch them—they're still bonded evidence, so we have to be careful with them—just walk around the tables and look at and see if you make heads or tails out of any of them. They're all from the cavity inside the wall in the room where the fire was. There were definitely more papers there, but some burned completely, and others are still in an ATF lab in Houston for chemical tests."

The group got up and milled around the tables. A few of the staff recognized some Scantron-style answer sheets. One of them suggested, "You know, those cards look a little like the answer keys we use for grading Scantrons by hand."

After a few minutes, a small woman pointed at some of the papers and said nervously, "I know what those are. They're student rosters that we use to show grade summaries by year groups. All of those answer sheets look like our standardized tests. Look, there's some from TAKS and the older TAAS tests. Boy, those are old—the state hasn't used TAAS since 2003. And those others are SAT and ACT answer sheets."

"And who are you, again, ma'am?" Bourgeois asked.

"Ruthie Gray. I'm the guidance counselor, and I handle papers like this all the time. Well, the rosters, anyway. Margo has handled all of the test materials for a while," she looked down with tears in her eyes.

"Margo? Margaret Schmutz, right?" When Ruthie nodded, Bourgeios asked, "And did she normally use that box in the wall for things like this?"

Ruthie shook her head, "No, I don't think that thing has been used for years and years. In fact, she had Ed put her cabinet right over it. I always figured it was because it wasn't being used anyway. We kept the student records in locked file cabinets."

Bourgeois' eyes narrowed, "And will you tell me again what Ms. Schmutz kept in the cabinet?"

"Well, that's where she stored the most sensitive standardized test materials," Ruthie answered. "All of the official test packages went in there, before and after every test. She kept it locked for security purposes and always did her work behind a locked door too. She was a stickler for that."

"Now that you mention it, I've heard something about that already," the Ranger said, recalling Nancilee's statements, "and who all had a key to this cabinet?"

"Only me and Margo, and I never used mine. The one time I did she kinda bit my head off," Ruthie said. "Like I said, she was a stickler for doing it all her way."

"Is there anything that stands out about these particular papers? Whether it's the specific information that's on them, the type of test, or anything?" Bourgeois asked.

Ruthie looked blankly at the papers strewn across the tables, shrugged and said, "The records are all written on, that's different. We don't usually do that. But, you know, we've had problems with low scores on these tests for years, and there have been auditors here many times. Maybe these are the kids with the lowest grades." She bent closer to look, "It's weird, I remember most of the kids who are highlighted, and they're not the ones in trouble. Look here, you can see their grades. These are all good students. I don't know what these are for."

"Maybe she was helping these kids cheat on tests. Is that possible?" Bourgeois asked.

"I don't know how she could," Ruthie said, shaking her head. "Besides, I can't remember how long it's been since any of our students did very well on these tests. That's why we've been under the microscope."

"How could we find out? If we wanted to check the test scores for any of the kids marked off in these records, how would we do that?"

One of the school district representatives spoke up, "We have the records for the state tests. You'd need to contact the College Board and ACT Incorporated about their tests. They have their own security procedures. We can help put you in touch with their people who monitor things like cheating, although Ms. Gray is right; I don't know how all or any of these kids could have been cheating."

Bourgeois nodded, "One thing at a time. Get me the contact information, and I'll reach out to these test people. Maybe they can help sort this out."

The Ranger stopped by the Orange County Sheriff's evidence room next, where he asked Bobby Powers to meet him. Scanning the evidence list, Bourgeois pointed out several items and asked Powers, "How much of this do you still have from the house, and how much has the ATF taken?"

"The metal shelves and desk are out in our warehouse, so's a bunch of burned-out computers. We also have a lot of burned books and notebooks bagged up here still. ATF took some of it for testing, and they took all of what's left of some smaller things, like some cell phones. Looks like this guy had his own Radio Shack going."

"I'm following up on some papers from the school fire that may give us an idea what was going on there," Bourgeois said. He added, thinking out loud, "Maybe there's something we're missing in the stuff from the house too."

Two hours later, they had sifted through ten large plastic tubs of charred books, papers and memorabilia, most of it barely recognizable. Seeing Bourgeois looking curiously at the remains of a half-burned notebook, Powers said, "That one got my attention too, since it wasn't as burned as the rest. It was in the middle desk drawer—the *metal* desk drawer, surrounded by that old metal desk. The thing was built like a battleship, so it was almost fireproof, although the right edge of the desk was literally melted away. Crazy."

Bourgeois used tweezers to lift burned sections of a notebook and said, "Here, hold this up while I turn the other pages." He noticed the deputy's furrowed brow, "I don't know, it may be nothing, but like I said, maybe there's a clue in here."

Powers leaned to look over the Ranger's shoulder, "I told you he was some kind of geek. What is that stuff?"

Shrugging, Bourgeois said, "Beats me, looks like something electrical though." He turned several more pages where they found a handwritten table with headings like "material, tube length, burn time" and random notes. He turned a few more pages then closed them again and said to Powers, "That's it. I'm calling Meyer over at ATF. Some of this has to be connected to those gadgets Mr. Schmutz made for those professors. Maybe Meyer's guys will find something in it that makes sense to them."

• • •

In April, Tina answered the phone at home, and a woman said, "Hello, I am calling for Jimmy Faison from Faison Law, and we have a legal matter that needs the attention of Genevieve and Tina Davis. Am I speaking to one of them?"

"You are, but I am sure neither of us has any business with the Faisons."

"Well, if you could come to the office, I am sure Mr. Faison can explain everything," she persisted.

"No thanks, I already have everything I will ever need from them," and Tina hung up.

After two more days of calls like this, Tina reluctantly agreed to allow the lawyer to visit her and Jenny at home. They were both surprised when Jimmy Sr. walked in behind Jimmy Jr. Although eighty-five years old and retired from practice, Jimmy Sr. still projected an intimidating presence that matched his decades-old reputation.

The four of them sat at the kitchen table, and after introductions, Jimmy Sr. said, "Thank you for allowing us your time. You've probably guessed by looking at me that I'm just an old retired lawyer, and you'd be right. When it comes to all of the details about our business today, my son and the firm will handle it, not me, but I felt obligated to explain it all to you personally at the request of an old friend.

"You see, that friend, Mr. Ken Hammock, passed away last week. I don't believe you knew Mr. Hammock, but shortly before he died, he learned of your acquaintance with his son, Mark. For reasons of his own and none of my concern, the elder Mr. Hammock modified his will, leaving his entire estate in a trust to the two of you," the old man said matter-of-factly.

"What? Why us?" a confused Jenny asked with tears in her eyes. "We didn't even know the man, and he sure didn't care enough about his only son to stay in his life,"

"I can't answer for Mr. Hammock's relationship with his son, but I can say that the estate is not insignificant. First, there is the sum of $500,000 that is yours as the sole beneficiary to Mark's life insurance, and it is completely separate from his father's estate. There was some confusion about that, or you would have already been contacted. We're already taking steps to remedy that for you. There's also the father's estate with approximately $3 million in various equity and cash accounts, and another $2 million in real estate. There are a few things we'd need to prepare for your signature on all of these as part of inheriting Mr. Hammock's estate."

Jenny turned to Tina and shook her head. Tina put an arm around her mother's shoulders and told the two lawyers, "I already told your secretary, we don't want any of Mark's father's money or estate or anything else that he wasn't willing to share with his son. I think we're both surprised about Mark's life insurance policy, but I guess that's different since it's from Mark, not his father."

Before Tina could say anything else, Nancilee walked through the front door, home from school. Jimmy Sr.'s eyes widened at the sight of her. Seeing her grandmother's tears, Nancilee hurried to kneel beside Jenny's chair, the old attorney's eyes following her intently as she went. Jimmy Sr. turned to look at his son while the three women talked, the grandmother and mother explaining why they had visitors. Jimmy Jr. sat stone-faced, glancing furtively once at Nancilee, then back at his father without changing expression.

Jenny sat straight, folded her hands, and said in a formal, businesslike tone, "Sir, thank you for explaining all of this to us. As my daughter said, we're more than happy to accept Mark's generosity, but we are not interested in any further business with his father or with you. So, I'd ask you to respect our wishes and please leave." Tina and Nancilee both glared at the two Faison men.

Jimmy Jr. started to answer, but his father held up a hand and said, "Yes, yes. As you wish. We'll provide your contact information to the life insurance company for Mark's death benefit." He stood and a confused Jimmy Jr. did also. The older man bowed his head briefly, "My condolences for your loss, ladies. Good day," and both men walked out.

In the car, Jimmy Jr. grumbled, "You just can't help some people. In their situation, living in a trailer park, how could they turn down Hammock's estate? Who cares if he didn't hug his son enough?"

The old man ignored his son's outburst and turned a steely look at him, "Don't you tell me that you didn't see what I just saw. That girl, I know you saw her."

"Yes, I saw her. And?"

Jimmy Sr. narrowed his eyes, "That young girl could have been one of *ours*. Everything about her . . . the hair, the eyes, her cheekbones." A visibly uncomfortable Jimmy Jr. started to answer, but his father cut him off, his voice now measured and barely masking his anger, "You had better not tell me you didn't see it. Instead, why don't you tell me whatever it is that's got you so squeamish."

Jimmy Jr. sighed and said, "Alright. There *was* something years ago that involved the boys, back when Teddy was still in high school. It involved the Davis woman named Tina, when she was also in high school with him. I didn't know her name then, and I didn't know it was her today until the daughter came in." He then explained the boys' run-in with Tina and Mark years ago at Grayton Pond.

"You knew this all of this time?" his father asked angrily.

"No, Dad, I didn't *know* all of this time," Jimmy Jr. answered. "I had my suspicions that something may have happened, but I didn't know there was a child. I was more focused back then on Hammock roughing up my boys—*your grandsons*—and they obviously didn't tell me the whole story about the little tramp at the time."

His father raised his eyebrows skeptically, then turned away with a serious expression that Jimmy Jr. had seen countless times as the older attorney strategized through one legal maneuver or another. When they pulled into the firm's parking lot, Jimmy Sr. said, "I want you to get everything together in Ken Hammock's estate . . . trust papers, every account, real-estate parcel, *everything*. I'll want to go over the game plan with you in the morning."

The next day, Jimmy Sr. visited Jenny, Tina, and Nancilee again at the end of the day at their trailer. Although they were still not interested in any dealings with the Faisons, Jenny felt some sense of obligation to accept the request from the statesman-like lawyer, out of respect for his age, if not basic civility. Sitting at the kitchen table again, this time Jimmy Sr. looked less like the famous and intimidating elder attorney and more like an anxious old man.

He began tentatively, "Now, Ms. Davis—all of you—please hear me out before you make a decision. And please trust that I have no agenda but to help. In fact, the firm intends to handle all of the legal proceedings, transfer the full estate, establish the new trust, and even manage the sale of the Hammock land parcels if you so desire. One last thing that I did not mention yesterday, at Mr. Hammock's request: Our firm would like to provide all counsel during any criminal or civil litigation involving the events in February. And we will do all of this at no fee to you or the estate. It was important to Mr. Hammock that we make this as easy an experience for you—and as lucrative, I might add—as possible. And we are committed to doing just that."

Jenny and Tina exchanged a curious look, then Jenny said, "Mr. Faison, I don't want to be unkind, and I am grateful for what Mr. Hammock tried to do for us and for your firm's offer of so much legal help, it's just that—"

"It's alright," Jimmy Sr. interrupted in a low voice, looking sadly at Nancilee, "and it is not you who has been unkind . . ."

Tina blurted out, "What my mom is trying not to say is what we've already said—we don't want anything from you, and certainly don't need any gifts or charity from the Faison family."

The old man nodded resignedly, "I understand. But please don't consider this a gift, and it isn't charity. It was very important to Mr. Hammock that he honor his son by doing as much as he could for you three who were so important to Mark. It would be *your* gift to Mr. Hammock, his son, and their memory for you to benefit from the estate, an estate that would have rightly passed to Mark and then to you under different circumstances. And as for my law firm," he paused as his eyes reddened, "please consider it a chance for an old man to do a small thing for the right reason and to pay his respects to such fierce Texas women, who show no appearance of needing anyone's charity."

Tina looked up at the ceiling, shrugged, and said to Jenny, "It sounds like we *do* need a lawyer, Mom." She looked across the table at Jimmy Sr. and said, "But only you and your son. We don't want to have anything to do with your grandsons or their sons."

"Of course," he replied, looking relieved. "I'll keep my hand in things just to keep tabs on everything, and only my son will handle any of your business. Expect to hear from our office tomorrow when everything is prepared."

They all stood up when Jimmy Sr. did, and he shook each of their hands, lingering for a second or two longer when shaking Nancilee's hand and looking into her eyes. "It's been my pleasure and honor to meet you all, ladies."

That evening over dinner the Davis women were in good spirits and joking about being millionaires. Tina told her mother and daughter, "You know what this means, right? This is a gift from Mark, and maybe it's also his way of telling us everything's going to be okay; it's okay for us to keep going."

Jenny looked puzzled. "Keep going?"

"With life. Keep living it and following our dreams. For you specifically, you're less than a year from being finished after all of this time, so how about getting on with it? Keep going by going back to school this summer and get back on track to be the first Davis woman to graduate from college."

After more cajoling and more tears as they swapped stories about Mark, Jenny listened to her daughter and re-enrolled to finish her senior year at Lamar University, starting that summer.

• • •

With less than a year until he retired from the Texas Rangers, Mason Bourgeois was anxious to keep pressing on the investigation to see it resolved while he still wore a badge and could push it along. His tenacity paid off by mid-summer. After tedious work combing through Ed's notebook and sifting through burned fragments from the garage, the ATF had pieced together enough detail to subpoena his credit card history, where they found a clear trail to his incendiary experiments. After trading data with investigators in Mexico, there was an even more compelling case.

In July, Bourgeois participated in a press conference at the Orange County Courthouse. Seated with him at the front of the conference room were the District Attorney, Orange County Deputy Sheriff Bobby Powers, and ATF Agent Wayne Meyer. The DA cut right to the chase: "After a broad investigation spanning several crime scenes, we now have sufficient evidence to close this case. The investigating officers from the Sherriff's Office, the Texas Rangers, and the ATF will review that evidence with you. In the end, you will see how the officers were able to demonstrate that Mr. Edwin Schmutz, a Grayton resident, is the architect of the devices that caused three horrific fires—two here in Grayton, and another, incredibly, in Mexico."

After all three lead investigators reviewed the evidence and the resulting insights each provided, the DA returned to the dais, "Again, it is now clear that Mr. Schmutz created these devices. We still do not have evidence to explain his motive, and, given his death and the destruction of so much of the physical evidence, we may never learn it. Although there is an on-going and related investigation that also implicates Mr. Schmutz's wife in the two fires in Grayton, her motive is also not clear, and she, tragically, also perished in one of those fires.

"However, let me also say that—at the *suggestion* of the esteemed defense counsel, Jimmy Faison, who is in the back of the room there, to keep me honest—we do have sufficient evidence to formally clear Miss Nancilee Davis from any role in these fires, as well as Miss Jo Deming and Mr. Mark Hammock, both of whom lost their lives in the Grayton High School fire."

The reporters then spent another hour asking a barrage of questions, trying to understand the links between Ed, Margo, Nancilee, Jo, Mark, the school, and Mexico. When the press conference ended and people in the room were leaving, Jimmy Sr. walked to the front of the room to shake the DA's hand. As he approached, he noticed, curiously, the Texas Ranger staring at him. At the same time, Powers stood to say goodbye to Bourgeois, "Well, this has been a heck of a ride, Mason," the deputy said with a grin. "Hey, I've been wondering, what is it about this case that it means so much to you? You've hung on to this like a bulldog, and I'm not sure we'd have made all of the connections if you hadn't kept at it personally."

Bourgeois stood, turning his attention from Jimmy Sr. to Powers as he shook the deputy's hand, "You're, right, it *is* personal to me. Forty years ago, I was a deputy sheriff right here in Orange County. I was the investigating officer for an incident that involved Margaret Schmutz, one that took her parents' lives and several others." He looked back at

Jimmy Sr., making eye contact when he said, "I even sat in a review in the DA's office right across the street from here, where we didn't do the right thing in the investigation. It's always bothered me. Maybe this was me stepping up like I should have then."

Jimmy Sr. had stopped listening to the DA and stood blinking, facing Mason Bourgeois. After a few seconds, the two men nodded curtly to one another and both turned and walked out of the room.

On his way back to Houston, Bourgeois stopped at a cemetery on the edge of town and walked through the rows of graves. Inside the funeral home, the funeral director watched through a picture window as the Ranger walked by, pointing toward him as he told his apprentice, "You just never know about people. That big fella there volunteered to pay for the burial and headstone for a woman who was headed toward the indigent cemetery in Beaumont. He never said why, just that he was no relation and wanted it to be anonymous. Something about 'it was still too little and too late.'"

The funeral director shook his head, "The way he said it got to me somehow that I can't explain. After all, in this business, it's not like it was my first touching story. You know? But I gave him the headstone at cost and the county covered the burial. It just felt right."

Outside, Mason Bourgeois stood at the foot of a new grave with his head bowed and his hat in his hands. Standing next to Cy and Lois Cormier's graves was a single, large headstone bearing two names:

Margaret Anne Schmutz	Edwin Henry Schmutz
May 10, 1954–February 13, 2014	February 8, 1954–February 13, 2014

Now at peace

The Ranger spoke softly to the headstone, "I guess it's finally over for you. I'm sorry that that day all those years ago took so much from you. I wish we had done more for you then." He cleared his throat and wiped a tear, "No, I won't hide behind *we*. *I* should have said more and tried to do more for you and your husband. Maybe it wouldn't have changed anything—probably wouldn't have, I guess—I don't know. Still, I shouldn't have dropped it, and I knew that at the time. I wish you could know how much that lesson stuck with me. For what it's worth, I taught my boys and everyone who has ever worked for me the same lesson: Never leave something undone or unsaid that you'll be sorry for later."

Bourgeois stood silently looking at Ed and Margo's headstone and her parents' and remembering that day years ago. He closed his eyes, listening to the rhythm of his breathing as a distraction from a familiar, old self-reproach. After a few minutes, he nodded slowly, put on his hat and smiled faintly. Then he turned and walked away.

• • •

No longer a suspect in the fires, Nancilee returned to Grayton High in the fall of 2014 for her senior year. With everything that had happened in the spring still hanging over her like a dark cloud, she kept a low profile, not returning to work as an office aide or joining any student groups. Although most of the students she passed in the hallway or saw in class kept their distance, not knowing what to believe about Nancilee, the fires, and the deaths, to her great relief her group of "misfits" welcomed her back with quiet and tearful hugs.

Still, school without Jo no longer had the attraction for her that it once had. Nancilee went through the motions, but she was simply trying to get through it. After weeks of watching her daughter's resignation,

Tina spotted a flyer for the SAT on the kitchen counter one afternoon and asked her, "Hey, kid, are you taking this again?"

"No, why bother, right? You saw my scores last year. I can't get into any of the schools Jo and I used to talk about anyway. So, I kinda figured I'd just follow you and Gramma to Walmart or something. Nothing wrong with that," she said with a shrug.

"No, there isn't," Tina agreed, "but it's not really what you want, now is it? You and I both know what Jo would say, 'Just take it again.' And she'd be right. It doesn't cost much, and you never know. Besides, I don't like the idea of you not at least trying, so do it for me and your gramma."

Nancilee sighed and was going to argue, but she saw from her mom's expression that she may as well give in rather than fight the inevitable. In October 2014 she spent what she knew would be a wasted Saturday at school retaking the SAT, this time with Ruthie Gray, two managers from the school district, and someone from the College Board there to manage the process. She then waited without real interest for her test scores to come by mail. Like everyone else in Grayton, she knew better than to expect good news.

• • •

By the time school had started two months earlier in August 2014, it had become clear to all involved—the Orange County Independent School District, the Texas Education Agency, the College Board, and ACT Inc.—that they had a complicated puzzle and problem on their hands. Although the criminal investigation had all but wrapped up with an understanding of Ed and Margo's complicity in the fires, it had not yet unraveled what Margo had been up to with the full range of standardized tests, for how long, and how that may have affected student and the school's performance. That left headaches for them all, from how to solve Grayton High School's performance challenges to protecting the integrity in all of the state and college exams.

The state-appointed interim superintendent—who was transferred in from Houston to get the school district back on track—was also at a loss. It was up to him to save a failing school and a school district in decline, but to do that they also needed to solve this puzzle and understand how it contributed to the performance problems. The evidence consisted of a confusing stack of partially burned papers and separate and private databases of school records, test scores, and test materials, some belonging to the district, others to the state, the College Board, and ACT Inc. He wasn't yet familiar with Grayton High's records, and he did not have access to the outside databases. It would take all of it to understand what they were dealing with.

Their best chance materialized unexpectedly when the superintendent received a phone call, which he explained in a special session with the school board and the state. "We have an opportunity to piece this together for everyone concerned. Given the circumstances of his removal, Theodore Markus is still unemployed, and he reached out to me for a reference last week. I met with him a few days ago, and we've reached an understanding. He has agreed to lead a joint team assessing all of the existing data in order to understand what Margaret Schmutz's scheme was all about and where that leaves us in repairing Grayton High School's and the district's performance ratings. We've put together a one-year consulting contract for the board to approve. In it, we agree to formally clear his record and give him full credit for whatever clarity he is able to bring to this situation."

Not one to let a good plan go unchallenged, school board member Lanita Westchase asked skeptically, "And just what makes you think Mr. Markus can get this done?"

"Well, first of all, *Dr.* Markus is a brilliant young man with a sterling reputation. I can tell you that he is just as concerned with setting the record straight as we are, both for his own sake and for the sake of the program he put in place at Grayton. In fact, at his suggestion and with his help in the negotiations, we already have commitments from the state and both college board groups to give us full access and help in assessing their records. I really think this is our path out of the woods, and everyone can win. Or we can keep going like we have been, and everyone loses."

After more debate, the school board approved Dr. Markus's contract and strategy. His team then spent months copying and studying test materials and records and comparing them to transcripts. By the end of the year, they had painstakingly traced ten years of Grayton High School student performance in standardized tests and school transcripts, not just in high school, but through their middle school records.

In December, Dr. Markus reviewed the team's findings in a private session with the school board, the Texas Education Agency, and the governor's office. "We'll show you much of the raw information and can go into as much detail as you'd like, but first I want to cut right to the chase on our conclusions. For reasons we'll never really know, it is clear that Margo spent at least fifteen years changing as many as half of Grayton's students' standardized test scores—and not to improve their scores, but to lower them. You can really see it in the data when we plot the average top 25- and 50-percentile scores in those years compared to the previous fifteen years. When we superimpose the top 25- and 50-percentile average GPAs in those same years, you can see that in their normal curriculum, grades were solid, while at the same time the standardized test scores were plummeting. In fact, when you look further back to middle school for every Grayton High School class in the last fifteen years, you can see that average academic performance is seamless from sixth grade into high school, but there is a pronounced step down in standardized test scores."

Markus paused to let the data sink in, then he went on, "The overall effect has been huge. The lower state tests directly affected the school's rating, ultimately resulting in Grayton being reduced to academically unacceptable. The lower college boards then disqualified most Grayton graduates from any competitive colleges. Look, let me walk you through the data, and you'll see what we mean." He spent the next hour explaining the details as they understood them from the papers that were retrieved from Margo's hidden chute, combined with all of the test and academic records.

"Just look at the test scores from this past October. When Margo was no longer there to 'help,' we can see an enormous jump up in scores in all of the top percentiles, most visibly in the top 25 percent." Everyone in the room looked stunned. He nodded after a moment and said, "Thankfully, the College Board and ACT Inc. are both bending over backwards to help us do the right thing now. They have already offered to repeat their exams in the spring for all Grayton students who have taken them in the last year and at no charge. Any who retake it and score higher will have all previous test scores nullified. We're working with them now to make the same offer to any Grayton graduate from the last ten years."

Chatter started around the room, and one of the school board members sounded shocked, "Isn't that just asking for us to be sued by everyone who did badly on those tests in those years?!"

The superintendent stood up and answered, "We all need to face the fact that if a tidal wave of lawsuits could come from this, they're already coming. What's done is done—Margaret and Ed Schmutz did their damage, and we can't change that. Dr. Markus is reminding us today that we have a chance to show good faith to the community and do the right thing. It may not make up for all of the damage that has been done to a lot of our students' lives, but it's a step in the right direction. Who knows, maybe it will convince some not to sue, and maybe it will convince even more not to give up."

The room started buzzing again until the woman from the Texas Education Agency spoke to the room, "I know this a school district decision, not the state's, but the commissioner asked me to pass on to all of you that he has already spoken with the governor, and they both endorse this plan. They agree with what we all just heard, this is the right thing to do."

"There you have it," the superintendent said to the group. "I suggest the board convene informally now, and if the district endorses this plan, let's get on with it right away." He sat down and winked at Dr. Markus, then watched as the school board talked in whispers.

The board quickly approved the plan, and press releases were issued the next day. In January 2015, twice as many Grayton juniors and seniors took their college board exams as had the previous fall, and all of the state literacy tests from the previous spring were readministered at Grayton High School. Results across the board were higher than had been seen on these exams in more than ten years. During the next year, 230 former students from as far back as 2007 showed up to retake their college boards, many with no intention of doing anything different with the lives, and some having already graduated from college. They simply wanted their records and their consciences to be cleared.

• • •

In May 2015 it had been just over a year since the fire, and the "family" gathered eagerly at Joe's house for a much-needed happy occasion to celebrate the graduations—Nancilee's from high school and Jenny's a week earlier from Lamar University. Nancilee and her grandmother came through the doors hand in hand, both wearing graduation gowns, and both blushed as they were met with cheers. After hugs and congratulations from everyone, Jenny said, "Well, I may have been the only grandmother walking across that stage, but I definitely have the loudest support group!"

"Loudest and proudest, and that goes for both of you!" Tina said with a laugh as the cheers went up again. "And Mom doesn't like to brag, but she's already been told she's being promoted into the management track. How about that?"

"Yeah, not bad for an old broad, right?" Jenny laughed while she hugged Tina and Nancilee to her. "And don't we have one more little announcement to make?" Jenny asked, looking at her daughter and granddaughter.

When Nancilee's eyes widened and she didn't speak up, Tina said, "Well, young Nancilee here did better on her SAT last fall than she thought she would. We didn't tell anyone yet because we weren't all on the same page about what to do next. It took awhile and some tearful conversations, but she came around. Guess who just got herself admitted to Texas A&M University?"

Nancilee smiled as the congratulatory hugging started again and interrupted everyone, "Mom's not telling you the whole agreement. What I said was, '*I will if you will.*' How was I to know she'd take the dare? So, yes, I'll be at A&M in the fall, and *Mom* will start classes at the junior college and then transfer to Lamar after a year and get the same degree Gramma just got."

Smiling through tears, Jenny said loudly, "How about that for the Davis girls?! And we never could have gotten here without all of you."

The next several hours were like old times for the first time since the fire—too much food and drink, and just the right amount of laughing and warm talk. After dinner and with everyone settling down and relaxing in the large great room, Tina elbowed Joe, who was sitting next to her on a couch, "Hey, do you think I could run some things by you—financial things? Now that the Faisons have everything settled with the trust and all of that insurance money Mark surprised us with, Mom and I need some help with how it's all invested. We don't want to do the wrong things with it, and being a big business owner, I thought you could help point us in the right direction."

Joe looked surprised, "Well, sure. I'm no Warren Buffett or anything, but I'm happy to give you whatever help I can." He drew an exaggerated serious face, "Why don't we step outside away from all the commotion so we can talk serious business, ma'am?"

Walking out to the back deck, Joe thought about it and added, "Tell you what, let's walk down there to Jo's thinking spot. Just watch your step, it's kinda dark tonight with the Moon back behind the clouds."

As they stepped off the stairs and strolled through the grass, Joe said, "I have to tell you, it doesn't surprise me one bit that Mark left that insurance money to your mom, and not just because they were going to be married. You guys were his family, *all* of you."

Tina nodded, hooked her arm around Joe's with a nostalgic smile, and said quietly, "He really was like a father to me, in his way. You already knew that Nancilee called him 'Uncle Mark,' right?"

"Oh yeah, that always made me smile, and I know he loved it . . . and loved *her*, all of you, actually."

"He loved Jo too," she answered with tears in her eyes. "Without a doubt he loved that girl, her mom, *you*, and your folks. Isn't it funny how life is? He had such a terrible life for so long, and then Jo's mom came along and touched something in his heart that brought him back. She did that literally just in time for him to be there and step in when I needed him as a kid in trouble years ago. And he's been there for us all ever since."

She started to cry softly, and said, "I'm sorry. I loved them both so much. I don't know if I can ever get over losing them."

Joe put an arm around her shoulders and pulled her closer as they walked. After a few steps he said, "Hey, don't be sorry," and then added hoarsely as he tried to keep his voice from cracking, "there's no shame in missing the people you love when they're gone."

As they stepped into the clearing, Tina wiped her tears, laughed at her own weepiness, and tried to think happier thoughts, "You know, I always loved it when Jo called me 'Mom.' Did you know that she did that?"

Joe smiled, took his arm from around her shoulders, and turned slightly away as he blinked away tears, "No, I didn't know, but I'm not sure I would have noticed, now that you mention it. Her calling you that makes sense to me. Like Mark, Jo loved you—loved you *all*—like you were family. You *were* family to her, to all of us. You still are."

After a pause, he went on, "You know, Nancilee still calls me 'Dad,' and it always makes me smile. Sometime back, I stopped even noticing when she said it. It's just always seemed natural. She was so close to Jo, I guess some of that same closeness rubbed off on me. For a long time now it's been like she was my own, even before . . ."

He felt the light touch of her hand on his arm and turned back to see her nodding as she said, "I know what you mean. Those two really were like sisters, maybe even closer than most. You couldn't help but feel it when you were around them. It always made me feel like we were doing something right."

"It's funny you should say that, because I've had that same thought for a long time," Joe said. "I still do when you all are here."

They stood facing each other silently, both of them thinking about life and love. As the clouds shifted, the clearing filled with the Moon's white light. Joe saw Tina's face looking up at him, and his heart skipped a beat. Standing this close to her, with all of this emotion flowing through both of them and her dark eyes glistening in the moonglow, he could hide from it no longer. He glanced up at the bright white circle and thought, *Jodie, darlin'? Oh my sweet girls, what would either of you say if you could be here?*

A warm and light evening wind rustled through the trees, and he closed his eyes, memories of Jodie and Jo flowing over him like the soft breeze on his face. He shook his head slightly with a smile to himself as he could almost hear them both whispering as they kissed his cheek like they had so many times in this place. *I feel you, babe; you too, punkin. I will always love you too.*

Joe bowed his head briefly, then touched Tina's cheek softly and stepped closer, "I think I should have done this a long time ago. I hope it's okay." She pressed his hand against her face and took his other hand as he kissed her.

• • •

Over the next several years, more Grayton High School students than ever took their college boards every year, and scores in those tests and the state literacy tests went back to levels unseen since before Margo started her project. Like Nancilee, growing numbers of graduates were again mustering the courage to take on some next achievement, from applying to their dream colleges to enrolling in vocational schools or following some other passion.

Two of the most successful, and considered by some most unlikely, were Tim Wolf and Matt Lyons. Following Nancilee's lead, they enrolled in Lamar University's computer science program but quickly chafed at the structured curriculum. While taking classes, however, they went from one small software project to another through their connections at the Orange Junior College programming club. As more of their work involved writing code to manipulate large databases for private companies, the two spent years developing and tweaking a program that could automatically ingest database structures and create the base code for each new project.

Matt summed up their original goal to Tim after a long night writing code, "Dude, there has to be an easier way. We keep doing the same things at the start of every project. If we had an app that would do some of that up-front work for us, we could be asleep right now."

Instead of simply easing their workload, the new code took weeks out of the time required to finish each job, and the demand for their work skyrocketed. They left college after two years, both to get away from the classical education environment and to make time for their business. By the time they would have earned their bachelor's degrees at the tender age of twenty-three, the two quiet giants from Jo and Nancilee's "misfits" had licensed their automation-code to several major database companies and were set financially for life.

With his reputation significantly recovered at the end of his work for Orange ISD, Theodore Markus was recruited to re-energize a charter school network in St. Louis. His last contribution to Grayton High School before he left in 2015 was to establish an endowed scholarship program. To Dr. Markus's great surprise, the Faison law firm not only took care of the legal framework at no cost to the program, but Jimmy Sr. personally lobbied with businesses throughout East Texas, ultimately cobbling together a $25-million initial endowment—$2 million of it from his own family trust—providing $1,000 per year of undergraduate and vocational school assistance to every Grayton graduate who maintained passing grades in a degree or certificate program. The Faisons made only two requests: first, that the scholarship be named The Jo

Deming and Nancilee Davis Award; and second, that the Faisons' role remain private and unacknowledged.

• • •

Four years later, in May 2019, Grayton High School's graduation ceremony had to be moved to the Orange Junior College football stadium. Much had changed in the mood at the school and in the town since the fire in 2014 and its aftermath. There was hope again, a renewed faith that effort and passion led to happiness, and there was gratitude. Some of the gratitude was tangled up and a part of the newfound hope, and some was very specific. It was the specific gratitude felt towards Jo and Nancilee that had drawn so much interest in this year's graduation. Most Grayton High School families and many from previous graduates turned out to hear Nancilee Davis give the commencement address and to pay their respects to the two girls who had made Grayton's recovery possible.

Nancilee had taken some convincing by the family to accept the invitation months earlier during her last spring break at home. At dinner with the newlywed Joe and Tina, Nancilee said nervously, "I know why they want me. It's because of me and Jo, I get it. But who am I? I don't have any great message to give them all . . . I'm nobody's motivational speaker!"

After much discussion, it was Joe who settled her nerves, "Hey, kiddo, don't overthink it, and don't try to sound like someone you're not. Think of it like this: 'What would Jo want you to say?' Or maybe, 'What would *she* say if she could?'"

"But they all think I was some kind of hero," Nancilee said, looking down at the table, "when I didn't do anything. What could I say?"

"So a lot of people may be there to hear you talk about the two of you? Fine, who's a better authority on that subject than you? Focus on what is most important in your memory of the two of you together. That will be more than enough and better than trying to make something up," and he pulled her close for a reassuring hug.

On the morning of May 25, 2019, Nancilee stood at the podium in front of a capacity crowd, all of whom were standing and cheering before she had spoken a word. Standing in the front row to the right of the graduates was her family: Joe and Tina, Jenny, Hal and Jessie Deming, and Ben and Dina Lucky. After the crowd had quieted and sat back down, Nancilee started, her voice shaking at first, but she gained confidence as she spoke:

> Hi, everyone. Boy, thanks for that warm reception! It's always good to be welcomed home. And thank you for the invitation to be here with you today. I hope I don't make you regret your choice.
>
> I have to tell you, I was worried about having something meaningful to say about life. You see, the truth is, I'm not much older than these graduates. I just finished college two weeks ago, so I can tell them about which professors to avoid at A&M maybe, but life? Yikes, I should be asking you!
>
> Instead, I'd like to say just a little about the most important lesson I learned here in Grayton and much of it at Grayton High. Maybe that does mean something about life for all of us. Some of you may have heard about the ongoing debate about "nature versus nurture" in how people turn out. I believe both play a part in shaping us, but I think there's something more to it still.

First, there's "nature." Nature is funny. It's like a lottery. Some of us are taller, or stronger, or faster than others. Some of us may be smarter, or better natural athletes, or singers, or some other talent. We also often think of it in terms of tendencies and personality, and that we're all wired to be how and who we are. Some are funny, or outspoken, or shy, like I am—even though, here I am on this stage talking to all of you!

Then there's "nurture." How we are, the way other people experience us, is also so dependent on the "nurture" we each find in life from the family, friends, and teachers who show us the way of the world and how to be in it. And our experiences with these people and where we happen to find ourselves experiencing them, can also affect our "wiring," maybe even rewire us in ways that take advantage of our gifts and talents—our nature—or rob us of them, if those experiences aren't good or helpful.

But however we are wired and in addition to whatever nurturing we experience, we also each have *choices* throughout life. Our good choices tend to help us—help us be more successful, to be better people—for ourselves, the people we love, and everyone around us. Other choices get in our way. Sometimes we make choices that feel good in the present but still hurt us in the long run.

Like our nature and nurturing, all of our choices contribute to who we become and where we go.

I don't believe that we can all make those good choices in spite of our nature or our nurturing. In some cases, the odds stack against some of us who, in another situation, may have made a better choice. But that would have been another, *better* situation they didn't have.

Still, we see examples of people who did make those better choices, even in the worst of conditions, or who come from backgrounds that do not presuppose success. But I don't think it's as simple as concluding that if *anyone* could have succeeded in those situations, then *everyone* could.

Because there is one more contributor. Life. It happens. Things happen. I learned five years ago that there is no karma or fate, that when life happens, the bad things don't happen only to those who we may think deserve them. They sometimes just happen, even to the best of us, another of life's lotteries, but often with a cynical outcome.

As dark as that sounds, it is how it is.

But . . .

My best friend has been gone for five years now. I can hear Jo's voice and feel her presence every day, reminding me to keep thinking about this lesson, and not give in to sadness, anger, and injustice—just like she always told me her mom still did for her, even after she had lost her. Because we can never know all of the little ways we influence others. The tiny happiness we may help someone see and feel, or the small slight we may help someone avoid or heal from. And through the days and years, just trying to make our own better choices whenever we can, can lead us each to a happier place and help others reach a happier place for themselves as those tiny happinesses ripple out through the world.

Does any of that guarantee we'll all be happy and live a life of butterflies and rainbows, or that we'll simply avoid some terrible life experience? No. Life still happens, and sometimes not in the way we all wish.

But we can still keep choosing right, keep choosing the light and the good, even in the small things. Because that's how we keep our hope alive. That's how we make it through each step of our journeys. That's how we help each other to keep hoping and make it through the journey. And that's how so many of us will look around from time to time and realize the happiness and wonder our journeys have brought us.

Again, I'm not saying everyone gets their happy ending. I'm also not saying we should all be trying to find or help the next Albert Einstein, or Jonas Salk, or Mozart, or Stephen Hawking, or Martin Luther King, or Neil Armstrong, or any other heroic or great person—or that we should be trying to do some incredible, life-changing thing for anyone.

But . . .

We can be like Jo . . . or at least try a little harder to be. She was never trying to make any grand gesture or to be Mother Teresa. She was just . . . Jo.

To understand what I mean, instead of rainbows, think about butterflies. The miracle of butterflies is that they exist and simply do what they do, leaving joy and small miracles in their path as they go, because they can, and it is simply who they are. That was my sister, Jo.

If I had one thing that I could say that was miraculous in who Jo was and the things she did, it's that she was who she was, every day and effortlessly, and she made us all better by living this simple idea. The greatest gift she gave me was being my friend and allowing me to bear witness to this in little moments every day, to learn from her example every day—as hard as it was for me on some days—or just to have the benefit of that tiny bit of encouragement.

We don't always recognize our butterfly-moments when they happen, although we sometimes remember specific ones in hindsight, those "I dodged a bullet" or "only by the grace of God" experiences. So often, those moments include some simple act of kindness, generosity, patience, teaching, and even forgiveness. For most of us, life is a series of butterfly-moments, most very small and seemingly innocuous. No matter how small—at the risk of suggesting I learned something in my English class here—each can be a moment, as William Shakespeare wrote,

Which, taken at the flood, leads on to fortune;
Omitted, all the voyage of their life
Is bound in shallows and in miseries.

We also don't always recognize the butterflies in our midst, or in our lives. Most of you and most of the world will never have the joy and privilege of knowing my sister, Jo, except through stories like this. But you may run across some *other* Jo in your life though, and if my story doesn't inspire you to be a little more like *my* Jo, maybe it will help you recognize your own Jo when she comes along. When you do, thank God, providence, or the universe for your good fortune.

Try to make her gift your own, even just a tiny gesture every day. It can change your life and the lives of everyone around you, and you will make the world a better place.

Nancilee didn't notice the standing ovation at the end of her speech. As she wiped happy tears from her eyes, she saw only her family beaming back at her, and she couldn't escape the feeling that Jo was there smiling with them.

When the graduation ceremony ended almost two hours later, most in the audience were still moved by the young woman's words and went through the rest of the day with a sense that the world was a happier place than it had been the day before. Several left unexpectedly and profoundly inspired. Although through the years and with the blur of time, they would forget the connection to this moment, they would each go through their lives with an unshakable optimism, and people who would meet them felt their own burdens eased and were reminded, even if only briefly, of some forgotten joy.

As the crowd walked out, reflecting quietly on the happy occasion and what they had just heard, a single butterfly zigzagged overhead. Hundreds of smiling faces turned to look and hearts beat with joy when a five-year-old girl's voice rang out happily, "Oooh look, Mommy! A butterfly!"

EPILOGUE

Life is a journey—each path chosen contributes to the journey, but how we journey determines who we are.

Mexico City (World News): Scientists cannot explain the unprecedented recovery of the monarch butterfly population. For a species that had been decimated, reduced to a single acre, and feared to be heading to unavoidable extinction in 2014, it is nothing short of miraculous that just five years later they are now estimated to cover 15 acres. The Executive Director of Butterfly Preservation National Autonomous University of Mexico, Dr. Jorge Osorio, speaking to reporters at the largest reserve in Mexico, said, "Although this critical species has suffered and is still at risk, what we've seen since should give us great hope."

On a fateful day eight years earlier, Ed Schmutz walked out in the middle of a lecture in the Grayton High School gym with a dark idea forming in his mind. Had he stayed, he would have heard Dr. Baker also say,

> Yes, life is tenuous. Life is also tenacious.
>
> Just as it appears to wait for just the right conditions to spring into existence, life can also shift ever so subtly over generations in response to environment changes, including man-made challenges. In this way, some species don't really disappear; they evolve—they adapt, survive, and live on.
>
> Still, the reality is, in the best of days, not all butterflies make it. The world takes many, whether we "help" in the taking or not. But some do make it. And as they do, they touch the lives around them, often without trying, always without knowing how widely and wonderfully their influence has helped others.
>
> We can all *aspire* to protect and help them when we can.
>
> And if not, we can *hope* that we aren't inadvertently doing something to make it harder for them, and that they will keep coming back, helping the world one touch—one life—at a time.
>
> Smile when you see one—for the gifts they are and for the beauty, hope, and life they carry with them.
>
> Pray it isn't the last and do what you can to help them.

REQUEST FOR REVIEWS

I hope you enjoyed *The Last Butterfly*. Would you do me a favor?

Like all authors, I rely on online reviews to encourage future readers. Your opinion is invaluable. Would you take a few moments now to share your assessment of *The Last Butterfly* at review sites of your choice? Your opinion will help the book marketplace become more transparent and useful to all.

Thank you very much!

Printed in the USA
CPSIA information can be obtained
at www.ICGtesting.com
LVHW040851151123
763329LV00002B/3/J